PRAISE FOR ANNE D. LeCLAIRE

Listening Below the Noise: The Transformative Power of Silence

"Luminous."

—*PBS NewsHour* with Jim Lehrer

"Eloquent and moving . . . Although technically a memoir, this book moves beyond that genre into spirituality and philosophy. LeClaire's reputation as a novelist may draw readers to this lovely book, which should also have cross-over appeal to spiritual seekers of any religion and no religion."

—*Booklist*

The Lavender Hour

"LeClaire packs this winning novel with resounding life lessons and a resonating set of romantic relationships."

—*Kirkus Reviews*

Entering Normal

"Exquisite . . . A beauty . . . If you love the feel of Anne Tyler's novels, then this has your name all over it."

—*Daily Mirror* (London)

"In rich and limpid prose, LeClaire shifts the point of view . . . focusing on the small acts that get us through the day, or the night, or not. A woman's book in the best possible sense, this will leave readers warm and satisfied."

—*Booklist*

"An emotional wallop comparable to that produced by Sue Miller's *The Good Mother* or Jane Hamilton's *A Map of the World*."

—*Publishers Weekly*

"A gentle, spirited novel about friendship and survival."

—*USA Today*

Leaving Eden

"A light, breezy novel about serious subjects. It's eventful, with a lingering death, a murder, a secret revealed, to say nothing of a makeover."

—*Boston Globe*

"Artfully crafted characters resonate within this emotional novel detailing one girl's ability to face the hardships of her life."

—*Romantic Times*

The Law of Bound Hearts

"Recommended . . . LeClaire has crafted authentic characters and successfully portrays the power of forgiveness."

—*Library Journal*

"A gripping, emotional intensity and depth of feeling highlight this poignant and lyrical novel, which illustrates how precious life is."

—*Romantic Times*

THE
HALO
EFFECT

THE
HALO
A Novel
EFFECT

Anne D. LeClaire

LAKE UNION
PUBLISHING

Text copyright © 2017 by Anne D. LeClaire
All rights reserved.

Published by Lake Union Publishing, Seattle

www.apub.com

Amazon, the Amazon logo, and Lake Union Publishing are trademarks of Amazon.com, Inc., or its affiliates.

ISBN-13: 9781503943186
ISBN-10: 1503943186

Cover design by Rex Bonomelli

Printed in the United States of America

For Bernard Cornwell:
Partner in Crime and First Lines

PROLOGUE

~

Every day is ordinary. Until it isn't.

On this early-October morning, the townspeople in Port Fortune wake before dawn to an ordinary day with its ordinary sounds: the groaning of trawlers straining against lines in the mist-shrouded harbor, the metallic chorus of gear being loaded on board underscored by the fog-muted, early-morning conversation of men, the deep-throated tolling of the marker buoy in the outer harbor, and over at Cape Port Ice the drone of the giant ice-making machines. They wake, too, to the town's ordinary smells: at the docks the distinct miasma of salt air, diesel fuel, ripe bait, and mug-up coffee, and at the Loaves of the Fisherman Bakery on Prospect Street the aroma of anise, cardamom, sugar, yeast, Frialator oil, and cappuccino, scents so thick they nearly coat the air. These every-day noises and smells are not dissimilar to those of her sister fishing ports along the Northeast Coast and yet are somehow so particular to this place that a lost and sightless child could find her way home.

At the police station, the shift changes, and Detective Dan Gordon retrieves his service revolver from his locker, where he has stored it since the birth of their daughter the year before. His wife insists on this precaution. Holly no longer wants a gun in the house, not even one he swears he always unloads and secures in the small gun safe in the basement. He is not unsympathetic to her request. Even in this small town, he has seen the sorrow caused by weapons that are believed to be unloaded, not to mention the grief resulting from those deliberately loaded and fired in hot passion or cold foresight.

At the Church of the Holy Apostles, Father Paul Gervase unlocks the front door and prepares for early Mass amid the comforting aroma of incense, wax, and the oil soap Mrs. Mason uses on the worn oak floor. Not long ago, the church was kept unlocked, but a recent uptick in crime changed that. The local paper ran a series about the town's growing drug problem, particularly the OxyContin scourge that has led to a heroin epidemic, the lead story for a week until it was crowded off the front page by reports about nearly a dozen girls at the local high school getting pregnant. The world is changing, and no one knows this more than Father Gervase. He waits for the first parishioners to arrive, Italian and Portuguese wives and widows for the most part, holding tight to the rituals of a lifetime as if by this they can slow a world spinning beyond their control.

At Port Fortune High School, Wayne Jervis, the custodian who moonlights part-time doing work at Holy Apostles, arrives and turns up thermostats. He unlocks classroom doors and then enters the faculty lounge, where he switches on the automatic coffee machine and adds water and grounds. Lastly, as he does every weekday, he goes to the girls' locker room. The *bitches'* locker room. He knows what they call him behind his back. Jervis the Pervis. *Bitches.* In recent months, nine of them have become pregnant, and despite the denials by the school principal, the girls, and their parents, a rumor persists that these are deliberate decisions, the result of a pact among the girls. *Bitches. Sluts. Whores. The lot of them.* If they are so hungry for cock, he'd be happy to show them what a real man can do. And a lot better than their high school boyfriends can. Jervis enters a stall and takes a long piss, leaving the seat up and the toilet unflushed when he is done.

At the Loaves of the Fisherman, Manny Costa, Leon Newell, Caesar Amero, and Portuguese Joe arrive early. The four have spent a lifetime rising before dawn, and although they no longer fish, the old habits die hard. At their regular table, they drink coffee, eat sweet rolls, and talk about the things that occupy their conversation every morning: the weather, town politics, how maybe the foreign fleets haven't completely killed the industry but the restrictions of new federal fishing regulations surely will.

Gradually the fog lifts and the sun inches upward, striating the horizon and casting a roseate glow over the eastern sky, the harbor and icehouse, the station, the bakery, other businesses, and homes. Slowly the rest of the town awakes.

On Chandler Street, Rain LaBrea hears her brother revving the engine of the thirdhand, piece-of-crap Mazda he thinks is such a big deal and curses him for not waiting to give her a ride to school. She texts her friend Lucy about how she now will have to take the bus like the dweebs do. There is no use complaining to her parents unless she's up to enduring one more lecture about how she should get up earlier if she wants Duane to give her a ride. Duane, her mother's Golden Boy who, in her eyes, can do no harm.

Across town, on Governors Street, Sophie Light raps twice on her daughter's door. "Lucy? Are you up?" She listens for a moment, and reassured by the noises inside the room, she descends to the kitchen and crosses to where Will is pouring coffee into two mugs and brushes his cheek with her lips, smoothes an unruly lock of hair with her fingers, a cowlick that spins in a counterclockwise directions that not even a comb and application of hair gel could tame.

"What time did you finally come to bed?" she asks.

"Around midnight. The game went into overtime." He hands one of the mugs to her. "Did I wake you?"

"I was so wiped last night I wouldn't have moved if Hannibal and his elephants bivouacked in the room." She takes a sip of coffee, smiles her thanks. "So who won?"

"Green Bay."

"Is that good?"

"Not for Chicago." He starts to say more, but at that instant he hears Lucy coming down the stairs. When their daughter enters the kitchen, his smile of anticipation morphs into a frown as he observes the snugness of her sweater, the length of her skirt that in his mind should be illegal, then intercepts a look from Sophie. *Let it go*. She's accused Will of being overly protective. "What would you prefer she wear? A caftan?" she recently asked him. Clearly she is better at handling their daughter's nascent sexuality than he, but doesn't she understand that a man's central purpose and desire is to protect those he loves? Now he looks at the contours of Lucy's breasts and her long thighs still tinged with the last of her summer tan. Their daughter is developing into a beauty on the cusp of womanhood, but it seems to Will she is remarkably innocent of the power this will give her. Yes, a caftan would be fine with him.

They eat what he has prepared. Cold cereal with sliced banana. Sophie pours them a second mug of coffee. Lucy gulps OJ. They sit in a comfortable domestic silence broken only by the faint tapping of Lucy's thumbs on her iPhone, the digits moving faster than Will would think possible on the screen's miniature keys and icons. If he'd done this at the table, his father would have cut off his hands. He wishes they would ban those things. Cell phones, social networking, Facebook, Twitter—ridiculous name. All the things pulling their daughter from them. He starts to speak but gets another look from Sophie. *Let it go*. Then, as if a switch has flipped, the morning ritual ends, and there is a flurry signaling departure. Sophie grabs her briefcase. At the door, she turns to ask, "Shall I stop on the way home and pick up dinner at the Kottage Kitchen?"

"I've got tonight covered," Will says.

Lucy kisses his cheek, and he smells the banana on her breath, inhales the apple-scented shampoo of her hair, the sweet fruitiness of her, and he knows a moment of fear and again the desire to protect her from danger large or small.

"Bye, Da," she says in a voice still morning husky.

He nods his goodbye. He kisses Sophie, a lingering kiss that draws a mock sigh from Lucy and a "Hey, you guys, I'm still in the room," but when he looks over at her, she is grinning. Then they are gone, and he resumes the morning rituals, wiping off the table, stacking dishes, turning off the coffee, already slipping into his own day, thinking now of the painting waiting upstairs on the easel, the supplies he'll need to order before the weekend. It is Tuesday, the day Sophie holds after-school rehearsal for the chorus and Lucy stays late for French club, then a field hockey scrimmage. Eight hours stretch before him, an ocean of quiet with no husbandly or fatherly obligations, and he feels a fleeting twinge of guilt at the pleasure the idea of this brings him.

An ordinary day in Port Fortune.

Until it isn't.

Until Lucy Light doesn't come home.

PART ONE
SINNERS
~

CHAPTER ONE

~

First they sent the priest.

Looking back I can see the inevitability that it should be the priest who would come, but of course that morning, not given the knowledge of foresight, I had no idea of how our fates were to become entwined. It was one of those warm and gentle days of late spring, and I'd opened the eaves window several inches, so the echo of a car door slamming floated up to the attic where I was working. I wondered if it was Sophie. I hadn't expected her, and things were often strained between us now, so I wasn't sure whether to go down or stay in the studio—a simple enough decision but just one of the many things I was no longer certain of in the unmoored ship of my life. My one or two absolutes, no one wanted to hear, least of all my wife.

I crossed to the window and looked down at the drive, but the black sedan parked next to my gray Prius was unfamiliar. A man stood beside it; I recognized the garb. A priest. Instantly I understood. Sophie was behind this. I heard the echo of her voice, the words she'd spoken the last time we'd talked, her voice soft with concern but steady, firm in her conviction. *You need to talk to some-one, Will. You need to talk to someone about your anger, about the way you've isolated yourself, shut yourself off from everyone.* Well, screw that. I didn't need to talk to anyone and certainly not a goddamn priest. Reflexively I stepped to one side so the angle of the attic shadow would conceal me from view if he looked up, but the priest, who was carrying a small yellow parcel, didn't raise his eyes, his attention focused on the flagstone walk where shallow puddles lingered from the rain that had fallen in the early morning, a shower much welcome, for the water table was low that year. Petals from the early-blooming azalea floated on the puddles like confetti. I watched as he negotiated around them carefully, made his way to the steps. Even from this distance, I could see his frailty, evident in the way he grasped the railing with his free hand, the way two-footed, like a child, he made his way slowly up the wide steps that rose to the front porch, planks I had reclaimed from disrepair, sanded bare and stained with Sherwin-Williams WoodScapes Exterior. *Rookwood Amber.* Not long ago, I'd found satisfaction in poring over color charts as if they were oracles. Just as once, not so very long ago, I'd found a comforting, nearly meditative pleasure in cutting cracked putty from sashes and replacing and repointing window panes, restoring elaborate wainscot, and planing the bottom of doors until they again swung free. How quickly what once were priorities could be upended. The man below disappeared from my line of vision, but I continued to stand at the window. I watched a car pass in the street and heard the engine of a low-flying plane overhead, something I normally would not have heard since I usually kept the window shut and all sounds from outside were silenced by thick walls, one of the benefits of houses built more than a century ago. Our street was lined with such well-constructed buildings. The doorbell rang, and again, a moment later, came a second chime. I knew I could outwait him—eventually even a man of the cloth schooled in patience would have to acknowledge defeat. *Man of the cloth.* How readily that antiquated phrase came to mind. I heard in it my mother, who'd had an idiosyncratic affection for outdated expressions. And for clergy, too, now that I thought of it, though our family had been Episcopalian, not Catholic. Yes, I *could* have waited up there until the priest left. Over and over since then I have wondered how things might have changed if I had never gone to answer his ring. Instead, determined to conclusively settle this matter that had brought the priest to my home—goddamn it, I did *not* need to talk to anyone about my anger—I wrapped my brush in a square of foil, found a rag, and wiped my hands, got them as clean as they would ever be. Before I went down, I remember switching off the large fan, an industrial one I'd installed myself to protect my family from toxic fumes, to keep them safe.

To keep them *safe*. Even now I taste the irony.

I did not hurry as I descended the three flights. When I reached the second-floor landing, the chimes pealed once more, and again as I crossed the foyer, and I knew a small, mean satisfaction at keeping the priest waiting. Through the wavy glass of the sidelights, I viewed an ordinary man edging out of the north side of middle age. Although it was cool for May, he was bareheaded, and the wind lifted the short strands of his hair into spikes, like the gelled pink hair of the teenage clerk at the market where we now shopped. In my limited experience, I have always found priests to be fat or skeletal, as if they were either wasted or well fed by their faith. This one was thin, scholarly looking, with shoulders beginning to stoop. From the weight of his calling, I remember thinking. All those untold burdens. I felt no sympathy. Don't talk to me of burdens.

If stripped of the clothing of his profession—the black suit, white band collar—the priest could be any professional. An accountant. Banker. Teacher. Salesman. Well, broadly speaking, I supposed he was all of those. Just not on my damned turf. I unlocked the deadbolt and opened the door.

"Yes?"

"I'm Father Paul Gervase." Given his slight build, the priest's voice was deeper, more resonant than I expected but still held the softness and lack of aggression I associated with the lower strata of the male Catholic hierarchy. I couldn't imagine why Sophie would think I'd ever talk to this inconsequential functionary, this man apparently not bothered by the prospect of time squandered on a fool's errand.

"From Holy Apostles," the priest said. He hesitated. "I, ah, I don't know if you recall me."

I stared blankly, waited.

"I celebrated the Mass for your daughter. For Lucy." He ran a palm over his head, smoothed his hair flat. His color was pale, tinged with gray, the look of a man with a disease not yet diagnosed. There was a saffron-colored smudge on his left lapel, a color I associated with the pollen of daylilies. A shade of marigold or cadmium.

It took a minute until I was sure my voice would be steady. In fact, I barely remembered the priest, but then I'd managed to block all details of Lucy's funeral, a Catholic service I had agreed to only because it meant so much to Sophie. "Yes?" I said and steeled myself for the inevitable opening, the empty words, the unbearably condescending expression of pity or sympathy wrapped in infuriating platitudes. In the past months, I'd heard enough of them to last a lifetime. *I don't know what to say*, people say. And then they would say it anyway. One woman had actually had the nerve to tell Sophie she was young enough to have another child, as if a dead child could be as easily replaced as a burned-out lightbulb. The woman had added that if we had a second child, we would again be a family, the loss might be diminished. Like that horrid phrase the Brits used for the royal family. An heir and a spare. What a fucking dumb-witted thing to say. The priest looked straight at me, blue eyes gazing out from behind wire-rimmed glasses, revealing nothing. I waited, then broke the silence. "You're wasting your time, Father."

Father Gervase smiled, an unexpectedly appealing smile but not false. "This isn't the first time I've heard that."

I bet, I thought.

"May I come in?"

Our eyes caught for a long moment, reminding me of a schoolyard game of chicken. Ridiculous really. I stepped back and invited the priest in with a sweeping gesture, an Elizabethan mockery of a welcome. The priest coughed, a noise as dry and insubstantial as the riffling of the pages of a missal, and then stepped inside. He looked around, admiring the foyer, the crown moldings, the parquet floor with inlaid marble squares, the rococo sideboard. What had Sophie told him? What had he expected? Dirty floors? Empty booze bottles? Food-crusted dishes?

"Amazing," the priest said. There was a note in his voice I couldn't identify.

"What's that, Father?"

The priest seemed not to have heard. "Amazing," he murmured again. Finally he roused himself. "This house," he said. "I grew up in a Victorian very much like this. In Milwaukee. Yes. Very like this one."

Was this true? I wouldn't take odds. I trusted nothing, no one, least of all priests, especially the small talk of this one.

"Is this the original flooring?"

I nodded.

"It's beautifully restored."

Once I would have taken pride in the compliment, but no longer. We should have sold the damned house. *Damned* was not too strong a word for all that had happened, but there really was no question of moving. In spite of everything, there remained too much of my father in me to just let the place go completely. Even today I can hear my father's words—*we are but caretakers of our belongings*—and I can recall the Saturdays of my boyhood when, in a companionship that required little conversation, we undertook weekend chores. Scraping worn shutters. Re-grouting bathroom tiles. The first gift I remembered receiving from my parents was an undersized carpenter's box with my name stenciled in navy blue on the side. It contained a nail set and hammer, screwdriver and miniature crosscut saw, socket wrench and pliers, a wooden hinged rule. I still have it somewhere in the basement. *For future generations*, my father would say as he instructed me in how to rewire an outlet, how to miter a perfect corner as if salvation could be found there, how to replace a washer. Of course that was back when faucets came with washers. When things were simpler to fix.

"Izzy bell tower," the priest said.

"Pardon me?" I said.

"Is that a Belter?" The priest pointed at the intricately carved sideboard.

"It is." I was forced to a quick reassessment. Counting myself, I doubted there were more than five or six people in the entire state who would recognize the cabinetmaker's work. "I inherited it from my grandparents."

"My parents had a bench of his."

I nodded, realizing how easy it was to forget that this priest had a history that predated his vocation, a prior life that even vows couldn't erase. Once, he was only a man, before that a boy.

Father Gervase coughed again, setting off a spasm. "I wonder," he said when he regained his breath. "Might you have a glass of water?"

No, I thought. *No, I have the only goddamn house in the state without plumbing.* "Yes," I said. "Of course." As we crossed the hall, for the first time I noticed the priest walked with a limp. Arthritis? Surgery? It seemed like every week Sophie relayed news of someone else she knew who was having a knee or hip replaced. People in their forties and fifties, for God's sake. In the kitchen, I retrieved a tumbler from the cabinet, turned on the tap. While I let the water run cold, I stared out the window at the last of the vernal flowers on the elm in the backyard. My eyes were caught by movement, and I watched the invisible hand of the wind stir the swing hanging from a low branch. I'd made it for Lucy when she was not quite two, too small for it really. She could only use it held in the safety of Sophie's arms. I'd taken a photo of them the day we put it up, a picture I can see clearly even now. Sophie in a long peasant skirt, Lucy dressed in miniature overalls. Pink, I remember. Both sheltered by a canopy of ovate leaves. That snapshot had been the start of a tradition. Each year I'd photograph Lucy on the swing, a visual record taking her from toddler to girl to teenager. The memory pains even today, although now of course for a different reason. A soft rustling behind me brought me back from the reverie. The priest had settled himself at the table, set his package on an empty chair. It was a mistake to have let him in. Too late, I understood this. I filled the glass and passed it to him. In the light cast through the bank of windows that lined the south wall, he appeared younger than I'd first thought.

"Tan zoo."

"Pardon?" I said.

"Thank you," the priest repeated.

"No problem." Lately I had been having hearing difficulties. Words were jumbled; there were long moments when entire chunks of conversation were lost or when the CD or television audio went silent, as if I had hit the mute button. Sporadically, I heard ringing, a persistent pestilent tone. Tinnitus. I hadn't mentioned this to anyone, least of all Sophie, who would have insisted I see someone. Was I going deaf? Developing a tumor? Well, what if I was? That was not the worst that could happen. The worst that could happen had already happened. At least that was what I believed on that spring day. Had you asked me I would have told you I had nothing left to lose, but of course there is always more to lose. I poured the last of the morning coffee into a mug and nuked it. I made no apology for not offering any to the priest.

"Myself, I never learned the knack," Father Gervase said.

"What's that, Father?"

"Brewing coffee."

"It takes no great skill." A fleck of paint rimmed my thumbnail. Cadmium yellow. Like the smudge on his clothing. "It's in the measuring."

"Now my maternal grandmother, a first-generation Swede she was. She could perk a pot that would make Satan himself weep. She'd spoon in the grounds, add water and an egg, and smash it with a spoon. Shell and all."

I could picture it—the brown coffee grounds, the shards of shell, the viscous strings of albumen, the bright splash of yoke bleeding into the mix—and I felt slightly queasy. A memory rose, unbidden. Lucy at the breakfast table, refusing to eat her scrambled eggs with implacable determination because her sixth-grade science teacher had informed the class that an egg was the embryo of a chicken. A band tightened across my chest. That was the cruelty of memory. The way it could ambush you. Take you out at the knees. Our entire house was a minefield. Once I'd come across Sophie sitting in the living room with tears running down her cheeks, a bronze hair clip she'd found in the recesses of the sofa held in her palm. Or I would find a note Lucy had scrawled and left unfinished in the back of a drawer, and the sight of her handwriting would take my breath away. So many things in this minefield. A simple word. An empty swing swaying in the breeze.

"Have you ever heard of that?" the priest was saying.

"What?"

"Beating an egg into coffee?"

"No." I managed a breath. "Can't say that I have." To steady myself, I concentrated on words. *Egg. Eggplant. Egghead. Eggbeater. Egg in one's beer. Egg on. Eggnog.*

"The idea is that the shells bind and settle the grounds."

Egg timer. Egg tempera. Eggcup. Egg roll. Egg hunt.

Egg hunt. Easter. In the field of memory, land mines were buried everywhere, easily tripped. Lucy with a purple straw basket, systematically searching the yard for the foil-covered eggs Sophie and I had hidden in the night. She was a methodical child, our Lucy. Sophie used to tease her about it. *Lucy, you're an old lady dressed in a girl suit.* A pain heated my chest. I forced my mind to the present, to this room. "I doubt you're here to talk about coffee, Father."

"No. No, of course not." The priest took a sip of water.

"Well, I'm afraid you've wasted your time coming here. I'm sorry for your trouble." The hypocrisy was not even a small bone in my throat. Of all I had to regret and mourn, the inconveniencing of this priest didn't even make the extended list.

"You know why I've come, then?"

"I assume Sophie asked you to come by."

"Sophie?"

"Yes. Sophie. My wife."

"Ah, Sophia. Well, no, actually it was the archbishop who sent me."

I frowned, confused. What the hell could the archbishop have to do with anything?

"Cardinal Kneeland," Father Gervase said.

"I don't understand."

"Of course. Of course. How would you?" He smiled, sipped again from the glass. "I should have explained. He wants to meet with you."

"Well, I have no interest in meeting with him." So I had misunderstood his mission in coming. This whole business had to have something to do with Sophie's work, a futile, do-good mission I wanted no part of.

"Let me explain. He wants you to come to Boston. Of course, I'll drive you. I'm happy to drive. We wouldn't expect you to drive." A slight tremor of his hand on the glass revealed the priest's nervousness, or, it occurred to me, perhaps an early symptom of Parkinson's.

"If your cardinal wants to see me, he could have come himself. We're wasting time here, Father."

"Yes, well." The priest hesitated, then forged on. "It's about the new cathedral," he said. "He wants you to see the cathedral."

At last I got it. Money. "You've got the wrong guy, Father. I'm not interested in donating to the building fund." If the cardinal wanted someone to pay for the damn cathedral, then let him ask the Vatican to open its coffers. A trace of a smile flicked across the priest's face, as if we shared a secret. "I won't change my mind," I said.

"No. I don't imagine you will." Now the priest did smile. It was like fencing with a cloud. I wondered what it would take to offend him.

"But it isn't about a contribution," Father Gervase said.

"Then what?"

"Are you at all familiar with the new cathedral?"

"Not intimately. I know an awful lot of people think it's a mistake to expend money on a monumental building when it would be better spent elsewhere." *Restitution for victims of priest abuse, for instance*, I thought but managed not to say.

"I'm not unaware of the controversy about the cost," the priest said. His tone held a wry note that surprised me. "No, I've come because Cardinal Kneeland wants to commission you to paint portraits of the saints. To hang in the nave."

"Saints?"

"Yes," Father Gervase said. "A series of paintings of the saints."

The *saints*. I nearly laughed. "Sorry. I'm not interested."

"You know that before you even talk to the cardinal? Before you hear what he has in mind?"

"I know that."

"I wonder," Father Gervase said. "Might I ask why?"

"Why what?"

"Why you dismiss the idea so readily. Why you won't consider it?"

Which reason do you want? I thought. *Because I want nothing to do with your church. Because I don't believe in your saints. Because the very idea sickens me. Because I want to be left alone.*

Father Gervase waited patiently, his eyes kind.

Perhaps it was this show of kindness, but I surprised myself by saying, "I don't have the heart for it. Not anymore."

The priest studied me for a moment. "You might be surprised at the capacity of your heart."

Christ, I thought. *Next he'll be giving me some shite about turning the other cheek.* "I'm not your man, Father. Tell your cardinal he'll have to find another artist."

A small sigh escaped the priest's lips, the briefest of exhalations. He began to speak and then stopped.

"I hate to be rude, Father, but if there is nothing else, I'd like to get back to my work."

"Of course. Of course." The priest rose, slowed by hips that clearly pained him.

Still holding my coffee, I led him to the foyer, both surprised and relieved that he had surrendered so easily.

At the door Father Gervase turned toward me, his eyes studying my face in a way that gave rise to a deep discomfort which I must have betrayed, for he broke the gaze and said, "It was kind of you to see me."

"Not at all." Now that I was nearly rid of him, I could be generous. I allowed myself a flash of sympathy for this man sent on the orders of his superiors. *Orders of his order*, I thought. I offered my free hand.

Father Gervase enfolded it in both of his but said nothing. His blue eyes again fixed on me, and I was acutely aware of being assessed. "All right, then," he finally said, and then, as he turned to go, "Doughnuts in pairs."

I closed the door, thought, *That was freaking weird.* I carried my empty mug back to the kitchen, left with an uncertain sense I had missed something. It was then I saw the yellow packet on the chair.

Anne D. LeClaire

Swearing, I grasped it and hurried to the door, but I was too late. Even as I shouted and lifted my arm, waving the damn packet like a semaphore, the priest backed out of the drive. I shouted again, but he pulled away. I exhaled my irritation in a long sigh. Either he would return when he realized what he had forgotten, or I would have to drive over to the rectory and deliver it. Neither option appealed.

I felt from the package's contours that it was a book. Without hesitation—I owed the priest nothing—I slipped it from the bag. *The Illustrated Book of the Saints.* I snorted at the cover, a garish depiction of Gabriel kneeing before Mary. The Annunciation in gaudy purples and magentas and greens. I could just imagine the art inside, if one could call it art. I pictured romanticized renderings in Technicolor. Golden rays of light spilling from the heavens. Lutescent halos big as meat platters. Illustrations similar to those in the Bible I'd received as a child, another of my parents' gifts. I could picture them still. Joseph and the coat of many colors. Daniel in the lion's den. Mary and Joseph in the stable. Bowdlerized Disney versions of biblical history. No cow dung in that manger. I understood then that the priest had fully intended to leave it behind. And what? This was supposed to make me what? Make me want to paint saints? I snorted again, this time at this pathetic transparency.

Instantly the rage—the anger that lay low but never disappeared, that had been stirring since the moment in the attic when I'd looked out and seen the priest walking up the steps, the anger Sophie told me was transference and thought would ease if only I would talk to someone about it, the anger she said was driving us apart and she could no longer live with—this rage woke. I flung the book at the door, narrowly missing a sidelight, and it fell to the floor with a thud. *Screw you, Father Gervase,* I thought. *Screw you and the horse you rode in on.* I was trembling. Sophie was right to be afraid of my anger. So dangerous. Unpredictable. A grenade, pin pulled, ready to obliterate all that had not already been destroyed.

Perhaps, like my wife, you are repelled by my anger, but before you judge me imagine yourself in my shoes, and just by doing so can't you feel the heat spreading through your chest, the release of it? Can't you understand? Once I would not have believed this, but now I understand too well that there is in all of us, even the most pacific and composed, an enormous capacity for rage, asleep maybe but present nonetheless, waiting for the single thing that will uncage it.

A faint hissing echoed in my head, then ringing, and then all was muted, as if I were paddling underwater. In this liquid void, the priest's parting words rose up.

Doughnuts in pairs.

CHAPTER TWO

~

Doughnuts in pairs.

Even through the veil of rage, I could picture this nonsensical image, saw them partnered in a glass-fronted pastry case. Pairs of chocolate-covered rings and irregularly shaped halos with dustings of cinnamon and sugar or coated with coconut. Chopped nuts. Plump glazed ones. Crullers. I could almost smell the grease, taste the coating on my tongue, as if I were standing in the Italian bakery on Prospect that Lucy and I would walk to on Saturday mornings and take our time selecting cannoli or ricotta tarts from the case to bring back home for a late breakfast. Our weekly father-daughter tradition.

Of course, I had misheard the priest. But what could he have said? I played with the phrase, came up with another possibility. Doughnuts in air. That made no sense either, but I saw them rise up out of the case, floating past until the ether was dense with them, dancing and twirling and tumbling, each pair linked by stick cartoon arms. A scene from *Fantasia*. Lucy's favorite movie. *Land mine. Land mine.* My head buzzed with memory. On the second-floor landing, a thought ambushed me and stilled my step. Maybe it wasn't that I was going deaf but that I was going crazy. Losing my mind, not my hearing. Going round the bend.

Loony tunes. Daft. Nuts. Bonkers. A finger of fear shot through my chest, and I considered the idea that my hearing loss was psychosomatic, some kind of PTSD symptom. I wondered if Sophie was right, if I *should* talk to someone, but instantly a cone of self-protection snapped in place. I thought of how she would drag me around from doctor to doctor with that determined, take-charge look on her face. *Let's get some answers, see what we're dealing with here.* Physicians and psychiatrists. Otologists and audiologists and neurologists. Hell, maybe even proctologists. She would cover all her bases. Corporal and emotional. Spiritual. I saw her kneeling in a pew, lighting candles, praying. To whom? Was there a patron saint of loose screws? I wouldn't have bet against it.

Early on, when we'd been at that mad and ardent state of courtship that trembled near a welcome madness, when everything she'd said struck me as either endearing or terribly clever, when if she had suggested I crush a goblet and eat the shards I would have happily agreed, when any weakness or flaw was not so much forgiven as unseen, when I could barely trust—let alone test—the miracle of her love for me, she'd told me that for every condition there was a saint who could intercede on one's behalf. We'd gone out for beer and pizza. Hawaiian, I remembered. Pineapple and ham. Her choice. She'd cut her slice neatly using a knife and fork, the first time I'd seen anyone eat pizza with such precision, and I had thought that this was a person who could be relied on to organize one's life. I trusted, too, the way she spoke with such certainty. Lately it seemed to me that women had begun to talk like children, their declarative sentences rising at the end as if in question. *I bought a new pair of boots today?* Didn't they know if they purchased shoes? *That new restaurant just got a rave review in the* Globe? Did they think this verbal tic in some way charming? Or did they believe it made them appear less threatening, the way an animal would roll over in submission to reveal a soft underside? It unnerved me. I liked people to be straightforward.

Saints, Sophie had told me in her confident tone, *could be invoked for most afflictions or important life situations.* I'd laughed, of course,

23

unable to believe she wasn't joking, that a bright and educated woman who seemed savvy about people in ways I wasn't would seriously buy into such shite. (*Shite.* Now there is a word. Proof positive that a semester in London could upgrade one's vocabulary.) *Useless superstition*, I'd teased and slid another piece of pizza on her plate, refilled her glass from the pitcher. *Is not*, she'd insisted with an earnestness I had found enchanting and a certainty I could almost envy. *Saints for every vocation*, she'd said, sipping her beer. *And every country. Saints to protect the innocent and the criminal.*

Which am I?

She had taken a sip of beer and gazed at me, considering. *You're an artist*, she'd said. *Patron saint: Luke.* How had she known this? Had she had to memorize a roster of them along the way? Some kind of catechism of the saints required of Catholics? Or had she looked it up before our date the way another girl might check a man's astrological sign? *There are saints for arthritis and gout*, Sophie had continued. *Headaches and earaches. Heartaches?* I'd said. A premonition? She'd laughed. *Even the plague. Everything is covered. Dandruff?* I'd teased. *Acne? Hangnails? Hangovers? Knock-knees and nose hair? Lost pets*, she'd countered. *And lost causes.*

Well, I thought that morning as I stood on the landing, *now we know better.*

Unlike Sophie, who continued to believe, *believed even after all we had lost*, I didn't believe in saints or in their power to intercede or comfort, and I certainly didn't need them at that instant. What I needed was a drink. I was overtaken with a desire that shot through thirst and went directly to craving. I could almost feel the heft of the bottle, almost see the pleasure of amber liquor in a tumbler, nearly taste the raw jolt of the first swallow, followed by a curling heat that could warm places nothing else could touch. Booze. I craved booze. I checked my watch. Eleven o'clock. Not even noon. Noon I might justify. Mac, my college housemate, had rationalized an early drink by saying, "It's five o'clock somewhere," grinning as if he had invented the phrase. I pushed the desire down, not from self-control but fear. I'd been down that slope earlier in the winter and had fought my way up. Best not to ski that trail again. Who was to say if this time I would find my way back? Plus, I'd promised Sophie. There would be hell to pay if she stopped by and found me drinking this early in the day. I started up the next flight of stairs, each step a victory over temptation.

On the top landing I inhaled the scent of oil paints and turpentine sinking down from the studio, and I was taken briefly by the familiarity of it and was comforted. For a moment I understood why Sophie had fallen for the science—the *pseudoscience*—of aromatherapy, why she had selected hand soap scented with eucalyptus, furniture polish imbued with the oil of lemons or oranges, and why, at night, she'd sprayed our pillows with a mist of lavender—ordered online and shipped from France—that was supposed to induce deep sleep. *Used* to spray, I thought and wondered if, when she'd moved to the rented condo three weeks before, she'd packed the blue aerosol bottle along with her bath salts and body lotions. It was all I could do not to go down to the room we'd once shared and check, afraid that if the spray was gone it would hold a significance I was not ready to face.

I switched the fan back on and returned to the worktable where I took up my brush, unwrapped it from the foil, and approached the easel. In the past, I had received a certain level of renown for my portraits—features in the arts sections of the *New York Times* and *Washington Post*, a four-page spread in *Arts in America*; exhibits in Germany and China; commissions from corporations, politicians, actors—and I gathered it was this attention that had led to Cardinal Kneeland's offering the commission. No doubt I would have refused anyway—even before September I would have avoided getting involved with the church—but since Lucy was murdered I had no interest in portraits and the necessary intimacy they involved. When I'd finally begun to paint again, I had turned to still life, finding in it a distance that allowed me to breathe, as if it were a door opening to another world. There remained a narrative in the work, but no people. I had never been very social, but after Lucy was killed I had given up on people. And who, knowing my story, could have blamed me? In still life I found something remotely identifiable as, if not truth, at least escape. I have never understood people who mistook still life for static. There is so much there in the line and light and composition that contains the power to stir me and draw me in and allows me—momentarily—to almost forget. And even if it was only an hour or two of reprieve, I would take it. As I stood there, I wondered again if Sophie knew about the commission. Had Father Gervase told her he was coming? I remembered another of our recent arguments. "Maybe you're content to spend every waking hour just going through the motions, mad at the world," she'd said. She turned to me then, and I'd seen the gleam of tears in her eyes. "I'm really sorry, Will. Really, I am. The thing is, maybe you can live that way, but I don't think I can."

Of course she couldn't. Not Sophie. I knew she was frightened by my anger, fury that at times shook even me, a force field that repulsed others and isolated me. Nights I would wake from the nightmares I'd had ever since the fall, when the police had given us the news, when I had gone to formally identify our daughter's ruined body, I had lain in the dark and—fueled by this rage—held on to the grim hope, the weak consolation, that someday I'd be able to find and kill the unknown person who murdered our daughter. Almost from the first I began to devise elaborate plots of torture, graphic plans involving things I wouldn't have believed my mind was capable of inventing. I hadn't yet learned the deeds we are capable of. That knowledge would come later, in the summer. Those fantasies and my newborn capacity for violence, my need for retribution, I kept to myself. Once—in the early-morning dimness and tired of being alone with these thoughts—I'd woken Sophie. *Soph, I'd said, if you found out who murdered Lucy and you absolutely knew you wouldn't get caught, do you think you could kill that person?* She had turned to me, not even trying to conceal her horror. *No, of course not,* she said, and then added with a conviction I did not share, *Nor could you, Will. Violence is never the answer to violence.* Well, the truth is we have no earthly idea how we will act when faced with the unimaginable. So I continued to exist in a deep and private grief from which I was cut off from everyone—even Sophie, especially her—and left to my own sorrow. I had lost my daughter, and I had lost my way, and it wasn't getting better.

The painting I was working on that morning depicted an Anjou pear, a wedge of cheese, and an ornate silver fruit knife, all on a blue-rimmed plate I'd selected from the collection of goblets and platters and teapots we'd picked up over the years. I put brush to paint, and as I looked at the order and simplicity of the arrangement on the canvas in front of me, I experienced a mix of relief and guilt to know that while I labored to capture the sharpness of a fold in the cloth that draped the table, the precise shade and texture of the fruit's flesh, I would be able to escape not only the past but the reality of life outside this room, as if I had entered a great tunnel leading to a parallel world.

I looked at the fruit on the blue dish and then thought: *Pears. Not pairs. Pears.* Perhaps that was what the priest had said. *Doughnuts and pears.*

CHAPTER THREE

~

"Do not despair."

As he pulled out of the driveway, Father Gervase heard the echo of his parting words to Will Light and recalled Will as he'd stood in the foyer, his face molded by the strange beauty of sorrow, a grief so personal and manifest he wore it like second skin. He remembered, too, the man's posture, his closed-up body that spoke loudly of his rage, and he knew how facile, how empty, those words must have seemed and felt the insufficiency of them, knew full well his own inadequacy. Surely there was something he might have said that would have comforted or consoled, or even indicated by holding silent that he had seen Will's pain, a witnessing that in itself could comfort. He hesitated for an instant, considered going back, but didn't. Will—his anger and grief—had unsettled him. Still, this did not acquit him. He was aware of his cowardice and was ashamed.

He wrenched the steering wheel, took the corner too widely, veered into the oncoming lane, saw, at the last minute, the motorcycle, and swerved. The bike skidded sideways and then straightened, avoiding a collision by a matter of feet. Maybe inches. As the biker roared off, and even knowing he couldn't possibly be heard, Father Gervase murmured,

"Sorry. Sorry." He felt slightly light-headed. The noise and color outside the car seemed to intensify and press against him, flustering him, and for a moment everything was unfamiliar, as if he had taken a wrong turn. He lowered the window for some air and sighed. A dry and shaky exhalation. Like someone's grandmother. Like his own Nana Gervase.

He was weighed down by the world, and more immediately, in this very moment, he was encumbered by the burden of failure. Double failures. He had failed the archbishop, and all too well he understood he had failed Will Light. This was, in his mind, the greater of the two failures. His foot eased on the accelerator, slowing his return to the rectory.

He needed time to quiet his heart. It all had been so unexpected. Although Sophia Light had spoken to him about her concerns for her husband, he'd been unprepared for not only the man and his grief and rage, but for the house itself and the flood of childhood memories the foyer had awakened, the echo of the past that had washed in. For a moment, hijacked by a vivid memory, he saw his sister, Cecelia, at ten, kneeling on the parquet floor in her Ursuline Academy uniform, pleated green jumper, the white sleeves of her blouse pushed up to her elbows, ribbon-tipped braids swinging forward, intent on a game of jacks. He experienced the old sorrow anew, anguish he had believed long ago metastasized into dead and shiny tissue. What was it Faulkner wrote about the past? It wasn't dead? It wasn't even past? The burden and bitter truth of this haunted.

A horn sounded, startling him, and he realized he was creeping along, slowed to a pace just short of a dead stop. The driver in the car behind him was practically attached to his bumper. Father Gervase flicked on his right turn signal and edged over to the curb. As the driver pulled past, he recognized her as a member of the parish, yes, the mother of one of the former altar boys, and struggled to pull up the name. Beth LaBrea. He felt the victory of this recall, even remembered the name of her boy. Duane. That was it. This small success pleased him. A sweet, reclusive boy, he recalled. And there was a daughter too.

A girl with an unusual name, but that he could not recall. As she passed him and sped off, Beth glared at him, off with one final dismissive look. Everyone was in such a hurry these days. Rush, rush, rush. *And to get where?* he wondered. The inevitable fate that awaited everyone? But this encounter shook him further. His hands trembled, and he tightened his grip on the steering wheel. The car idled at the curb, its engine whispering of futilities. And of failures both ancient and new. What should he have said to Will? What could he have said to blunt the acuteness of his pain? That with time things would get better?

He thought again of Cecelia. No, grief was not healed by time. Eventually, the edges crusted over and no longer ran scarlet, but the best one could hope for was the blessed way that memory faded at the edges, for the numbness of a scar in place of a wound or its fragile, webbed scab. Well, whether a memory grew clouded, a scab or scar, he knew fully how grief permanently changed one's world, how it gave rise to doubt and despair, and even to questions about the nature of faith. Countless times over the years he had sat in the rectory study facing parishioners seeking consolation, desperate for answers because their world had been shattered and they were lost as to how to pick up the shards and start again. And it was an immutable fact that the loss of a child violently shifted the tectonic plates of one's world. If he knew anything it was this. A current of unrest, ephemeral as the wake of a passing wasp, rippled through him, and he brushed it away. He reminded himself that faith was not faith if it had not been questioned and that even grief had a purpose. And hadn't he delivered a homily on this very subject just weeks back? "Suffering points us to the good," he'd quoted Pope John. "It creates the possibility of rebuilding goodness." As he'd looked out at his parishioners, he'd felt the stony, near-hostile stare of Andrea Doucette, who had lost her husband three years before when the *Alva Josephine* went down off Georges Bank, and the hopeful, trusting gaze of twenty-seven-year-old Mary Silveria, whose husband had so recently been buried in the watery grave of the bank. His eyes had fallen next on Sophia Light, her face sober and purposeful. The grief of these women had disconcerted him—as if the Fates or the Weird Sisters had materialized in the wooden pews that morning—and before them he'd felt insubstantial. For a moment, he'd lost his place in the text. When he continued, he'd spoken of the link of suffering to love—a radical and resolute love in the passion of the cross—and had hoped that his words would reach them. "It is not our concern," he'd said, "to erase or regret the scars of grief, but to find opportunity in the wounds that wrought them. Our faith," he had told them, "must triumph over both our sorrows and our fears."

Now he thought of Sophia's husband. He doubted Will would have sat through his homily. Certainly the man he'd seen earlier would reject any philosophical or theological discussion of the mystery and meaning of suffering. And again, at the thought of Will Light, he was swept by an anxiety so sharp it verged on apprehension, actually—impossibly—closer to premonition than perturbation.

He was brought back by the sound of a policeman tapping on the passenger window.

"Father Gervase?"

He rolled down the window, and Michael Callahan peered into the car. In spite of the uniform, Father Gervase could see the child the officer must have been—a skinny kid, an altar boy with a splash of freckles across his nose.

"Is everything all right, Father?"

"Fine, Michael. Fine. Thank you."

The policeman seemed uncertain.

"I'm just thinking for a bit," Father Gervase said. He repeated the words. "Just thinking." As if it were his regular practice to plant his car and sit in meditation in what he now saw was a no-parking zone. At that moment, a convertible with the top down swept past, crammed with teenagers. He counted six in the backseat: three boys and, sitting on their laps, three girls, two of whom he recognized as members of the parish. They seemed to him as exotic as tropical birds. For the third time in minutes, he thought of Cecelia, remembered seeing her in their father's old Nash, riding around town with her best friend, May, windows down, radio blasting, so filled with life and joy that even strangers smiled at the sight.

Michael Callahan watched the car as it took the corner with wheels squealing.

"Gotta go, Father," he said.

"I'll see you on Sunday, then, Michael? At Mass?"

"If I'm not on the duty roster, Father."

"Good," the priest said, as if the officer would show up, playing out the pretense his own mother maintained back in Milwaukee when she waited until after eleven on the Sabbath to phone his brother, as if Joe had actually gone to a ten o'clock Mass. Father Gervase waited until he had gone, then shifted the car into gear, pulled back onto the street, and headed, as was inevitable, to Holy Apostles.

The church rose on the hill, visible even from the harbor, and the priest was pleased by the sight of it. It had been built by Italian stonemasons at the turn of the century and seemed to him to be what a church should be—solid and traditional with the patina of age and prayer. There was nothing modern or stark about it, unlike the new cathedral in the city, whose interior was all steel arches and ribs and seemed to the priest like the innards of a ship before the deck was in place. It was this exact echoing starkness that concerned the archbishop, whose solution was to fill the walls with canvases of the saints. "Paintings of saints," he'd told the Arts and Furnishings Committee. "In the tradition of Catholic wall art. And aren't we fortunate to have one of the most noted portrait artists in the country living not a half hour away, a man whose work has been compared to the Flemish masters."

The committee's vote had been unanimous.

Now the only one who wouldn't cooperate was Will Light.

Father Gervase realized his approach to Will had been ineffective, weak, lacking the details that might have made the artist accept. He should have explained why Will had specifically been chosen by the archbishop and the head of the committee. And although matters of finance would naturally be the purview of Cardinal Kneeland, he could have hinted at the size of the commission.

Father Gervase sat for a moment outside the rectory. The next time they must select someone else to approach Will Light, for without a doubt there would be another attempt. The archbishop was a man accustomed to getting his way, and he was determined to have his way on this business. But with a sinking heart, the priest suspected he would be directed to return. The heft of his own failures and weaknesses weighed heavily.

At last, he got out of the sedan, uncharacteristically slamming the door behind him, a sound that echoed on and on.

CHAPTER FOUR

~

Again, the slamming of a car door broke into my focus, reminding me why I usually kept the window shut, the outer world completely muted.

I assumed it was Father Gervase returning on the transparent pretext of picking up the book he had so conveniently left behind. *Well*, I thought, *I'll be damned if I'll answer the door.* I waited for the chime, wondering how persistent the priest would prove to be. Minutes passed, and when the bell did not sound a trace of concern shadowed my irritation. Had he fallen? Had a heart attack? Stroke? I hoped the hell not, but I remembered the priest's ashy complexion and pictured him slumped on the steps. I set down my brush and crossed to the window, but when I looked down on the drive I saw not Father Gervase's car but Sophie's green VW Bug and again was taken by a clutch of emotions too complicated to separate.

Sophie was nowhere in sight. But she was home, and the tight fist beneath my ribs released. And why shouldn't she be here? This was still her home too. So far we had avoided speaking about what the future held. At least she hadn't spoken to me of it. I had no idea what she told others, what she confided to her friends and her therapist any more than I had a clue of what our future held, but it was clear that our marriage was undergoing a slow and sad erosion, and I felt unequal to the chore of shoring up the ground, making it solid again. Although I knew better than to hope we could return to how we had once been—hope, that sucker's emotion, the resort of fools that led only to more heartbreak and in the end proved as useless as saints—I couldn't still the flicker of possibility at the sight of her car in the drive. For the second time that day, I wrapped my brush and descended, remembering to switch off the fan and close the window before I left. The stair runner muffled my steps, and when I reached the first-floor landing I saw that Sophie had not heard me. She stood in the foyer holding *The Illustrated Book of the Saints*. I watched her, attentive as a spy, as she leafed through several pages. She wore faded gray tights and a matching T-shirt with a purple logo across the chest that I didn't recognize. Some abstract design, as I remember. In the past week she'd had her hair cut, and the style struck me as too severe. Still, in spite of the hair and our rift, heat tightened my belly. I couldn't remember the last time we'd had sex. What I remembered was how in the first days following Lucy's murder when I sought, *needed* the connection and comfort of sex, I had reached for her and her shocked rejection in response. Was that the beginning, the first crack in the mortar that had connected us, too swift and silent to be noted for what it was?

Finally she sensed me and looked up. "Hi."

"Hi." My awkwardness was a third presence in the hall. I didn't know how I was supposed to be, how to be natural with her. Should I have hugged her? Kissed her? The moment passed.

"I rang, but you didn't answer," she said. "I didn't want to surprise you, but I won't take long. I just stopped by to pick up a couple of things."

"No problem." I was irritated by my uncertainty, by my complicated emotions, and by her composure, the way the ball now always seemed to be in her court.

"I won't be long."

So. Not coming home. "I was finishing up anyway," I said. Christ, we were so goddamn formal, it absolutely killed me, but I was determined to stay calm and to be civil. To prove to her that I was changing, that I could be what she needed. If she needed her space for a while—her *space*, we used to joke about couples who talked like that—well, then I would go along with it. Whatever it took so that *space* wouldn't turn into an unbreachable rift. Mortar not just cracked but crumbled. In spite of everything, what it came down to was I couldn't stand to lose her too.

"How's it going? The work?"

"Okay," I said. "It's going."

"Good. That's good. I'm glad for you."

What's happening here? What's happened to us? "Look, I really was about ready to knock off for the day. Why don't we have a glass of wine?"

She lifted an eyebrow. *For Christ's sake, it's just wine*, I wanted to say. But I'd be damned if I'd start justifying. "Or tea if you prefer."

She hesitated, looked down at the book she still held. I could see her struggle with the decision, and then she attempted a smile. "Wine would be welcome, Will. It's been a tough day."

I was able to breathe again. I expected her to follow me to the kitchen, but she went into the living room, as if she were a guest in the house, for Christ's sake, and I swung back to irritation. I grabbed a bottle of Cab from the rack and chose two goblets from a shelf. They were hand blown, part of a collection begun when we'd started dating. Whenever we took a weekend away, we'd buy two matching wine goblets as souvenirs instead of the usual tourist crap, a tradition we continued after we married. I can still recall where each pair came from. Block Island. Provincetown. San Francisco. The East Village. The anniversary trip to Florence. The squat-stemmed glasses in my hands came from a craft show in Quebec City, goblets that once represented the future we were building, a future as it turned out that was as fragile as crystal.

When I returned to the living room, she was sitting in one of the Morris chairs, lost in thought, staring intently into the far distance. Again, as I had in the foyer, I studied my wife. She had changed, and it was more than the haircut. I searched for the words. Seriously self-contained. No laughter shining in her eyes, though that had been gone for some months. I tried to see in her something of the woman I'd married, the girl who laughed with ease of a child, who wore not only her heart on her sleeve but her mind and soul as well, nothing concealed, the person I'd tried to comfort through the long fall and winter just past when we were fellow survivors clinging to the lifeboat of each other. I remembered that day last November when I had come down from the studio in the midafternoon to find her in the kitchen sobbing. She'd been dressed in a blue sweater the shade of cornflowers that fell softly to her hips and a charcoal skirt, black boots, an outfit she'd chosen for lunch with Jan and Alicia, an outing I had encouraged and taken as a sign that she was on steadier ground. "What's wrong?" I'd asked. "Tell me what's wrong."

Between shuddering sobs, she'd related the story, how in the middle of lunch, she had broken down and fled to the restroom of the restaurant until she could regain control. Later, on the way back to the table, she'd overheard Alicia saying, "I don't know what to do with Sophie. She's a mess. She's just a mess." I had held her, let her cry, her tears wet on my shirt. "I'm not a mess," she kept repeating. "I'm not. Can't they understand that I'm grieving?"

"Alicia is an ass," I'd said. It was Alicia, I remembered, who early on had told me grief was like having a house burn down. It took a long time before you realized what you had lost. For an instant I feared I might strike her. "I know exactly what I have lost," I managed before I walked away. I recalled, too, the day in mid-December, the first day Sophie had said she was not going back to school. She'd notified the superintendent that she was quitting. "You quit?" I'd had absolutely no idea she was even thinking of this. Her counselor had encouraged her to return to work, had told her the routine of work might be helpful, and although I admit I had had some reservations, I'd supported her decision. After all, she loved her job as choral director at the school. She loved the kids. How many times had she said it was the kids who made the job worthwhile? The rest of it—administration, rules, regulations—were joy robbers.

"I can't do it anymore," she'd told me.

"It's okay," I'd said. I'd assumed she no longer had the energy to fight the battles her job entailed: convincing the school committee that the majority of choral music was sacred but that this didn't mean she was trying to bring religion into the school, battling the athletic department for a share of the students' free time after classes.

"It's not okay."

I'd tried to embrace her, as I had after that lunch with Alicia, but this time she'd escaped my arms. I'd struggled to think of what to say, to find some way to go on, but she wouldn't talk about it. She walked up the stairs to Lucy's room and crawled into Lucy's bed. "It still smells of her," she whispered to me when I went to find her, and her words struck me hard. Lucy's smell. The fruity mix of apple-scented shampoo and the deodorant that smelled faintly of baby powder and beneath this the singular indefinable scent that was our daughter.

Sophie stayed there that night. And the next. And for weeks after, long after the last traces of our daughter clung to the bed linens. I'd tended to her, bringing her soups and bowls of milk and toast, as if she were an invalid, one suffering a terrible and terminal illness. I was helpless in the face of this collapse.

During those weeks, her sister, Amy, drove down from Maine for several weekends, dismayed and worried about Sophie's condition and as helpless as I had been in the face of it. I fielded calls. She didn't want to speak to anyone, not her friends or her parents, who phoned from Arizona, or her therapist, who called regularly, or Amy, who, after she returned to Maine, called each night.

"Please," I'd begged as the weeks passed. "Please. At least come downstairs."

"I can't," she'd say. "I can't do any of it, Will. Surviving is the most I can manage right now." I saw then, as some part of me had known all along, that our journey through these days was a solitary one. Separate lifeboats.

It was someone from school who pulled her from—if not grief, at least from the bed. Joan Laurant showed up at the door one Saturday morning early in March and asked to see Sophie. "She's not available," I'd told her. "She's still in bed."

Joan was the high school PE teacher, and according to Sophie she never really fit in with the rest of the faculty. "It isn't because she's a lesbian," Sophie said. "It's that she's incapable of putting up with the bullshit the job requires. If they didn't want to risk a lawsuit, she probably would have been fired."

Now she stood in our foyer, a fit and attractive woman, brusque nearly to the point of rudeness. Before I could stop her, she'd brushed aside my concerns and charged up the stairs like a train without brakes. As if guided by radar, she'd gone directly to Lucy's room, where Sophie lay, duvet pulled nearly over her head. Joan took one look at the lump that was my wife and said, "Come on. Let's go. We're going out."

Sophie stared over the edge of the blanket, listless and wan.

"Get up, kiddo. We're going to go fight."

"What?"

"Fight. You know. Punch. Jab. Hit. Box. *Fight*."

I'd started to intercede, to protect Sophie from this bullying, but to my astonishment, she'd risen obediently, as docile as a dairy cow, and—not changing out of the tatty sweats she'd slept in for weeks—headed out with Joan. Later she told me they'd gone to a gym where she had laced on gloves and punched a body bag until she was so exhausted her arms trembled and she could no longer lift them.

Now I shook off the memory and crossed to Sophie with the wine. "I assumed you'd want red." She reached for it, gave me a tired smile. She had said it had been a bad day, and I saw the truth of that in her face. She still held the book and raised it toward me, a question in her eyes. I took a swallow of wine, made myself wait until she had a sip before taking a second, then asked, "Did you know he was coming?"

"Who?"

"Father Gervase?"

She placed her glass on the table. "He was here? He brought this?" Her surprise seemed genuine, but I didn't totally trust it. I knew she continued to go to Mass each Sunday and talked with the priest.

"He left it."

"Why?"

"The archbishop of Boston sent him. Apparently he wants to meet with me about painting portraits for the new cathedral in the city. A series of the saints."

"Really?"

"So your priest tells me."

"And the book is for research?" She couldn't mask the hope in her eyes.

"No. I need to return it. In fact, if you want to drop it by the rectory, I'd appreciate it."

Her chest rose, then fell in a silent sigh. "You've decided not to accept the offer? Just like that?"

"Yes."

"It could be major," she said. "For your career."

I didn't bother to respond. I'd had that kind of attention before. In the end, like so many things, it had proved empty.

"We could use the money."

I couldn't argue with her about that. In the past months, without her working, with me no longer arranging openings, pursuing commissions, funds had flowed steadily out. Savings that had once seemed more than comfortable had dwindled. Only the fund we had established for Lucy's college tuition remained untouched, now designated as a reward fund for anyone with information leading to the arrest of her killer.

"If the church has money to throw around," I said, "let them give it to the poor. Let them hand it over to the victims of pedophile priests."

"Right," she said. She leveled her gaze at me, and I could see that I had again disappointed and saddened her. I watched her place the book carefully on the end table next to her wine.

I sat in the other Morris chair, allowed myself another swallow. "Shall I build a fire?"

"Oh, don't bother."

"It's no bother."

"I can't stay."

"Can't? Or don't want to?"

"Will," she said, her voice soft but steady. "Please. Let's don't start."

"Right," I said. I looked at her and again thought that it was like gazing at a stranger. It wasn't even the haircut or the self-control. Even the contours of her body had changed. Once she'd been soft, womanly. I remembered with a pang that was physical how I used to hold her, stroke her curves, her stomach, and once more felt the hot dart of desire that refused to be extinguished in spite of everything. Even now I remain amazed at how persistent our most primitive desires are. Sex. Survival. Revenge. "I'm getting a pot," she would say when she caught herself in the mirror as she climbed out of the bath or as she undressed for bed. "You're not," I'd respond, not in any automatic, husbandly, reassuring way but because I truly loved her body, the slight rise, the mound of her belly. I couldn't have imagined her with plank-flat abs, couldn't understand the appeal of that. "You have a body born to make love to," I'd tell her back in a time that was far distant. Now she was thinner, her chiseled arms evidence of the hours she spent in the gym. She had taken up kickboxing, she had told me, and could bench-press a hundred and ten pounds. She wanted me to be proud of this, but I couldn't. Couldn't even fake it. I resented the way her body had been transformed. This woman I did not know. I wanted my wife back. I felt the impossible longing to have my life back. My old safe, comfortable life.

Recently—the previous week? Over the weekend?—Sophie's photo had been in one of the Boston papers. She was a font of information. Nearly eight hundred thousand children go missing every year. Two thousand a day. Twenty thousand children murdered in past years, she'd told the reporter. *Twenty thousand.* The figures had shocked me. Still, I deeply resented how this had transformed Lucy into a symbol, a statistic. A month before, Sophie had been interviewed on the noon news of the local NBC affiliate. She had become a media icon. Practically beatified. The Voice of Our Murdered Children, they called her. I had watched the show, amazed at how articulate she had become, how fierce, Sophie who used to have a glass of wine to fortify herself before attending school committee meetings. She had coined a term to describe the culture that allowed the abuse and killing of children, a culture that glorified death and violence in games and movies and television. *Murdertainment.* She'd told reporters that speaking about this was a way something positive could rise from the loss of our daughter. When she talked about what had happened to Lucy and other children, her anger was apparent, but it hadn't consumed her. In some way, it had made her stronger. The balance between us had shifted precariously.

"Will?"

When I looked over, I saw her expression. Part irritation, part concern.

"What?"

"You haven't heard a word I've said, have you?"

And I hadn't. That was another of the things we'd argued about recently. "You don't listen to me," she complained. I would parrot back what she had said on an automatic pilot of recall, but of course now she was right. I hadn't been listening. I had gone to the hollow place of non-sound. Perhaps I really was going deaf.

"I've been asked to go to Washington," she said.

"Washington?"

She caught me up, explaining that she had been asked to testify at Congress before a subcommittee on violence in the media and its effect on society. I saw only the futility of this, the inevitable disappointment for her, as if anything she could possibly say would make even the smallest dent in the profits generated by violence. It was always about money.

"The committee hearing is on Tuesday. Do you want to come with me?"

That I wouldn't do. In the days immediately following Lucy's disappearance, I'd allowed myself to be convinced to appear on television with Sophie. We had watched the clip of the interview later that evening when it was re-aired on the eleven o'clock news, and when the cameras returned to the anchors at the end of the segment I had been shocked to hear one of them say to the other in an offhand way, *The father struck me as very calm.* As if they could possibly know what the fuck I was feeling. That was the last time I'd allowed myself to be put on the stage of public opinion.

Sophie waited for my answer. "Why don't you ask Amy?" I said. "She'd be better company."

"I knew that's what you'd say."

Then why ask?, I thought.

"I'll drive down on Sunday. So I'll be there on Monday."

She put an odd emphasis on *Monday* and looked at me as if I should understand. Had I missed something? "Monday?" Was there another interview she had scheduled? A symposium? A panel? I waited for a clue.

"I can't stay here in town. I just can't." She stared at me. "You've forgotten." Her voice was flat. Not a question. "Seven months," she said, finally. "Monday it will be seven months to the day." Her gaze was both accusation and indictment.

Somewhere deep in my chest I felt as if a rib had broken.

"I can't believe you could forget," she said.

"I didn't forget." But of course I had. And she knew I had, which made me defensive. "I just don't keep track of the—the anniversaries. I don't like to make a . . . a goddamn holiday of it." God knows it was difficult enough to get through the formal calendar days—Christmas, Valentine's Day, Lucy's birthday—without marking each passing month too.

"You think that's what I do? Make a *holiday* of it?"

"I don't know what you do. I just think keeping exact track of the weeks and months seems—" *Morbid*, I thought but did not say. "I mean, what's the point?"

"Well, what would you rather I do, Will? Shut down? Shut everyone out? Give up hope? Pretend nothing happened?"

"Jesus, Sophie. How can you think it is remotely possible for me to pretend, to forget—"

But Sophie was not listening. "Is that what you want me to do?" she continued. "Shut everyone out and retreat to the attic while the world falls apart around me?" *Like you* was unspoken, but the words hung in the air so present she might as well have screamed them.

"Soph—" I began, but saw it was too late.

She stood, her face set.

"Don't go," I said.

"I can't stay."

She left, not bothering to pick up whatever she had come for. I stood at the door and watched her walk to the car. Walk away from me.

CHAPTER FIVE

~

Evenings, I walked.

So the day Sophie left for DC, I headed out, as I often did, with no particular destination in mind, propelled only by the need to escape the vast and haunting stillness of the house. On some nights, I would walk to the harbor, a sight as familiar to me as breakfast toast, and I'd pause to sit on a bench and smell the sea, staring at the fishing fleet as the boats bobbed at their moorings like tethered boxcars or whales. I had read somewhere, probably a chamber of commerce brochure, that our harbor was the safest on the East Coast.

Sometimes, if there were no high school kids horsing around on the basketball court, I'd walk by the community playground. Several years back, a group of townspeople had spearheaded a drive to raise money to hire a big-name builder famous for his all-wood playgrounds, but when we learned our children had been playing on structures built of arsenic-laced timbers, it had had to be torn down. Now the swings and slides and jungle gym were all plastic and fiberglass, and parents hoped that they hadn't been too late in discovering the danger of what they themselves had brought into town. After the playground, I'd walk over to the promenade that fronted the town beach, passing the house with a collection of owls set on glass shelves in the street-facing window, dozens of them in glass and brass, ceramic and wood, a collection that had fascinated Lucy when she was a child. I'd continue on, pass the statue honoring fishermen lost at sea and the memorial wall etched with their five thousand three hundred names—*the harbor may be safe, the ocean not so much.* I understood that some found comfort in these numbers, found consolation in knowing that they were not alone in grief, that they were but part of many who had walked the sorrowful path of fractured hearts and spirits, but screw that.

At other times I'd find myself cutting through an unfamiliar neighborhood, miles from our home, with no idea of how I got there. More than once I'd hiked all the way to the Eastern Point Lighthouse, and it would be after midnight before I returned home, feet sore, sometimes blistered, my legs worn as stumps, the exhaustion a relief. Again and again Sophie had told me it was foolhardy, dangerous to walk alone so late at night. She said it made her sick with worry to wait in the late dark for my return.

"What do you want me to do?" I'd asked her. "Get a gun?"

"A gun?" She had looked stunned.

"For protection. If you're so worried."

"Oh, for God's sake, Will. That's the last thing I'm suggesting. I'd just feel better if you weren't walking around out there half the night."

But once the idea of a gun had been seeded, it grew. For protection, I'd told myself, a small handgun. The true, darker reason I had admitted only to myself. I would need it when I found the person who killed Lucy. It would have to be unregistered. Untraceable. According to news reports, there were thousands of illegal guns floating around. How hard could it be to get just one? In the end, it had proved easier than you would have imagined. A trip to Portsmouth. A visit to a pawnshop. A number scribbled on a paper. A hurried meeting in—at another earlier time I might have laughed at the irony—the parking lot of a white-steepled church. Methodist I think, if I am remembering the sign in front correctly. Cash exchanged for a weapon. Extra for the ammo. The entire exchange took no more than five furtive minutes, no questions asked. When I took the bag, I had expected it to be heavier, the weight reflecting what it contained. *Ironic* doesn't begin to cover that moment. One of the few petitions I had ever signed was one to ban assault weapons. By the time I'd driven out of the lot, I couldn't remember what the man had even looked like, only the thin, hyped-up sound of his voice that made me suspect he was high on something. At home, I'd taken the brown bag up to the attic studio and after locking the door had practiced loading it, weighing the cold metal shells in my palm. Finally I stashed it beneath a paint-stained rag on a shelf behind my worktable, where Sophie wouldn't ever look but where it would still be handy.

In October, when I began these walks, I'd drop by the police station. At first, the duty officers manning the front desk were cordial, offering me coffee, their voices, if not warm, at least neutral, but gradually their tones became less sympathetic, more guarded. "Go home, Mr. Light," they'd say. They had nothing new to tell me. The case was still active and open. Let them do their jobs. They would call. I really didn't expect them to call. I knew the odds, the dark statistics of these things. With each month that passed it became less likely that there would be any development or resolution. To find who killed our daughter and make him pay. Once I'd shown up at the station intoxicated—not just tipsy but drunk to near incapacitation—and they'd threatened to put me in protective custody, for my own safety they'd said, but in the end one of the cops on patrol had driven me home.

On those autumn evenings and well into the winter, I would prowl, as I now knew the police did, restless and vigilant, searching faces for what lurked beneath the human masks. A teenager on a skateboard. The jogger with a blue neoprene sleeve on his knee. A man in a gray top-coat. The police recruit on bike patrol along Main Street. Or the burly young man walking a Gordon setter. It could be anyone, I would think. Anyone could have killed Lucy. I knew that if I could look into the face of the person who had murdered her, I would know it absolutely. Of course now the irony of this slays me, and I wonder if those I passed—the dog walker, the recruit on patrol, the jogger, any of them—would see, on looking at me would glimpse the rage, the need for revenge, the slumbering violence of which I was capable or even if I, on looking into the bathroom mirror as I shaved, if even I was blind to the depth of what I was capable of. And so I walked and searched the faces of the people I saw for the stain of guilt. It had to be someone, I'd think. *Anyone.*

In the early spring, before she moved out, I had shared my thoughts with Sophie, believing she would understand, but instead she warned me I was growing cynical. No, I told her. Not cynical. Realistic.

"What about you?" I'd said in defense. "You haven't changed?" I pictured her in a fighting stance, her kickboxing class, her taut body.

"Of course I've changed, Will. But what would you have me do? Isolate like you? Sit around and cry? Well, I've done that. It doesn't help. It's just that—we can't let our hearts grow hard."

"And you think you haven't done that?" I'd thought of her talking to reporters, spouting numbers about the thousands of dead children.

"No," she said. "I haven't."

"Right."

"It's possible to be an activist, you know, to believe it's possible to change things, and to still have an open heart."

"*The voice of our murdered children,*" I'd said, unable to strip my voice of sarcasm.

"Oh, Will," she'd said. Her look of pity had made me shiver. "Can't you see? We can't afford to grow cynical. If we do that, they've won."

"That's cheap sentiment," I'd said. "Like what people said after 9-11." The truth was they had won. And we had lost our daughter.

And still that spring, I searched faces. The person who killed our child—again and again the image of her blood-soaked tote, the annihilated cell phone, her broken body, would cloud my vision—this person was walking in the world undetected. Laughing. Eating a burrito. Buying a six-pack. Or a bottle of booze. Or a pair of new shoes. Planting a lawn. Tossing a Frisbee to a retriever. Watching a ball game. Having sex. Going on. Unpunished. Undetected and not likely to be detected. Unless he made a mistake. Unless there was another child.

Seven months.

That evening I wandered aimlessly for a bit. I headed toward the playground, but as I approached I saw a group of boys shooting hoops in the growing shadows, serious go-for-broke, smack-talking ball, their voices breaking open the quiet of the night. Despite the chill of early evening, they had stripped to the waist and sweat glistened on the skin of their chests, their naked backs. The air seemed to shimmer around them—a force field. On a bench at the far side of the playground, a boy sat alone, his concentration focused on the electronic device he held. He was thin, and there was in his posture a vulnerability, someone others would bully, the kind who would try to will himself invisible. I had a vague recollection of the boy as someone Lucy had known, but I wasn't sure. I turned away and continued over to Stacy Boulevard. There were more dog walkers there, out for a last stroll before heading home for the evening. A wind blew in off the water, the blue expanse broken by chevrons of white. I buttoned my jacket against the chill. It was only May. I should have worn something warmer.

Seven months.

I pictured Lucy back in October on the last morning of her life, her quick, banana-scented kiss and "Bye, Da," as she flew out the door, innocent of what lay ahead, and I was burdened by every month, every week and day and hour that had passed since, the bleak horrors of Thanksgiving and Christmas, the seasons melting from fall to winter and now spring, edging into summer, the mornings when I woke and for one cruel nanosecond life seemed normal and then memory cut like a lash and with it the impossible grief, the actual physical pain of it, and the knowledge that nothing would ever again be the same.

Seven months of this with no indication that it would ever ease.

Does my grief tire you? Do you want me to get on with my life? Try to understand how impossible that is. Try to imagine what it is like to have your daughter, your beautiful, kind child, murdered and then tell me to get on with my life. Seven months and here is what I imagined as I walked and searched for the face of her killer. I pictured what she suffered before she died. And I imagined her fear at the end. Wondered how the end had actually come and hoped it had at least been swift, a single small mercy. Had she pled? It didn't bear thinking. And yet I couldn't stop thinking about it, ruminating on the horror of it. And truth be told, if it happened to you, I don't think you would either, and I hope you never have to find out. So this was what I was left with. This was what had led to my new self—an angry man who drank too much and had an illegal handgun hidden in his attic studio against the day when he found his daughter's killer.

I reversed course, walking back past the Owl Lady's house, past the playground, now dark and empty, the boys gone home. In the town center, a Coors Light sign flickered neon in the window of the Crow's Nest. Forget it, I told myself. Go home. A promise was a promise. I thought of Sophie in Washington, off on her crusade.

The Nest was crowded, and as soon as I entered I was assaulted by body heat and noise. The place stank of stale beer, of something faintly musty, of cigarette smoke although years ago the state had passed a no-smoking law. You could wash the place down with a fire hose and it wouldn't cleanse the air. I paused, almost left, thought of the promise I had made to Sophie. Just one, I thought. One beer and I'd leave. I took a quick look around. The crowd was young—mostly fishermen and a few women, two men engaged in a game of darts—no one I recognized except for Gilly behind the bar. Each stool was occupied, and I muscled in at one end, pushing against a brawny twentysomething, jostling his draft. The man, still in his fishing garb, whipped toward me and our eyes met. I didn't know him but watched recognition dawn on his face and then, swiftly, saw it shift from belligerence to embarrassment and then pity. A look I knew too well. Even strangers gave me that glance. I might as well have been wearing a T-shirt proclaiming, *Something terrible has befallen this man.* And if it wasn't pity I saw in the faces of others, it was suspicion. "You're imagining that," Sophie told me when I confided in her, but I wasn't. I knew the police hadn't immediately cleared me in the beginning. I remember the cadaver dogs brought in by the state police before Lucy had been found, German shepherds sniffing the ground of our backyard, even rooting around in our basement. *Our basement.* The implication clear.

"Sorry," the fisherman said as if he were the one who had shoved in, spilled beer.

I felt let down. Although I had not been in a fight since high school, I would have welcomed it that night. The release of it. Something solid to punch, not phantoms. Had that been my intent in coming to the Nest? To seek the physical release of a fight? Though the truth was the fisherman was younger, fitter, and in any confrontation I would have gotten the worst of it. Hell, those days Sophie of the muscled arms could probably have bested me.

Gilly made his way toward me. "Hey, boss," he said and slapped a cardboard coaster in front of me. "So what'll it be? Draft?"

Seven months.

I can still recall every detail of that October day as if it were etched in granite, a monument of loss. It had begun in an ordinary way. I'd made breakfast. We'd eaten together, and then Lucy and Sophie had left for school. I'd welcomed the time ahead—eight full hours because it was a Tuesday and my wife and daughter wouldn't return home until nearly five. After classes Sophie had chorus, already in rehearsals for the concert that signaled the holiday break; Lucy had French club and a field hockey scrimmage.

I put in a full day painting—probably forgetting to eat lunch without Sophie there to remind me. I was that way with work. At some time late in the afternoon I'd descended to the kitchen to start dinner preparations: chopping onions, mincing ginger, pureeing garlic, seasoning and browning the lamb. I took satisfaction in the cutting and dicing, the sound of oil sizzling in the pan. Cooking grounded me after a day in the studio. It was a segue between the two passages in the symphony of my life: painting and family. At one point I had looked out the kitchen window and noticed the last of the serrated leaves from the elm cartwheeling through the air. As I often did when I stared at the tree, I'd taken a moment to admire the graceful architecture of the arching branches. I'd poured myself a glass of Cabernet to sip while I worked. Back then, drinking hadn't been an issue. I rarely had more than two glasses at night. Occasionally, Sophie and I might allow ourselves a short pour of something later, before bed. Asked how I felt, I'd have said, "Content." I was pleased with the progress of my current painting. Dinner was under way. The prospect of a family evening lay ahead. Content.

I'd heard the front door open and called, "In here." Minutes later, Sophie entered the kitchen. She had looked so happy, as she often did after a rehearsal with her chorus. She loved those kids, and the feeling was reciprocal. They even phoned her at home. I'd lift the receiver and hear a young voice asking for Mrs. Light. Many of them came to her with their problems or for advice, things they could have taken to the guidance counselor or their parents. I used to wonder if the administration knew the kids called her, if she could get in trouble for it. I knew how territorial educators could be. I'd tease her, ask her if the school paid her extra for the counseling. Once she had asked me if I thought Lucy minded this, this sharing of her mother, but the truth was Lucy was supremely confident in her place in both of our hearts and openly proud to have a mother who was so loved by her peers. The previous spring, before the prom, two of the senior girls asked if they could come by to show Sophie their gowns, and a boy called to ask whether he should buy his date a wrist corsage or pin-on one. Last summer vacation, two of the girls—altos in the chorus—had called her and told her they were pregnant, confiding in her even before they told their parents. She had been deeply upset by their news.

"Imagine if it were Lucy," she'd said.

"Well, where were their parents?" I said. "Didn't they know what was going on in their daughters' lives? What were they doing, letting those girls run wild?"

"Oh, it's so easy to blame the parents, but it's not that simple, Will." She'd paused and reached out to stroke my arm. "I think we like to affix blame because it makes us feel safe. Like it couldn't happen to us."

"Well, we don't have to worry about it happening to us. To Lucy. She's a great kid."

"That's the thing, Will. These girls—Cassandra Lewis and Heather Church—they're really great kids, too."

So that last afternoon, radiant as a girl herself, she'd come into the kitchen. She paused by the iPod dock, made a selection. A clarinet concerto. Von Weber, as I recall. "Hmmm," she'd said. "Something smells delish."

"Lamb tagine," I'd said and poured her a glass of the Cab.

She took it, kissed me lightly in thanks. "Is this the same meal you made when the Rogerses came for dinner? With all the spices?"

I was impressed she had remembered. We didn't entertain much, and that evening with Larry and Jenna Rogers was more than a year before. "It's the one." I'd set down the spoon and crossed to her, stood behind her, and folded my arms around her midriff. I'd nosed her hair off the column of her neck, pressed my lips to her nape, inhaled. "Coriander." I kissed the sweet spot of skin beneath her earlobe. "Cumin." She tilted her head back, and a light moan slipped from her mouth. I shifted her, turned her to me, and slid my tongue down the underside of her jaw, tasting the salt of her sweat. "Ginger," I said. I had a hard-on before I reached her throat.

She pressed herself against me. "A chef and lover, too. Careful, Will, if the word gets out, you'll have them lining up at the front door."

I kissed her deeply, pulled away only to unbutton her blouse. That was the last carefree moment we had.

Her hand stayed mine. "Lucy," she said. "Is she upstairs?"

"Didn't she come in with you?"

We pulled apart. A flicker of unease but even then it was no more than that, a flutter, while we tried to sort out what lapse in communication there had been. Sophie buttoned her blouse.

"I thought you were driving her home after French club and hockey," I said.

Sophie scowled. "No. She wasn't there. I assumed she must have called you earlier to pick her up. I thought maybe she didn't feel well. Remember how yesterday she said she thought she was coming down with something?"

"I'll check upstairs," I said. "Maybe she slipped in earlier when I was in the studio. Maybe she fell asleep." I allowed myself to be reassured by the knowledge that occasionally in the past Lucy had done that after school, fallen into a sleep as deep as that of an infant until one of us had had to wake her for dinner. She would be slow to stir, as if rising up from a coma.

"I'll go with you," Sophie said.

"No need," I said. "I've got it covered." But she followed me from the kitchen. As we crossed the hall, I checked the chair by the sideboard where Lucy often flung the blue L.L.Bean tote she used as a book bag. Not there. I forced myself to take the stairs calmly.

"Lucy?"

Her room was just as she'd left it that morning: PJs hanging on the door that led to her bath, the bed neatly made, teddy bear propped on the duvet, curtains pulled open. Everything in it was a reflection of her—our daughter—half girl, half woman. Another bear, this one an oversized panda, on the armchair next to a bed. Atop the wicker basket she used for laundry I saw a pair of balled-up pink underpants and the Boston College sweats she liked to wear while studying. Her iPod was on the desk next to an empty apple juice box. On the shelf hanging above the desk were small stuffed animals from infancy and plastic figures from cartoons and movies, a collection of the toys we had given her over the years. A small basket of cosmetics and another of jewelry were on top of the dresser flanked by two photos, one of Lucy with her best friend, Rain, and the other of the three of us, taken in Camden that summer, the rocky coastline a blue cradle in the background, Sophie and Lucy and me in the foreground, tanned and happy. A family.

The room smelled of her. Nothing was missing. Except Lucy.

I turned to check the bathroom, but Sophie was already ahead of me.

"Lucy?" she called.

"Lucy?" I said.

"Where do you think she is?" Sophie asked, and still there was no fear in her eyes or in her voice, just the slightest apprehension.

"Are you sure she didn't say she was going to Rain's after school?"

"No, but that's probably where she is."

We returned to the kitchen. I started to turn the heat off under the lamb, as if dinner was going to be long delayed, and stopped myself. Lucy would show up any minute. An hour from now the three of us would be sitting down at the table as we did every night, reviewing our days, sorting out where the mix-up had occurred. Sophie insisted on this. "Families that eat together stay together," she said. And Lucy teased her about this. "What are we, the Brady Bunch?" But I knew she liked it as much as we did.

I stirred the stew, fought a growing unrest. Until Lucy was born, I had never thought of myself as a person given easily to fear, but taking her infant body into my arms was like holding eight pounds and three ounces of naked vulnerability that was my charge and duty to protect. And I had. I held to all the rules my mother had enforced in my own childhood. *No swimming for a half hour after eating. No running with a Popsicle stick. Or scissors.* "If you're not careful, you'll turn her into a neurotic worrier," Sophie had said. She was the more carefree one of us, more trusting that all would be well. Behind me she switched off the music and picked up the phone; I listened as she questioned Rain. "She hasn't seen her since their seventh-period class," she reported after she hung up.

"Try Christy," I said, but she was already dialing.

I checked Lucy's room again, as if we'd somehow missed her the first time, checked the bathroom, even looked in our bedroom. Sophie stayed on the phone. Other friends and classmates. The principal. Coach Davis. "He said she didn't show up for hockey scrimmage," Sophie reported, her voice tight. "No excuse or anything. She just didn't show up." She didn't have to say what we both were thinking. That was not like our Lucy. So responsible. So dependable. Even last year on the officially sanctioned "Freshman Skip Day," she had gone to class.

At six we called the police.

I would go over and over that morning, searching my memory for some clue I had missed and still not believing it possible that she was gone. The missing child. It was a story that was a staple for made-for-TV movies and on the big screen, in novels and on the front page of city papers and the six o'clock news, horribly, unthinkably trite in its familiarity. A mother weeping, pleading for anyone with news of her child to call the police, a father—stoic and strong at her side, jaw tight. *If you've seen our daughter . . . Kelly, please, if you are hearing this, please come home . . . Amanda, please come home . . . Jessica, we're not mad. We love you . . . Please, everyone, please help us find our daughter. Please, if you have our daughter, bring her back to us.*

It was a standard plot line of fiction. And of heartbreaking fact.

One you never thought could ever happen to you. Not to you.
Seven months.

I knew I should go home. I thought again of the promise I'd made to
Sophie. No more heavy drinking. In the far corner where the men were
playing darts, I caught the glimmer of steel as a missile flew toward the
segmented board. Gilly waited for my order. The noise in the room
grew in volume, and the ringing in my ears started again. Go home, I
told myself. Make some coffee. Have a glass of wine. And then what?
Sit before the television. Alone. Judge me for my weakness if you will,
but then think, what would you do in my place? How would you go
on if someone had murdered your child? You cannot imagine what it
takes to go on. "Bourbon," I said. "Straight."

"Bourbon?" Gilly said. "You sure?"

"Positive."

The barman paused. "Bar brand okay?" he finally asked.

"Fine."

"You want something with that? Burger? Fries?"

"Just the drink."

"Okay. Bourbon. Straight up. On its way."

Seven months.

CHAPTER SIX

~

Seven times.

For the seventh time Rain counted backward from one hundred to zero. Nearly ten minutes had passed since her parents walked past her door, their steps slowing outside her room before continuing down to their own. When she had finished the counting, she opened her door and listened to the hush of the house. She knew her parents would fall asleep quickly, lulled by the dinner her mother had served—a totally disgusting meal, total carb city; she'd barely been able to manage two forkfuls—followed by an evening of mind-rot TV, one of those stupid reality shows with the pathetic contestants and a panel of has-been judges, the kind of show that asked the viewers to call in their votes. Totally lame. And fixed of course—any idiot knew that—but still her parents continued to watch, sitting there in the den as dull and patient as a pair of shoes. Seriously. She didn't know how they tolerated their lives. Just shoot her now.

Carefully, allowing herself to step only on the lurid peonies woven into the pattern of the worn runner, she crept down the hall away from her parents' room. She was meticulous in this, as she was in everything. If she stepped off a blossom, as she occasionally did, she would return to her room and start over. Tonight there was no misstep, and she proceeded quietly to the end of the hall, then in darkness descended. She felt the pressure beneath her breastbone, the stretch of too-tight skin on her body, but she would not allow herself release until she had finished what she had to do. Once downstairs, she crossed to the front door. "Button lock," she whispered and fingered the little brass bar in the knob to ensure it was set in the horizontal position, not the vertical. Check. Next she tested the deadbolt, made sure it had been shot home. Check. Finally she tested the chain. Check. Six more times. *Button lock, deadbolt, chain. Button lock, deadbolt, chain.* She intoned the order softly to herself. Buttonlockdeadboltchainbuttonlockdeadboltchain. Deep breath. Still the fist in her chest was clenched. The control box for the security system was affixed to the wall to the right of the doorframe. The alarm button glowed red, signaling that it had been armed. Earlier she had watched as her father triggered the sensors on the doors and windows, the exterior motion detectors but not the interior ones. Rearming it would cause it to beep, and that might rouse her mother, who had the hearing of a doe, so she had to content herself with tapping the box with her index finger. Seven taps.

Finished in the front hall, she went to the dining room, finding her way in the dark. When she'd first begun her rounds, she'd carried a small Maglite until it occurred to her that someone watching from outside could follow her progress through the house, and so now she moved in darkness unless there was a full moon throwing its glow through the windows to light her way. He could be watching and waiting. *He.* The person who had killed Lucy. Tonight there was cloud cover blocking celestial light, and she crept through the dark room as she checked the two windows on the southern wall. Seven times she checked the locks. She repeated her ritual in the living room and the den, the kitchen. Finally she reached the back hall and the door that led into the garage. It too had three locks. Button knob, deadbolt, chain. Seven times she checked them.

Recently she'd overheard her mother complain to her father, "How much longer must we keep this up? We've got this place locked up tighter than Fort Knox." As if that could keep anyone from trying to break in. And what did they know about security anyway, about how robbers and kidnappers, rapists and murderers, thought? Seriously. The extent of their knowledge they got from TV shows. *CSI. Law & Order* reruns. Pathetic. Her parents were epically stupid. As she passed the basement door, she saw a line of light seeping beneath the bottom crack. Duane was down there glued to his computer, another mind-rot machine. Duane the Lame. She had no idea what her brother did down there. For all any of them knew, he could be clicking on porn sites. Maybe he was smoking dope. Or doing something hugely illegal. Or researching how to build bombs, like that kid in Oklahoma. Or those brothers in Boston. She imagined SWAT teams in full riot gear smashing down their front door, leading him off in chains, the disbelief on her parents' faces. She imagined the town overrun with reporters—like right after Lucy had disappeared—platoons of them, interviewing neighbors and teachers and the other kids, all as clueless as her parents. "What will people think?" was one of her mother's favorite cautions. Well, this would certainly give them something to talk about. She could almost feel sorry for her parents—raising two complete losers. Two noobs. Although, of course, her mother thought Duane was perfect. But maybe he was down there sleeping. Or cramming for final exams. She knew nothing about her brother these days. She thought he might slip out at night, because more than once she had heard their mother tell their father that he'd forgotten to set the alarm the night before when Rain *knew* it had been set. The only explanation was that Duane punched the code in and escaped the house. But where would he go?

When she had finished her rounds, she returned to the second floor, again stepping only on the runner's faded blossoms. The pressure in her chest was painful now, burning. In her room, she wedged a chair under the door handle. She'd asked for a lock, for some *privacy*, but her mother had said there was no need—privacy was a foreign concept to her mother—and that was the end of that, so she was reduced to this half-ass measure. She pulled the curtains tight across the window (always aware he—the murderer—could be watching) and then turned on the small bedside lamp. The light glared flatly, revealing the slippery-looking chintz on the spread and curtains, the god-awful furniture—fake French provincial. Her mother's idea of sophistication. Rain's idea of ugly. Ugly. Ugly. Ugly. The fist in her chest shifted to her belly, clenched so tight it was like a menstrual cramp.

She opened the second drawer of her bureau and took out her pajamas, then stripped, turning away from the mirror so she wouldn't have to look at herself. She didn't need a reflection to know how she looked. Her thin body, her badly shorn hair that she'd cut with a pair of her mother's sewing shears. A pixie cut, her mother had called it, in the way she always tried to transform a disaster into something else. *Are you eating lunch at school? I can pack something if you don't like cafeteria food.* Her mother would rather eat fingernails than mention her worst fear. *Anorexia.*

D-Ni-Al was her mother's middle name. Seriously.

Rain couldn't wait until she was old enough to leave this house for good, although sometimes she would see her mother standing in the kitchen or her father walking in from the garage and a memory from her childhood would surface—something as simple as her mother letting her eat a spoonful of raw chocolate-chip or peanut-butter dough while they readied a batch of cookies for the oven or her father hoisting her up on his shoulders so she would have a clear view of the Fourth of July fireworks over the harbor—and a swift tenderness would wash over her. And then something would happen—her mother would criticize her for something stupid or her father would fart right there in the room—and the unexpected surge of softness would evaporate, gone as if it never existed, and be replaced by disgust.

It was her father who first noticed the scars. It had been a Sunday and they were having dinner. She'd grown careless and had worn a short-sleeved sweater instead of her usual long sleeves. She'd been staring at her plate, pushing the mound of potato around with her fork, wondering how she'd get through the meal, how soon her mother would let her be excused, when she heard her father say her name.

He was staring at her arms. "What in the name of Pete happened to you?"

"Nothing." She'd hugged herself tightly, concealing her arms with their faint crosshatching of lines.

"What do you mean nothing?" He reached for her arm, turned it over. "You're all scratched up."

She had pulled her arm free, thought fast. "Oh, that. Dee's cat. I was trying to pet her."

Predictably, her mother chimed in. "A cat? Did you wash with soap after? Cats carry diseases, you know. I don't even want to *think* of what their claws have been in."

"Don't worry. I washed and put on antiseptic cream."

When she dared look up, her eyes met Duane's, and instantly she saw that he knew. *Freak*, he'd mouthed. She'd held her breath, afraid he'd say something, but for once he hadn't. Once caught, twice sly, she had been careful not to slip up again. She let her arm heal, started cutting places concealed by clothes, places her parents wouldn't see unless they demanded she strip. And for months she'd been success- ful, fooling everyone. Until one evening last week when her mother had walked into the bathroom just as she was getting out of the shower. Rain had whipped a towel around her body. "Pleeeze," she'd said. "Can I have a little privacy here?" Too late. Her mother had stared at her thighs, the scars and scabs and fresh cuts, and for once was yanked out of the la-la land of happy thoughts and into a total freak-out.

"Oh my God. Who did this to you?"

"No one *did* it to me, Mo-ther."

"Don't lie to me. Was it that boy? What's his name? The one who keeps calling the house?"

By "that boy" her mother meant Chuck Meadows from biology class who had phoned exactly twice in the past three months, each time to check up on a homework assignment.

"My God, what have you got yourself into?"

"Nothing. Just get out. Get out and let me get dressed."

Her mother left, but Rain heard her outside the door, waiting.

It had begun in October—in European history class. They were studying the chapter on the period leading up to World War I, and Mr. Marshall was droning on and on in his pale, limp voice about the shooting of some prince or duke or something. Rain had felt so jumpy she didn't know if she would make it through even one more minute. After Lucy was murdered, she hadn't wanted to go to school, but when a week had gone by, her parents had said, *Enough. It will be better if you get back to the normal routine.* Like they had a clue what she needed. Like it was even possible to return to normal. Sometimes her skin felt too tight on her body; other times she felt as if she had no body at all, as if she might rise up off the chair and float right out of the room and no one would even notice that she was gone. Just like, after the first few weeks of circling a wide swath around Lucy's vacant desk and chair in homeroom, classmates walked right by it as if they were invisible. Now she felt as if the chair she occupied was as empty as Lucy's, as if she had evaporated or nothing more dramatic had happened than Lucy had transferred to another school or something. She'd shut out the teacher's voice and picked up the biology report due for her next class and pried the staple off that had been affixed at a forty-five-degree angle as Mr. Neuben demanded or you got five points deducted from your grade. Idly, she unbent it until it was straight as a wire, tested the point of one end with her thumb, and then, with no more thought than if she were doodling in the margin of her textbook, she drew the point across the smooth inner skin of her forearm. A scratch appeared, a white line against her faded summer tan. She traced the line with the end of the staple, and then again, harder now, breaking the skin. She was amazed to see blood bead on the surface in a row of tiny red pearls. For the first time in weeks, it seemed that she could breathe, as if she were no longer invisible. She drew a second line. And a third. "Hey, spaz. Whatcha doing?" Ferret-faced, syruphead Danny Weston was watching her. She pulled her sleeve down to cover the marks, shoved the staple between the pages of her text, lifted her face to Mr. Marshall. But she couldn't forget what it had felt like, couldn't forget how for a moment she had been able to breathe.

She thought about it for several days, ran her finger over the scrapes as they healed. Then, one night, while getting ready for bed, she could no longer ignore the claustrophobic tightness of her own skin, the growing panic, and so, as if in some part of her brain she had been planning this all along, she unearthed the green leather manicure case her grandmother had given her for Christmas and slid the tiny scissors from the silk loop that held them in place. Slowly she drew the smaller of the two blades across her arm, shocked to see it made not a scratch but a cut. The pain—and the relief—was immediate. She pressed the blade against her skin, made another cut. And no one knew. Until last week when her father had noticed. So her mother had done the total freak-out scene, threatening to call the police, so sure was she that someone had done this to her daughter.

"Who did this?" she kept asking. "And don't hand me any nonsense about cat scratches."

And so Rain had told her the truth, which set off a different kind of hysteria. The manicure set was confiscated. Lectures began. Whispered conferences between her parents at night while Rain eavesdropped from outside their door. "Well, I've had it," her mother said. "It was bad enough with all the locks and that ridiculous security system that's costing us an arm and a leg, but I'm done humoring her. I mean it. Now she's gone too far."

"Maybe it's some kind of phase she's going through."

"A phase? A phase?" Her mother's voice rose. "She's *cutting* herself, David." Her father murmured something, too low for Rain to hear. "I mean it. Enough is enough," her mother said. "You've got to do something."

"What do you expect me to do, Beth?"

Then her mother started to cry. "I don't know. I don't know. I just know this is beyond me. I can't handle this."

Rain had retreated to her room, sick with shame. In the morning, her parents announced they were sending her for therapy. *A shrink*, she thought—*to shrink me*. Though if she got any smaller she would disappear for real.

She placed her pajamas on the foot of the bed and slipped on a clean pair of panties—totally nude she felt too exposed, even thought the shade covered the window. Then she opened the bottom drawer and pulled it free from the dresser and carried it to the bed, emptied the contents and turned it over. She knew her mother snooped in her room when she was at school, going through it like a customs inspector, and she was relieved to see she hadn't discovered the razor blade in its hiding place. She picked at a corner of the Scotch tape from the underside of the drawer, freed the blade. The tightness inside her body made it hard to breathe. She took the blade and drew it across the pale skin of her left hip, felt the relief as blood surfaced. After a minute she drew a second line. She was *real*. She *existed*. She shivered, her near-naked body now cold. She pulled a Kleenex from the box on her dresser, folded it into a precise oblong, and pressed it against the new cuts, holding it there until the blood clotted. The cramp in her belly eased, nearly disappeared. She retrieved a large Band-Aid from her stash hidden in the bottom of a tampon box, tore off the paper, and placed the bandage over the cuts. She was always careful that there were no traces of blood on her clothes or bedding. She always flushed the old Band-Aids and bloody tissues down the toilet in the morning. She had never been a devious child, but she had become adept at fooling grown-ups: her sad-eyed father; her mother, who went through her room every day, searching for clues; and her teachers.

Duane was right. She was a freak. A loser. A total screwup.

CHAPTER SEVEN

~

Instantly, even hungover, I realized I had really screwed up.

When I heard my name, I believed Sophie had come to me in a dream; then she spoke again, was in the room with me. Not a dream. Here. Not in Washington. I scrambled up from the sofa where I'd passed out the night before and stumbled, momentarily dizzy. My head throbbed, my bladder ached, and my mouth was parched, but even with the hangover, I was acutely aware of my wrinkled undershirt and shorts, the sour smell of my body.

"Hey, Soph," I said.

"Oh, Will." Her body was rigid with an anger as sharp as a blade, and with disappointment, too, the more penetrating weapon. "You promised."

What could I say to that?

She glanced around the room. "Jesus, Will."

"I wasn't expecting you," I said, my brain racing, wondering what she was doing there. Shouldn't she still be in Washington? I realized I didn't even know what day it was. I looked around, saw the mess as Sophie must have seen it. Empty bottles. My shirt and pants draped over one of the Morris chairs. Shoes on the floor. A blanket and pillow on the couch. Food on the coffee table. She *hated* the room looking like this.

"What's going on, Will?"

A *thong*? Why was she asking me why I was wearing a thong? What the hell could that mean? I looked down at my shorts, was instantly shamed to see they were stained. "What?"

"What's going on?" she repeated.

Oh. I took in the plastic forks and boxes of half-eaten food on the coffee table—a pizza carton and half-empty boxes of cereal—and tried to calculate how long the binge had lasted, tried to remember how long she had told me she would be in Washington. She had left for Washington on Monday. Her testimony had been postponed until Tuesday. So this had to be at least Wednesday. I closed my eyes as if that simple act could possibly make the mess disappear. Instead of answering I said, "Let me get us some coffee." I would have sacrificed a foot for a cup of coffee. Or a Coke. Water. Anything liquid. That and a piss. I retrieved my pants from the arm of the chair and pulled them on, relieved to see they were not stained too. With forced casualness, I made an effort to straighten out the room. I was aware of her eyes following me as I folded the blanket, gathered the cartons. I focused on each movement, willed my hands to stop shaking.

She remained standing. "So you don't remember." Her voice was flat. This was a statement not a question.

Remember what? Now I would have sacrificed both feet for a triple dose of caffeine. "Let me get rid of these," I said, indicating the boxes. If I could get her to the kitchen, I could turn on the coffee. But the kitchen looked no better. An open peanut-butter jar. Cracker bits and bread crumbs and dirty knives in the sink. A carton of souring milk on the kitchen table. Empty ice trays on the counter. Moving as quickly as the hangover allowed, I dumped the milk down the drain, wiped the counters. I measured grounds, poured water into the coffee machine, careful not to spill. The need to piss was urgent. Sophie was talking to me from the living room.

"What?" I yelled. "I can't hear you. Can you come out to the kitchen?" There was silence, and I could feel her weighing my request. As I reached for two mugs, my gaze fell on a squat cobalt-green teapot, and it brought on a rush of memory. The sprawling flea market set up on the edge of a farmer's meadow. The autumn day. A lifetime ago. The moment Sophie fell into my life. Literally.

The teapot had been in the back of a narrow table crowded with used and chipped china. Together, at exactly the same moment, we had reached for it. As our fingers touched, two children raced by, jostling Sophie, and she fell into my arms. Instinctively, immediately, I had cradled her, felt, as I steadied her, a nearly primitive need to protect this soft woman with the round face and wild blonde-streaked hair, this creature dressed in a denim skirt, off-the-shoulder blouse in a green—malachite, I remember, a shade that most women can't wear—and boots with heels so insanely high I didn't know how she was able to walk in them. And even with those heels, she regained her balance with the grace of a Balinese dancer. Her head just brushed my shoulder. Moments later, I handed money to the woman behind the table—the asking price, no haggling—while Sophie cradled the pot in her hands, just as shortly before I had held her. She laughed up at me then and looked directly into my eyes. "Our first purchase," she'd said with a confidence I would never have dared, even joking, as if our future had already been decided and we could cut through the dance. So easy. So inevitable. With an innocence nearly arrogant, with not an inkling of what lay ahead.

Another lifetime ago.

Sophie came to the threshold but didn't enter the room, and I was pulled back to the present. "Don't go anywhere," I said. "I'll be right back." In the bathroom I peed a long stream, the smell acrid. The cabinet mirror above the sink confirmed the grim news. Unshaven jaw, red-shot eyes, bags underneath, face deeply lined. I opened the cabinet door, shook two tablets out of the bottle, swallowed them dry. The headache was killing me.

When I returned, Sophie hadn't moved from her spot in the doorway. "You don't remember calling me, do you?"

Shite. A dim recollection surfaced. Sometime—the previous night?—I'd phoned her at her hotel in DC. The Mayflower. Big mistake, I realized now. Big, big mistake. Huge. I debated whether admitting I remembered the call would escalate the magnitude of my error or if it would be better to plead amnesia. Didn't matter. Either way was an admission I'd been smashed out of my skull when I'd phoned. Here was an idea: someone should invent a phone with an internal Breathalyzer that would prevent drunks from making calls. It was the kind of crazy concept that once would have made her smile. I could imagine her response and how we would have played with the idea. *What would you call it?* she'd say. *Intoxi-not. Dry-dock. Designated no-call.* Think of the friendships it would save, the relationships rescued from rupturing. The coffee was brewed, and I poured two mugs, offered one to Sophie, which she ignored.

"So what was so pressingly important that you had to wake me at two in the morning? Or was it just for some middle-of-the-night drunk talk?"

Yeah, I sure could have used the no-call gizmo. I stalled for time, set her mug on the counter, drank from mine. I was playing catch-up here, trying to nail down the day, what I'd said during the call. Had I been telling her I needed her? Asking her to come home? Begged her? I thought I remembered crying. God, I sincerely hoped not. She hated drunken conversation, the slurred sentimentality. I didn't blame her. Every inch of my skull ached—behind my eyes, my temples, jaw—and I was nearly cross-eyed from the pain.

"You need help, Will. You're a mess."

A mess. "Christ," I shot back. "That's rich." As simply as that I was drawn in to starting an argument.

"What?"

"That you'd tell me that. Have you forgotten?"

"What are you talking about?"

"Last fall. Remember when you had lunch with Jan and Alicia and you overheard them say you were a mess? What did you tell me when you came home? You weren't a mess. You were grieving. So what is it? You're allowed grief, and I'm not?"

I was gratified to see she was contrite.

"You're right, Will. I'm sorry." She entered the kitchen, picked up the mug, and pulled out a chair at the table. "I don't want to fight."

"I'm sorry, too, Soph. I really am. I screwed up. I know it."

"Yeah, you did."

"Okay, we agree on that."

"I don't know what to do, Will. I can't handle this."

"Handle what?" I said, afraid of her answer. Did she mean the drinking? Our marriage?

When she spoke, her voice was heavy with sorrow. "I don't know, Will. I've tried, I really have, but I just can't do this anymore."

The void between us was growing wider, and I feared it couldn't be crossed. How had it come to this? Once I would have bet our marriage was solid enough to withstand anything, but I was no longer confident. I wondered if in even the strongest of marriages there always existed a fault line and it just took one major, earth-shattering disaster to reveal it. "I'm sorry, Soph. What can I say? I feel like a total shit."

"So what happened?"

I sat at the table and dropped my gaze to my mug, unable to meet her eyes. "I don't know. It wasn't anything I planned." I considered telling her I'd been lonely with her off in DC, and although I was tempted—even scared and on the defensive—I couldn't use such an unfair accusation as a weapon. "I was out walking and thinking about—you know—"

"No. I don't know, Will."

Lucy. I didn't allow myself to say her name, afraid I would start weeping. "Everything," I said. "And I was walking by the Nest, and, I don't know, I thought I'd go in for a beer. Just one beer."

"Not one of your best ideas, Will."

"You think I don't know that? It's just so hard, Soph. Sometimes I just need to forget."

She reached over and laid her hand on my arm. "Drinking never erases memory, Will. It just makes you drunk."

She was still upset, but I saw the conversation was calming her down. "I know. I know that." But that wasn't completely true. Drinking did help me forget, at least for the moment. And for this brief respite I was able to block out the pain of losing a daughter and how utterly I had failed my family. My head throbbed so badly I wondered briefly if I had a tumor.

"Will?"

"Yeah?"

"We really need to talk."

We need to talk. Nothing good could come of that.

I struggled to come up with a response.

"Oh God," she cried out.

"What?" I said. "What's wrong?"

She was staring out into the backyard. "Lucy's swing," she said. "What happened to Lucy's swing?"

I shifted my gaze to follow hers, saw two ropes hanging freely from the elm tree, saw on the ground beneath it the plank of the wooden seat.

She crossed to the sink for a better view. "Look. It's been cut," she said. "Someone came into our yard and cut down Lucy's swing? Who could have done this? Why would anyone do something like that?"

"I don't know." A boozy recollection surfaced. The hacksaw in my hands, the dark, lit only by the glow of the back porch light and the echo of light cast from the Eatons' house next door. No longer able to bear the sight of the empty swing, I'd sawed away at the ropes, as if they were responsible for our loss. I remembered, too, the wind overhead in the night air and the drunken moment when I thought it had called out to me in Lucy's voice. "I don't know," I repeated.

Something in my voice or my face alerted her.

"Will. Tell me you didn't . . . tell me it wasn't you."

But of course she knew, could see the truth plain on my face. The silence filled the air between us, as wooden and flat as the useless seat that accused me from the lawn in our backyard. "Soph—" I began.

"Don't," she said. "Just don't." She set her coffee down on the kitchen table and, her posture rigid, left without another word.

I heard the front door slam her departure, the rumble of the VW's exhaust as she backed out of the drive. I stood motionless as granite while minutes ticked off and the mug grew cold on the table, but she did not return. I must have stood there like that for half an hour. Staring into the emptiness. Then a fury of motion took me. As I tore through the rooms as if possessed, I remembered what Sophie had once said about an acquaintance, a woman who never seemed to stand still. *Can't hit a moving target*, she'd said. That best described me as, in spite of the searing headache, I began a frenzy of cleaning, as if setting the house straight would be the start of getting everything in order. I started in the kitchen, working as if to eliminate the criminal evidence. In the living room, cleaning as an act of atonement. I dumped the accumulated trash into a plastic bag, dusting, hauling out the Hoover. As I pushed the wand of the vacuum cleaner beneath the skirt of the sofa, it struck something. A shoe, I thought. I knelt, the motion causing a momentary wave of nausea, and reached under the sofa, knew instantly a shock as I felt the cold contour even before I withdrew the pistol. Or revolver. I didn't know the difference. I cast a swift glance toward the hall, afraid

Sophie might have returned, but of course she hadn't. I had absolutely no memory of retrieving the weapon from the studio where I'd hidden it, but obviously at some point in the past days that was exactly what had happened. A thought chilled me. What if instead of under the sofa I had left it out on the table or on the sofa cushion? What if Sophie had seen it? I stared at the gun in my hand, knew it was no longer safe to keep it in the house. But where? The car was a possibility, stashed in the trunk. Or the glove compartment. I remembered I didn't have a—what was it called?—a license to carry. Hell, I didn't even have a license for a weapon, never mind driving it all around town. I tried to think. I abandoned the vacuum there in the middle of the floor and went upstairs. I needed to get sober and devise a plan. I carried the gun into the bathroom with me, shoved it in a vanity drawer, and turned on the shower, adjusting the water until it was as hot as I could stand, and gradually, as it streamed over me, washing away my sour stench, a plan formed. I dressed, then retrieved the pistol and headed out, intending to drive to our bank and open a safety-deposit box where I could stash the gun, but before I had even turned on the engine, it hit me that the entire purpose for the gun was to have it on hand. I sat behind the wheel, and my gaze fell on the backyard shed. Sophie never went there. It was dark inside, and I paused to allow my eyes to focus, then settled on a row of paint cans, three of which were empty, waiting to be recycled. I pried open the lid on one that had held the stain I used for the front steps, wrapped the gun in one rag, the ammunition in another, and dropped both in the can, reassured that now the weapon would be safe from Sophie but available for when I needed it. Available when I finally learned who had killed our Lucy.

CHAPTER EIGHT

~

The Illustrated Book of the Saints was still on the side table in the living room.

In the past days, Father Gervase had not returned for the book, nor had Sophie dropped it off at the rectory as I had asked. Again, as I had been the first time I had glanced at it, I was put off by the gaudy sentimentality of the cover art, the blatant piety. The book was thicker than I would have thought necessary. I had no idea how many saints there were but estimated there must number no more than one or two hundred. But then my knowledge of this realm could fit in a thimble with space left for my thumb, just bits and pieces I had gleaned from Sophie over the years: they had suffered for their faith, lived holy lives, many had been martyred and rewarded by sainthood. I thought of the childlike sentimentality it must take to believe in the supernatural power of these beatified to comfort or console, to intercede or heal. And yet people did believe.

One day while walking down an aisle at the local grocery store, my attention had been drawn to a shelf displaying votive candles with images of different saints on the glass cylinders. One might have expected this at one of those shops dealing in religious icons and books and other kitschy paraphernalia, but at the Safeway? Even more surprising was a smaller grouping of aerosol cans that flanked the candles, each containing the scent connected to a particular saint. *Spray and pray*, I'd thought. I had never understood it, this bizarre conception that saints could intercede in one's life. I remembered as a child riding in the backseat of Jimmy Harrington's family sedan and watching the oval medal of Saint Christopher as it swayed on its chain from the rearview mirror, hung there, Jimmy's mother explained, to protect them on all journeys. And I had seen ads in the classified pages of the *Globe* beseeching Saint Jude for help and seen, too, over the years, the occasional television reports documenting the hordes of pilgrims descending on Lourdes for healing, clinging to their last hope, arriving by the thousands, in wheelchairs and on crutches and being transported on gurneys. I had always been both unexpectedly moved by them and equally dismayed. I thought, too, of the front-yard shrines throughout Port Fortune with statues of the Virgin Mary ensconced in the upended bathtubs—Mary on the Half Shell people called them—and of the adults who had placed statues of Saint Francis in their gardens. I even knew a couple who'd buried a miniature replica of Saint Joseph by their front door in the belief that this would facilitate a house sale. "You have to bury him upside down," the wife had told us over a dinner at the seafood restaurant by the harbor. "And when the house sells, you must unearth him and bring him to your new home," her husband added. These were intelligent and educated people, skeptical in matters of politics and commerce and in no other way given to superstition. Their gullibility stunned me. It was all such shite. Although Sophie would have argued with me, I thought it was not much different than the Greeks and Romans and Norse with their pantheons of gods. But this was the twenty-first century, for Pete's sake. What would it take to believe in all this shite? A lobotomy would be a start.

Early in our marriage, Sophie and I had reached a truce on these matters. She didn't try to convince or convert me; I didn't ridicule or subvert her faith and believed I was successful at hiding my true feelings. The only thing she asked of me, even before we married, was that our future children be raised Catholic, and I had agreed without hesitation. Thus I had surrendered our only child to this church. By its priests Lucy was christened and confirmed, and within the stone walls of Holy Apostles a funeral Mass had been said for her. In the end all the rites and rituals had offered no more protection for Lucy than Saint Christopher had for Jimmy's family when their Ford Fairlane got hit by a drunk driver.

I flipped the book open to a random page and was surprised to see a painting that was not the mediocre schlock I had expected. I was arrested by the image of a man as slender as a boy, with a boy's face, clad in what looked like white Jockey briefs. In the painting, he was lashed to a post and four arrows pierced his flesh, one each in chest, thigh, rib, and abdomen. Saint Sebastian, I read, a martyr who, when he refused to sacrifice to the gods, was shot with arrows and then clubbed to death. The protector of archers, athletes, and police officers. I turned to another page. Saint Apollonia, virgin and martyr, and protector of dentists. When she refused to renounce her faith, heretics broke out all of her teeth and then burned her alive. *Protector of dentists*. On another page, I saw a painting of Saint Bartholomew. He was depicted with a thick beard, receding hairline, and was holding a curved butcher's knife. The text beneath the painting informed that Bartholomew had been flayed alive and was the patron saint of butchers and tanners. So you were shot with arrows and made the protector of archers, had your teeth broken and became the protector of dentists, were flayed and protected tanners? I doubted the church deliberately intended this to be ironic. As I thumbed through the pages, I scanned passages depicting lives dedicated to supreme good works and charity and lives ended by torture, a listing of the hunted and haunted, the beheaded and burned, crucified and stoned. The accompanying paintings were works of the masters, of Rembrandt and Caravaggio, El Greco and Holbein. I found these renderings to be deeply disturbing. It was hard to tell from the faces whether they were in agony or ecstasy.

What did I believe in that, in the face of torture and inquisition, I could hold tight? Lucy, I knew instantly. I would have suffered anything to have saved Lucy. And Sophia. That was my list. My daughter and my wife. My country? I considered the question. I had never been one of those people who needed to wear a flag in my lapel proclaiming proof of my allegiance. I had never served in the military, and in college I had signed a petition opposing a certain government policy. I didn't hang a flag from our front porch, not even on the patriotic holidays when the entirety of Port Fortune was swathed in red, white, and blue. And yet, standing in the hall, staring at the faces of the saints and reflecting on the question, I believed I would not betray my country. But, then, who knew, when put to the test, what a man would do, what a person could withstand in the face of torture? Who knew what a person was capable of? As it turns out, we are all capable of much, much more than we would have dreamed.

Shadows crossed the room as the sun moved lower in the sky. I flipped to another page and was completely unprepared for what was depicted in the painting. A woman—nude to the waist—was having her breasts torn off with pincers. Saint Agatha, the text instructed. Protector of wet nurses. A wave of nausea swept me. I'd had more than enough of martyrs and of saints, of the torture and murder of virgins elevated into something sacred instead of profane. I was taken by an anger so violent I was queasy with it and slammed the book shut. I wanted the goddamn thing out of my house.

CHAPTER NINE

~

Father Gervase closed the book and lowered it to his lap.

Earlier a brief thunderstorm had rolled through, leaving the lilac leaves a magnified and brilliant green. The bench where he rested was still damp, but this hadn't deterred him from coming out to sit in the garden situated between church and rectory. It was five thirty in the afternoon, and soon Holy Apostles would be on the summer Mass schedule arranged to accommodate tourists and returning seasonal residents, but for now this hour was free and the meditation garden was hushed and cool. There was a narrow stone bench nestled in an arc of lilacs and another in the shadow of a juniper, and this was where the priest sat. He inhaled the nitrogen-charged air deeply, almost greedily, drinking in not only the ever-present scent of the sea but also the daylight, which wouldn't edge toward shadow until after seven, compensating for the enforced confinement of past winter days that he found more challenging each year. Lately he had daydreams about slowing down and moving to a warmer part of the country, a place of extended daylight. A reassignment to a seminary or retreat in Arizona, perhaps, or New Mexico, although he would miss being near water. There was always Florida, but he did not seriously consider it. Geography called to one, and, in spite of the climate, Florida had never appealed to him. The San Francisco area was a possibility. He had never been there and yet could imagine it—a more laid-back Boston with cable cars and the Golden Gate Bridge. His ideal spot would be somewhere with a temperate climate and a suggestion of seasonal change. He had little control over the wishes of the church regarding his placement, but he liked to dream. He pictured a small place with a garden, one similar to the site where he now sat and that gave him such pleasure.

He had always liked this hour when the world slowed down and he could claim a slender window of it for himself. Even as a boy he'd looked forward to this time. School would be over and homework could be put off until later in the evening. His mother would be busy in the kitchen preparing dinner, his father not yet home from work. His brother, Joe, would be off somewhere with a posse of friends, playing baseball or shooting hoops, depending on the season, or hanging out at the home of his current girlfriend. Cecelia would be occupied too, playing jacks with her friend May or jumping rope, always with an intense concentration that to this day he associated with his sister. Unlike his siblings, he would not seek company but would slip away to a corner of the laundry room where he could read undisturbed, enveloped by the lingering smell of laundry detergent and wet cotton spinning in the dryer, and enjoy the quiet pleasures of solitude, as he did even now.

Often these days he changed into gardening clothes and donned gloves to tend to the ferns and hostas that lined the walk in the shady section or to take up a trowel and rough the ground around the bed of daylilies that edged the front path, a narrow strip that received direct sun. The garden was not overly large and required little care: the plucking of weeds from the border beds and crushed clamshell paths, the cutting back of shoots that sprang up at the base of the lilacs, the dividing of an overgrown hosta that threatened to choke adjacent plants, chores of basic maintenance he relished in spite of the way his energy seemed to wane lately and despite the disapproval of Lena MacDougall, the president of the Rosary Society, who hinted that weeding was beneath his station.

"We have a gardener for that, Father," she said the first time she spied him on his knees in the lily bed, her lips pursed thin. "You shouldn't be doing it."

"Laborare est orare," he replied. *Work is prayer.* He'd spoken to her of how such work could uplift one and, if done consciously, celebrate existence and contain the teachings of life, but she had not been swayed by this philosophy. She believed his work should stay inside church walls and not involve dirt beneath his fingernails and had even complained to Father Burns that it reflected poorly on Holy Apostles to have Father Gervase doing the job that was the responsibility of the hired gardener.

"After all, we are not First Baptist," she had reproved, "and we mustn't act like it."

A sigh escaped the priest's lips as he thought of Lena, who believed *her* duties involved policing the parish and enforcing her personal standards of behavior. And didn't she have a bee in her bonnet about the weekend janitor. "There is something off about that man," she'd said. "I just don't trust him." And just last month she'd created a stir about Miriam Endelheim coming to pray in the sanctuary. "She has her own synagogue," she'd complained. "Why does she have to come here?"

At that moment, the priest had found himself praying for the virtues of patience and acceptance. "Mrs. Endelheim has a special affection for the Blessed Virgin. She likes to sit with her," he'd explained, then added, smiling, "Don't forget, Mary was the original Jewish mother." His attempt at humor had fallen flat as it often did with her. And his explanation for Miriam Endelheim's presence in the sanctuary hadn't satisfied Lena any more than his equating manual work with prayer had. Father Gervase rarely allowed himself the luxury of disliking people, but Lena reminded him of a creature of prey. But in spite of her sniffing disapproval, Mr. Jervis was still employed to clean the sanctuary and chapel, Mrs. Endelheim continued her regular visits to the Virgin Mary, and he went on working in the garden.

The love and pull of the land was bred in his genes, handed down from his paternal grandfather, a Wisconsin apple farmer. Throughout his teen years he'd helped in the summer orchards. Autumns, during the harvest, he operated one of the farm's cider presses, an old John Deere machine that clattered and whirred as the air filled with the heady scent of apple mash and the buzz of intoxicated yellow jackets. He had loved his hours at the farm, certainly some of the happiest of his childhood, and imagined a future spent there. But occupations, like geography, called to one, and another life outside Wisconsin awaited him. Still, had he not entered the priesthood, he would have been content tilling soil, growing crops. Or reading poetry. Now there was a job that should exist. To spend one's days in the company of Blake and Dickinson, Yeats and Hopkins, Auden and Milton. To fill one's mind with their wisdom, the music of their words.

Today he did not weed or rake, but he had brought with him to the garden a volume of Neruda's poetry. He read only a few lines before setting the book aside. Will Light intruded on his concentration. Since his visit to Will, Father Gervase had replayed their conversation, unable to escape the lingering knowledge of failure, a burden that had not lessened with the passing days but had seemed only to reveal and magnify his previous ineffectiveness and shortcomings, failures that, in the face of Will Light's grief and anger, festered like splinters beneath flesh. Late in the game, Father Gervase realized that too often he had been tone deaf to the needs of those needing help or comfort. In response to these needs, he had quoted scripture, promoted faith, parroted the words of mystics and saints and popes. Better to have said nothing. Better to have listened. Or simply laid a hand on Will's shoulder. Better to have handed over an anthology of poems.

On the matter of Will Light, and in spite of Father Gervase's report, Cardinal Kneeland hadn't given up. "Perhaps we need to speak to him about the amount of the commission," the archbishop had said, his mind that of a Medici banker.

"I'm sure that will not make a difference," he'd replied.

"Well, you have planted the seed," the archbishop told him. "When you go back, it will have taken root."

In this, as in so much, Cardinal Kneeland's faith was stronger that his own.

Determined to be better prepared for a return visit to the artist, two days ago he had walked over to the Port Fortune Museum of Art to familiarize himself with Will's work, something it occurred to him he should have done sooner. The museum, a two-story Greek Revival, had been donated to the art association by the heirs of its original owners. Inside, the walls were filled with work he found somewhat predictable: oversized canvases of seascapes at sunrise, landscapes captured at sunset, smaller oils of pink roses draped over white fences, pastels of peonies in full bloom. A docent directed him to the second floor, where two rooms were dedicated entirely to Will Light's work, the majority of which were portraits. They'd struck Father Gervase as Vermeer-like in composition. A teenage girl behind the counter of a coffee shop. A child crouching at water's edge, surf sucking at her feet. A young fisherman in yellow oil-skins, on loan from the permanent collection of a Boston museum. An older fisherman sitting on a barrel by a shack mending nets. A woman seated at a vanity, her image reflected in the mirror. Another painting of the same woman looking through a window out to the sea, her face drawn with sorrow. After he had seen the entire exhibit, he circled the galleries again, going slowly from room to room, this time looking more closely at each painting. Shadows reflected on foreheads and cheeks; soft smudges of vermilion furred edges; clear, translucent glazes from morning light filtered through clouds and raked flesh once vibrant as embers, now captured with mineral earth and linseed oil. He returned to the old fisherman, the child at the seashore, a young boy crossing a meadow captured on the cusp of manhood, the woman at her dressing table. Exact moments held in time—a morning light, a constant gaze, a flushed life—caught by a deft hand. As he studied the portraits he saw they had, at first glance, a quiet, contemplative focus, but there was also incorporated in each a second layer of suggestion and a meaning beyond the obvious. He could now understand fully why, beyond the artist's fame, the archbishop was set on having Will accept the commission to paint the mural of the saints.

Movement at the periphery of his vision pulled Father Gervase from his reverie, and his eyes widened. As if his preoccupation with the artist contained a conjuring power, the priest saw standing at the edge of the garden Will Light. His heartbeat quickened and with it the knowledge that he was not as afraid of failing the cardinal as he was of failing Will. Well, no time now for a quick retreat, and he vowed to do better, to reach out and . . . What? Save? No, that was not yet in his mind. To help.

CHAPTER TEN

~

Just as I entered the garden the little priest looked up and caught sight of me, and the moment for a quick retreat escaped.

I'd planned on dropping the book at the rectory office, but it was after five by the time I arrived and the door was locked, staff departed for the day. In search of someone else to take the goddamn book off my hands, I'd wandered into the garden, where I ran into the priest.

"Will Light," Father Gervase said and started to rise.

I motioned for him to sit. "No need to get up, Father. I won't disturb you further."

"Not at all," the priest said, standing. "Not at all. I was just enjoying a few minutes in the garden. Glad to have you join me. You know what they say about pleasant moments."

"What's that?" The priest was even smaller than I remembered. And frailer.

"Pleasure shared is pleasure doubled."

"Yes, well, I can't stay. I just—"

"Is Sophia with you?"

I knew Sophie often stopped by to sit in the garden or the chapel at the end of a long day and that more than once she'd sought the priest's counsel. If he didn't know, I wasn't about to tell him about Sophie's move into a rented condo. "No, she's having dinner with a friend."

"Well, please tell her I continue to hold you both in my thoughts and prayers."

"I'll do that, Father."

A silence stretched on so long it verged on awkward before the priest broke it. "You know, Will, it's rather amazing that you came along just now. Rather amazing."

"Really? Why's that?"

"I was just thinking about you, and then I look up and here you are." I managed a noncommittal shrug.

"Now some people would say that this is nothing more than coincidence. Happenstance."

"Yes, well—"

The priest removed his glasses, held them at arm's length, and checked the lenses. "But there are others who believe there is no such thing as coincidence." He lifted his gaze from the glasses to me. "They believe that everything is connected and that these connections—what we call coincidences—are meaningful signals from the universe."

"I guess that's not something I think about much." I wanted to get rid of the goddamn book, not be drawn into some inane discussion about coincidence. And my head still ached from the hangover.

"Oh, I've always been interested in these things." Father Gervase slid his hand into his pants pocket and withdrew a soft green square of something that looked like silk. "You know what I mean. In astonishing occurrences of synchronicity that defy explanation."

"Hmmm, well—"

"I remember reading of one story in particular. A story of identical twins who had been separated at birth and adopted by different families." He polished the lenses with the cloth, attentive to the task until, satisfied, he returned the green square to his pocket and put the glasses back on, fitting one earpiece at a time behind each ear. "Amazing tale, really," he said. "It was about two boys, separated at birth by adoption. They grew up to marry women with the same first name, who both gave birth to boys on the same day and named their sons the same name. Now that's a coincidence that challenges belief."

"This chance meeting hardly rises to that level, Father."

"Perhaps not." The priest reached out and absently stroked a fern. "Perhaps not. Still, I've read this interesting fact somewhere—" He looked up as if searching for an answer in the branches arcing above the bench. "Now where was it?"

I shifted the book from one hand to the other. "Listen, Father, I just wanted to—"

Father Gervase's gaze again landed on me. "Well, I don't remember where I read it, probably not important. The thing is, according to the article, and I'm probably not getting it exactly right, but the gist is that scientists believe we are hardwired to connect anomalies in meaningful ways. You see? The mind wants, even needs, to make these causal connections."

I remembered too late the priest's inclination toward conversational sidetracks. "No. No, I didn't know that."

"Oh yes. Yes. According to the article, researchers believe it's this ability that's at play when we learn a language."

"Interesting," I said, my voice just short of curt. Christ, would I never be able to escape.

"Isn't it." Father Gervase studied me for a moment, leaned toward me. "So here's the question at the core of it: Are life events random, or do they represent a deeper order?"

"And what's your take on that, Father?" I asked in spite of myself.

"On coincidence?" He smiled. "Well, I don't know about the scientific aspect, but there is something at work. I think of it as spiritual timing. God's timing."

I could guess where this conversation was headed and derailed it before it could pick up speed. The last thing I wanted to hear was any shite about God's timing. "Well, I just stopped by to return this. You left it at the house." I extended the book, but Father Gervase made no move to take it and instead headed toward the side door of the rectory, motioning for me to follow. There was a damp circle on the seat of his trousers from where he had been sitting on the bench, and this patch caused an unexpected softening in me. I found myself trailing the priest into the rectory, thinking I'd just get rid of the book and get out of there.

The living room where he led me held the smell I associated with my father's home after my mother died, a place of men who lived without women, a stale, slightly sterile smell that made me feel claustrophobic. The room was furnished with two couches, a rather discouraged looking recliner, and a television—one of those new flat-screen jobs. Plasma? LCD? Not that I knew the difference. Our television was so old it was surprising the Smithsonian hadn't requested it. There were a couple of side tables and a coffee table on which were magazines and a newspaper folded open to the television guide, a room not unlike that of an average family. I had pictured something more austere, more monk-like. There was the requisite crucifix on one wall, a box of tissues on one of the side tables along with a framed photograph of two men in clerical garb. I wondered if this was where parishioners came for counseling or if there were more formal offices for that. I tried to imagine the priest spending evenings here, watching television, waiting until it was time for bed, and I thought what a lonely existence it must be. I suppose not unlike mine during those days.

Father Gervase set the book he had been reading down on one of the side tables. "Can I get you something to drink, Will? Coffee? Or a glass of wine? Sherry, perhaps."

Before I could respond, another priest entered the room, his clerical collar nearly concealed by a crewneck sweater. He was balding, younger, and beefier than Father Gervase, and he wore the bright smile of the perpetually cheerful, and beneath it a barely concealed air that verged on preoccupation, as if his thoughts were often somewhere else. Someone you might imagine managing a minor league baseball team.

"Oh, sorry to interrupt," he said. "I didn't know anyone was in here."

"That's perfectly all right," Father Gervase said. "Perfectly all right. In fact, if you care to join us, we were just about to enjoy a glass of wine. Have you two met? No? Will, this is Father Burns. Father Burns, Will Light."

The younger priest extended a hand. His grasp was firm, the skin of his palm slightly rough. "Please," he said. "Just call me Father Joe." A flash of recognition crossed his face. "Will Light," he said. "The artist."

I nodded. Extricating myself was becoming more and more difficult, and I regretted the impulse to follow the older priest into the rectory.

"Have a seat," Father Gervase said. "Have a seat. I'll get the wine and be right back." Then, elusive as quicksilver, he slipped away.

"I'm so glad to meet you," Father Joe said. "Paul has told me about you."

Paul? It took a moment to realize he meant Father Gervase.

"He tells me I must get over to the art association and see your paintings. He was quite taken with them, I gather."

"Yes, well, most of them are older work. Not the kind of thing I do anymore."

Father Joe checked his watch. "I'd like to stay and talk, but I'm due at Rose Hall Manor. It's my turn for pastoral calls. We'll have to talk another time."

Not bloody likely, I thought.

"My apologies for dashing off, but I'm sure Paul will be right back." He slipped out as quickly as Father Gervase had.

All the comings and goings—it might as well have been a French farce. The only things missing were housemaids and mismatched lovers. I crossed to the framed photo and recognized the two figures in it. The former pope—the one with the Nazi past who shocked everyone by retiring from the job—and Father Burns at his side. I turned from it and picked up the book Father Gervase had set on the table, assuming it was a volume of scripture, and saw it was a collection of poetry by Neruda. The little priest was full of surprises.

I was trying to decide whether I should just slip away when he returned, carrying a tray with a carafe of wine, three small cut-glass goblets, and a plate of biscotti, which he set on the coffee table.

"Father Burns has left?"

"Off to Rose Hall Manor." I noticed that the priest had changed into dry trousers.

"Of course. Of course. I forgot it's his evening there." He poured the wine.

"I hope you like sherry."

"Really, I can't stay. I only stopped by to return this." I set *The Illustrated Book of the Saints* on the table next to the tray, relieved to finally be rid of it.

"No need to return it. I meant it for you." Father Gervase held out a glass. "Here you go. I hope you like sherry. Amontillado. A gift from one of our parishioners."

I took it. One glass. Hair of the dog, I thought. And then I would be out of there.

"To your health," Father Gervase said.

"And yours, Father." I took a deep swallow, winced at the sweetness of it.

The priest offered the biscuits, which I refused, then settled himself in the recliner. "You know, I went to the art association this week. I found your work remarkable."

"Thank you," I said, refusing false modesty.

"I see now why Cardinal Kneeland wants you to paint the series of the saints."

I set my glass down so sharply the remaining wine slopped over the rim, wetting my fingers. "I told you I'm not interested. I don't give a damn what your cardinal wants."

Father Gervase reached for the tissues, pulled one from the box, got up, and brought it to me.

I mopped at my hand, shamed at my outburst. "Sophie tells me I have anger issues," I said and stopped before I could blurt out more.

The priest returned to the recliner. "Yes, well. Sometimes it is hard—" He fell silent.

I waited. "What's hard?" I finally asked.

"To distinguish anger from grief."

"Oh, believe me, Father, I know very well what grief is." I lifted the sherry, drained the glass.

"Yes. Yes, I would guess that you do." Father Gervase took a sip of wine, looked into the distance, sat for a long minute. "What do you think of it?" he finally said.

"Grief?" My voice was sharp with disbelief that I would be asked this.

"The book." The priest nodded toward the table where I had placed *The Illustrated Book of the Saints.*

For an instant, I considered lying, saying I hadn't opened it. Instead I said, "Frankly, I found it repugnant."

Father Gervase leaned forward, smiling as if nothing I might have said could have given him greater pleasure. "Really? Tell me more, Will."

"What else do you want to know? I found it repellent."

"Ah. And what was particularly disturbing about the book?"

"Christ," I said. An image from the book materialized in my mind—Saint Agatha, breasts torn with pincers—and a heat of rage began to rise. I recalled Sophie's view that the glorification of violence edged near pornographic. *Murdertainment.* "All of it. The violence. People stoned to death. Burned. Beheaded. Hunted and haunted. Tortured." *Lucy's ruined body. The bloody book tote.* My worst fantasies of what she must have suffered rose up.

"Ah, the early saints," the priest said. "Yes, there was a good deal of that. Of course, we have to read the stories through the lens of their times. Actually, the range of saints is quite wide."

"I have no interest in your saints, Father."

"They came from all races," the priest continued as if I had not spoken. "All ages. Those born into poverty and those born into wealth. Hermits and kings."

I set the empty glass on the table. "Let's get this straight, Father. I have no interest in your saints, and you can tell your archbishop I'm not interested in your commission. I don't paint saints."

Father Gervase made a flicking motion with his fingers. "But you do, you know."

"What?"

"You do paint saints. I saw them at the exhibit."

"What are you talking about?"

"Your portraits." The priest rested his head back against the chair back and stared at the ceiling, reflecting. "The fisherman mending nets," he said. "The young woman at the coffee shop. The woman at her vanity. Go back and look at their faces, Will. You were capturing the faces that could be saints."

"Oh, spare the sentimental shite," I said. I no longer worried about offending this priest. All I wanted was escape. "What you saw, what I painted were just people. Ordinary people."

"And that is my point, Will. The saints were ordinary people."

I didn't bother with a response.

"They were people just like us. They worked hard. They tried to find solutions. Some of them were sinners. A good many of them, in fact. Sinners who kept on trying."

I had had enough. I was so full of rage my hands trembled with it. "I mean it, Father. I'm finished with this. Find another artist. Tell your cardinal to find someone else to paint your goddamn saints."

CHAPTER ELEVEN

~

Find someone else to paint your goddamn saints.

I supposed I should have felt feel ashamed at my outburst and the way I'd stormed out of the rectory, but I felt only relief at escaping from Father Gervase and his sanctimonious talk of saints. In weakening daylight that muted the outlines of the buildings along Main Street, I walked home. The air had turned cool. Porch lights cast a soft glow through windows and reflected in puddles from the earlier storm. As I continued, the cloying taste of the sherry lingered in my throat, just as anger continued to simmer. I need you to understand, as Sophie so clearly did, the source of my rage. It wasn't the little priest's conversation or his persistence about the saints. It was the truth of what had happened to Lucy that simply couldn't be borne, so weighty and opaque I was surprised I was able to walk upright or speak. I had a keen need to wash it all away and thought the hell with promises I'd made to Sophie. The hell with everything. Much later, I would wonder how events might have been altered if I had gone straight home, if she still lived there instead of renting a condo. But of course blaming her for my behavior was an easy way to ease my conscience. I switched directions and headed toward the Crow's Nest.

When I entered the tavern, the highlights from the previous night's Sox game were showing on ESPN, the sound muted. It was early for the dinner crowd, but business was brisk at the bar. There were two empty stools at the far end, and I slid onto one. A bartender I didn't recognize approached. She was tall—at least five eleven—with one arm covered from wrist to elbow with a sleeve of tattoos that looked like a piece of garish fabric. She looked too young to be serving legally, but it was getting more and more difficult to gauge ages. Half the ball players playing for the majors looked like they belonged on a Little League team.

"What can I get for you?"

"A draft."

"Anything in particular?" Her voice held a husky undertone.

"Sam Adams," I said.

When she crossed to the tap, I observed the others at the bar watching her. "Why do men do that?" Sophie had asked me once. "Why do they check out every woman who walks by?"

"Oh," I'd answered, "I believe it's hardwired in the male chromosome," but I'd learned not to do it when I was with her. Not that other women interested me once I had met Sophie. It had been easy to be faithful.

A memory came. A snowy February night. The three of us watching some mindless rerun of a rerun, a docudrama about a woman who had disappeared and her husband who, it turned out, had been having an affair with her best friend. The show was narrated by that writer who died, the one whose daughter had been murdered after which he had become famous for covering murders and scandals of the famous and the wealthy. The name came to me. Dominick Dunne.

During the commercial break, Sophia had gone to the kitchen to make cocoa and get a bowl of cheese popcorn. Lucy turned from the screen and fixed her eyes on mine. "Jeannie's dad is cheating on her mom," she said.

"Wow," was all I could think to say. "That's rough."

"She hates him. Jeannie does, I mean. Not her mom. She doesn't think her mom knows."

"Wow," I said again, wondering how much longer Sophie would be. She knew how to field things like this.

"You'd never cheat on Mom, would you, Da?" Lucy said.

"Jesus, Lucy."

"Well, you wouldn't, would you?"

"Of course not. I can't believe we are even having this conversation."

"Well, people do."

"Not this people, honey. No worries there. Your da's a two-woman man. Just you and your mom. Forever." How smug that sounds now. An innocence bordering on arrogance, as if there were some kind of protection from the human condition, some prophylactic against the pain, loss, and betrayal in store for all of us. But of course if we knew what awaited—the losses and disappointments and grief that are inevitable, the unthinkable things we will prove capable of—the knowledge would paralyze us.

The bartender returned with the draft and set it in front of me along with a plastic bowl of salted nuts. "Anything else you want?" She emphasized *anything* in a way that seemed suggestive, but I had to be imagining it. I had a good twenty years on her.

"I'm good. Where's Gilly?"

"His night off. I usually have the weekend shift, but they asked me to cover for him today." She lingered, belatedly sliding a coaster under my glass. "So what do—" Her question was cut off when one of the customers farther down the bar signaled for her and she strode off, walking with what Sophie would call attitude. I took a deep swig of the beer. It helped wash away the taste of sherry but did little to erase my lingering anger. I stared up at the TV, watched the Sox botch a double play, finished the beer, thought about heading home.

The bartender returned. "Another?"

I stared at the glass, surprised to find it empty. "Why not?"

In an efficient motion, she tilted my glass beneath the tap, filling it until foam spilled down the sides. "I haven't seen you here before," she said.

"I don't come in often." Her hair was pulled back in a low ponytail, revealing ears that were well shaped and flat against her head, a row of silver studs piercing the lobe of each. I thought briefly of telling her what pretty ears she had, but I rejected the idea immediately, knowing how it would sound. "How long have you been here?"

"I started about a month ago. I used to work up in Portsmouth. At the Strawberry Banks pub. You know it?"

I shook my head.

She extended her hand across the bar. "Jessica."

I took it, registering the softness of her skin, the firmness of her grip. "Will," I said.

She smiled. "So will you or won't you?"

Will you or won't you? What did that mean? Or had I not heard her correctly? I no longer trusted my ability to clearly understand simple conversations. I was saved from responding by another customer calling for service from the far end of the bar.

"Don't go away," she said. "I'll be right back."

I stared up at the TV, felt the presence to my right as someone slid onto the stool.

"Evening, Mr. Light."

I recognized him. "Detective." A silence stretched between us, both unsure of how to open a conversation, an awkwardness broken only when Jessica returned.

"What can I get for you?"

"Coffee. Black." Gordon turned toward me. "I'm on the evening shift this week. My wife and daughter are visiting her parents on the South Shore, so I'm on my own for the week."

I nodded, could think of nothing to say. Our relationship—if you could call it that—had always been strained, as if from first glance he had detected a capacity for violence in my face.

Jessica set a mug in front of him. The steam curled up, scenting the air with richness of coffee. "You want something with this?" she asked.

"What's the special?"

"Chicken burrito or fish tacos." She lowered her voice. "Not that I'd recommend either one."

Gordon laughed. "I'll have a bowl of chowder. And a burger. Medium."

"Anything on the burger? Cheese? Onion?"

"Have them throw a slice of swiss on it."

She punched the order in the bar computer.

Gordon grabbed the sugar dispenser, poured a steady stream in his coffee. I remembered that detail: the amount of sweetener he liked in his coffee. And that one specific image triggered a flood of memories. I remembered Gordon sitting in our kitchen, adding spoonful after spoonful into his coffee, remembered the horror of that first night. The night Lucy hadn't come home.

CHAPTER TWELVE

~

It had taken less than five minutes from the moment I called the station to report Lucy missing to when a patrol car pulled into our drive.

Before the two patrolmen even got out of the car, I had the front door open and was waiting at the threshold while they crossed the walk and up the steps. I led them in and introduced myself and Sophie. Both men were large, and their presence, magnified by the holsters on their hips, crowded the hall. The taller of the pair, the more fit, took the lead. "I'm Detective Gordon," he said. "This is Officer Slovak. We're responding to a report of a missing child."

"Yes. Our daughter. Lucy."

"Full name?"

"Lucy Light. Lucy Leigh Light."

Slovak, a man with a beefy build but not soft, as if he spent his spare time power lifting in the gym, stood to one side and let Gordon take the lead. The detective pulled out a pad, flipped it open, retrieved a pencil from his jacket pocket, and scribbled down some words without looking at me. I noticed his ring finger was bent at an odd angle as if he had broken it at some point and it had not been properly set. Sports injury, I guessed.

"Age?"

"Fifteen. Lucy is fifteen."

"When did you notice that she was missing?"

I checked my watch, amazed to see that nearly an hour had passed since we had found Lucy's room empty. "A little after five."

Sophie spoke for the first time. "She didn't come home after school."

"When was the last time either of you had contact with her?"

"This morning. At breakfast. Before school," I said.

"I saw her at lunch," Sophie added. "We passed in the hall when she was walking to the cafeteria."

"You were at the school?"

"I teach there. We both had lunch at the same period. I was on my way to the teachers' lounge."

"What time would that be?"

"Twelve thirty."

"Did you speak with her?"

"Yes. I asked how she was feeling."

Gordon raised an eyebrow. "How she was feeling?"

"Yes. She hadn't felt well yesterday, and we thought she might be coming down with something. But she said she was better. She said she was going to the hockey scrimmage and would get a ride home."

"And that was all?"

"I made her promise if she felt sick at all to skip hockey. I told her to call home so Will could come and get her. She promised she would."

Gordon turned to me. "And where were you?"

"Here. I work at home." That evening neither of them asked me the pointed questions—if I had gone out at all during the day, if there was any way or anyone who could verify I had been home alone all day—those would come later.

"And she didn't call you?" Gordon said.

"No. I assumed she was coming home with her mother."

"What about siblings? Brothers? Sisters?"

"No. Lucy is our only child."

Slovak looked up from his pad. "Have you contacted her friends? Chances are she's with one of them and just forgot to call home."

"Of course we've called her friends. It's the first thing we did." I fought to keep irritation from my tone, but Jesus, did they think that we hadn't already thought of that?

"What we'd like to do is search the house," Gordon said.

"Why?"

"To make sure she isn't here."

The thought of them going through our home was so invasive I couldn't conceal my reluctance. "We've already done that. I'm telling you, she isn't here."

A swift glance passed between the men. "We understand," Gordon said. "But it's standard procedure. We'd just like to check to make sure."

"You'd be surprised," Slovak added. "Sometimes a kid will fall asleep in the basement. Or curled up in a closet while talking on her cell. Or texting."

"I'm telling you, it's a waste of time. Lucy isn't here." My voice rose, tightened. Sophie touched my arm, silencing me.

"We'll just check. Like we said. Standard procedure."

"Where is her room?" Slovak asked. "We'll start there."

"I'll show you," Sophie said.

"That's okay. We can find it," Gordon said.

"If you don't mind, we prefer to do this alone," Slovak said.

And if I do mind?, I thought.

"It's upstairs," Sophie said. "On the second floor. Third door down the hall on the left." We waited in the kitchen, listening to doors open and close as the two men made their way through the house. I closed my eyes, imagining them in Lucy's room, remembered seeing her pink panties tossed atop the laundry basket when I'd checked the room earlier, and I felt helpless that I was unable to protect our daughter from this violation. I stared through the kitchen windows, out at Lucy's swing. The sky was turning from dusk to dark.

"Where do you think she can be?" Sophie asked.

I didn't want to give voice to my fears but wondered if she was having them too. An accident? Some kid in school who'd offered her a ride. *Use your seat belt, Lucy. Always use your seat belt. Seat belts save lives.* The promise we had extracted from her that she wouldn't drive with Jared Phillips, that boy who had been driving the car that had killed a classmate, a girl, the year before. I pictured a mangled mass of steel, a tree.

"I asked them all—Rain and Christy and Jeannie and the rest—to start a phone chain," Sophie said. "To check with everyone they could think of."

"Good. That's good thinking."

"Upperclassmen, too," she said. "Everyone with a car."

Again I thought of the Phillips kid, imagined a wreck. Darker, more atavistic fears I didn't contemplate. Back then, before I knew better, when I was still protected by a glorious ignorance, it was incomprehensible, unthinkable, to imagine that those kinds of things could possibly happen to people like us. The sound of doors closing grew distant, and I realized the men had reached the top floor. I waited. Narrow bands tightened across my skull, signs of a headache onset. I thought about going for aspirin but stayed seated, reluctant to leave Sophie waiting alone in the kitchen.

"Do you want some coffee?" she asked.

"No. Thanks."

A minute passed, and then she got up anyway and measured out grounds, started the machine. I understood her need to do something, anything. Twice she tilted her head, said she thought she heard a car in the drive and, before I could move, went to check only to return and shake her head. The waiting stretched on. We heard the men as they descended the stairs, went down into the basement, wasting time. Lucy was somewhere out in the night.

Eventually, the men returned.

"She's not in the house," Gordon said.

"We already told you that."

"Are there any other buildings on the property? A shed or garage?"

"There's a garden shed in the backyard."

And so more minutes passed as they went to check the shed. It hadn't occurred to either Sophie or me to look there. Why would we? Lucy had no reason to go there, a small structure crammed with all the gear for outside maintenance. A lawn mower, emptied of gas, serviced and retired for the past season, two ladders, tools, a couple of snow shovels, a five-pound bag of salt left over from the previous winter, all manner of odds and ends. Within minutes the men returned, the futility of their search plain on their faces. I rolled my head from side to side, trying to reduce the tension. The pain was settling in, the pressure mounting behind my eyes, and I rubbed my temples.

"You all right there?" Gordon said. "You look kinda pale."

Was I all right? Jesus, what the hell should I have looked like? Our daughter was missing. I don't think I realized how even that first evening, even while they were maintaining that Lucy was probably out with friends, that seeds of suspicion were already taking root.

Uninvited, Slovak took a seat at the table while his partner went out to the patrol car, returning moments later with a laptop that he set on the table and flipped open. "We'll start by getting her info in the system," he said. "It will go out to other stations in the area. And to hospitals."

Hospitals. Sophie reached over and took my hand. I could feel her tremble. Our once-safe kitchen, the hub of our domestic life, had been converted to something alien and cold.

"We'll need a physical description. Color of eyes and hair. Height. Weight. Distinguishing marks."

I answered for both of us.

"What was she wearing when she left home this morning?"

I could picture Lucy clearly. I described the sweater, the short skirt.

"That's good," Gordon said. "You'd be surprised how many parents can't describe what their kids wear."

How many times had the police had to ask parents these questions? What kind of parents didn't pay attention to their kids?

"But she would have changed for hockey," Sophie said. "Blue sweat shorts and a white tee. And maybe her gray Boston College sweatshirt."

Gordon took down the info.

"Except—" Sophie paused.

"Except what?" Gordon said.

"We checked with the coach, and she didn't go to hockey. She didn't even see him about getting excused from the scrimmage. So maybe she hasn't changed clothes."

Unable to sit any longer, I crossed to the counter and got out some mugs. The lamb tagine, long forgotten, lay cold and congealed in the pot. The memory of that afternoon—of chopping vegetables, preparing dinner—seemed far distant. It belonged to Before.

"We'll need to have a list of her friends, starting with the ones she is closest to. Also her teachers. Her coach. The other members on the team. Anyone you can think of she might be with. Neighbors. Maybe a family she babysits for. Relatives who live nearby."

I let Sophie handle this, listened as she gave the names, watched Slovak write them down. Names of friends I recognized. Rain LaBrea, of course. And the Hayes family, our neighbors she used to sit for before they divorced and Ellen moved away with their son, a boy so disabled he couldn't walk, a fact Sophie believed led to their divorce. A few names I didn't know, specifics of our daughter's life I'd missed. I checked my watch and saw another hour had passed since the police had first arrived.

"Would anyone like coffee?" Sophie asked.

"Please," Gordon said.

"Not for me," Slovak said. He picked up the list he'd made of Lucy's friends, her teachers and coach. "I'm going to follow up on some of these."

We watched him leave. I poured three mugs of coffee, brought them to the table. One of the mugs had a slight chip on the lip, and I gave that to Gordon. "Sugar?" I asked.

"If it isn't a bother."

Sophie started to rise, but I rested a hand on her shoulder, squeezed gently. "Sit," I said. "I'll get it." We both watched as he shoveled spoonful after spoonful into the cup until I couldn't imagine how it could be drinkable. He took a sip, then returned to the questions.

"Have you noticed anything unusual lately?"

"What do you mean?"

"How has Lucy been acting? Has there been any change in her mood or behavior? Has she been depressed?"

"Lucy? No. Not at all."

"Any problems at school? Have her grades dropped?"

"No."

"What about at home?"

"What do you mean?"

"Any reason she might be upset? An argument with one of you?"

The idea was ludicrous. "No," I said, my voice tight.

"Maybe something she wanted to get back at you for. Has she wanted to go to a party or a concert, something you've forbidden?" Gordon smiled, as if to say, *You know how teenage girls can be.*

Not Lucy. Not our teenage girl. "No. Nothing like that."

"Does she use social media?"

"What?"

"Twitter. Facebook?"

"She's on Facebook," Sophie said.

Again I remembered that morning, Lucy texting at the breakfast table.

"Do you know her password?"

"No," I said.

"Selkie," Sophie said.

"I didn't know that," I said, feeling a spark of what?—jealousy—that Lucy had shared this with Sophie and not with me.

"Selkie?" Gordon said. "Could you spell that?"

"S-E-L-K-I-E," I said. "From the Irish myth." Sophie and I exchanged a quick look, and I knew she was remembering too. Lucy swimming, her long hair plastered against her scalp as her arms knifed though the water, and then emerging. *You're like an otter child*, Sophie had told her. *Or a selkie*, I'd said and told her about the mythological sea creature who shed her sealskin to take the form of a woman and how a fisherman had hidden the skin and taken her for his wife. How enchanted Lucy had been by the tale, and being Lucy and curious about everything, she had researched the subject until she knew every version of the myth.

"Does she have a boyfriend?"

"No. I mean, she has a group of friends, boys and girls, but no one special. She isn't dating anyone." Sophie's voice was steady, but I heard the urgent undertone and knew she too was aware of the minutes ticking off on the wall clock.

"What about alcohol? Drugs?"

I stared out the far window into October darkness. "This is ridiculous."

"Please." Sophie leaned in toward Gordon, her voice pleading. "You aren't listening to us. Lucy is a good student with a group of good kids as friends. She doesn't drink or use drugs. She's the president of SADD, for God's sake. And she would never just not come home. She always calls if she's going to be late. Always. Why aren't you out trying to find out what happened to our daughter?"

"Mrs. Light, until there is a reason to think otherwise, we start with the premise that she left voluntarily."

Until there is a reason to think otherwise. The words hung in the air, stunning us with their implication.

"What about a driver's license? Does she have one?"

"Christ, weren't you paying attention? She's fifteen. Of course she doesn't have a license."

Gordon ignored the outburst. "Does Lucy have her own cell phone?"

"Yes." I recited the number.

"Good. This will help. We'll contact the service, ping her phone. If it's turned on, we'll get the exact location. If it's off, we'll get the time and location where it was last used."

All the times I had wanted to take the damn phone and toss it, now I was grateful Lucy had it, prayed it was on and the battery was charged.

"Like I said, as soon as this info goes out, we'll get a report from every hospital and police department in a fifty-mile radius."

Sophie rose. "I can't," she said to me. "I can't do this. This can't be happening."

Gordon looked up from the computer. "Please, Mrs. Light. I promise you, we'll do everything possible to find your daughter. Believe me, I know what you must be feeling."

"Do you?"

He started to say something then stopped. "Just a few more questions. Help us out here, okay."

Sophie sank back into her chair, the little fight she had in her gone.

"What about a credit or debit card? Does she have one?"

Sophie nodded. She found her purse, handed two cards to Gordon. "She's on both of our accounts."

Gordon copied down the numbers. The radio on his hip squawked—the words indistinguishable—and without looking, he reached down and lowered the volume.

"I'm almost done here. One last thing. Is there a recent photo of Lucy you could let us have?"

Sophie left and reappeared moments later with two photos—one from Lucy's bureau, the photo taken of the three of us in Maine, and the other her freshman class picture—and laid them on the table. Lucy smiled up at the three of us.

"We'll get these back to you," Gordon said as he picked them up.

After he left, Sophie came to me, leaned against me. "This can't be happening," she said again.

By the next morning, the news had spread throughout the town. Tracking dogs were brought in by the state police, searched our grounds. Our basement. Our *basement*, for God's sake. A rapid response was set in motion. Volunteers organized a search team to aid the police. By nightfall, posters of Lucy appeared tacked to telephone poles and trees around town. We grew used to the phone ringing, to police arriving and departing. We were again asked to account for our whereabouts the day Lucy disappeared. They asked if there was anyone who could verify my actions that day.

"We have to ask these questions, you understand," Gordon said, his voice apologetic. He was our liaison and kept us informed of every step of the investigation. He reported that Lucy's friends, her fellow students, and faculty were being interviewed again. He reviewed with us the press release appealing for information before it was sent out. He told us that security tapes from the school had been gathered and played and that they were continuing to amass what he called "electronic and forensic footprints." To no effect. All these efforts resulted only in dead ends. Lucy's cell phone held no signal. There were no ATM withdrawals or charges on the credit card. No reports of accidents involving a fifteen-year-old girl matching Lucy's description.

That first week, friends and parents of Lucy's classmates stopped by. They dropped off platters of food. Casseroles and cakes, roast chicken, a huge pot of chowder, the kind of things people brought after a death, something I supposed I should have felt grateful for but that only added to a sense of violation. Most of the food ended up tossed in the garbage, just like the lamb tagine I had scraped from the pot in what felt like a lifetime past. The Before life.

Amy drove down from Maine. She helped deal with the reporters—"the cameras," she called them—who swarmed into town, jackals on the scent of a story: *Young, pretty white girl missing. Daughter of an internationally noted artist.* There was speculation about kidnapping. We were walked through the procedure and told that if a kidnapper got in touch with us we were to notify them and absolutely not try to handle it on our own. News vans sprouting satellite dishes rotated from the street outside our home to the police station to the school, where they interviewed Lucy's friends, her teachers. Each time I opened the daily paper or flicked on the television news and saw a picture of Lucy staring back at me I felt a punch in my solar plexus. They'd used the class picture Sophie had given to Gordon and another of her in shorts and tank top holding a tennis racket. Where they had gotten the last one I had no idea. One of her friends I supposed. Amy manned the phone, urged us to rest, to eat. But we slept little, subsisting on endless mugs of coffee. Sophie swung between hope and fear. Several times I found her in Lucy's room, a rosary in her hands. The days stretched out in one long nightmare that eventually ended, only to be replaced by a far more horrific one.

"Can I get you another?"

The bartender's voice pulled me back. "What?"

She nodded toward my glass. "Another?"

I needed to get out of there. Without a word, I tossed a twenty on the bar and headed for home.

CHAPTER THIRTEEN

~

Rain wished she was at home, wanted only to be left alone, but it was crystal this was so not going to happen.

"How could you forget?" Her mother, as usual, was on a rant. "I told you and told you what time we needed to leave, and you said you'd be ready. Now look at us. We're already fifteen minutes late."

Fifteen minutes late because earlier they'd fought about what she was wearing. She'd put on her favorite pair of cutoffs, the ones long enough to cover her scars, but her mother had said they were *inappropriate* and had told her to go put on a dress. *A dress.* Like that was going to happen. She compromised by putting on a denim skirt.

"It's bad form to be late for an appointment," her mother said in her scolding voice. Her furious voice.

Bad form? Really? "My B."

"And drop the attitude, Rain. It's not productive."

Seriously? Seriously? What was so totally not productive was wasting a Friday afternoon. Right now Christy and Jeannie were at the mall scoping the stores for sales, Jeannie probably looking for something to lift from Macy's or CVS. They had started stealing a couple of months back, and Rain could not believe how easy it was. Like the stores were asking for it.

Her mother slowed the car to check a road sign. "Cedar Street. This is it. Now look for the third house on the right." They passed a brick ranch. "That's one," her mother counted.

Rain dropped her hand to her upper thigh and pressed her fingers against the cut she'd made earlier that morning.

"That's two. And here it is. Three." Her mother swung the car into a gravel drive and switched off the ignition. Hands locked on the steering wheel, she twisted her shoulders so that she could face Rain. "Listen to me, young lady. I want you to give this a chance."

Rain stared straight ahead through the windshield and eyed a two-story Cape with clapboards painted white and green shutters framing the windows. She had expected an office building or something in the new medical center out by the highway. "This is it? The shrink's office is in her house? What kind of shrink has her office in her house?"

"Doctor," her mother said automatically, completely missing the point as usual.

"Whatev."

"And yes. Dr. Mallory sees patients in her home. Which is so much nicer. More relaxing, don't you think?"

If her mother had a clue what she was thinking, she'd probably have her shipped off and locked up in some hospital for loonies, which was exactly what Sally Sampson's parents had done to her last year. A major freak-out over drugs or something. Now Sally was at some lame school for troubled girls. *Just shoot me now.*

"When I spoke with Dr. Mallory, she said we were to use the side entrance. She said she'd be waiting for us."

We? Us? No way Rain was going in there with her mother. "I'm going in alone."

"Are you sure?"

"I'm not a baby."

"I know that. I just thought you'd feel better if I came with you."

Like she was going to let *that* happen. She darted an *over my cold corpse* look at her mother.

"Okay, then, if you're absolutely sure." Her mother released one hand from the wheel and lifted her hair off her neck, flipping it to one side. She looked tired. Rain could almost pity her. Last summer, when she'd been looking for a bracelet she wanted to borrow, she'd come across a book in her mother's top bureau drawer, stashed beneath a pile of scarves like it was some kind of porn. *How to Look Ten Years Younger.* Well, whatever advice the author gave, it wasn't working. Her mother looked like hell. It had to suck to be old and getting older.

"I'll be back in an hour."

"I'll walk home," she said, like that was even a possibility. She knew her mother would be waiting when she came out.

"Please, Rain. Try. Okay? Give this a chance." Her mother's voice had morphed from tight impatience to that pleading, weak note that Rain hated. She reached over and rested her hand on Rain's arm. Rain remained completely still—frozen—and finally her mother withdrew her hand.

"Yeah. Okay," she said, her tone sullen. She unlatched the door and escaped before her mother could kiss her or give her one of her pep talks. Or worse, cry. Her mother meant well. In her most generous mood, Rain allowed her that, but she was missing some essential gene in the mothering department. *I've tried with her*, Rain once heard her say to her friend Joyce. *It isn't as if I haven't tried.* As if mothering were like baking a cake using the recipe in some old grease-stained cookbook, but in spite of following all directions, Rain had still come out of the oven lumpy and half-cooked because there was some essential ingredient that was missing from the mix. So Rain's fault, not her mother's. When she was younger, Rain used to study the other mothers she saw around town and try to imagine each of them as her own mother, as if they were auditioning for the part. A mother who wouldn't criticize and who always thought to bring extra boxes of juice to the playground. A mother who would get the recipe right.

A narrow brick walk rimmed by forsythias past bloom curved to the side door. She could feel her mother's eyes on her back as she headed toward the house. Like what? She was going to run off and the ditch the appointment? Not that the idea hadn't occurred to her. It would serve her mother right if she did run away, take off for some city and live on the streets. It drove her bug-fuck nuts the way her mother was always lecturing her. *As long as you live in this house, young lady, you will do as you're told.* In spite of the antiperspirant she'd applied that morning, a trickle of sweat dampened her underarms. Just as she reached the door, it swung open. A child stood there. A child with gray hair.

"You must be Rain. I'm Dr. Mallory."

This was a huge mistake. Colossal.

"Please, come in." Dr. Mallory beckoned her into a narrow hall. Rain glimpsed a padded bench along one wall and a carpet on the floor that she bet was one of those cheap knockoff Orientals. A single door in the center of the wall to her left was open, revealing an office. The place smelled weird. Doggy. Her stomach began to ache. The trickle of sweat had turned into a river. She pressed her palm hard against her thigh and followed, her gaze now fastened on the shrink's shoes, black with flat, squished heels like someone's great-aunt from the last century. Or one of the old Italian grandmothers at Mass.

Dr. Mallory stepped aside and motioned for her to enter the office. The dog smell was stronger here. There were two upholstered chairs, a moss-green crocheted throw folded over the back of one. A table placed between the chairs held a square glass vase filled with white tulips and a copper bowl filled with cellophane-wrapped butterscotch candies, the kind her granddad always brought when he used to visit.

On the opposite wall there was a bookcase with four shelves, each one crammed with books. An old analog clock and a framed photo of a full moon rising over the Port Fortune harbor rested on the top. A small desk was placed at an angle in one corner. And in another corner, she saw a pile of cushions and a wicker basket containing children's toys. Rain's skin tightened.

"Where would you like to sit?"

Anywhere but in this stupid room. She plopped down on the chair without the crocheted throw. She expected Dr. Mallory to claim the chair at the desk, but instead she took the other chair, slipping off her ugly shoes and tucking her legs beneath her, like a child would. A bubble of laughter caught in Rain's throat. This was a shrink who had shrunk.

Dr. Mallory picked up the copper bowl and held it toward Rain. "Would you like a candy?"

"No." The cut on Rain's thigh began to sting, and she pressed her fingers against it. She looked around, avoiding the shrink's gaze.

"Maybe later." Dr. Mallory placed the bowl back on the table.

"Do you have a dog?"

Dr. Mallory smiled. "I do. Are you allergic?"

"No. It just smells really doggy in here."

"Does it bother you? If it does, I can put him in another room."

"It's in here?"

"Yes." As if called, a small dog crawled out from behind the desk and regarded Rain with huge brown eyes.

"His name's Walker." At the sound of his name, the dog padded across the room, *bounced* really, long ears swinging with each step. "Short for his AKC name. Golden Prince Johnny Walker."

"Like the booze?" Back before he switched to beer, her father swilled the stuff.

"Yes."

"That's lame."

"Do you think so?"

"Who names their dog after booze?"

"What do you think would be a good name for him?"

"I dunno." *Really? Really?* Were they going to spend the whole session talking about this ratty animal? Not that Rain gave a shit if they did, but her mother would go into orbit if she learned this was what she was spending money for. *Good money*, as she had reminded her about every two minutes. Not that Rain had any intention of sharing anything that went on here with anyone, especially not her parents.

"Tell me about your name. I've never met anyone named Rain before."

"Whatev." The dog stared at her, creeping her out. The whole place was creepy. She hated it. Hated everything about the room and everything about being here. This totally blew.

"Is this a name your parents gave you when you were born, or is it one you chose for yourself?"

As if her parents would allow her to change her name. She could just imagine the freak-out if she even suggested it. "My parents gave it to me." Rain knew the whole pathetically stupid story about how she was named, about how on one anniversary her parents had taken a trip to Nantucket and how it had stormed the entire weekend and how they'd spent almost every minute in their room at the inn (a very *romantic* inn, her mother always said when she told the story in case Rain missed the point), and how that was where she had been conceived and so they'd named her Rain. As if she wanted to know that kind of creepy detail about her parents. She hated that story. Hated imagining her parents in the inn on Nantucket. The whole thing was too gross for words. Major gross-out. Colossal.

"How old are you, Rain?"

"Fifteen."

"Any brothers or sisters?"

"One brother."

"And how old is he?"

"Seventeen."

"Is his name Thunder?"

"What?"

"I meant it to be funny. Rain. Thunder. "

"Oh. Yeah. I get it." A joke. Epically stupid and not the least bit funny. The spiky hand inched along the face of the clock atop the bookcase. Rain pressed harder against her thigh.

"What is his name?"

"My brother?"

"Yes."

"Duane." Duane the Lame.

Dr. Mallory observed her for a moment. "I know it's your parents' idea for you to see me."

Not her parents. Her mother.

"How do you feel about that?"

Rain picked at her thumbnail. She thought it was colossally idiotic. "I dunno." She darted another glance around the room, noticed a basket of magazines next to the shrink's desk, a copy of *Psychology Today* on top.

"How do you think I may be able to help you?"

Rain shrugged.

"Did your mother tell you anything about me?"

She slouched down in the chair. "She said you were a shrink and I had to come here." Jesus, it must bite big-time to be an adult in such a small body.

"I gather you don't want to be here."

Really? Really? How brilliant. "Like you said, it wasn't my idea. I don't need to come."

"Do you have any questions you'd like to ask me? It isn't fair for me to be the one always asking questions. Is there anything you want to know? I'm open to talking about me."

116

This was worse than being with her mother. Why were adults always trying to get you to talk? *What's on your mind, dear? Penny for your thoughts.* Always prying and prying. Her mother staring at her like what she'd really like to do is grab a veggie peeler out of the drawer next to the sink and scrape back the covering of her skull and get a good look inside. Not that adults ever really listened even if she did talk. She crossed her arms, hugging her midriff, feeling a meanness rise inside. "So where do you get your clothes?"

"What?"

"Your clothes. I mean, it can't be easy finding stuff small enough to fit."

Dr. Mallory said nothing.

"Do you have to shop in the children's department?"

"Sometimes. Why? Does fashion interest you?"

"Not particularly."

"I see. What does interest you? Shopping? Music? Do you play sports?"

Rain shrugged. "I dunno." What really interested her were rocks, not that she'd tell anyone. She liked the way the different kinds sounded, like poetry. Metamorphic. Sedimentary. Igneous. She knew the names of dozens of kinds of rocks. Her granddad told her there was even a name for the study of rocks. Petrology. When she was ten, he'd returned from a vacation in the Southwest and given her a polished rock that hung from a silver chain. It was called an Apache tear, he'd said, and then he told her about the legend, how all the men in an Apache tribe had been driven to the edge of a cliff, and rather than be taken prisoner or killed by their enemies, they had all jumped off the cliff. The women had been hiding in a cave, and when they heard what had happened they wept, and their tears had turned to stone. Rain tried not to imagine it, the women weeping while the men died. It was a kind of obsidian, her granddad told her when he gave it to her. When you held it in your palm it looked black, but when you held it to the light you could see through it. He told her life was like that—sometimes things seemed dark, but if you held them to the light, you could see your way clear. No. She wasn't about to tell any of this to the shrink.

"What about school? Do you like school?"

"What difference does it make if I do or not? I have to go. Just like I have to come here." *As long as you live in this house, young lady . . .*

"What would you rather be doing?"

"Now?"

"Yes. If you had the afternoon to yourself, what would you like to do?"

Rain thought of Christy and Jeannie shoplifting a tube of lipstick or a pair of socks. She recalled the thrill that ran through her body the time she'd taken a scarf and how she had tossed it in the trash on the way home so she wouldn't have to explain it to her mother. She shrugged again. She was done talking. She'd just sit and wait until the hour was up and she could escape. The silence stretched on. She glanced across at Dr. Mallory, but the shrink didn't seem to be pissed or frustrated. Unlike most adults Rain knew, she didn't seem to need to fill every moment with words. Which suited Rain just fine. In the stillness, she listened for other sounds, the ordinary noises a house made—the humming of a refrigerator motor, the click and hum of a furnace or air conditioner, the scratching of a branch against a window—all the ticking, purring, creaking sounds of a house—and then she listened for the sounds from the world outside, a car passing in the street, a plane overhead on approach to Logan, but silence enveloped them. She wondered if this was what it was like before you were born, in the womb. But no, there would be sounds there, liquid, pulsating sounds. Her skin itched just thinking of it.

The dog—Walker—looked from one to the other, then sat up and crossed to Rain's chair and gazed up at her. "What kind is he?"

"A King Charles spaniel. Would you like to hold him? He enjoys being held."

Hold him? Seriously? She imagined leaving there covered with hair and smelling doggy. "No."

"You don't like dogs?"

"Not especially."

"Do you have pets?"

"I had a couple of fish once. They died."

"How did you feel about that?"

"They were just fish. Fish die." The fish had been another gift from her granddad. Not regular goldfish like you might expect, but two iridescent blue fish with tails twice the size of their bodies that waved back and forth in the tank like fans. She had named them Fin and Min. Her granddad had said that sounded like a vaudeville team and then had explained what vaudeville was.

Dr. Mallory clasped her hands in her lap. Rain noticed a wedding band. She couldn't imagine who would want to marry such a short person. But maybe the husband was freaky short too. She stared at her knees and plucked at a few gel-stiffened strands of hair. Until she'd chopped it off, she hadn't realized how much her hair had shielded her from the world.

"I didn't speak with your mother at length, Rain. She's not my patient. You are. And what you and I share is confidential. But your mother is concerned for you, just as you'd be concerned for a daughter of your own."

"Yeah, well, I'm not going to have a daughter." She wasn't like those stupid cows at school who were so proud of getting pregnant. "I'm never getting married."

"Never is a long time."

Another brilliant observation.

"Do you have a boyfriend?"

"No."

"A girlfriend, then?"

"What, like a *girlfriend* girlfriend? I'm not gay, if that's what you're thinking."

"Would it bother you if I thought that?"

"Whatever. It's a free country. I'm just saying, I'm not gay."

Dr. Mallory nodded. "You mother told me you've been having a hard time."

I bet she did. Probably couldn't wait to tell you what a freak her daughter is.

"She told me a little about your friend who died last fall."

Rain swallowed the tightness in her throat. *Died.* Like the true word—*murdered*—mustn't be said.

Dr. Mallory leaned forward. "I'm sorry, Rain. Sorry about your friend."

Her skin felt prickly, tight, and her throat ached. "There's nothing to say."

"The loss of a close friend would be enormously hard for anyone."

Rain concentrated on breathing.

"I haven't had exactly that kind of loss, Rain, but I've had other kinds." Dr. Mallory paused, studied Rain for a moment, then continued. "Two years ago my husband died. The only thing that got me through was that I had people to talk with, people who were there to support for me at a very difficult time. I would like to offer that kind of support for you."

"Yeah, well, I don't need support. I'm okay. No matter what my mother told you."

"Everyone feels what you're feeling, Rain. That's normal. And even people who are strong and well need other people."

Rain glanced at the clock. "Aren't we supposed to stop now? The time is up."

"Is it?" Mallory smiled. "I don't always go by the clock. Some sessions are shorter and some are longer. It depends on what makes sense.

If you think this is enough for today, that's fine. Do you want to stop now?"

An hour ago. I wanted to stop an hour ago. "Yes," she said. She nudged the dog away with the toe of her shoe and rose.

In a surprisingly graceful movement, Dr. Mallory unfolded her legs and stood. She slipped on the ugly black shoes and crossed to the desk, where she flipped open her appointment book. "We can meet next week at this same time if that works for you."

"Whatever." What would work for Rain was to get the hell out of there.

Dr. Mallory came toward her, and for a horrible moment Rain thought she was going to hug her or something, but the shrink only held something toward her.

"Here's my card, Rain."

Rain made no move to take it.

"As you can see, this is my home, and I'm here all the time, days, nights, and weekends. I always answer the phone, and I want you to feel free to call." She pressed the card into Rain's hand. "If I don't answer, it's because I'm out briefly, and I'll get back to you."

"Right." Rain shoved the card in her pocket.

"And I'd like you to call if something is troubling you or if you just want to talk."

Like that was ever going to happen. "Sure."

Mallory opened the door. "Take care of yourself, Rain. If you aren't able to take care of yourself, please call me."

"Sure."

"Until next week, then."

As she expected, her mother was waiting in the car. Rain opened the door and slid in the front seat, exhausted, as if she had been running sprints.

"How did it go, dear?" Her mother's face was all expectant and hopeful. "How was Dr. Mallory?"

"Short. She was short." She could sleep for a solid month. "Where did you find her anyway? The circus?"

The hope faded from her mother's face. "Dr. Mallory is highly recommended, Rain. Mr. Clarke was very enthusiastic about her."

"Mr. Clarke? You asked Mr. Clarke for the name of a shrink? Well, that's great. Just great." Now the whole school would know. The teachers weren't supposed to talk about the students, but good luck with that. They were a nest of vipers, and the guidance counselor was the worst of all. "And I'm not going back." She jammed her hand in her pocket, scrunched the card Dr. Mallory had handed her. "And there's nothing you can do to make me. Nothing."

CHAPTER FOURTEEN

~

There was nothing I wanted to do but go home.

Yet I was glad for the walk, for time to shake off the memories that had risen in the Crow's Nest and get my head straight from the two beers. But in spite of the walk and the evening air, the memories lingered and I still felt the effects of the alcohol, probably more than I normally would have had, either because I'd had the sherry with the priest first or because I'd had all of it on an empty stomach. Whatever the reason, there was a low buzz in my head, as if the A string on a guitar had been thumbed. Not entirely a bad feeling as it took the edge off, but this was not necessarily a good thing since the desire to deaden pain and quash feeling with booze had proved dangerous in the past. The trick was to hold steady at the buzzed stage before it flipped over to flat-out drunk, but that was a trick I hadn't mastered. The best I could manage lately in spite of my best intentions was to try to stay away from the hard stuff.

I was a half block from home when I saw the car parked in my drive. In the glow cast from the streetlight, I made out a shadowy outline on the driver's side. As I approached, a woman stepped out. She was in her midthirties, hair in a blonde bob, heavy makeup, gray slacks, black blazer. She looked vaguely familiar, but I couldn't place her.

"In sight," she called out.

What was in sight? Or had she said *insight*? One word. Who the hell was she? What did she want with me?

"Mr. Light?" she repeated.

Oh. "Yes?"

"I wondered if I could have a moment?"

I was still trying to place her, aware of the oily odor of tar in the air. I glanced over and saw that once again Payton Hayes had resurfaced his drive. The guy did it twice a year or something. Talk about overkill. I hated the smell of asphalt. If hell had a signature smell, it would be that emanating from his driveway, not sulfur.

"I'm Melinda Hurley. I'm a reporter with the *Boston Herald*," the woman said.

Recognition snapped in. She wore her hair in a different style, had done something to lighten it, but it did nothing to soften the sharp features and searching gaze that were so suited to her work. She was one of the ferrets who had covered the story of Lucy's murder. One of the cameras. Last fall, the press had practically moved into town, nosing about and invading every aspect of our lives, questioning Lucy's friends and teachers, our friends, showing up at our neighbors' doors. It had been beyond invasive, closer to cruel.

"I wonder if I could ask you a few questions?"

Anger uncoiled in my belly.

"I'm working on an update," she said.

The anger rose to my chest. Christ, how I hated these people.

"Earlier today I spoke with the chief, and he told me there've been no new developments on the case."

The case. I felt as if an artery has just been ripped opened. "I have nothing to say to you."

"It's been seven months. Have you lost hope that your daughter's murderer will be found?"

I brushed by her, circled toward the steps.

"Mr. Light. Just a few words. Our readers wonder how you and your wife are doing."

I swung on her, shouted, "Just how the fuck do you think we're doing?"

Instinctively she stepped back, then raised her hand, palm open, and made a calming motion. "Whoa. Take it easy. I'm just doing my job."

"Your job?" Drops of spittle flew from my mouth.

The reporter recovered her poise. "I'm trying to help, Mr. Light. Keep the case in public consciousness."

"Bullshit. You don't give a flying fuck about us or our daughter. You just want a story. Now get the hell off my property."

The reporter held her ground. "Mr. Light," she said. "Just one more thing. I am also doing a follow-up story on the teenage pregnancies in town."

"You people—" My heart was pounding. "You people have no sense of decency. No idea of how it feels to have your personal life invaded. Can't you just leave us alone?"

"I have to ask. It's my job. Many of the girls have now had their babies, and we are following their stories. I understand that some of these girls were schoolmates of Lucy, and I wondered if your daughter might have been—well, if she might have been pregnant when she was killed."

A pain cut through with such thrust it might have been a hunting knife. In an action immediate and without thought, I shot my arm out and, palm against her chest, shoved her away from me with so much force that she stumbled and fell. That was the first time my rage escaped my control, but it wouldn't be the last. Her tote and notebook arced through the air and landed in a puddle left from the earlier rain. I stared down to where she lay sprawled on the walk. She stayed there for a minute, mouth open in shock, and then she scrambled to her hands and knees and stood. One pant leg was ripped, and blood had already started to seep through. Her face was pale.

I turned away and strode toward the house.

"Wait," she called. "Wait just a damn minute."

I mounted the steps, breathing hard, as if I had been in a battle.

"Hey. You can't do this. I don't care what you've been through. You can't do this."

I just did. When I climbed the steps, she was still calling my name, demanding that I turn around, anger now in her voice. My hands trembled on the porch rail. Once safely inside, I didn't bother listening for the sound of her car starting up. I rubbed my chest, as if I had sustained an actual wound. *I wondered if your daughter might have been pregnant when she died.* I headed straight for the kitchen, found the bottle of bourbon I'd shoved in the back of one cabinet, as if in spite of all intentions I had known I was going to need it. Think me a fool if you will. Or weak. But don't judge if you yourself haven't been lost, despairing. You may think you know how you'd behave, but the truth is we have no idea of what we will do when faced with a nightmare. We like to believe we will be brave, the person who jumps in the way of danger to save another, the person who will face horror with resolve and courage, who, when tested, will rise up. But believe me when I say we have no idea. I do know now that we are both stronger and weaker than we could ever imagine. And we are capable of things we would never have dreamed possible. I filled a tumbler half full, didn't bother with ice, and drank a good part of it down in one swallow. I remembered the bitch all right. Remembered them all, the way they had appeared at our home only moments after Chief Johnson arrived.

We had been in the kitchen when he came. It was ten thirty in the morning on the second week of Lucy's disappearance. When the doorbell rang, Amy went to answer it. She still hadn't returned to Maine, and we had come to rely on her to run interference for us. Moments later, she reappeared and told us the police chief was there and wanted to speak to me. Me, she had said. Not both of us. Sophie's eyes met mine, and she came with me when I went out to the hall. Whatever it was he wanted to say, we needed to hear it together. Back then—Before—we were still a team, partners. His face telegraphed the message of bad news.

"You found Lucy?" Sophie said. "Where is she? Is she all right?"

"No," he said. He turned toward me. "There is no easy way to say this."

Sophie took hold of my arm, her fingers pressing hard. "What is it?" I said.

He swallowed once, looked at Sophie. "You might want to sit down."

"Tell us," I said.

"Your daughter is dead."

"No." Her word was a whisper, a long, low sound of denial, as if that single syllable could reverse time, make the chief evaporate.

I pictured, as I had the first night, a car crash, a metal frame twisted against a tree on some back road, our daughter inside.

"Her body was found this morning. A woman walking her dog found her in the woods outside of town. We'll have to wait for the coroner's report, but it looks like homicide."

People say things like *time stood still*, and I always thought it was just a facile expression, but it is true. At that moment everything froze, and yet at the same time, I was aware of everything. Sophie clinging to me, the pale echo of her moan in the air. Amy standing in the background.

"How—" I began, but was interrupted by the sound of engines outside, of cars pulling up and then the doorbell.

Amy went to check. "Oh God," we heard her say. "I can't believe this," she reported when she returned to the kitchen. "There are three network vans out front on the street."

I turned on the chief in a fury. "You told the press?"

"Of course not."

"They're here, aren't they? How else would they know?"

"They live in scanner land. There's nothing we can do about it."

Nothing we can do about it. Vultures. Predatory bastards. Now seven months later one of them was back to feast on what meat had been missed, to strip bones, suck marrow. I finished the first tumbler of bourbon and poured another. Time passed but I had no sense of it, nothing beyond those walls. After a while I was aware of, somewhere in the muted distance, the sound of thunder and then, later, of rain against the window over the sink, as if the storm that had pushed through earlier that day had reversed course and was returning. And then, later still, I heard the sound of the doorbell, remember thinking that the parasitic bitch would never give up. I stumbled and caught myself on the table, stumbled again in the front hall. I swung open the door, fist raised. Detective Gordon stood there. His shoulders were spotted with rain from where he'd run from the cruiser to the porch.

"Hey, pal. Take it easy there."

I lowered my fist but could not swallow the rage.

"Are you all right?"

"I'm fine." The words were slurred.

"Glad to hear it, Mr. Light. Because, well, I have to tell you, you don't look so good."

I leaned against the doorjamb, spoke with the careful precision. "Actually, I'm a little high. Not against the law for a man to get high in his own house, is it?"

Gordon looked behind me, into the house. "May I come in?"

I stepped aside, stumbled, and then regained my balance.

"You sure you don't want to sit down somewhere?"

"I wanna be left the hell alone." What was he doing here? I couldn't think straight. My brain was mush.

"How about coffee?" Gordon said. "I could use a cup."

"Sure. Why not." I led him to the kitchen. The bourbon bottle was on the table. Nearly empty. I threw it in the trash. I tripped again as I walked to the counter, spilled coffee grounds as I tried to negotiate the suddenly impossible task of brewing coffee.

Without asking, Gordon took over. "Have you eaten anything?" he asked as he spooned grains into the filter.

"Not hungry."

Gordon poured water into the receptacle, pressed the brew switch. Then he opened the refrigerator and foraged until he found bread and a jar of peanut butter. He opened drawers until he located a knife, then made a sandwich and set it in front of me. "Here. Eat this." He poured us both coffee, watched while I drank it. The absurdity struck me. A detective in my kitchen making me a sandwich like it was some kind of after-school snack. I remembered the first time Gordon had been in our home—the night Lucy hadn't come home—and suddenly was seized with panic that wiped the fog from my brain as it occurred to me why he was there. "Sophie," I cried. "Has something happened to my wife? Is that why you've come?"

"No." Gordon rested a hand on my shoulder. "No. Nothing like that."

I could have wept with relief.

Gordon looked around. "She isn't here?"

I rubbed my hand over my eyes, imagining her reaction when she heard about the events of the evening, wondered if there was a way to keep it from her. "No."

"Listen, Mr. Light. Will—" In the months since we first met, this was the first time the detective had called me by my given name. "I probably shouldn't even be here, but I thought you should know. An hour ago a reporter came by the station. She said she wanted to report an assault."

"Assault?"

"She said she sustained an injury when she fell. She said you pushed her."

The last traces of haze cleared from my head, like an eraser swiping a board, and I was near sober. "Is that all she told you? Did she tell you what the hell she was doing in my yard? Why she'd come here?"

Gordon's gaze was not without sympathy. "We didn't get into that."

"I just bet the hell you didn't."

"According to her, you pushed her so hard she fell. There was evidence of a cut."

"So what—you're here to arrest me?"

Gordon gave me a steady gaze. "That's what she wanted."

I held my hands out, wrists up, mockingly, as if to be cuffed. "So go ahead. Arrest me."

"Well, from what she described, what happened here qualifies as a nondomestic assault. A slap, a shove—these are all classified as misdemeanors. They're not cause for an actual arrest."

"So why the hell did you come?"

Gordon gave me a steady look. "Like I said, I probably shouldn't have come. Just wanted to let you know. Give you a heads-up."

"I see."

"Will, right now we aren't involved. Okay? As I told the reporter, because the incident wasn't witnessed by the police, we can't do anything. For this to go forward, she'll have to go to the courthouse tomorrow and file a private complaint for assault and battery."

I was exhausted, tired of it all. "Then what?"

"Let's hope it doesn't come to that. With the night to think it over, there's a good possibility she'll drop the whole thing. People do that. In the heat of the moment, they want to file charges, but by the next day they've calmed down and don't want to bother following through, going to court."

I recalled the reporter screaming at me, remembered her sprawled on the ground. I didn't hold much hope she'd forget. "And if she does go ahead?"

"The court will schedule a probable cause hearing to see if there is enough evidence to justify the complaint. You'll get a notice of the hearing and the date."

I pictured her torn slacks, the blood. "She wanted to ask me about Lucy," I said. "She asked me if Lucy had been pregnant when she was killed."

Gordon's eyes widened. He exhaled and again reached a hand out to my shoulder. "That's tough."

"Right. Tough."

"Listen, you screwed up."

I nodded. No argument there. "So what do I do now?"

Gordon got up, put his mug in the sink, his job finished. "Like I said. Hope she cools off overnight."

"Okay."

At the door, we shook hands, as if an agreement had been made. "Thanks," I said. "Thanks for letting me know."

"No problem." Gordon headed for his cruiser, then turned. "You might want to take it easy on the booze."

"Right. I know."

"And it might be a good idea to get yourself a lawyer."

A lawyer. Christ. Sophie would be furious when she found out.

CHAPTER FIFTEEN

~

In the cool light of the next day, the whole thing seemed overblown, but still, there I was sitting in my neighbor's law office.

Payton's room was all chrome, leather, and glass with thick carpeting you could lose a shoe in, far different than the colonial he lived in. He greeted me with a strong handshake. His jacket sleeve inched up, and I noticed the oval gold cuff links. He flashed a smile revealing teeth so white a dentist had to be responsible.

"Thanks for fitting me in," I said. When I'd called earlier that morning, his secretary had said his schedule was full. I'd been surprised when he had called back minutes later and said he could see me at noon.

"How's Sophie?" he asked.

"She's okay," I said and wondered if from his vantage point next door he had noticed her coming and going, her car absent from the driveway for days at a time. Although I already regretted bothering him. Payton and I had never been particularly close. Sophie and Ellen had made some effort to have, if not a deep relationship, at least a neighborly one limited to a shared barbeque once each summer, cookies exchanged at the holidays, called greetings across the yards when both were outside. When Ellen had sought a divorce, I'd been surprised but

Sophie hadn't. As usual when it came to others, I was pretty much clue-less. After Ellen moved, taking their handicapped child with her, Payton had kept to himself, and gradually an odd distance developed between us. As I said, we had never been close, and with Ellen gone, there was even less reason to get together. Still, when Gordon had suggested I get a lawyer, he was the first person I thought of.

He leaned back in his chair, ran a thumb over his chin, over the beard he had grown after Ellen left him. "I'm not a criminal lawyer, Will. Our firm handles probates, trusts, wills. Property and estate matters."

I knew that. He had drawn up simple wills for both Sophie and me and helped us plan for a solid future for Lucy if the unthinkable happened and Sophia and I both died before our daughter was an adult. Another irony in a necklace of them.

"I can recommend another lawyer. I can give you a couple of names."

"I don't want another lawyer." Better the devil you knew. "Can't you represent me?"

"I'd be more comfortable if you got someone who handles these things."

These things. His tone was neutral, but I still felt as if I'd stepped in dog shit and carried it into the office and soiled the rug. "It's probably nothing. Even the police said it will probably come to nothing. I just want to cover my six, ya know."

Payton stared at me for a moment and then reached for a pad, again revealing the cuff links that I now saw were monogrammed. "Have you talked this over with Sophia?"

Had I? Oh yes. Knowing she would find out anyway—small towns keep few secrets—I had phoned her that morning, and we'd argued about it for what felt like hours. I was reluctant to follow Gordon's recommendation, and she was set on my seeing a lawyer. Looking back I think that the argument had become heated because all the unspoken hurts and resentments of the past weeks, things that would have been unthinkable Before, had served as invisible fuel and had left both of us quite shaken. "Yes. In fact, she suggested I call you."

"She did?" He looked pleased. "How is she?"

I had no idea how to answer that question, and my silence seemed answer enough.

"Okay," Payton said. "Give me some more details. You say this happened Wednesday?"

"Yes. Yesterday. About dark."

"Okay. Take your time. Go through it step by step."

So I began relating how I'd come home and found the reporter in my drive.

"Name?"

I frowned. "I don't know. Can't remember. She's with one of the Boston papers. The *Herald*, I think."

He jotted down a note. "It shouldn't be difficult to find out. You say you were coming home and she was waiting for you?"

"Yes."

"Where were you coming from?"

"I'd gone out on an errand. Stopped by the Crow's Nest." I doubted he had stepped foot in the Nest since his last semester at Harvard. Moved up in the world. Country-club bars for him.

"So you'd been drinking?"

"A couple of beers. Two. That's all." I didn't mention my visit to Father Gervase, the glass of sherry.

Payton scrawled another note. "And if necessary the bartender will attest to that? Two beers?"

"Sure."

"His name?"

"Her. Her name. Begins with a J, I think. Jennie. Jessie. Something like that. Tall woman with tattoos."

He added it on the pad. "Go on."

I detailed it all, how the reporter had showed up, the questions she'd asked, how I'd told her to get off my property and she'd persisted and then how I'd shoved her—just a little push really—and she'd fallen. When I reached that part—pushing her—a queer expression flashed crossed his face.

"Were there any witnesses?"

"No."

"What about Sophia?"

"She wasn't home."

"I have to emphasize, Will, I'd be more comfortable if you got someone who handles this kind of thing."

"But you can do it? Right? I'm asking you."

Payton reviewed the few notes he'd made, then stretched back in his chair, again stroked his beard with his thumb. "As I said, this isn't my bailiwick, and I'm a little lost here."

I stared at him, unwilling to plead.

"Look, here's what I can do. I have a colleague who spends a good deal of time in the courthouse. Let me see if I can get hold of her. She knows the clerk, and at the least she can see if a criminal complaint has been filed."

Criminal complaint.

"Would you like anything while I'm making the call? I can get one of the girls to bring you coffee."

"I'm fine."

"Bottled water?"

"No. Nothing. Thanks."

He went through another door to an inner office, probably a conference room. The courthouse lawyer must have taken his call immediately, for I heard him start to speak. "Hey, Gillian, Payton here. Glad I reached you." Unable to stomach more, I went in search of a restroom. When I returned, he was back at his desk.

"Do you want the good news or the bad?"

"The good, I guess."

"My colleague checked with the clerk. As of noon today, nothing has been filed."

"So what's the bad?"

"You're not out of the woods yet. The reporter has up to three years to apply for a criminal complaint."

Three years? For a little shove? Insanity.

He uncapped his pen and wrote something on a notepad. "Here's the name and address of my colleague. She said if you can get over there tomorrow afternoon at two, she can see you."

I glanced at the paper. Gillian Donaldson. A WASP name. "I don't know," I said. "Maybe I should just wait and see how it plays out."

"You came to me for advice, Will. Here it is: you don't want to be behind the curve on this. Go see Gillian."

CHAPTER SIXTEEN

~

The address was at the far end of Seaside Drive, a summer cottage converted to a private law office.

A discreet black-and-gold quarter board on the front said *Gillian Donaldson, Attorney at Law.* There was no doorbell. I opened the door and entered a vacant reception room. Empty water bottles filled a trash basket that looked as if it hadn't been emptied in days, and the surface of the vacant receptionist's desk bore rings left by beverage cups. An ancient air conditioner, its grille coated with grime, was wedged in the window. So. No thick carpet or Mont Blanc pens here. Donaldson appeared from an inner office. She was older than I had expected, perhaps fifties, with dull brown hair that fell to the collar of a cotton print shirt. The vision of a lightweight blonde faded away.

"Gillian Donaldson," she said. "Gillian." She extended her right hand, on which she wore a black orthotic wrap. "Carpal tunnel," she explained.

"Will Light," I said. Her grip was stronger than I'd expected.

She indicated the room with a sweep of her hand. "Pardon the mess. I'm between receptionists."

What was the story with that? Had the previous receptionist been fired or quit? No matter. I had no intention of returning. Somehow this whole thing had gotten out of my control, blown out of proportion. I suspected Payton might have made more of a drama than the situation required. Donaldson led me into her office, which was no neater than the outer room. She motioned for me to sit in the wooden chair that flanked the desk and then took her chair. "Payton gave me a quick overview of the situation when he called, but it would help if you told me in your own words."

I was tired of the whole thing and wasn't sure I could summon the energy to go over it again. My stomach rumbled. I'd skipped breakfast.

"I understand you're concerned that a reporter . . ." She trailed off and lowered her gaze to check a note on the desk. "A woman named Melinda Hurley might file a complaint against you."

"Right. Listen, I don't want to waste your time here."

She arched an eyebrow.

"The thing is, I think maybe Payton overreacted."

"How so?"

"Well, it's been a couple days, and I haven't heard anything more. It seems to me if something was going to happen, I'd know by now. Like I said, I don't want to waste your time."

"Well, since you're here, why don't you tell me what happened." She leaned forward, bracing her elbows on the desk, and hooked an errant strand of faded hair behind her ear, an unconscious gesture I'd seen Sophie do a million times. "Start from the beginning."

The beginning. What beginning? What had led me to this second-rate office because I'd shoved a woman? At what point had my life irrevocably shattered? When Lucy was killed? When Sophie moved into the guest room? Or had it all been set in motion long ago? Was it all payment for some karmic debt I had incurred? Although I didn't believe that shite, I couldn't push the thought away.

"Will? Are you with me here?"

"What? Yes. Right."

"What day did this happen on?"

"Day?" I pulled my attention back. "Wednesday. This past Wednesday."

"Start with anything. What was the weather?"

"Raining. It had been raining." Gradually I recalled the day. The visit to Holy Apostles to return the book to Father Gervase. The glass of sherry. The stop by the Crow's Nest, the two beers I'd had there. Gordon coming in and triggering memories. My return home to find the reporter in our drive.

"Good," she said. "You're doing great."

I recounted the conversation with Hurley. When I got to the part when I'd pushed the reporter, I tried to gauge Donaldson's reaction, wondered if her sympathies would lie with the other woman, but her face remained impassive. I told her about going into the house and leaving the reporter screaming at me and then how later that night the detective had come by. On this retelling of the episode, the fourth time I had gone over it, I felt distanced from it all, as if I were recalling a movie I had seen long ago. She listened with a disconcerting attentiveness, her eyes never leaving my face except to take a few notes. When I was finished, I'd given her a complete picture of that day and evening. I sank back and waited for her to join the chorus of people who had told me how I'd screwed up.

"There are no worms," she said after several minutes.

"No worms?" Christ, what a disaster it was turning into.

"Words," she said. "There are no words I can say to convey how very sorry I am about what happened to your daughter."

I shifted my gaze to the room's one window and stared out on the street.

"Okay," she said, her tone now all business. She reached into a small refrigerator—the squat, blocklike cube like those students kept in dorm rooms—removed two bottles of water, and handed one across the desk to me. The phone on her desk rang, and she pressed the mute button and let the call go to voice mail.

"Let's start with this. I don't think you're overreacting. The fact is that you pushed her, she fell, and as a result sustained an injury."

"A scrape. For Christ's sake. She just scraped her knee."

Again she arched her brow. "And apparently was upset enough to report it to the police."

"But hasn't followed through on it."

"Look, Will, I'm not here to debate you," she said. "If you decide to go ahead with me, you need to understand that I'm here to represent you, to act in your best interests."

No problem there. I had no intention of going ahead with her. I had seen Payton Hayes, agreed to see Donaldson. In my mind I had fulfilled my promise to Sophie, and I just wanted to leave and get something to eat. I was light-headed with hunger.

"And in return I ask that you tell me everything so if we go ahead with this, I'm not hit with any surprises down the road."

"As I said, this is probably a waste of both of our time. I think the best thing is for me to wait and see if this whole thing just goes away. Certainly that seems to be what is happening."

Her eyes—green I now noticed—searched my face. "And you're okay with that, with waiting to see?"

"I don't see much choice."

"There is always a choice."

"Really?" I didn't bother to mask my sarcasm.

"Let's say you're right—the best-case scenario is Hurley doesn't follow up on this. From what you've told me the injury wasn't serious, discounting bruised pride, so she might decide this isn't worth the trouble to pursue." She paused to twist the cap off the bottle, took a drink. "So you're right. You could sit tight and see how it plays out. But there's another way this could be handled. Another choice. A more proactive approach."

"Proactive?"

"You could stop any action on her part before the court system gets involved."

"How's that?"

"She came to your home to interview you, correct?"

"Right."

"So you phone her."

"I phone her?"

"Yes. You defuse the situation. You apologize. Say you were caught off guard with her questions, tell her how traumatic the year has been."

"You've got to be freaking kidding."

Donaldson continued as if I hadn't spoken. "And then you give her what she wants. You agree to an interview."

"Forget it. Not happening."

"Why don't you take the weekend to think it over. To consider it."

"No need. It's not happening." I pushed out of the chair. "What do I owe you for today?"

"Today is a consultation. There's no charge. If after you think it over you decide you want to continue, or if the reporter does follow through and swears out a complaint, I'll require a retainer. From that point on you would refer everything to me. Anyone who contacts you—police, her lawyer, reporters, anyone at all—you'd refer them to me."

"Nothing is going to happen."

She studied me for a moment. "Okay then. We're done here then."

She ushered me to the door. "Good luck, Will."

Outside, in spite of the warmth of the May sun, I shivered.

CHAPTER SEVENTEEN

~

Despite the burnished light of late afternoon and the mild temperature outside, Father Gervase regretted not having worn a heavier sweater when he'd come out to the chapel.

May had turned to June but the stone-slabbed floor still held a lingering chill of winter, and now it seeped through the thin soles of his shoes. Set at the edge of a small plot behind the church, the chapel had been built decades ago at the bequest of a parishioner as a place in which to hold small weddings, baptisms, and other services and as a quiet retreat for those who wished to use it for meditation or prayer, but since the custodian reported finding several syringes beneath the pews and even, to the Rosary Society's horror, used condoms, parishioners wishing to use the space were required to sign for the key.

The rectory study was warmer, and certainly he would be more comfortable there, but he'd formed the habit of retreating to the chapel when writing a homily for the Sunday masses. There he was less likely to be interrupted, and the stillness allowed him the necessary space in which to reflect. Now, as he absorbed the quiet, a lambent ray cut through the chapel at a low angle, and its beam fell beneath a pew to his left, where it settled on a small object, obviously overlooked the last time that Wayne Jervis swept. From a distance, it was not clear what it was. The priest hoped their part-time custodian hadn't neglected to lock up after he cleaned, once more leaving the chapel open for illicit meetings or drug dealings. At one time it would have been inconceivable to use a holy space for such things, but it was Father Gervase's sorrowful knowledge that times had changed, and not even church property was exempt from fornication and theft. As he returned his attention to the homily, he made a note to retrieve the object when he left.

It was unusual for him to leave the writing of the homily to this late in the week, as he usually had it written by Wednesday, but the past three days he had been overwhelmed with duties. In addition to the usual demands of his schedule, there had been two funerals—Manny Costa's on Monday and Elizabeth Spellman's on Tuesday afternoon—and on Wednesday morning the christening of the Rodriguez infant. Christenings and funeral masses, he thought, the bookends of the earthly Christian life. And then on Thursday, there had been the extended counseling session with Joseph and Sylvia Ramos. In spite of his best efforts, it was clear that their union was on a paved path to divorce and heartbreak. Another failure on his growing list of disappointments, although the Ramos family would be a challenge for even the most skilled counselor, which Father Gervase had never claimed to be. According to Sylvia Ramos, their problems began last fall when their sixteen-year-old daughter became pregnant. She said Joseph placed the blame at her feet, but from all the blustering Joseph did and the way he avoided looking at either of them directly, Father Gervase suspected there was truth to the rumor that another woman was involved. Patiently, he had listened to them both, had spoken about how at various times in life one was faced with the long process of feeling hurt and lost, betrayed and abandoned, but with work it was possible to come out on the other end of these experiences wiser and more compassionate. The couple had stared at him as if he were speaking a foreign language and one

Anne D. LeClaire

they had no interest in learning, let alone mastering. How he wished they had gone to Father Burns for pastoral guidance.

And overshadowing everything all week was this business with Will Light. Father Gervase could still hear the echo of Will's words when he'd left the rectory two weeks ago: *tell your cardinal to find someone else to paint your goddamn saints.* He lacked the courage to pass this message on, even discreetly edited, and so had been avoiding the bishop's calls. At some point he knew he'd have to report in. All in all, a difficult week, and it was the weight of this long week that had given rise to the subject of this homily. He stared down at the notepad on which he had copied the words of Paul, one of the most prolific of the apostles. *We are subjected to every kind of hardship, but never distressed; we see no way out, but we never despair.* Second Corinthians. This scripture had proved a source of comfort to many, himself among them, and yet in spite of the wisdom of sacred writings and the power of prayer, he understood too well that despair and hardship remained a daily condition. His thoughts returned to Will Light, and he knew that even if the artist listened to his homilies they would be no match for the depth of his anger, rage he had recognized on his first visit and feared the risk it posed to Will. In the past Father Gervase had seen the damage rage could do when it morphed into violence. He had been plagued with a growing belief that he had somehow been called to reach Will and help him. *The call.* Wasn't that the word Father Gartland had used? The older priest had been the spiritual director when he was at the seminary and one day told him he saw in him the potential to be an excellent counselor. "In fact," he said, "I think you have a calling for it. You might ignore it, but it will not ignore you. For what are we asked to do but counsel? And console. Remember, Paul, when the call comes, you must answer it."

He tried to turn aside these thoughts. He was too old and too tired for this business with Will Light, which technically was not his job anyway since the fact was that Will was not a member of the parish, not even a member of his faith.

He shifted on the bench, unable to get settled. The cold crept up his ankles and calves. In addition to the discomfort of the chilly chapel and elusive words for his homily, there was the growing distress in his stomach, indigestion brought on by the dish Mrs. Jessup had served for lunch, a heavy kale soup loaded with kidney beans and chunks of linguica that now caused him to belch and rub his belly, regretting every spoonful. He no longer tolerated rich or spicy foods as easily as he once had, a function of aging, he supposed. He'd broached the subject with Mrs. Jessup several times, but her back stiffened at his comments, which she took as criticism of her cooking. "Father Burns has no complaints," she'd said through thin lips. Mrs. Jessup had raised eight children and ruled the rectory kitchen like a tyrant, and in truth he was afraid of her. Just the thought of approaching her again about the delicacy of his digestion made him weary. Perhaps he should lie down for a bit. But no. He had the homily to write.

He returned again to the fundamental questions of humanity. Why did we have suffering, evil, pain? How did we build resiliency? How did we hold steady in the midst of the storm? He closed his eyes to reflect. From the near distance, the noise of a lawn mower reached him, and he was comforted by this ordinary, domestic sound. A few minutes passed. In spite of the chill that had now reached his knees and the discomfort of gas beneath his ribs, his breathing slowed, his chin dropped, and his mind drifted from the task at hand. He closed his eyes and soon slipped into the space his mother used to call twilight time, where he was neither sleeping nor fully awake, a suspended limbo land between dream and consciousness. The chapel grew warmer, as if a heater had been switched on, and he relaxed into this unexpected warmth.

Minutes passed, and later Father Gervase would believe he had fallen asleep. Behind his closed lids, a vision materialized: a young woman clothed in a simple gown of linen, a cowl draped at the neck and a halo of braids coiled around her head. There was a sense of the familiar about her, and as recognition dawned, a sensation spread through his chest that was a blending of pain and joy and pulled him fully awake. The vision was Cecelia, his sister grown into the adulthood she'd never known in life. His family history trembled like a timber hut built on fault lines. The notepad slipped from his hand, and he tried to put the tragedy of Cecelia back in the past where it belonged, but it remained with him like a suitcase he had carried on a long journey. All possibility of finishing the homily faded, and he knew the futility of continuing to struggle with it while haunted by the past. He closed the notebook and clipped his pen to the cover, then stood. He took a moment for blood to flow to his protesting arthritic joints, knew the inevitability of a cane in the near future.

Before he left the chapel, he remembered to pick up the piece of trash beneath the pew. He was relieved to see it was not a needle or worse. Only a child's toy, a small plastic figure. He slipped it in his pocket and departed, taking care to lock the door behind him. Then as he often did when his mind sought perspective and his heart sought calm, he walked not back to the rectory but down to the harbor and the sea.

CHAPTER EIGHTEEN

~

I walked across the sand toward the wooden bench where Sophie waited.

Earlier that day when Sophie had suggested we meet at "our bench," and I'd felt a stirring of hope. On summer evenings shortly after we married, we'd formed the habit of taking an after-dinner stroll here, and although alcohol was forbidden on the public beach, we would share the illicit pleasure of drinking Chardonnay while the sun set over the water.

That day, for obvious reasons more compelling than town bylaws, I walked toward my wife with hands devoid of wine. "Hey, Soph," I said. Her hair had grown out a bit from the severe cut and framed her face softly, making her look more like the woman I married. The woman from *Before*. I sat at her side, close enough to smell the fragrance she was wearing, something spicy and unfamiliar. I hesitated, then brushed her cheek with a kiss.

She slipped off her sandals and flexed her toes, digging them into the sand. "I've been waiting to hear," she said.

I was lost. "Hear what?"

"About your appointment with the lawyer Payton recommended. How did it go?"

More than a week had passed since I'd seen Donaldson, and in truth, I had put it behind me the moment I'd walked out of her office. "I think we can let it go for now. It's probably a big to-do about nothing."

"Nothing? I don't know, Will. It doesn't sound like nothing. You're charged with assault and you call it nothing?"

"Not charged. There's no charge, Sophie."

She stared at me, skeptical.

"I've got it covered, Sophie."

"You've got it *covered*?" A couple walking past turned and looked at us. "Exactly what does that mean?"

"What it means is, like I said, a charge hasn't actually been filed. Jesus, Soph. I didn't hit the woman. I pushed. She fell down."

"Still."

Still.

"Oh, Will, Will. What were you thinking?"

I wondered how many times we were going to go over this. "I wasn't thinking. I reacted. Okay? *I reacted*. Look, can we just drop the subject? It's in the past. Nothing has come of it and I really don't need another lecture on my behavior."

A curtain of silence fell between us. Sophie looked down at her hands, now clasped together in her lap as if in prayer. At the water's edge three children played. The boy was busy with a pail and shovel. Another child, smaller, sprawled prone, making snow angels in the sand while her sister turned cartwheels. Farther down the beach a group of high school kids were tossing a Frisbee. One of them had brought a black Lab, and the dog darted from player to player, following the arc of the toy. I watched as the disc again sailed through the air and the Lab, with perfect timing, made a twisting leap and took it in midair, then ran from the group. Several of the boys gave chase while the girls cheered the dog on.

"Will?"

A tall boy had turned from the pursuit and now veered toward the most slender of the girls, a blonde who stood a head shorter. Sensing his intent, she ran but he caught her easily, then lifted her in the air, as if she weighed no more than a leg of lamb, and headed for the water, threatening to throw her in. Watching them, I remembered what Sophie had once said about the teenage boys she saw each day at school, how their testosterone levels were so high the air around them shimmered with it and a person could get pregnant just walking by. The girl's shrieks of mock distress floated up to where we sat. The muscles tensed in my thighs, my shoulders, knotted my jaw. I watched as the boy swung her over the surf, her toes skimming the surface. The rest of the group had turned their attention from the dog and gathered at the water's edge to observe. "Do it, Eric," one of the boys called. "I dare you to throw her in." For a minute, it appeared Eric was going to follow through and that the girl, defenseless in his arms, would land in the water, but at the last minute, he set her down in the sand. "Coward," another boy taunted.

I swallowed against the sour taste rising in my throat, against my intense and sudden hatred of these boys. *It could have been anyone*, I thought. *Anyone.*

"Will." Sophie's voice yanked my attention back, although the thought still circled in my head. *It could have been anyone.* I knew not to share this with her.

"Hiss at them," she said.

"What?" Had she read my mind?

"I miss them."

"Who?"

"Them." She nodded toward the group of teenagers. "I hadn't expected to miss them this much."

"*Them?*" I spit the word out. "You miss them?"

"I do."

"Even knowing . . ."

"Knowing what, Will?"

I could no longer stay quiet. "It could have been one of them. It could have, you know."

She made a sound.

"What?" I said.

"Oh, Will." She shifted on the bench until she faced me directly. She reached across the short distance that separated us and laid her hand on my knee, warming the patch of skin beneath the fabric of my trousers. "It hurts me to see you this way."

"What way?"

"Bitter. Angry. Looking at everything—everyone—with cynical eyes."

"And what exactly would you have me do? Pretend the world is all good? Pretend evil doesn't exist? If I'm sure of one thing, Soph, it's that evil exists. It lives right here in this town. And that's the truth."

"There are many truths, Will. We decide what truth we choose to hold."

"Spare me."

"We do, Will."

"And what truth do you hold?"

"That goodness exists here too. I choose to focus on that."

"And what about your work? Aren't you focusing on evil when you spend your time raising awareness of all the children who are harmed, taken, or murdered each year?"

"But not out of cynicism. Surely you can see that, Will. I do it out of a desire to bring attention to what needs to be changed. I can't sit here and look at the world and see everyone as a potential criminal."

"And you think that's what I do?"

"Isn't it?"

I had no answer.

"The work I do, Will, I guess I mean it for Lucy. Have you thought about what you could do for her, in honor of her?"

"Christ, Sophie. Don't pull that guilt-trip bullshit on me."

"It's not bullshit, Will. It's truth. She would hate this, you know."

Again I looked out at the harbor, ignoring the group of teenagers, instead fixing my gaze on a sailboat as it tilted into the wind and curved around a buoy with ease and headed for the horizon.

"She would hate knowing she was the reason you're drinking." Her hand still rested on my knee, and she moved it an inch or two until it was on my thigh, spreading the warmth. "Or that you hit that reporter because of her."

"Not *because* of her, Sophie. Never because of her. Because of what happened to her."

"She would still hate it."

"Well, we don't have to worry about that now, do we? She'll never know."

A spasm of pain crossed her face. "You're a better person than this, Will. Can't you be that person? If not for me, then for Lucy."

"I might have been that person once, Soph, but this is the person I am now."

She didn't move, but I could feel her withdraw, pull into herself.

"Last month," she said, "in Washington, I had a lot of time to think. I couldn't stop thinking about the work Father Gervase came to see you about. The painting of the saints."

"I told you, Soph. I'm not interested."

"I think you should consider it, Will."

"Why?"

"For Lucy. You could do it in honor of Lucy."

"I can't."

"Of course you can. What you're saying is you won't. You don't want to."

I didn't bother to respond.

"Here's the hard truth, Will. These past months have been beyond horrific. A nightmare. But we didn't get to choose that. What we do get to choose is how we react. We get to determine how to make sense of something that's fundamentally senseless. And we get to—and I don't mean to sound righteous about this, Will—but we have an opportunity to make the world better. I know if Lucy had lived she would have made the world a finer place, and you know that too. She was robbed of that chance, but we can do it for her, Will. We can do it for her."

Again, as I had in past months, I had the feeling that Sophie and I were in separate lifeboats, drifting farther and farther apart in our sea of grief.

"Lucy's gone, and nothing we do will change that, Will. We can't make that go away, and I don't think the grief will ever go away. How could it? But at least we can choose to find meaning in it. I guess that's what I was trying to say a minute ago. We can dedicate a part of our work to her. We can try to make the world a better place."

"Yeah, well here's a news flash for you, Sophie. The world isn't a better place."

On the beach, the students had begun to gather their coolers and the Frisbee and started heading toward their cars. The sailboat I saw earlier was a white speck on the horizon. I considered what it would be like to wade into the water, walk until I was waist deep and then swim, swim for that horizon, swim beyond the jetties and buoys, swim until exhaustion-weighted muscles and water claimed me. For a moment, the pull of the idea, the release it offered, the seductive possibility of it, shook me.

"Will?" Sophie shifted again on the bench. "I worry about you, Will."

The white sail grew tinier. "No need."

"Why not get away for a bit?" she said. "Take a break from everything. You know that Amy and Jim would love to have you visit them."

I didn't bother to respond.

"Or you could go somewhere else."

"Where?"

"I don't know. Anywhere. Manhattan. You haven't been there in a long time."

"Ah, the geographic cure. Brilliant."

"I'm just trying to help, Will."

"I know." Maybe her suggestion wasn't such a bad idea. I tried to imagine being someplace where every day, everywhere I went and everything I saw wouldn't hold reminders of Lucy. But even as this thought occurred, I knew the futility of it. Wherever I went, as long as I was alive, I carried it with me.

"Think about it, Will. You haven't left since—well, since we lost Lucy."

"We *lost* Lucy? You make it sound like we misplaced her. We didn't lose her. She was taken from us." I should have stopped there, but of course I didn't. Looking back now I see how lost I was in my grief. "She was murdered."

Her cheeks reddened as if I had slapped her, and she lifted her hand from my thigh. Her expression hardened, and I saw I had lost her. Again.

"Soph—"

"Forget it, Will. I can't talk to you about this."

"No, I'm sorry. Listen. You're right. A change might be good. Let's get out of here. Let's drive up the shore, have dinner somewhere." For one split moment, it almost seemed possible to slip back to our former selves, to a prior life that held spontaneous car rides along Route 1, exploring side roads, discovering restaurants and antique shops, stopping at small motels, checking in without luggage, driving toward a future that held more hope than despair. Hope that wouldn't end in despair and more grief.

"I don't think so, Will." Her voice was flat, and her posture, when she rose, was defeated. "Not tonight."

"Soon then?" I held on to the fleeting glimpse of that other life.

"I don't know, Will."

"Soph—"

"I don't know where we are heading, Will. I just need—time."

"Right," I said. End of conversation.

She bent over and pressed her lips against my cheek. "I love you," she said. "Nothing will change that."

I watched as she walked away, her footsteps in the sand forming a parallel line to the shoreline and the incoming tide. I followed her progress back toward the harbor, past the child constructing a castle and his two little sisters, now both of them making snow angels in the sand.

CHAPTER NINETEEN

~

It made Rain furious the way everyone was acting like Lucy was some kind of angel.

She sat in the passenger's seat, and the school yearbook that had triggered her anger almost glowed through the fabric of her backpack as if emitting some kind of radiation. If wishes came true, the book would disappear, evaporate into the ether. In fact, she would have thrown it away, but her mother the customs inspector would ask what happened to it and no doubt was waiting to take possession of it when they got home and would pore through the pages as if they contained a secret code to Rain's behavior.

Her mother, completely clueless as usual, drove on toward Dr. Mallory's. At the thought of the session ahead, Rain slid her hand over her outer thigh and pressed down on the latest cut. Her heart beat hard and loud in her chest. It would serve her mother right if she had a stroke or some kind of attack right here in the car. At least that would get her out of her appointment with Dr. Mallory. But no. No such luck. Not even one minute late, they turned into the shrink's drive. As she made her escape, she grabbed the backpack from the floor.

"Why don't you leave that with me, dear," her mother said.

Rain pretended not to hear and, bag slung over her shoulder, walked toward the house for the torture appointment.

"Don't forget," her mother called after her. "Duane will pick you up after."

Right. Like she should get on her knees in gratitude that Duane the Lame had agreed to give her a ride.

Dr. Mallory waited for her inside. "Hello, Rain. How was your week?"

Seriously? Seriously? Did the shrink really think she was going to walk in the door and just start spilling her guts? Well, good luck with that. "Okay."

"Just okay?"

"I guess."

"I was just about to pour myself a glass of tea. Can I get you one too?"

Rain wanted to refuse, but thirst stopped her. In fact, she was feeling light-headed.

"Sure. I guess."

"I made some fresh this morning." Instead of heading into her office, Dr. Mallory walked toward a door at the end of the hall and disappeared into a separate part of the house. Rain paused. Was she supposed to wait in the hall or what? Then Dr. Mallory called for her to come along, and so she followed the voice through the far doorway, walking past several packing cartons stacked in a hall and into another room, one that smelled of bacon and a hint of wood ash. It contained an oven, refrigerator, table, and sink, so it obviously was the kitchen, but it was unlike any Rain had ever seen. A huge fireplace dominated nearly an entire wall. The brick hearth was flanked by a wooden rocking chair on one side and an armchair upholstered in plaid on the other, the fabric so worn that the stuffing poked through in places. A dog bed in a green-and-blue plaid fabric that matched the chair was placed directly in front of the hearth. The wall adjacent to the fireplace contained shelves from floor to ceiling, each crammed with books. Piles of even more books were stacked on the floor. Rain had never seen so many books outside of the library. The extent of her parents' book collection would fill one shelf.

"This was originally the living room, but years ago we converted it into the kitchen." Dr. Mallory retrieved a container of iced tea from the refrigerator and took two tall tumblers down from an open shelf. "Do you take sugar?"

Rain nodded. "Why did you?"

"Why did we what?"

"Why did you switch rooms?"

"Well, it just made sense. My husband and I both liked to cook, and the original kitchen was tiny and dark, not a place you'd want to spend a lot of time in, so we decided to take this large room and turn it into the kitchen. One or two spoonfuls?"

"One."

Dr. Mallory stirred in the sweetener. "So we took our old sitting room, a larger space with the fireplace, and turned it into this kitchen." She handed the tea to Rain. "Here you go."

"I didn't know you could do that."

"Do what?"

"Switch rooms around like that."

"Why on earth not?"

"I don't know. I guess I thought a kitchen had to stay a kitchen. I mean with the plumbing and everything." The tea tasted faintly of mint and something citrus. Maybe orange.

"Oh, things can always be changed. That's what Benji said."

"Who's Benji?"

"My husband. Benjamin." She poured herself some tea, added sweetener. "He believed you could change almost anything. He'd say that the secret is first to get very clear on what you want, on what makes sense in your life, whether it's a kitchen or a career, a garden or a relationship. Once you can visualize it, when you can see it plainly in your head, then you only have to put in the required time and effort to make it happen."

Rain looked around the kitchen, tried to imagine her own parents turning a sitting room into a kitchen. "It must have been a lot of work."

"Now that's another thing Benji understood. How satisfying hard work can be. How rewarding in the end." Dr. Mallory set her glass on the counter, crossed to one of the shelves, and reached for a framed photo that was braced against the books. She gazed at the image a moment, then handed it to Rain.

Even in the photograph, Rain could see the man was tall. Tall and handsome, with a slender build and white hair. He wore cream-colored pleated pants and a matching V-neck sweater and held an old-fashioned brimmed hat in one hand. Rain couldn't imagine why he'd married the dwarf shrink. Something about the photograph stirred a meanness in her. "He's very tall. He looks like some old movie star," she said. She waited a beat, then added, "Oh, sorry. I mean that about calling him old."

"Oh, no need to apologize. He was old when that photo was taken. Just a month before he passed." She took back the frame and returned it to the shelf. "You know, Rain, you must never apologize for speaking a truth."

Good luck with that. In her experience, telling the truth led to nothing but trouble.

"It's how we speak a truth that is important. That and the intention behind it."

"The intention?"

"Yes. Whether we mean to hurt another with our words. Honesty requires a measure of kindness with it."

Rain's cheeks warmed.

"I wish he could have met you," Dr. Mallory continued. "He would have liked you."

Right. I'm so sure. She knew better than to trust compliments.

"He would have, you know."

"Why do you say that?"

"Well, for openers, you're smart. And feisty. Those are qualities he admired. And he'd like the way you question authority."

"Yeah, well, a lot of people don't think that's a good thing."

"Oh, it may make things tough right now, Rain, but in the long run, it will serve you well. Now let's get you some more tea, and we'll head into the office and talk about how I may be able to help you."

Help. The cut on Rain's thigh burned at the word.

They sat in the same seats they had chosen last time. Today there were peppermints in the copper bowl. The green vase held white peonies. As soon as Rain settled in the chair, the old spaniel stirred from beneath the desk and crossed to settle at Rain's feet.

"He likes you," Dr. Mallory said.

Again Rain felt the meanness rise in her. She looked around for a place to put her glass.

"Oh, just set it on the table," Dr. Mallory said with no fuss about coasters or making water marks. She placed her own glass on the table by her side. "I guess school must end pretty soon."

"Yeah. We have two more weeks and then we get out."

"And what are your plans for the vacation?"

"Plans? Like what?"

"What are you going to do? Do you go to summer camp?"

Camp. Seriously. Just shoot me now. "No."

"What do you usually do?"

Rain thought of the summer stretching out in front of her: hanging at the mall, sunning at the beach, endless arguments at home, her mother nagging her to help out around the house. It all seemed hugely pointless.

"Nothing much. Just hang out, I guess."

"If you could do absolutely anything, what would it be?"

"Anything?"

"Yes. If you had a magic wand and could do anything, go anywhere this summer, what would it be?"

"Well, that's a stupid question."

"Why?"

"Because I can't go anywhere or do anything, so why think about it? It's a colossal waste of time."

Dr. Mallory reached for the candy bowl and offered it to Rain, who refused. "Daydreaming. Imagining. These are never a waste of time. It's the rich territory that holds our deepest longings that can guide us to our daimon."

"Our what?"

"Our daimon. It's a word from the Greeks. It means our soul's purpose. Our destiny. The expression of our gifts."

Rain's heart began to beat hard again.

"What do you want to do after high school? Beyond this town?"

"I don't think about stuff like that."

"Really? You seem like a person who would have a lot of dreams."

She and Lucy used to talk about a future, even imagined adventures they would take together. Once they had talked about going on a car trip around the country. Maybe to the Southwest. Lucy was the only one she had told the story about the tribe of Apache women hiding in the cave, their tears turning to stone. She had told Lucy about the different kinds of rocks. They found special ones and exchanged them, called them their Lucky Strike stones. Once Lucy's parents had taken them on a day trip to Mount Tom, and when they were hiking they had found a shiny black stone. When she showed it to her grandfather, he'd told her it looked like babingtonite, which wasn't really a stone. It was a mineral. And then he'd told her the difference between them. He'd also told her she and Lucy had happened to find the one mineral that was the official mineral of Massachusetts, and what were the odds of that. She still had the babingtonite, and it was the luckiest of all her

160

Lucky Strike stones, even if it was really a mineral. They'd talked, too, of taking a trip to Europe after they graduated. "We can get a Eurail pass," Lucy had said. "And stay at hostels." As if Rain would ever be allowed to do that.

"Rain?"

"What?"

"What would you like to do with your life?"

"I don't know."

"If you could be anything at all, what would it be? Just tell me the first three things that come to mind."

Rain smirked. "The pope." *Geologist.*

"Interesting." Dr. Mallory reached for one of the red-striped candies and unwrapped it. "Close your eyes, Rain."

Rain stared, open-eyed.

"Just for a minute. Good. Okay, think back to when you were ten. The ten-year-old Rain is lying on the ground staring at the sky. The grass is soft and your entire body feels supported. It's warm; there is a little breeze, and it feels like a soft hand on your cheek. It is quiet. You are happy."

In spite of her reluctance, Rain felt herself grow quiet, dreamy.

"You are imagining the future. You see your adult self."

The spaniel snored. The clock on the bookshelf ticked off the minutes.

Rain opened her eyes. "This is bullshit."

"Why?"

"Because just because we want something doesn't mean we can get it or be it."

Dr. Mallory leaned toward her. "But you do have dreams, passions. What would you like to be, dear?"

"A geologist," she blurted. "Okay? Now can we stop this stupid game?"

"A geologist? What sparked that interest?"

Rain didn't answer. She was done with this foolishness.

"You know it's a good thing to have ambitions and aspirations, Rain," Dr. Mallory said. "The root word of *aspiration* comes from the Latin, meaning to take in breath. To have life. Our aspirations fill us with life."

Rain shifted in the chair. A memory rose up. She and Lucy lying on Lucy's bed. *Someday I'm going to live in Paris. I'll speak perfect French and be a writer for a magazine there. I'll write about food and travel and what's it like to be an American living in Paris. And you could come and stay with me. Wouldn't that be the coolest?*

Her stomach ached and she curled her fingers into a tight fist, pressing her nails into her palms, harder and harder. Her gaze fell on the backpack, still on the floor where she'd left it when she'd entered the room what seemed like hours ago. Silence filled the air, broken only by the sound of Walker snoring at her feet.

"We got the school yearbook today." The words slipped from her mouth of their own will. She squeezed her hands tighter. "The senior class dedicated it to Lucy."

"Was that a surprise?"

"Well, usually the book is dedicated to the class advisor. I mean Lucy wasn't even a senior."

"Ah."

"And there's one whole page at the beginning with Lucy's photo and this really stupid quote, and a poem Lucy wrote for sophomore English composition."

"That must have been a shock. How do you feel about that?"

"The poem?"

"About the dedication."

She shrugged. "Okay, I guess."

"Really?"

"Sure. Why not?"

"There are many feelings this could evoke. Sorrow. Grief. It's possible some people might even feel a little resentful."

"Why?"

"Because of the attention."

"That would be just sick."

"Why?"

"'Cause Lucy was—well, everybody knows what happened to her."

"Do you want to talk a little more about that?"

"Not really."

Dr. Mallory sat quietly, waiting for her to continue.

"It's just that the kids at school act like she's some kind of saint," she blurted.

"Have they always?"

"What?"

"Acted like she was a saint."

"You mean since before she was—before she was gone?" *Dead*, she thought. *Murdered.* She imagined Lucy's murderer still walking around and shut her eyes against the thought.

Dr. Mallory nodded. "Yes. Did they treat her that way before she was dead?"

Rain considered this. "No," she finally said. "No. They treated her normal. I mean, she was popular. Everyone liked her and stuff. Except maybe for the mean girls like Bethany and Allison—but they don't much like any of the other girls."

"But it makes you angry about the yearbook?"

"Yeah. I guess it's wrong to feel that."

"Not wrong. Feelings aren't right or wrong. They just are."

Right. What planet does she live on? Everyone knew it was wrong to feel angry. Or jealous. Or mean.

"Our feelings can sometimes feel uncomfortable, but they are not wrong." Dr. Mallory smiled. "Let's talk a bit more about why you are upset."

"Let's just forget it, okay."

"That's another thing about feelings, Rain. They're not so easy to deny or forget."

"I'm just saying, everyone forgets Lucy wasn't perfect." She was lucky to get a C in algebra. And she could break rules, too. Rain remembered the time when Lucy had called her from the Hayeses' one night when she was babysitting and had told her to come over. It had been Lucy's idea to open the liquor cabinet and taste the gin. They both hated it, agreed it tasted like pine needles. Wouldn't everyone be surprised to hear about that? Or about the fib she told her parents about riding in Jared Phillips's car. "Now just because she's dead everyone is acting as if she was."

"I'm sure she wasn't perfect."

"What?"

"Well, Lucy was human, so she was flawed. Just as we are all flawed. That's part of being human. So go on, Rain. Let's talk more about the yearbook dedication."

Again anger took hold. "Half the kids in the senior class didn't even know her that well. Now they're acting like—like she was their best friend."

"And she wasn't."

"No."

"Who was her best friend?"

Her throat ached and she swallowed against tears, but one escaped and slid down her cheek. Dr. Mallory didn't tell her everything would be all right or try to hug her or even reach over and touch her hand. She just waited until Rain's tears stopped.

"Sorry."

"Why are you sorry?"

"I'm not a baby. I don't usually cry."

"Oh, child, tears are one of the most healing things on the earth. 'The cure for everything is salt water—sweat, tears, or the sea.' The writer Isak Dinesen said that. Do you know of her?"

"No."

"She was another feisty, independent woman. Her given name was Karen Blixen, and she was born in Denmark. She moved to Africa. She was a pilot and a writer. I think you might enjoy reading her."

"I don't read much," Rain lied.

"Tell me, Rain. What's hardest about missing Lucy?"

"I don't know." *Laughing. Having secrets. Having someone to have your first taste of alcohol with. Having someone to trust absolutely.* One of the great things about Lucy was if you told her a secret she would never tell anyone. "I guess having her to talk to."

"Yes. I understand that. Having someone to talk to, a friend like that is a great gift."

Rain nodded.

"I know I can't take Lucy's place, Rain. But I hope I can be a person you can learn to trust. A person you can talk to."

Fat chance. Rain noticed that the time was up. Dr. Mallory crossed to the desk and her appointment calendar. "Same time next week work for you?"

"I guess." She picked up her backpack, vowing it would be the last time she'd come here. What could her mother do if she refused? Put her in jail?

At the door, Dr. Mallory touched her shoulder. "Wait one minute. There's something I have for you before you go." She walked away in her worn black shoes and returned a minute later and handed Rain a book. It was so thin at first Rain thought it was some kind of brochure, or like the monthly devotion pamphlets in the rack by the entry of Holy Apostles. "I think you might enjoy this."

Rain read the title on the cover. "Babette's Feast," by Isak Dinesen.

"Dinesen understood a lot about dreams, about destiny and courage."

"Whatever."

"One more thing, Rain. I'm going to ask you to do something."

Rain waited.

"Do you have a favorite shell or something like that? Something small you found or someone gave you?"

"I don't know." *The Lucky Strike stone.* "Why?"

"I want you to carry it with you. And when you feel sad or angry or overwhelmed, take it out and hold it in your hand."

"That's it?"

"That's it. Can you do that?"

"I guess. It sounds pretty stupid." But it wasn't. Not really. She and Lucy used to carry the Lucky Strike stones around with them.

"You know, in some cultures there are traditions of carrying amulets, touchstones, and charms. Worry beads," Dr. Mallory said. And then, as she had at the end of Rain's first appointment, she said, "Take care of yourself, Rain. And if you aren't able to take care of yourself, call me."

As if.

Outside, the driveway was empty. No big surprise. She could have predicted it. Duane had forgotten he was supposed to pick her up. She swung the backpack over her shoulder and started walking, knowing when she got home and told her mother she'd had to walk somehow it would turn out to be her fault. Another predictable thing.

She had gone two blocks when she heard the sound of his for-shit Mazda slow down beside her, but she wouldn't give her brother the satisfaction of looking over. The car crept along beside her.

"Hey there."

Not her brother. It was that pervert custodian from the school. Jervis.

"Need a lift?"

"No thanks." Like she'd ever get in his car. Creepy.

"It's pretty hot to be walking. Where are you heading?"

She walked a little faster and stared straight ahead. She'd kill Duane when she got home. If she got home. Thoughts of Lucy popped in her head.

"Come on. Hop in and I'll give you a ride."

"No thanks."

A car headed toward them. It slowed down as it approached, but Jervis continued to creep along at her pace, the smell of his car's exhaust clouding the air. The other driver glanced over at her and then continued on. Rain swung her book bag from one shoulder to the other so it hung between her and Jervis.

"Hey," he said again.

She stopped and turned. "Look," she said. "I don't want a ride, okay. My brother is on his way to pick me up."

He smiled. "Yeah? Looks like he forgot."

"He didn't forget. He's just late."

A car pulled up next to Jervis, and Rain recognized it as the one that had passed moments before. The driver rolled down his window.

"Any problem here?"

Relief swept her. She knew him. Mr. Hayes. So funny he should appear, as if she had conjured him by remembering the time she and Lucy had tried his gin when Lucy had been babysitting for his little boy.

"Hey, you don't want a ride, that's okay. Suit yourself." Jervis floored the gas and took off, trailing the scent of exhaust.

Rain looked at Lucy's neighbor. "Thanks," she said.

"No problem. Glad to help."

"My brother was supposed to pick me up, but I guess he forgot."

"If you'd like I could give you a ride," he said. "Or if you prefer I can drive and you can walk and I'll escort you home, ride shotgun as it were. Keep away unwanted advances."

Rain had to laugh. She scanned the street. Still no sight of Duane. "That's okay. I don't want to bother you."

"No bother. If we see your brother along the way, we'll flag him down."

"Okay," she said. "If you're sure it's no bother."

He reached over and opened the passenger door for her. "You're one of Lucy Light's friends, aren't you?"

"Yes. Her best friend." It came out like she was bragging, and she wished she had only nodded.

"I haven't seen you around for a while."

"No." Even for someone older, he was good-looking. She wished she had worn something a little prettier, wished the polish on her toenails wasn't all chipped.

"Buckle up. Got to keep you safe," he said.

Her cheeks heated, and she reached for the strap and engaged the buckle.

"So, where to?"

"Where to?"

"Where do you live?"

"Oh, right." He must think she was an idiot. "Chandler Street."

"So what were you doing in this part of town?"

"Oh, nothing. Visiting a friend." She could only imagine what he'd think if she told him she was seeing a shrink. Too soon they turned onto her street and he pulled into her driveway.

"Here you go," he said.

There was no sign of Duane and his piece-of-shit car or her mother's Volvo, which saved her from spending the next hour being cross-examined about how she got home. "Thanks again. For everything."

"Anytime."

Anytime?

"I'm always glad to help a damsel in distress."

Damsel in distress.

What an old-fashioned thing to say. But she played the words over. Damsel. In distress. Rescued. And for a moment, for one of the few times since Lucy was murdered, she felt protected. Safe.

CHAPTER TWENTY

~

I'd had a week of fitful sleep and felt as if I suffered from some kind of wasting disease.

A partially completed canvas waited at the easel, but I stared blankly at the painting that had once been so promising. Technically the composition—five oysters on the half shell set on an indigo plate—was not the problem. It was fine, I could see that, the light refracting off the flesh of the mollusks was exact, yet I had lost interest in it, cared no more about it than I would a dead houseplant, as if an unseen yet powerful force had stilled my hand. So even this last refuge in my life, the slender modicum of peace I had found in the studio, was to be taken from me. From the hollow, aching emptiness of the house I heard the phone ringing. Finally the caller gave up and the echo of the ringing evaporated and, as always, Lucy's absence crowded in, a deafening presence. This absence was like the sky, covering everything. It was like living in a room hung with heavy curtains. Unable to bear the claustrophobic silence any longer, I fled the house.

The market was nearly deserted. It was far too early for the after-work crowd, and the morning shoppers had come and gone. I grabbed a basket—no need for a cart—and negotiated the aisles, shopping for the few items that now sustained me. I passed the long stands overflowing with fresh produce and turned toward the meat department, where a white-jacketed butcher was busy arranging cellophaned packages of chops and steaks, chicken thighs, and ground beef in neat rows in the display counter. Not for the first time, I was struck by the extravagance of it all, the waste implicit in such abundance, the food that would remain unsold past expiration dates, produce already decaying and destined for the huge garbage bins that lined the concrete wall behind the market. I had to resist the urge to abandon my basket there in the middle of the aisle.

Today the spike-haired cashier at the checkout sported two-inch strands dyed purple. Not any improvement over the usual pink. "Hey, Mr. L," she said. She looked at my groceries. "You find everything you need?"

I nodded, avoiding conversation. I no longer trusted my hearing. A sign hanging above the belt read, "Remove All Items from Your Cart or Basket at Checkout." Dutifully I emptied the groceries. Coffee. Bread. Peanut butter. A stack of frozen dinners I once would have considered inedible but that now comprised most of my meals. I sensed rather than saw another shopper push a cart into the narrow space beside me. The woman began to unload her groceries. I set the plastic divider between our orders and moved my few items along the belt toward the cashier.

"Hi," said a small voice from below.

Two toddlers stared up at me from the folds of the woman's skirt, the girl a miniature version of her mother, the boy, younger with a darker complexion. A baby was propped up in a yellow molded infant seat in the grocery cart. It was the girl who had spoken.

"Hi," she said again, staring up with clear brown eyes, steady and trusting.

"Hi." I pushed the word out and turned away. The cashier scanned each item with infuriating slowness. I reached for my billfold, as if that would make her quicken her pace. Beside me, the mother lifted the baby out of the seat, straddling the infant on one hip. She turned to lift the molded seat from the cart, and from the edge of my vision, I caught a glimpse of the infant just as he slid from her grasp. Motion seemed to slow—the open-mouthed mother crying out, her eyes wide, the cashier's hands frozen at their task, baby slipping, slipping, slipping, from hip to thigh to knee, toward the floor.

Without thought, I brushed aside the other children and lunged for the infant, felt my shoulders jerk as I caught him.

"Whoa. Great save, Mr. L," the cashier said. "You totally rock."

The infant was heavy in my arms.

The woman, shock fading, reached for her baby. We were separated by an arm's length, and I looked fully at her for the first time. As our eyes met, a faint memory stirred, a familiarity. *Do I know you?*

"Thank you," she said as she lifted her infant from my arms and cradled him close to her chest. Relieved of the burden, my arms felt lighter, emptier. Bereft. The mother held my gaze a moment longer, as if searching for something else to say. Again I was struck with a sense of knowing her. A hand tugged at my shirt hem. The girl reached an arm up to me, holding something toward me in her fist.

"Here, mister," she said.

I shifted my gaze from the child to her mother, as if for guidance, and was struck by the calmness she radiated, how peaceful she seemed, only moments after the near disaster. She nodded her okay.

I opened my palm; the child deposited a red chunk in it.

"Lick wish," she said in her tiny voice.

I tried to make sense of the word, one probably mangled by my hearing problem.

The mother smiled. "Licorice," she said. "It's her favorite."

Lick wish. A Lucy word. The familiar pain of grief stirred in my sternum. More memories surfaced, ambushing me. I managed to mumble my thanks, then grabbed my groceries and walked away, leaving in my wake a buzz of conversation, the voices of the teenage clerk and the woman, and then the higher voice of the girl. And then, just as I reached the automatic doors, a surprising ribbon of laughter, light and joy-filled, floated to me, and I knew without looking that it was the mother.

Even before I had crossed the parking lot, I discarded the sticky red chunk. *Lick wish.* In the car, I rummaged through the glove box until I found a tissue. I wiped my palm clean of the moist residue, but the vision of the woman, the weight of the infant in my arms, remained, and with it memory and the ever-present pain. I drove home in a cloud of despair, one that carried with it a hopelessness more powerful than any I had ever felt. I could not see a future that held more than this. Terrible solitude and utter isolation. It was a future I wasn't sure I could any longer bear to face. Certainly I was unable to return to the emptiness of the house that awaited me. In the driveway, I left the groceries in the car, the frozen dinners to melt in the heat, and walked away. My stride was fast, although I had no destination, not walking toward anything, just away from something. *Move on. Pick up the pieces and get on with life.* The directives echoed in my head. Others were quick with advice. One person had even told me it was unhealthy to stay stuck. You wouldn't believe the things people said. Maybe you are thinking of them too. Perhaps you want me to get on with it, but unless your life has been rent with violence, you cannot imagine how thoroughly it destroys the foundation.

I passed familiar places—the Crow's Nest, the market, the town's historical museum, and next to it the art museum. I passed, too, new places—a yoga studio where there had once been a dentist, a yarn shop. I continued past the town line and went on with no destination in mind. For the rest of the morning, I walked. And into the afternoon. I walked past hunger and thirst. My feet grew sore and my breath more labored, but still I kept going. Twice a cramp seized my left calf, a sign I knew indicated dehydration, but I did not stop for water. Twice, cars stopped, and each time a familiar face asked if I needed a lift home, offers I refused. Later, I would trace the route in my car and discover I had walked for more than thirty miles.

At last, well after dark, nearly disoriented with exhaustion and dehydration, I walked toward the next open business I saw, a gas station and convenience store. I went in and called for a taxi. Even exhaustion had not lessened or numbed the despair, despair as thoroughly a part of me as muscle and marrow.

At home, I managed to climb the stairs to my room and fell fully clothed on the bed. Just as I closed my eyes, the scene from the market played out behind my lids. I saw the woman from the market and saw again the moment the baby had slipped from her arms, my own reflexive action in reaching for the child, the damp weight in my arms. I recalled how the woman's shock so quickly turned to gratitude and how her eyes had looked into mine holding both serenity and something very much like sorrow. Again a twinge of recognition hit me, something faint about her expression, her eyes, but it eluded me. And then I recalled the ribbon of her laughter following me as I left the market. At last I escaped into a fitful sleep.

I woke at dawn and knew a half-conscious and too-brief moment of peace before awareness snapped in. Another long and pointless day stretched in front of me. More than one person had told me it would get better, that time did heal. As if such a thing were possible. Did pain ever become bearable? Fainter? I couldn't imagine.

I forced myself to move, to go through the morning routine. Shaved. Made coffee. Toast. I poured a second mug and carried it with me up to the studio where the oyster painting waited on the easel. Work I knew I would never finish. I straightened my worktable, cleaned brushes, moved about my space seeking purpose. I sorted through a stack of CDs, rejecting Schumann and Saint-Saëns, Bizet and Barber, settling at last on Chopin. I sat in the chair by the window and closed my eyes as the notes of the Concerto No. 2 filled the room. I stayed there for long moments. A ray of the morning sun cut through the pane and heated a stripe across my legs. Finally, I stirred and retrieved a sketch pad and drawing pencil. I have often wondered what led my actions that morning, for looking back I recall my sense of feeling almost in a trance. Certainly it was nothing I planned.

I hadn't attempted a portrait in months, and the work was halting at first. Outside, a car horn sounded, but absorbed in my task, I barely heard it. Gradually, my gestures grew sure, and an image appeared on the page as if rising up from beneath the surface of the paper. Raven hair framed a face more round than oval; the eyes, too, were round. And dark. There was something faintly foreign about her, suggesting a heritage either Portuguese or Italian. The likeness was not exact; I saw this even before it was completed. I was working from memory, and the line of the jaw was not precise, the arch of the brow not quite right, but I had captured something there that I had seen in the woman's features, the face both serene and sad.

"Will?"

I was so startled my hand jerked on the pad and left a ragged pencil line. I looked up and saw Sophie in the doorway.

"Sorry. I didn't mean to frighten you. I phoned but I guess you didn't hear."

"No."

"I don't mean to disturb your work."

"You didn't. I was taking a break." I set the drawing on the table, fought a growing dread. Were we going to argue again?

She was wearing a summery dress in some kind of gossamer material that danced around her as she approached the easel and looked at the abandoned still life. "This is good," she said. "Remember the critic who said you understood light like the masters did? It was in that feature in the *Times*, I think. Remember?"

"Yes." So long ago. *Before.*

"He was right. You do."

I didn't tell her I no longer cared about the painting.

She picked out a brush from a jar of brushes and rolled the handle in her fingers, a delaying tactic. I realized she was nervous.

"What is it, Sophie?"

"I'm going to go away for a while."

"Where?" I kept my voice steady although the shock of her words ran through me.

"Maine."

"How long?"

She played with the brush, smoothed the bristles. "Two months."

"For the summer then."

"Maybe longer."

I raised an eyebrow.

"I'm not going to Amy's. I'm going with a friend."

"A friend?"

"Yes. Joan Laurant. She's rented a place in Rockport for the summer, and she asked me if I wanted to come along. Apparently it's one of those old farmhouses with dozens of rooms and property that goes down to the water."

Joan. I recalled the way she'd barged in last winter and pulled Sophie from her bed and taken her to the gym to box.

"I need this, Will. I need to get away to think."

"You could have gone to Amy's." *You could have gone with me. We could have rented a place together.*

"I wasn't planning to go at all. This just came up. And when Joan asked me, I thought, *Why not?* And then I knew it was exactly what I needed. Time away from here." She looked at me a little shyly. "I might even try to write."

Write what? I wanted to ask. "And you can't do that here?"

She replaced the brush on the table, her confidence returned. "I'm not here to ask permission, Will. I just wanted to see you before I went. To let you know where I'll be."

"It's settled then? That's it? No discussion?"

She opened her bag and pulled out a notebook page. "I've written down the address. The phone number at the rental. I'll have my cell, but service is spotty there."

I stared at the paper.

"Do you want me to leave it here, or shall I put it on the kitchen table?"

"Doesn't matter." So this was a done deal.

"And Amy will always be able to reach me. Their house is only seven miles from where I'll be."

"When are you leaving?" I asked.

But Sophie didn't hear me. "Oh," she said, her voice soft. "This is lovely." She was looking at the sketch I had set on the table. "I didn't know you knew her, Will."

"Who? Knew who?"

"Mary." She picked up the pad and carried it to the window for better light. The skirt of her dress whispered around her legs. "Mary Silveria."

I realized then why the woman in the market had seemed familiar. In midwinter, Sophie and I, along with most of Port Fortune, had stood in line outside the funeral home, all waiting to go in to the wake for her husband. I hadn't wanted to go. I really didn't know the family, but Sophie had insisted. The woman was a parishioner at Holy Apostles. Her husband's boat had gone down off Georges Bank. The line of mourners had inched along until finally we were inside, standing before the woman who gazed at us with grief-stunned eyes, hands cupped in front of her swollen belly. Sophie hadn't told me she was pregnant. "I don't. Not really. I saw her yesterday and was just fooling around with it."

"It's good."

"Just a sketch," I said, my voice dismissive.

Sophie put the pad back on the table and came to me, slipped her arms around me. I felt, beneath my fingers, the sheerness of the dress, the strength of her body. I didn't want to let her go.

"Take care, Will," she said. "Be well."

My throat thickened. "You too, Sophie. I love you."

"I love you too, Will."

And then she was gone, leaving me alone to wonder how much love could withstand.

A great restlessness took hold for which I had no outlet. I replayed the scene, trying to make sense of it. I picked up the paper on which she had jotted down the address and fought the urge to tear it to shreds. I looked at the address: *13 End of the Road.* An odd name. And not a good omen. Then my gaze fell, as Sophie's had, to the drawing on my sketch pad. Now I had a name for the woman. I again recalled her standing in the funeral home, pregnant and bereft. And then pictured her as she had been in the market, a widow with two toddlers and an infant in her arms. Then I heard the echo of her laughter, light and joy-filled. How was it possible? How had this woman, widowed too young and left with three children, been able to not only go on but to come alive to joy? And for a moment, one single moment, the darkness that had filled me, the despair and grief that were as much a part of me as bone and marrow, lifted, warming me with a lightness of being as surely as earlier that morning a ray of light had streamed through the studio window, heating my leg.

I stared at the drawing as if the answer was held there, but the image stared silently back at me. Even as I put it away, her gaze stayed with me, haunting, beseeching. What did she want of me? What did any of them want of me? This woman? Father Gervase? Sophie? Couldn't they understand I had nothing left to give?

Then, as if the priest were standing there in the attic room with me, Father Gervase's words echoed in the silent studio.

The saints were ordinary people.

The saints were us.

You do paint saints.

CHAPTER TWENTY-ONE

~

But I did not paint saints. Or anything else.

After Sophie left for Maine, I closed the door to my studio and walked away. If I'd had a deadbolt on the door, I would have shot it home. I no longer climbed the flight of stairs to the top floor each morning. Instead, I poured my energy into chores that had been neglected for months. A faucet that dripped in the first-floor bathroom off the kitchen. The peeling paint on the sill over the kitchen sink. Tasks that required nothing of me but mindless labor. I finally got around to properly repairing a broken window in the dining room. Earlier in the spring someone had thrown a baseball through it, leaving a perfect hole in the center with a web of cracks radiating from it. The ball had landed on the table, chipping the ceramic bowl we had brought home from a trip to Italy. I had been infuriated that we were targets of such an act of vandalism and wanted to call the police, but Sophie had convinced me to let it go. "What on earth do you think they can do about it?" she'd said, her voice tinged with a bitterness she rarely betrayed. "If they can't find who killed Lucy, I doubt they will find who did this." There was no arguing with that, so I'd patched the worst of it with duct tape and waited for the new pane I ordered to come in, but I never got around to replacing it. So last week I had retrieved it from the basement and carried it outside, where I set it on the grass while I went to get the stepladder from the garden shed. As I'd worked cutting out the old putty, setting in the new pane, inserting glazier's points to hold it in place until the new putty set, I'd felt the ever-present anger stir that someone would target us for such vandalism. A boy, I'd imagined, one with an arm strong enough to hurl the ball across the yard, although it was far too late to do anything about it at that point.

Another day last week, looking for yet another chore to fill the time and searching for hedge clippers to tackle the shrubs along the back of the property, I found a pile of stakes in the shed and impulsively took them to mark off the lines for a patio in the backyard that I had once considered constructing. I had gotten as far as plotting the design for the bricks, a basket-weave pattern. I'd imagined it as a place where we could gather in the late afternoons or where Lucy could spend time with her friends. *Before.* I ordered four pallets of bricks, and while waiting for them to be delivered, I prepped the space, cutting up sod and leveling the ground (my father had drilled the importance of careful preparation necessary for every job, telling me that was where a project failed or succeeded), and was aware occasionally of eyes on me, in that inexplicable way one had when being watched. Once I saw Payton Hayes watching from his kitchen window. He'd waved and moments later appeared to ask if I wanted a beer or cold drink. We had spoken only once since I had seen him in his office. He had phoned to see how I had made out with Gillian Donaldson. I'd given him a brief report, and we had each gone back to our own lives.

The only other witnesses to my work were the finches that nested in the elm and the two ropes of Lucy's swing, which, with the seat now gone, swayed freely from a limb like severed arteries. Sometimes I would catch their movement out of the edge of my vision and imagined Lucy sitting in her swing watching me in silent companionship, a thought that brought sharp pain, but also an odd and completely unexpected comfort.

Once started, I worked on the patio obsessively, plying trowel and level and spreading stone dust, bending to the precise task of laying bricks in the pattern I had devised. It occurred to me it was a futile task as I no longer had a family to gather there, but still as the work progressed I felt the stirrings of something, not quite excitement or pleasure and certainly not joy, but a stirring nonetheless. At first I put it down to the satisfaction of doing the work, physical labor that helped me sleep better at night, but when I tracked it back to the first faint stirrings, I thought of the woman in the market, her laughter, the quick drawing I'd done of her.

You do paint saints.

Do it for Lucy.

I resisted. You have no idea how I resisted. I wanted none of it. Even the thought of agreeing to accept the commission caused a hot flush of irritation, as if it would indicate an acceptance of a religion I didn't believe in and a church I didn't belong to, surrendering to something I couldn't name.

What are you afraid of?

The more I struggled and resisted, the stronger the ghost echoes grew and the more a possibility took shape in my mind just as the patio took shape beneath my hands.

The saints were ordinary people.

You do paint saints.

Wherever I went these words of Father Gervase's stayed with me, a ghost staking out territory in my head as certainly as I had staked out the space for the bricks I now laid. If I were a more fanciful man—or a more superstitious one—I would say it was as if the little priest had put a curse on me.

I began to see saints.

I saw them in the streets and shops of Port Fortune. It wasn't that I was visualizing dead people in halos and robes, but instead flashes of something in the features of my fellow townspeople, glimpses that briefly transformed a face, revealing an essence of goodness or virtue or a wisdom born of pain. They fit no single profile. They were men and women and even youth with expressions that were worn or serene, gaunt or well-nourished, naïve or experienced, happy or worried or bitter. They were white, and black, and varying shades of brown. Ordinary people going about their daily business and spanning all of life's stages. A hefty boy on a trail bike. A fisherman with a face seamed with a web of deep lines. A balding man with stooped shoulders sitting at the bar in the coffee shop. One night I again saw, sitting on the wooden fence at the playground, the slight-framed teen with an expression at once desperate and proud and lonely, and I'd been reminded of the martyred youth who'd been pierced with arrows in the book of saints Father Gervase had brought to my house. Saint Sebastian.

The saints are us.

The irony was bitter. In the past months, ever since Lucy's murder, I had looked into the faces of the townspeople and seen only the possibility of cruelty and alienation, mean-spiritedness and the real potential for evil. Now, as if I possessed the vision of some other person—some stranger, a madman or monk—I began to see in them a fleeting aura of the possibility of goodness. A sort of halo effect. Regardless of what life had taught me, of what I had learned of humanity and its potential for pettiness, for betrayal and greed and envy and the most grievous of human sins, it seemed anyone might appear a saint. I remembered what the priest had told me. Saints come from every page in history and from every part of the globe.

The saints are ordinary people.

Gradually, despite my deep reluctance and resistance, a vision took shape. A gathering of the saints. Not on individual canvases but in two triptychs. Six panels. All ages and colors. Receiving Communion.

For Lucy.

And then, one day when the last brick was laid and the patio finished, without forethought or conscious intention, I climbed the stairs to the third-floor studio and unlocked the door.

PART TWO
SAINTS

~

Every saint has a past and every sinner has a future.

—*Oscar Wilde*

CHAPTER TWENTY-TWO

~

As always, with the arrival of summer, Port Fortune geared up for the influx of tourists and seasonal residents.

As if a page had been turned and in concert everyone had exhaled a long-held breath, the paranoia and fear that had held townspeople in its grip through the past months eased. Even the drama of the pregnant teenagers had morphed into something like acceptance, and after the birth of the babies, attention shifted to caring for the infants. There were hastily arranged marriages, one adoption, and two girls who remained single and kept their sons to raise alone. And as if by tacit agreement, there had grown a consensus among the townspeople that Lucy Light had been murdered by a stranger, an addict who had been passing through, and as awful as it was—those things happened, just look at the news—it was an aberration that wouldn't be repeated. In the face of the unimaginable, towns, like individuals, find ways to accommodate and compromise and go on. The green ribbons that girded trees throughout the town had faded to the palest yellow, their edges tattered and defeated. People again grew careless about locking their doors and relaxed the vigilance with which they watched over their daughters.

Concern and conversation now centered on the weather. A high-pressure area had stalled over the northeastern seaboard, and an extraordinary, record-breaking heat had descended. For five days the temperature hit ninety-nine degrees, and accustomed to the mitigating influence of offshore breezes even at the height of summer, the town was unprepared for the intensity of the heat. Every AC unit within thirty miles had sold out days ago, and brownouts occurred periodically as utility systems wilted into overload. At the *Port Fortune Sun Times*, the editor reported that historically heat waves had proved more deadly than hurricanes or tornadoes. He reminded readers to stay hydrated and to remain inside during the peak hours of the day.

Even in daylight, animals wandered into town. A deer was seen lapping water from a birdbath in Lucia Crowley's yard, and two streets away Alan Moore witnessed a fox drinking from the bowl he'd set out on the back stoop for his dog. Over at Cape Port Ice, there was a sighting of a brown bear on the ramp leading to the worn loading dock, and in Jules Cavanaugh's hives, the honeycombs began to melt in spite of the furious efforts of the fanning bees.

In four days, ten deaths had occurred: three elderly residents of Rose Hall Manor, one suicide, two dogs, and four of Ben Roark's hen pullets, whose bodies he discovered inside the coop, limp and covered with greenheads. People spoke of the heat as if it were an animal, a great creature that had crawled into their town along with the fox and deer and brown bear, suffocating all with its low-slung belly and fetid breath.

That Tuesday morning at seven thirty the thermometer mounted outside the town hall registered eighty-three, and by noon it edged closer to one hundred. At the Morning Glory Bed and Breakfast, Leola Simmons had installed window fans in each bedroom, but arriving tourists, on learning there was no central AC, canceled their reservations and demanded their deposits be returned. At the Loaves of the Fisherman, the temperature in the kitchen by the Frialator reached one hundred and twenty-three degrees, triggering the fire alarm. Leon

Newell, Caesar Amero, and Portuguese Joe sat at their regular table and recalled heat waves of decades past, the summers of '98 and '34.

At the town pier the *Johnny B Good* arrived in from a trip offshore to a pier so hot the crew felt as if they were stepping on the sun. Moving as quickly as the heat allowed, the men unloaded the trawler and re-iced their catch. Waves of white incandescence rose off the parking lot; tires on boat trailers sank into the softening macadam.

The police department issued extreme heat advisories, and Chief Johnson reminded residents that the elderly and animals were at the highest risk. Tempers flared as if in sync with the mercury, and Dot Hastings, the station dispatcher, dealt with a steady in-rush of calls reporting escalating bar brawls and domestic quarrels, people collapsing on the street, and homeowners violating the recently instituted ban on watering lawns. "This outdoes the full-moon mania," Dot said to Dan Gordon, who arrived at the station having just cited the owner of an Alaskan malamute for leaving the dog in a locked car while she was shopping in an air-conditioned market. Even at the beach there was no relief. Swimmers suffered sunburns; cranky children blistered their feet just by walking across the sand.

At Holy Apostles, fans had been set up in the sanctuary, and Father Gervase's garden was showing signs of stress. Each morning and evening he surveyed the brown-edged leaves of daylilies and the limp blossoms of hydrangea bushes, and mindful of the request to limit watering lawns and gardens, he convinced Mrs. Jessup to save her dishwater, which he carried in jugs to pour out at the base of the plants.

So life went on.

If people talked about the Light family now, they focused less on the mystery of the daughter's murder and more on the honor her father was bringing to Port Fortune. Will Light had been chosen by the archdiocese of Boston to paint the murals for that city's new cathedral, a series of the saints that would hang in the nave, portraits for whom he had asked some of the people of Port Fortune to serve as models.

CHAPTER
TWENTY-THREE

~

"Ya know, Jossie thinks this is pretty damn funny," Leon Newell said.

"What's that?" I was paying halfhearted attention to Leon's conversation. When some models posed they tended to be talkative, and over the years I'd learned to filter them out.

"This. Me posing as a saint. Jossie's laughing her head off about it. She says if I'm a saint, it has to be one with singed and broken wings."

"She must be thinking of angels. I don't think saints have wings."

"Well, she says that maybe me posing as a saint some of it will rub off. I told her not to get her hopes up."

I had to smile. As is true in many small towns, gossip was its lifeblood, and although I usually paid little attention to it, Leon's reputation as a drinker was legendary. In that he was not alone. When the cod stock diminished, a good share of the fishermen began driving trucks with bumper stickers that said, "Port Fortune—A Drinking Town with a Fishing Problem."

"We're almost ready," I told him. "It'll just take me another minute or two to get things set."

"No problem." Leon looked around. "I haven't been in this building in years. Used to be Louie Johns's place."

"That so?"

"Yup. I guess you've heard of him."

I ran the name through my mind. "Sounds vaguely familiar," I said.
"But I can't place him."

"No kidding. I thought everyone in town knew of him. He was a
boatbuilder. One of the best. A real craftsman. Wooden boats, ya know.
None of that fiberglass crap for him. You wanted a dory or a catboat
built, Louie was the man. Sloops, too. He had buyers coming up all
the way from Maryland. Even a couple of times from Florida. Seams
on his boats were so tight, they'd never sink as long as you kept them in
water. Here. Let me show you something." He stepped down from the
riser I'd built for the models to stand on and crossed to the back of the
building, walking with the rolling gait of a man who had spent years at
sea. "Ya see that beam? See those cuts up there?"

I stood beside Leon and gazed up at the beam, saw a faint hatching
of scars.

"There's one for every boat Louie built. Must be a hundred of 'em.
You can still see some of his earliest ones around the harbor. The nar-
rower ones. They're the ones that last longer. Boats are same as people.
Bigger they are the more they carry, and the body can't stand the extra
weight." Leon rubbed his thumb along his jaw. "Louie died a while
back. Must be—let's see. Must be ten years now. Kinda funny though."

"What's that?"

"You painting saints in here. I'll tell ya, most Saturday nights there
used to be some hell-raising going on in this place."

"That so?"

"Oh, you can't imagine. 'Course, everything is so dull these days.
Some guys I know turned into teetotalers. Attend those meetings. Like
they took the pledge. Not like the old days. Chappy Wilson—you heard
of him? No? Well, he'd bring in some of his home brew. High-octane,

that stuff was. Ya know what he put in it? Potato peelings. See? Vegetable stuff. Oranges."

A poor man's vodka, I thought and shuddered. "How'd it taste?"

"It wasn't the taste we was looking for. My Christ, but we had some good times. More than once someone called the police. Different times, those were. 'Course, after he lost his son, he quit the booze."

I looked up. "He lost a son?"

"Over in 'Nam. Caught in an ambush. The day he got the news, Louie quit the drink cold turkey."

A better man than I, I thought. I gazed up at the marks on the beams and wondered how many of them had been incised after the death of the boatbuilder's boy.

As Leon walked back to take his place on the riser, he looked around as if ghosts of past days still lingered. "How long have you owned the place?"

"Oh, I don't own it. I'm only renting it for this project." I would have preferred being in my own studio, but at the outset it had become apparent that the oversized dimensions of the canvases would require a large work space, and with the understanding that the diocese would absorb the cost, I'd negotiated for use of the barnlike building. There were two skylights in the high ceiling that, along with the rolling barn doors that opened to the water, offered good light. I had already grown used to the smell, an amalgam of wood and tar and varnish and the lingering must of a building that shouldered up to the sea.

"Okay," I said. "Let's get started. I don't want to take up your whole morning. I'm going to begin by taking some photos, a few different poses that I'll use as studies. As I explained earlier, your head, hands, and feet are all that will show in the final painting. The rest of you will be covered by a robe."

"Who am I supposed to be? Jossie was asking me. I know you told me, but I already forgot."

"Saint Brendan." I looked over at Leon's deformed hands, his seamed and weathered face, and saw in them a likeness of the ancient saint.

"Brendan, huh? Never heard of him."

"He was Irish. A sailor. I thought you might know of him, you being a fisherman and all. He's one of the patron saints of sailors."

"Hell, I was raised Baptist. No saints for us."

I gestured toward the far side of the room, where several stacks of books and folders were spread across the surface of a workbench. "You can read about him if you want. There's a folder with his name on it over there."

"Well, he must have been an ugly son of a bitch if you want me to sit for him. So what do you want me to do?"

"Stand there and look holy," I said.

"Jesus." Leon laughed. "That's one hell of a tall order."

"We'll start with your hands." People were most comfortable when I focused on their hands, and I began with those to put them at ease. If you pay attention, you'll notice how revealing hands are of a person's life. Looking at Leon's I was reminded of the smooth, plump hands of seventeen-year-old Tracy Ramos, whom I'd chosen for Rose of Lima, and the pale, thick-knuckled ones of the Portuguese baker who posed for Crispin of Viterbo. Leon's were thickened and worn, fingers permanently cupped from years of hauling nets.

"Okay, now if you'd just clasp your hands in prayer."

Leon shifted from one leg to the other, then joined his hands.

I never gave specific directions beyond that, just asking my models to hold their hands as if they were gathering for Communion. Some folded their hands, fingers interlaced tightly as if hiding something in their palms as Leon did then. Some cupped one hand over the other. Others pressed palms together, fingers steepled together, like a child's, while others aimed their fingers straight forward. What I noticed, though, was how when they stood there, robed and hands held in an attitude of prayer, people stood a little taller, a little straighter, reverent, and I was unexpectedly touched by this. And then, immediately, thought if I wasn't careful I'd find myself lighting candles. Or heading over to the grocery store to purchase some aerosol cans I thought of as spray and pray.

After Leon left, I rolled open the large barn doors on the water side of the building to take advantage of the slight breeze coming in from the harbor, although the movement of air did little to alleviate the already intense heat. It was impractical to air-condition a space that vast, but if the weather continued, I knew I would need to install a few more fans. I was scanning the photographic studies I'd done of Leon when a shadow fell across the workbench. I looked up to see Father Gervase standing there. The priest held two takeout drink containers, the sides beaded with sweat.

"I didn't want to bother you, but I thought you might like a cold drink," he said.

"Thanks." You might be surprised to learn I wasn't unhappy to see the priest. We had developed an odd relationship, not friendship but a peculiar sense of ease with each other. He would show up at the oddest hours, always with a cold drink or cookies he had purchased at the bakery. Sometimes he would just sit and watch me work, and other times he would chat, reminiscing about his childhood in Wisconsin or his work as a young priest in an inner city. Once he had been called by the police to talk to a man who held an entire SWAT team at bay with a gun. "He told us to get you," the cop had said. "You're the only one he'll talk to." Again and again the little priest continued to surprise me. "As a matter of fact, I was just about to take a break," I said.

Father Gervase set the glasses down and sank down on one of the smaller benches. "I also come with a message."

I didn't bother any attempt to withhold a sigh. "From the archbishop," I said.

He smiled. "From the archbishop."

"What does His Grace want now?" From our first meeting, the big-bellied and well-coifed cardinal had struck me as more a smooth and successful salesman than a priest—a salesman, I soon learned, who was adept at generating positive PR for the church. Once the many decisions, negotiations, and compromises intrinsic to the project had been settled and I'd signed the commission contract, the archbishop called a press conference to announce it. The surprise in all this had been Father Gervase, who was proving to be an unexpected ally. When Cardinal Kneeland voiced reservations about my idea of using the townspeople as models, it was Father Gervase who had reminded the archbishop that traditionally the greatest artists had employed local people as models, paintings resulting in some of the most famous examples of religious art. He knew of a former church in Rhode Island that had become renowned for its frescoes painted by an Italian artist in the 1940s, all of whom bore the faces of the church's former parishioners. And then there was the matter of selecting the forty-two saints to be painted, seven for each of the six panels. The archbishop had wanted to choose them, but Father Gervase pointed out perhaps the artistic vision should lie with the artist but I could submit renderings to the committee for review, presenting the idea so cleverly that the archbishop ended up believing it had been his own. Again, I realized how easy it was to underestimate the little priest. And it had been Father Gervase's quiet suggestion that one figure not yet sanctified be incorporated in the saints' Communion gathering, a figure who would represent the potential for sainthood in everyone.

"Cardinal Kneeland has a proposal."

"And who does he want included now?" It had been settled that I would choose the saints for the panels, but each week the archbishop "suggested" one he believed should be represented.

Father Gervase hesitated. "Well, he's been thinking about what an opportunity there is here."

"What's that?"

"The fact that you're painting here in this building, right by the center of town. He has an idea he thinks could be a win-win for everyone."

A win-win for everyone. I could hear the archbishop's silky voice in that phrase. "So what's the idea?"

"That you open the studio to the public so they can come in, look at what you're doing, see the work as it progresses." Noting my expression, he quickly added, "It's not proposing this for every day, you understand. Just one morning or afternoon each week."

"I don't think so."

"His thinking is that it would be good exposure for you and generate interest for the project."

"I don't work that way, Father. On display. I don't do sideshow art."

The priest nodded, then smiled gently, as if he had known before he asked that this would be my answer. "I'll pass on your response."

From my prior interactions with the archbishop, I doubted that this would be the end of it.

"How are things coming?" Father Gervase asked.

"No problems so far." *If one discounted the meddling of your archbishop*, I thought. "I've drafted the scheme for the first panel on the south side of the nave." I indicated the white board I'd nailed along one wall of the building where some of the photos were displayed. "The photographic studies for Rose of Lima, Crispin, Peter, Paul, Maurice, Brendan, and Ambrose are completed."

The priest inspected the photos. "Interesting."

"How's that?"

"That you have the baker posing as Crispin." He pointed to Alonzo America's head, black hair so abundant with curls they formed a cap. "Crispin. From the Latin. It means 'with curly hair.' And there's Jules Cavanaugh as Ambrose, the patron saint for beekeepers."

There's a saint for everyone, for everything, Sophie had said so long ago. *Knock-knees and nose hair?* I'd teased her. *Lost pets,* she'd countered. *And lost causes.* I wondered if she still believed.

Father Gervase leaned in closer to the photos. "Hands," he said after a minute. "So beautiful. So individual."

"Yes," I said, and found myself sharing with the priest my observation about the different ways the models held their hands in prayer and how they stood more reverently when they posed.

"And you find that unusual? Their reverence?" Father Gervase returned to the small bench by one of the worktables.

"I guess I don't understand the pull of religion."

"You never attended church?"

"As a child. But a very skeptical child." My parents had seen that I attended Sunday church school, but even then, as I'd listened to Mrs. Moulton read the story lessons, disbelief had surfaced. Alone in the bulrushes wouldn't the baby Moses have cried and been discovered? And in that den? Wouldn't a lion really eat Daniel? A *lion*? My questioning only grew as I aged. I couldn't understand the mindless acceptance of dogma, an acceptance people were quick to call faith. And I was repelled by the way everyone protected his own little plot, which of course involved making everyone else wrong. I couldn't understand the surrender of self to priests and popes that Sophie's religion demands.

"Outside of the structure of religion, the dogma you reject, do you find it so hard to believe there is a God?" Father Gervase asked.

I readied a flip reply, but the priest's sincerity elicited a more thoughtful answer. "I believe there is a mystery beyond our understanding. Why can't we leave it at that?"

"So you are a doubter. That's good news."

"Good noose?" I said. Was I to be hung for my lack of faith?

"Good news," Father Gervase repeated. "There is no true belief that isn't tested by doubt."

"I am not a true believer, Father."

"Even nonbelief is a kind of belief. And I do believe you are a believer, Will. For instance, you believe in art."

"Whatever." I was determined not to be drawn into a discussion.

The priest closed his eyes for a moment. His hands were folded in his lap. "Perhaps," he said softly. "Perhaps in the end it is not our beliefs that matter as much as it is our behavior."

I wondered how the archbishop would respond to this bit of theology. "Whatever, Father. I guess what I am saying is I have no use for religion."

"And yet here you are," the priest said. "Painting saints."

I laughed, a short laugh. "Yes. Here I am. Painting saints."

By late afternoon, the oppressive heat of the day abated a bit, and I left the studio and headed home, detouring first along the sea walk, observing a handful of swimmers and sunbathers enjoying the final moments of the day. A line of children queued up by the ice-cream truck, a vintage vehicle restored and operated by two college students. I replayed my conversation with the priest. I am not by nature an impulsive man, but in accepting the commission, I had acted on an impulse I couldn't explain. I knew that on some level—the archbishop wasn't the only one harboring hidden agendas—I hoped that it would bring Sophie back from Maine, would serve as a way of reconnecting us and bringing us together. Well, if that had been my expectation, it wasn't working. While she seemed pleased with my decision and had called several times expressing interest about which saints I was painting and asking how the work was progressing, Sophie remained in Maine. With Joan Laurant.

I left the beachfront. As I passed the playground, I heard a group of youngsters playing a game of tag, their laughter braiding the air. Off to one side, I caught sight of a lone teenager and recognized him as one I had seen there in the past. The boy was sitting on a bench and looking very much alone. I studied him from a distance, took in the narrow shoulders, now hunched, the bowed head, and saw a vulnerability so naked I nearly flinched from it. An image from the book Father Gervase had left at our home so many weeks before came to mind. Saint Sebastian. Pierced with arrows.

Sebastian was not on the list I had drafted and submitted to the archbishop, but that easily could be altered. I approached the boy. "Hello there," I called out as I grew closer.

The boy looked up, his expression wary.

"I don't want to bother you, but I wonder if I could ask you something."

The boy drew inward, and as he looked at me, his face was stricken and his eyes widened in fear.

CHAPTER TWENTY-FOUR

~

Heat-stricken by the weather—Father Gervase remembered a time when such high temperatures would not have bothered him—he walked slowly back to the rectory.

Although he knew boyhood memory was not to be relied on, summers seemed much hotter now than in the long-ago past. Or was it a factor of aging? Daily, he was aware of his aging. Why, just that morning he'd asked the man who mowed the lawns in front of the rectory if he would add more mulch to the perennial beds to conserve what little moisture the soil held, a job he once would have done himself. Easily. The yard-man had then reminded him that he had already asked him to do the mulching. So memory waned along with energy.

His hip was bothering him more today, and he limped along, shoulders slumped not only from the heat and aging, but from his visit to Will Light's new studio. Again, as he so often did after encounters with the artist, Father Gervase allowed his thoughts to land on his own inadequacies. Even now, after having agreed to take on the commission, the artist was clearly still mired in grief, and all he had to offer were empty words about the comfort of faith, something Light wanted no part of. Of larger concern to Father Gervase was the matter of Will's anger. Although it seemed to have abated, the priest knew it was there, beneath the surface perhaps but alive nonetheless. And so he continued to reach out to the artist, knowing it was the smallest things that could help. A hand on his shoulder. A cup of coffee. A bit of casual conversation. He still had misgivings about his own ability to help the artist and found himself making excuses that would relieve him of the mission. More than once he had spoken to his Lord about this. *I think you've called the wrong number.* Then he would remember that doubt made one cautious, made one stumble, and so he would return to the artist's studio, a willing if inadequate instrument of God's plan.

He rounded the corner and began to climb the hill toward the rectory. It was his turn on the rotation for the weekly pastoral visit to Rose Hall Manor, and he wondered if this once he might ask Father Burns to step in for him. What he needed was a cool shower followed by a tall gin and tonic and then to sit down and watch the Sox finish the last game in the series with Cleveland. The thought of this quickened his pace slightly, but then, before he could alter direction and avoid her, he saw the figure waiting on the rectory porch. The sight of her took the last of the stuffing out of him and with it all hopes of the shower and a drink and finding Father Burns. No help for it now. The priest braced himself as Lena MacDougall shot up from the porch rocker to greet him, her face full of righteous purpose. "Good afternoon, Lena," he said, noting her dress looked freshly ironed, her hair without a strand out of place. "Have you been able to keep cool amid the sweltering heat?"

She didn't waste a minute on small talk. "Have you heard the latest, Father?"

There was little doubt he was about to. He forced a welcoming smile, allowing himself the small sin of hypocrisy.

Without giving him a moment to reply, she began. "That man who is painting the saints," she said. Lena seldom honored people with their names. *That man. Her. That boy. Him.* As if Father Gervase should intuit who was the latest to head her complaint list.

"Are you speaking of Will Light?"

The color rose in her face. "It's a scandal," she said. "An absolute scandal."

"What's that?" *Lord grant him patience.*

"An absolute scandal. Someone has to do something about it."

Father Gervase was quite sure that by *someone* she meant him. The prospect of the shower and drink disappeared completely. He'd be lucky if he had enough time to change his shirt before he was due at the nursing home.

"It was bad enough when that Ramos girl was asked to pose. Well, you know how I feel about that. Not that my objections did the least bit of good."

Not something he could easily forget. Half the parish had heard her belief that it was completely inappropriate for an unwed mother to pose as a saint. An unwed mother *and* a teenager whose boyfriend declined to marry her, a position backed up by the boy's parents. He wondered what her latest objection would be. He resigned himself to hearing her out.

"Now he's chosen that woman."

"Which woman is that?"

"You don't know?" Her eyes glittered with a gossip's satisfaction that she would be the one to deliver the news. "I heard it from Lucia Crowley, who heard about it over at Amelia's Shear Pleasure. She said the woman herself was telling everyone, pleased as punch she was."

"What woman?" he asked again.

"Miriam Endelheim." The name was a sourness on her tongue.

"Ah."

"A Jew," she said. "That man has chosen a Jew to be one of the saints."

"I see," he said, keeping his voice as neutral as he could manage.

"It won't do. You have to do something about it. This time he's gone too far."

"I wonder," he began. "I wonder which saint Miriam is to represent."

"Well," Lena sputtered. "I can't see how that matters in the least."

"I would think perhaps Teresa Benedicta of the Cross."

"I never heard of her," Lena pronounced in a tone that suggested this failing lay wholly with the saint.

"A remarkable woman. She was born Edith Stein. She died at Auschwitz."

Lena was unmoved. "Never heard of her," she repeated.

"Or," Father Gervase continued, knowing it was weak of him to provoke her, but it was so easy to get her goat he found the temptation irresistible, "maybe Miriam is to be painted as Saint Martha. Or Elizabeth. Or perhaps even Mary."

She stiffened. "It's just not right. Not right at all."

He heard her out, and when he finally explained he was late for his duties at Rose Hall Manor, she left, begrudgingly and unappeased. He stopped by the kitchen long enough to swallow a slapped-together jelly sandwich, washed down with water, and thought about his exchange with Lena, a conversation salted with prejudice and impatience. He took solace in knowing that in the eyes of God everything could be forgiven.

CHAPTER TWENTY-FIVE

~

Rain woke in the dark, disoriented and still dressed in her T-shirt and tan capri pants.

Gradually she rose to full consciousness and was swept up in memories of the evening and the scene at dinner. The meal began as usual: her brother staring at his plate in silence, her father shoveling food into his mouth as if this were his last meal on earth or as if eating was a job to be finished as quickly as possible, Rain moving the congealing concoction of cheese noodles and ham around in different arrangements on her plate, waiting for the meal to end, and her mother, as usual, chirping on as if they were a normal family.

"How is the job going?" she had asked Duane. "Was it busy today?" Duane continued to stare at his plate and mumbled something that no one could comprehend. "Duane," her mother had said in her sharp voice, which should have been a warning, but if her brother had seen the storm signal, he'd ignored it. "I asked you a question, and I expect an intelligent answer."

Her father ceased his obsessive shoveling to look up. "Let the boy alone, Beth. I'm sure he's tired and just wants to eat in peace." Duane had spent the day scooping ice cream at the Eastern Point Creamery, a job their father had arranged for him but one Rain knew he hated.

With no warning, their mother stood up so fast her chair reeled back. "Why do I bother?" she'd cried. She threw her napkin on the table. "Why do I fucking bother?" The shock of hearing her swear (something she considered akin to one of the sins and for which, when they were younger, she had more than once washed their mouths out with a bar of Dove) was followed by a second jolt as she burst into tears and left the room. For a moment the three of them sat in stupefied silence; then, predictably, their father got up to follow her, to try to make the peace, and good luck with that.

Rain exchanged glances with her brother. "Another pleasant dinner with the Freak Family," he said, and then he got up and escaped down to the basement.

For a moment, Rain almost followed him so she wouldn't be alone in the room still echoing with her mother's outburst. Instead she cleared the table and put the plates and glasses and silverware in the dishwasher while the scene replayed in her mind. She wished she could turn back time, back to when they were younger and, at least in recollection, there had been less tension, when her mother seemed happier or at least more patient, and her father more available or at least less absent and preoccupied, less passive. A time when her brother actually liked her and would carefully explain the rules of a card game or let her ride behind him, astride the rear fender of his bike, when he could make her feel special just by smiling at her or laughing at one of the silly jokes she read from *A Child's Book of Jokes, Puns, and Riddles*. What happened? When had it changed? When had they all turned into members of the Freak Family?

When she had finished the dishes, she'd wandered into the living room and turned on the television, but after a bit of channel surfing, she switched it off. Silence echoed throughout the house. Finally she'd climbed the stairs to her room, her stomach tight with anxiety. She sat on the bed and stared at the bottom drawer of her bureau. She was nearly faint with the need to feel the razor blade against her skin and considered the risks, the door with no lock, her mother's strange and volatile mood. No. She would have to delay until it was safe. She rocked on the bed, waiting, and in the stillness, broken only by her own heartbeat, she heard the shrink's voice. *Take care of yourself, Rain. And if you can't take care of yourself, call me.* Well, good luck with that. Like a midget shrink with a stupid, smelly dog could change the world. Could make things right. Could bring Lucy back. Could make the police find the murderer and put him in jail. She sat stiffly, willing time to pass, willing the tears that welled to evaporate. But after a while, as if someone else had slipped into her body, she got up and rummaged through her desk until she found the shrink's card in the back of a drawer. It was stuck in that stupid little book she had never bothered to read or return. She sat on her bed with the book and the crumpled card and stared at the telephone number. *Call me.* It was all hopeless. Utterly hopeless. She fell back on the bed and gazed blindly at the ceiling, and after a while, exhausted as a two-year-old, she escaped into sleep.

Now, awake in the dark, she was aware of a deep ache in her stomach. Hunger pangs, she supposed—she had eaten almost nothing at the disastrous dinner—or perhaps something more serious. Serve everyone right if she had an ulcer or a tumor or something. She thought again of the razor taped to the underside of her bureau drawer. She swung her feet to the floor, flicked on the bedside lamp, and checked the time. Two a.m. Surely her parents were now asleep. In the pool of light cast by the bulb, she saw the shrink's card on the pillow and next to that the book. A miniature book, hardly bigger than an oversized deck of cards, just like Dr. Mallory was a miniature woman, with a little dog, living a safe and boring little life, nosing into other people's business. Rain didn't trust her one bit. And seriously, who had even heard of a book that small, anyway? It couldn't be much of a story. Hardly worth the trouble. She picked it up and flipped it over. From the back cover, a black-and-white photo of the author stared up at her, a woman sitting in an armchair, holding a book in one hand and a cigarette in the other with a serious, almost stern look on her face. Above the strong jaw, her lips were dark with lipstick, but it was her gaze which transfixed Rain. The author stared directly out at her with an intensity that made her want to look away. The dark eyes seemed to be seeing straight into her mind. Into her heart. Straight to the truth.

In spite of the heat—even at night there was no relief from the heat, and her mother thought air-conditioning was unhealthy so everyone had to suffer—Rain felt chilled. She pulled her feet back on the bed and slid beneath the sheet. Leaning back against her pillow, she opened the book to the first page. The first sentence took her far from Port Fortune, transported her to Norway and the fjord between tall mountains. She reread the words, soothed by their cadence, and continued on to discover the town of Berlevaag, the little child's toy town where the buildings were painted in pastel colors. And as easily as that she was drawn into the story. Something about it, the way it was written—*a toy-town painted many colors*—reminded her of the fairy tales her father used to read to her in the evenings before she went to bed. She wondered what it would be like to live in a place of many colors instead of the dreary gray shingles or white clapboards of Port Fortune. Once her grandparents had mailed her a postcard from Bermuda, a photo of pastel-painted cottages. That was the closest she would ever get to such a town.

The book was only fifty-four pages in length, but it took her longer to read than she would have imagined. Although she usually read quite quickly, she found herself deliberately slowing her pace, sometimes rereading whole paragraphs or pages, worrying over the individuals on the island. The last line, Philippa's telling Babette how she would enchant the angels, caused her throat to ache for reasons she couldn't understand. She clasped the book close to her chest and at last fell back asleep. She dreamed of a town painted many colors and peopled by a general who looked a bit like her father and a cook, a woman who looked nothing like her mother and who wore ugly black shoes and held out her arms to her. She woke at eight, the book still on her chest.

The story remained with her: the sisters Martine and Philippa and the mysterious Babette. Who would have thought such a small book could raise so many questions? Why would Babette spend all of the lottery money on the dinner? Why would the general return to the island? Did people really behave like that? *Lucy*, she thought. Lucy would have loved talking about the story.

"Rain?" Her mother's voice called from the hall. "Are you awake? It's after eight."

Rain slipped the book beneath her pillow.

It was later, in the shower, that she realized that for the first time in many months, a night had passed in which she had forgotten to scout the house after everyone slept, to check the locks on all windows and doors. The fear that had settled in her chest since Lucy disappeared eased, and she felt a flash of reckless freedom.

CHAPTER TWENTY-SIX

~

Two boys swept past me, their skateboard wheels skimming the sidewalk, and I felt a flash of annoyance and then a clutch of resentment at their wild and careless freedom.

I watched until the boys disappeared around the building's corner and then unlocked the doors to the boat barn. The air was a few degrees cooler inside, and I rolled the doors shut to keep the heat out as long as possible. There still had been no break in the temperature, each day melting into the next. I planned on beginning the scheme for the second panel on the north wall, a grouping that would include Columba, Leonard, Martin de Porres, Simon, Blaise, Augustine, and Monica. Five men and two women. A mother and son. From the start it had been decided that the saints should mirror the diocese's congregants in ages, occupations, and ethnicities, but culling the final forty-two from the hosts of the saints had proved more difficult than I would have imagined, and I still found myself debating some of my choices among the hermits and scholars, the fishermen and farmers, the lawyers and poets, merchants and bankers and ascetics, who peopled the ranks of the saints.

I had overslept that morning and was relieved to find Elaine Neal was not waiting for me. She had agreed to pose as Monica, and with her narrow face lined with suffering, she appeared every bit what I envisioned the old nun might have looked like, not dissimilar to the painting by Vivarini I had come across in one of Father Gervase's books. Elaine was a member of Holy Apostles and the owner of Port Fortune Books and had been enthusiastic about the project from the beginning. Occasionally in the past weeks she'd shown up at the studio with another volume about the saints to add to the library I was acquiring. Before I knew it, people would be gifting me with rosary beads.

"Hello," she called from the doorway. "Not late, am I?" She was slightly out of breath and leaned on her cane, a sturdy, serviceable stick of some hardwood—walnut or oak perhaps—with a knobbed top. In her other hand, she carried a folded copy of the *Boston Globe*.

"Right on time." It hadn't occurred to me to offer to pick her up, and I regretted this oversight.

"I was delayed at the store. A bit of trouble there."

I switched on a couple of fans. "Nothing serious, I trust."

"A broken window in the back door. Kids making mischief. Nothing taken, as far as I can tell. Just the inconvenience of it all. Vaughn's been after me to get a security system installed, but I just hate the idea of it, not to even mention the expense. But I have to admit it's a bit worrisome. Things like this didn't used to happen in town."

Was that true? Or did things like that happen and people just forgot? Had most of the townspeople already started the blurring of memory required to forget about Lucy, recollections faded as surely as the green ribbons tied around trees now limp and nearly white while my own memory haunted me daily? The memories plagued me mostly at night, but they never evaporated, even with dawn. I unfastened the straps of my backpack and took out my camera.

Elaine limped to the riser, her Birkenstocks scuffling along the floor as she went.

"If you'd like, you can sit," I offered. "I can get you a chair."

"Oh, this is fine." She tossed her paper on the chair. "It's walking that gives me problems. Standing's fine. By the way, did Valentina Walsh get hold of you?"

"Valentina? No. Why?"

"I ran into her yesterday, and she said she was coming to see you. Well, be prepared. Forewarned is forearmed."

I had to smile. Sophie used to say that with the wind at her back, Valentina could give a nor'easter a run for its money. I wondered what she could want with me.

"She has an idea," Elaine said, as if I had spoken. "I hate to spoil her surprise, but like I said, forewarned and all. Well, you know how she fancies herself a poet?"

"Yes." I recalled the sentimental, rhymed couplets that appeared on occasion in the *Port Fortune Sun Times*, leading Sophie to suggest once that the editor must be a close relative or accepting bribes.

"She wants to write a poem to go with each of the people you paint. She sees them as sort of companion pieces to the project."

"Oh Lord," I murmured.

"Exactly," Elaine said. Then, after a minute, "I suppose you know her story."

"Old Glory?" I said.

"Her *story*. No? That's right, you moved into town after that. Sometime in the early nineties, correct?"

"Ninety-two."

"Yes. Well, it all happened long before that. Still, I'm surprised you haven't heard. You know how this town is for gossip, and she gave them grist for the mill for quite some time." She looked up toward the skylights, lost momentarily in thought.

"What happened?"

"She always has been a little—well, not exactly strange—but unique."

My curiosity was awakened. I set the camera on the worktable.

"People put it down to her being a change-of-life baby. I think her mother was in her late forties when she was pregnant, and even as a girl Valentina was different. Eccentric, you know? For instance, she didn't start talking until she was almost four. And when she was about sixteen she started to dress completely in white. Summer. Winter. Didn't matter. All in white. Shoes and everything. Pretending to be Emily Dickinson or something. And she'd talk all whispery, so soft you could barely hear her, like a mouse she was."

I tried and failed to imagine the bold and bossy Valentina as subdued and mouselike.

"Naturally, right after the accident people were worried about her, afraid she'd disappear completely, have a total come-apart, but the funny thing is that just the opposite happened, a complete U-turn. She was nineteen at the time and started wearing so much jewelry she looked like a Christmas tree shot up with steroids. And scarves enough to give Isadora Duncan a run for her money. Then she started ordering people around, acting like she'd been elected mayor."

"She was in an accident?"

"Not her. Her fiancé. Drowned. The day before they were supposed to marry." Again Elaine paused in thought before continuing. "There was gossip, people being people and all. Some talk that it wasn't an accident. That he—James Wells was his name, the youngest son of Ellie and Peter Wells. You must know them. They own the gallery on West Main. Well, the talk was that James committed suicide. The strange thing was that his passing seemed to let something loose inside of Valentina. She was like a creature set free." She grinned and added, "Not that that improved her poetry a whit."

I tried to wrap my mind around the whole story: the quiet girl in white, the boy who drowned, the wild woman who now wrote drivel verse.

"Well, there's nothing for it," Elaine said, sweeping her cane like a golf club in an arc an inch from the surface of the riser. "There'll be no stopping her with this new poetry idea. Once she gets a hold of something it's best to just take yourself out of her path."

"Yes." I pictured Valentina's face and pondered the idea of asking her to pose. She was a little old for Saint Joan, but perhaps some other saint of a fierce and fiery nature. Or maybe, it occurred to me, maybe I could capture her as a mature Joan, the woman the real Joan hadn't lived to become. I wondered if she would be open to the idea. When I'd begun the project, I'd wondered how the people of Port Fortune would respond to my request to pose, but their reception had been more positive than I'd foreseen, and several people had even called to volunteer. Thus far, only one person had refused. The teenager in the park. I replayed the scene. How I had introduced myself to the boy and explained about the project, although most everyone in town had heard of it because of Cardinal Kneeland's publicity campaign and the stories that had appeared in both the local and Boston papers. When I'd asked the boy if he would be willing to pose, the request had clearly disturbed him. He had shaken his head violently. No, he'd said, and then had left the playground so quickly it seemed more an escape than a departure. I wondered if I should track him down and approach him again. There was something haunting about the teen. And his age would be a plus. So far Rose of Lima was the only one under twenty to be represented on the panels.

The boy would make a perfect Saint Sebastian.

I pondered the idea while I focused on Elaine's hands, her swollen and arthritic knuckles clasped in prayer.

My next model was Payton Hayes. Earlier in the summer, after the appointment he'd set up for me with Gillian Donaldson, he'd phoned to see how the meeting went and then again several weeks later to see if anything had come of the whole episode. I was happy to inform him that the reporter had never followed through with a formal complaint. Another man might have suggested we get together for a drink, but

I had never been that kind of men's-night-out kind of guy and our relationship remained what it had been, cordial but not close. So when I'd asked him if he would pose for Saint Vincent de Paul, he'd seemed surprised and hesitated so long I believed he would refuse, but then he'd shrugged and said, not without amusement, "Why not?"

After Payton left, I took a break to stretch, regroup, and have some water. The *Globe* Elaine had brought with her was still on the chair where she had tossed it and I scanned the front page, flipping idly through the front section. One headline caught my eye: "Study shows war veterans report hearing problems." The opening paragraph spoke of a study released by Johns Hopkins that reported on a number of war veterans returning home who were experiencing both distorted hearing and hearing loss. The story was continued further in the section, but before I could turn to it, I was interrupted by my next model and I set the paper aside. I had two more sittings that day and so stayed on late. It was after dark by the time I returned home, and later still—after I'd showered and eaten dinner—when I noticed the red message light blinking on the phone.

"Hi, Will."

My reaction to Sophie's voice was physical, a jolt that coursed through me.

"Just checking in to see how things are going. Is it still hot as hell there? We've had a nice breeze coming in off the water here today, and it's actually been quite comfortable. Call me when you get a minute. Okay? Nothing important."

I checked the time. Nine forty-five. Too late to return her call? Better to wait until morning? I replayed her message, listening hard to what she said, trying harder to hear what was left unsaid. The paper where she had written the number for her Maine rental was on the table next to the phone, and without giving myself time for second thoughts, I punched it in the keypad. I counted five rings and was about to hang up when Sophie answered.

"Hi," I said. "It's me."

"Hi, you." Her voice was soft.

"I know it's late, but I just noticed the message on the machine. Hope I'm not waking you."

"No. I was just sitting here with a book."

"What are you reading?"

She laughed, and I realized how long it had been since I'd heard that, the sweet, joyful sound of her laugh. "You wouldn't believe it."

"Something for your research?" I thought of the books she had taken with her. *The Plight of Our Murdered Children: Our Nation's Shame.*

"Hardly. Do you remember the cottage we rented for a week the first summer we were married?"

"By the lake in New Hampshire?"

"The very one."

Memory took me. The cabin with its splintery wooden dock jutting out into the lake. Early-morning swims and afternoons spent paddling a canoe across Sunapee. Simple meals cooked in a kitchen outfitted with a mismatched collection of dishes and pans. Fresh-picked blueberries and soda crackers in a bath of the cream-clotted milk purchased from a local farmer. Grilled trout, sliced tomatoes, and a salad of fiddlehead ferns. The one bedroom with a lumpy mattress on the double bed. The living room with wicker chairs and faded chintz cushions that flanked a fieldstone fireplace and, on the opposite wall, two plain pine shelves nailed between studs. "By any chance are you holding a *Reader's Digest* condensed book?"

She laughed again. "You got it," she said. "They even smell the same. You know? Kind of musty. I swear, this is the only time I can stand that smell. In an odd way, it's almost comforting."

I thought about the old boat barn where I was working, the smell of tar and salt, wood and must. "So what's the story you're reading?"

"*The Snow Goose*, by Paul Gallico."

"Sounds familiar. What's it about?"

"Love and loneliness."

I swallowed against a closed throat.

"The main character is a reclusive artist," she said.

"Oh yeah? How does it end?"

"I don't know, Will." She paused then as if we were talking about a different story. "I haven't reached the end yet."

"Should I keep my fingers crossed then? For a happy ending?"

Instead of answering, she said, "I'm glad you called."

Glad you called. I parsed the three words carefully, as if by doing so I could mine a deeper meaning. "Is everything okay up there?" I asked. "Are you okay?" *Are you okay?* Immediately I wanted to take back the question. How I had hated when people asked me that in the weeks after Lucy's death. As if anything could ever be okay again.

"I'm doing okay. I'm making good progress. What about you? How's your work going?"

"Pretty well. Today I started photo studies for the second panel. This afternoon I had Harold Weaver."

"Harold from the hardware store?"

"The same. He's posing for Simon. And Payton Hayes came in too."

"Really? I didn't know he was one of the models."

"He seemed surprised when I asked him. With his Van Gogh beard he's perfect for Vincent de Paul."

"Yes. I can see that. Did he mention Ellen? I often wonder how she's doing. We e-mailed a couple of times after they divorced, and she wrote last fall. A lovely letter expressing her sorrow for us and how wonderful Lucy had been with their boy. But then we fell out of touch."

Lucy. The sound of her name opened wounds, as did anything I associated with our daughter. "Payton didn't mention her. I got the feeling that's a chapter of his life he has left behind. This morning Elaine Neal came in. She's posing for Monica."

"How was Elaine? I haven't seen her in ages."

"She was Elaine, you know, the walking history of the citizens of Port Fortune. Oh, you'll appreciate this. She told me Valentina Walsh wants to do a series of poems about the project."

Sophie chuckled. "In rhyming couplets, no doubt."

"No doubt." I settled back in the chair, struck by the ease of our conversation. "Elaine also told me an interesting story about Valentina."

"You mean about her fiancé, the boy who drowned the day before their wedding?"

"You know about that?"

"Oh, Will," she said. "Everyone in Port Fortune knows. It's one of the local legends."

"Apparently. That's one of the odd things. I've been hearing a lot of local history from the people who come in to pose."

"Like what?"

I told her Leon's story about Louie Johns.

"Leon posed, too? I have to say that surprises me."

"Why?" This was the easiest conversation we'd had in months.

"I would have expected it of Elaine Neal and even Harold Weaver, but Leon doesn't seem the type."

"Actually," I said, "there's only been one person who hasn't agreed to pose."

"Who's that?"

"A boy. I don't know his name, though he looks vaguely familiar. I've seen him a number of times around town. At the playground. Always alone. When I asked him, you'd think I was suggesting he commit a major crime. He couldn't get away fast enough. The thing is, you should see him, Sophie. There's something about him, something vulnerable and proud. He would be perfect for Saint Sebastian."

"What does he look like?"

I pictured the boy as I'd last seen him, sitting on the wall, shoulders slumped. "I'd say he's around sixteen or seventeen. Thin." I did my best to describe him.

"Is his hair sort of reddish-brown, a little shaggy? Was he wearing yellow high-tops?"

"You know him?"

"You do too. It's Duane," she said. "Duane LaBrea."

"LaBrea?"

"Rain's brother."

It came to me then why the boy had seemed familiar. Once Duane had given Lucy and Rain a ride to our house after some event at the school, and another time he'd dropped Rain off for an overnight with Lucy.

"If you want," Sophie continued, "I could get in touch with him."

Did I want? Suddenly I was reluctant.

"I mean, I know him. He used to sing tenor in the chorus. If I asked him for you, he might say yes."

I didn't answer.

"Look," Sophie said, mistaking my silence, her voice more business-like. "I'm not trying to interfere. If you rather I stay out of it, I will."

Again I pictured the boy, imagined him as Sebastian, decided. "No. No. That would be great, Soph."

"I'll call his house tomorrow. If you're sure."

"I'm sure." I paused to draw a breath. "It's just, earlier, when you told me he was Rain's brother, it just took me by surprise. It was unexpected. And—" My voice trailed off. Rain. Lucy's best friend.

"I know, Will." I heard her deep inhale. "I understand. I do."

For the first time in months, we were in sync, understanding without needing words, like we used to be. Before. "I guess I better let you go," I said, wanting to hang up before the connection shifted.

"Will?"

"Yeah?"

"You sound—" She hesitated. "You sound different."

Was that a good or bad thing? "I do? Different how?"

"I don't know." Her voice grew thoughtful, tentative. "Lighter, I guess."

Was I? "And you sound happy, Soph."

"I am, Will. Or at least, if not happy, I'm feeling a kind of contentment. It's been good for me to be here. Will, I've been thinking. If you ever take a day off, maybe you could drive up. We could have lunch or something."

"I'd like that, Soph. Maybe some weekend? Would a Saturday or Sunday work for you?"

"Any day would work for me, Will. Just let me know."

"I've got people scheduled to pose for the next day or two. How about if we leave it loose. I'll give you a call when I can take a day."

Filled with the promise of that day, I lingered on the phone for no more than five more minutes and then hung up before the miracle of the call disintegrated.

CHAPTER TWENTY-SEVEN

~

For the next five days, I woke with an unfamiliar feeling I could not identify that lingered on into the day.

As I walked across town to the studio, I thought about it. The emotion was not hope or anything even close to approaching happiness. Certainly not that. It was more an absence, a lack of something that had been part of me for months, more neutral. An unfeeling of a sort, though not unpleasant. I recalled my last conversation with Sophie. *You sound different*, she'd said. *Lighter.*

The sky had been steadily darkening all morning, and I heard the rumble of thunder in the near distance. I quickened my steps and reached the studio minutes before the rain started, hard, pelting drops that struck the pavement and the drought-hardened earth like shrapnel, causing steam to curl up from the sidewalk. I was grateful for the rain, as we needed it. Lawns were turning brown and brittle; gardens were parched. Inside, I flicked on the lights against the encroaching darkness. Overhead, the rain pinged against the skylights with such force it could be mistaken for hail. There were no models scheduled for the day, and my plan was to finalize the scheme for the three panels for the south wall. After Lucy died, work had been no more than an escape from a life grown bleak and intolerable, but in the past weeks, it had become something more. I welcomed the discipline, one that seemed to flow into other aspects of my life. My desire for drink had waned. I ate simply. Days were spent either in research or working on the panels. At night I slept deeply, the hours disturbed not by visions of violence but by dreams peopled with saints. Later, I would come to think of these brief weeks as a kind of walking dream, an escape from reality, although reality would return soon enough. But for that time I found that life, so austere and monk-like, oddly satisfying and wondered if this paring down, this simplification, was what Sophie was finding so appealing about the Maine farmhouse, why she had sounded so content when we had talked. Nearly a week had passed since that conversation. Initially I'd planned on driving up the following Saturday for the lunch she had suggested, but the weekend came and went and I remained in Port Fortune. I told myself I needed to work, but I knew it was actually fear that kept me from driving north. Sophie hadn't phoned again, and I had resisted calling her, reluctant to test the reconnection we seemed to have arrived at during our last call, the fragile promise of beginning anew. *Next week*, I told myself. *I'll drive up next week*, but I still held back, afraid to test the hope that Sophie and I would somehow make our way back to each other. I couldn't believe that no matter how badly we had been devastated and pulled apart by our separate ships of grief and, as trite as it may sound, that love would find a way. I hoped my drawings of the saints might be part of forging that path.

I settled in at the worktable, pulled a sketch pad from the pile, and again contemplated the architecture of the first grouping. Brendan, the thick-bearded Irish abbot, face shadowed by the hood of his robe; Rose of Lima, the young and slender virgin, eyes lifted to the heavens; Peter, the bearded, old fisherman; Paul, the thin and fiery-eyed Jew; Maurice, the black-skinned soldier; Ambrose, the wise bishop of Milan, his face clean shaven beneath the miter. And lastly, the curly-coifed Crispin. The group was diverse, and their robes, appropriate to the era and geography of the individual saints, added to the distinction. Overhead, the lights flickered, and I swore softly at the threat of a power loss. A sound at the door drew my attention. A figure stood there in the shadow.

"Mr. Light?"

"Yes."

The voice seemed uncertain. Young.

I remained at the bench. "Can I help you?"

Again the lights flickered. The figure froze at the door, and then a second figure appeared. I could make out the form—a woman—could see the umbrella she stood beneath but little else in the shadow. The woman lowered the umbrella and shook rain from the fabric, spattering the floorboards, then snapped it shut.

"Hello," she said. "It's Beth. Beth LaBrea."

Beth LaBrea. In spite of the fact that our daughters had been best friends, that friendship had never expanded to involve our families. I could only recall a couple of times over the years that we had spoken, mostly on the phone to check on some plan the girls had cooked up. Permission for one to stay for dinner or overnight. That kind of thing. We never socialized, but as I have said, I'd never encouraged a social life, had, in fact, discouraged it. I had been completely satisfied with a life comprised of my family and my work. I dimly remembered a time just before Lucy and Rain were to start high school when Sophie had arranged a mother-daughter dinner out for the four of them, but if she had said anything about it after, I hadn't paid enough attention to recall it now. "Hello."

"You know my son, Duane." She pushed the boy forward.

I nodded.

She barreled on. "Your wife got in touch with us several days ago. She said you wanted to talk to Duane about posing as a saint for the mural. Of course we are absolutely thrilled with the idea." The boy stared at the floor, refusing to meet my eyes. The last thing Duane looked was *thrilled.*

"Is this something that might interest you, Duane?" I asked.

"Of course it would," his mother said and pushed the boy a few more steps forward.

Duane shrugged his shoulders and continued to stare at the floor.

"Duane," she said, her voice sharper. "Mr. Light has asked you a question."

"I guess. I mean, I'm not sure."

Thunder rolled, closer now, and again the lights flickered off, leaving the building dark for a moment before switching on again.

"Duane—" the mother began.

"I don't know," he stammered. "I mean, I have to go to work."

"You could come after work," his mother said. She turned to me. "Will you still be here later today?" she asked. "At four? He gets off work at four."

I studied the boy, could see some of the mother in his features. The heart-shaped face tapering to the chin, the narrow shoulders. "I expect to be here. Unless we lose power."

"Oh, the storm is just passing through," she declared with certainty, as if she were personally charged with controlling the weather. "This will all clear up by noon."

I found myself disliking her. The boy looked miserable, and as much as I would have liked him to pose I wanted to let him off the hook. "You don't have to decide now," I said. "If you want to take a few days to think it over, you can let me know."

"Oh, no need for that," Beth LaBrea declared. "It's settled then." Duane remained silent, his shoulders slumped in defeat.

I was puzzled by my reaction to the woman, my aversion. Even her bullying of her son didn't explain it. I remembered that it had been Beth LaBrea who had initiated the idea of tying the green ribbons on tree trunks and utility poles, green being the color of hope, she had told Sophie. It had also been Beth who had taken up a collection for us, as if money could possibly compensate for the loss of a daughter. I had been furious when she had appeared at our door with an envelope thick with cash. "She means well," Sophie had said. That night I'd tossed the envelope on our barbeque grill, soaked it with liquid fire starter, and set it aflame. I'd been aware of Sophie watching from the kitchen window, but when I went back inside she hadn't said a word.

"You can expect him at four," Beth said, and then they were gone as quickly as they had appeared, leaving only a puddle on the floor where they had stood as proof they had ever been there.

For the remainder of the morning, I occupied myself by sketching variations of the panel until I arrived at a scheme that satisfied. At noon, I locked up and, as had become my habit, walked over to the deli on Prospect for a quick lunch. As Beth LaBrea had forecast, the rain had ceased, and I found myself childishly pissed that she had been correct. Inside the deli, there was a long line at the counter, and I was resigning myself to a lengthy wait when the counter girl called my name.

"You here to pick up your order?" she asked with a wink.

I had no idea what "my order" was but recognized the gambit as her way of serving a resident before attending to the tourists on line, an acting out of the confliction many tradespeople felt at the influx of tourists each summer. On one hand they were grateful for the business. On the other, they resented the disruption in daily lives, the traffic jams and long waits at every restaurant in town, the squeal of air brakes on the tour buses that crowded the streets. The girl disappeared into the kitchen and returned with a brown bag. "Here ya go," she said as she handed me the bag, then gave me change for my twenty, which I dropped in the tip jar.

"Hope you enjoy," she sang out as I left.

"I'm sure I will," I said, even as I wondered what she had given me.

The morning's rain had soaked everything, covering benches and puddling walks, and although I often spent my lunch break at the park or by the beach, that day I headed back to the studio. I chuckled when

I opened the bag. The clerk had been paying attention to my choices over the past weeks. A veggie wrap with ginger dressing.

At three, although it would be another hour before Duane was due, I pulled out the first book of saints Father Gervase had left for me and flipped through it until I found the portrait of Sebastian. I checked the index of another book. I located the page for the saint and compared it to the first. In each of the paintings, the boy was clad in a loincloth-like garment. I wondered if it would skew the composition if only one saint in the panels was not garbed in a robe.

At four, I put the books aside, oddly antsy. Four fifteen came and passed. And then four thirty. By five, I resigned myself that Duane was not coming and was disappointed beyond what I might have expected. I carefully stored my work in the folders and placed them on the worktable.

CHAPTER TWENTY-EIGHT

~

The last of the women had left the church following the four o'clock Mass, and Father Gervase carefully slid his surplice on a hanger and placed it in the alcove closet.

He was fairly certain that the remainder of the day was free of obligations, but recently his memory was proving unreliable, and so he returned to the rectory office to check his schedule. He was relieved to find that it was indeed open. For the past several days, he had stayed inside, sheltered from the intense heat that had blanketed the town, heat that bothered him in a way it never had before (as a child he'd delighted in the warmest of summer days), but the thunderstorm had brought with it at least a temporary relief from soaring temperatures. Eager for some mild exercise after the spell of inactivity, he set out, skirting groups of boisterous tourists as he made his way down to the center of the town, relieved to find his hip was giving him a little less trouble today. There was a sense of celebration in the air, as if the rain had awakened and revived not only plants but people. Impulsively, and thinking of the prospect of Mrs. Jessup's canned-tuna-and-macaroni salad that sat on the first shelf of the rectory refrigerator marinating in a pool of mayonnaise, he decided to treat himself to an early dinner out. But first he detoured by Will Light's studio to see how the project was progressing. He enjoyed seeing the townspeople come to life under the power of the artist's hand and reflected on how Will had captured Tracy Ramos, the teenage girl who worked part-time at the coffee shop and an unwed mother with bold eyes, black-dyed hair, and a chippy attitude that hadn't been diminished in the least by the shame of her circumstances. In truth, Father Gervase had always found the girl a bit daunting. Yet caught by Will's camera and, later, by his initial sketches, Tracy had metamorphosed into a demure and innocent Rose of Lima. Now, whenever he walked by the coffee shop, he slowed his step to peer inside to catch a glimpse of her and could see her as Will saw her. Transfigured. And then there was Leon Newell. Aged beyond his years by drink, hard living, and harder work, the fisherman too had been transformed through Will's vision so that the lines in his face spoke more of sorrow than whiskey and windburn, and those rheumy, yellowed eyes held an unexpected wisdom.

Through his choices, Will was testing assumptions, encouraging others to see ordinary people anew. And yet there remained in each of his renderings a hint of shadow, of another past. How would the world change, Father Gervase wondered, if one could look for and see goodness, whatever human guise it was cloaked in, if one could see that potential in everyone and acknowledge not only the piousness of the saints but the complications of their past, the potential in sinners before they became saints. He thought of the gossips and warmongers, the venal and cranky, the gamblers and con men who stood among the ranks of the canonized. An idea occurred to him for a homily, but before he could reflect further, he arrived at Will's studio. The barn doors were open, but he stopped at the threshold as he always did before entering the studio and prayed for guidance. Will seemed steadier, less angry, these days, but still Father Gervase was concerned. He knew anger such as Will's did not magically evaporate, and one's need for vengeance could turn to violence, a violence that only begat more violence. Although he had not shared this with anyone, in fact had struggled with the call and tried to deny responsibility, he'd come to believe he was being asked to stand by Will as he walked the ground of grief until the artist was out of danger.

"Might as well come in, Father." Will's voice reached him from the far end of the studio.

"I don't want to bother you."

"What's up? Am I to receive another directive from His Grace?"

Father Gervase smiled at the edge of mockery. "No. No message. I just was taking a walk and thought I'd stop by. I don't want to disturb you if you're working."

"No problem. In fact, I'm done for the day. My last model didn't show up, and I'm about to head home."

"Oh. Yes. I see. Well, I won't be keeping you then." He lingered at the door.

"Is there anything else, Father?"

"No. That is unless—"

Will waited.

"Well, I was on my way to High Tide Café and—" He paused, suddenly awkward. "I know it's a bit early and all, but I wondered if perhaps you'd like to join me for dinner."

"Dinner?"

"Unless you've already made plans."

"No," Will said. "No plans."

"I know it's early," Father Gervase repeated.

"No. Not at all. Just give me a minute to lock up."

While Will closed the doors and secured the lock, it occurred to Father Gervase that implicit in the invitation to join him for dinner was the understanding that he would treat, and he hoped he had enough cash with him to cover the bill. Well, now there was no way he could check, and he hoped he would be spared the embarrassment of having to ask Will to pay for his own meal.

Other than one older couple at a table in the rear and a father with his young son who perched on stools at the counter, they had the café to themselves. The waitress led them to a four-top by the front window. "Specials are on the board," she said.

Father Gervase would have preferred a table less visible to those passing by on the street but was reluctant to make a fuss by requesting another. He stared up at the board. *Cod Reuben Sandwich. Fish Stew. Lobster Roll. Clam Chowder. Seared Tuna on a Bed of Greens.* Except for the occasional Sunday evening with Father Burns, he couldn't remember the last time he'd eaten a meal out with anyone. When he'd first arrived in Port Fortune he'd received a number of invitations from the parishioners, but uncomfortable in their homes, he had begged off, offering various excuses, and gradually the requests had stopped. In truth, he was most at ease in the rectory, reading or writing or working in the garden.

Once, sitting on the garden bench, he had overheard three women discussing him.

"It's like pulling teeth to have a conversation with Father Gervase," one had said.

A second had offered a defense for him. "Oh, I think he's just shy. And a little forgetful. It's kind of sweet."

"Sweet?" said the third. "Try socially awkward. He's either tongue-tied or rambling on and on about something."

He'd been mortified at their assessment. Was that how people saw him? He hadn't recognized the voices and remained grateful for that. He hoped they were not regular members of the congregation and comforted himself by thinking they were summer residents. Still, he found himself replaying the conversation. *Rambles on and on. Socially awkward.* Such a cold indictment. Had people always seen him that way? During high school and his first years at university he had dated, and his memories of those distant times were pleasant. One girl in particular came to mind. Cynthia Gibbons. A brunette with a frank and open face who played oboe in the high school orchestra. He remembered a kiss they had shared in the small room off the auditorium where the instruments were stored. That summer she had moved away. He couldn't remember if they had exchanged letters.

The truth was, he didn't mind being alone, preferred it actually, though he might have enjoyed having an animal. A small dog or cat. Even a bird. Oddly, the one person he had felt drawn to, the one person who didn't want something from him or seek his company because he was a priest and might bring a person one step closer to their Savior was Will Light. Again he worried about the bill.

"What can I get you to drink?" the waitress asked, pencil posed over pad.

"Do you have iced coffee?" Will asked.

"We have iced coffee and iced tea. The tea comes sweetened and unsweetened."

"I'll have the coffee. No cream."

She turned to Father Gervase. "And what can I get for you, Father?"

Coffee would keep him up all night. How did one drink coffee this late in the day and still manage to sleep? He really would have liked a glass of wine, but since Will hadn't ordered one, he refrained. "Just water, thank you," he said.

"Shall I get the drinks, or are you ready to order?"

"I'll have the seared tuna on greens," Will said.

"I'll have the same," Father Gervase said, although he was no longer hungry. He groped for a topic of conversation and settled on the weather, the first and last resort of the desperate. "A good rain this morning," he said. "For the gardens."

"We could use more," Will said.

"Yes. It's been a dry summer. One might even say arid. And after the spring rains, I had hopes for a good season for the gardens."

Their salads arrived, and the priest welcomed the reprieve from having to make conversation. He unfolded his napkin and spread it on his lap, relieved that Will seemed content to eat in silence. So many people didn't. The tuna was rare in the middle, and he wanted to send it back to the kitchen for further grilling, but Will was eating his, and again Father Gervase was reluctant to make a fuss. He shook salt on the slab of fish, then sliced a portion from the edge where it was most cooked. "How is Sophia?" he asked.

"She's in Maine. A friend has a cottage up there, and she went up to work on a project."

"A project?"

"Writing. It's a project exploring violence in our culture and the effect of it on all of us. She is especially focusing on violence against our children."

"Good for her. The world could use more voices of conscience sitting on its shoulders. She's that rare person, you know."

"What's that?"

"An activist without anger."

"Is that what she is?"

"I think so, yes. You know sometimes we go through an experience—a betrayal, a grievous loss—and we are left wondering how anything worthwhile can possibly come out of it." He took Will's silence as encouragement to continue. "But it is possible to emerge from such an experience with a greater capacity for compassion, you see. To have a change of heart or mind we could never have anticipated. It seems to me that is what has happened to Sophia. She has had a conversion experience. What we call a *metnois*."

"Yes, well, no offense, Father, but I'm not in the mood for a sermon."

"No. Well, I meant no offense. I certainly didn't intend to invite you for dinner and then spend our time together preaching." *Invite you.* There it was again, the implicit intention that he would treat. He removed his glasses—it was a puzzlement to him how they were always smudged—and reached into his pocket for the green silk square to clean them. As he lifted it to clean the lenses, an object fell to the table. Across from him, Will made a sound.

"What is—what is that?"

"This?" Father Gervase picked up the little Yoda figure. For no good reason, he had developed the silly habit of carrying it around with him.

"Where did you get that?" Will asked, his voice so agitated the older couple at the back table looked over.

"Why I . . ." The priest paused. "Why I don't remember exactly."

Will reached for it, and as Father Gervase surrendered it he felt the trembling in the artist's hand.

Will lifted it closer to his face, turned it over. "Where did you get this?" he asked again, his voice stricken.

The priest's brow furrowed with concentration. How had he come to have it? Had he picked it up somewhere on the parish grounds? On the street? "I don't remember exactly," he said, puzzled by Will's agitation.

"Please," Will said. "Try to remember."

"Is it important?"

"Did—did Lucy give it to you?"

It took a minute for him to follow Will's question. "Lucy? Your daughter?"

"Yes." Will clasped his fingers tightly around the toy. "This belonged to her."

"Are you sure?" Father Gervase said and immediately regretted the question.

"Absolutely." Will opened his fingers. "Here," he said, "this ear that's missing its tip. And here, on the bottom, the little mark. Lucy did that. This is hers. Did she give it to you?"

"No." That much he was sure of. He'd only started carrying it around in recent weeks. Could it really have belonged to Lucy? How was that possible? But Will Light was so certain.

The waitress approached the table but, sensing Will's distress, turned away. He closed his fingers tightly around the figure and shut his eyes, clearly trying to gain composure. "Think," he urged. "Try to remember."

Try to remember? As if it were that easy. He could recall so much from the past. The hazel of his sister's eyes. The bibbed red-gingham apron his mother wore when she kneaded bread. The smell of rising yeast in their kitchen. The soft surrender of Cynthia Gibbons's lips, though more than four decades had passed since that swift kiss. The sound of his brother's laughter. His father's handshake when he'd left home for the seminary. The warm halls of the seminary, steam heat fueled by the boiler in the stone-lined basement. All those were so easily retrieved that they might have happened yesterday. But more recent memories, things that in fact *had* happened yesterday—or last week— he found tucked in a vault beyond his reach. He stared at the tiny figure the artist held and tried to remember how it might have come into his possession, but this attempt was futile.

"Here," he said. "If it belonged to Lucy, you should have it."

CHAPTER TWENTY-NINE

~

It was futile to remain any longer in Lucy's bedroom.

I'd been sitting there on her bed for at least an hour, and it was growing dark but I didn't switch on a light. I stared at the tiny Yoda as if somehow I could be able to decipher the puzzle of how it had come to be in Father Gervase's possession. For it *was* her Yoda. Of that there was no doubt. For perhaps the hundredth time since the priest had handed it to me, I turned it over—as if to verify what I knew was there but couldn't quite believe—and stared at the sole of one little reptilian foot, saw the three interwoven *L*s, the personal logo Lucy had created for herself. Like a brand cowboys used to mark cattle, she had explained.

Lucy had fallen for Yoda when she was ten. I could recall as clearly as if it had been only last week the night she and seven friends had been having a sleepover with pizza and a marathon *Star Wars* viewing party. Once, in a lull between DVDs and as I was leaving the room after delivering the girls two more pizzas, I'd overheard bits of their conversation.

"Who would you rather have as a boyfriend," one girl said. "Luke Skywalker or Han Solo?"

The responses seemed to be evenly divided, and I remember wondering if this foretold their future dating choices—good guy or bad boy—and I'd hung at the door, ridiculously anxious about Lucy's response.

"Yoda," she had said.

"Yeew," one of the other girls said. "You're kidding."

"Nope," Lucy had said. "He's the smartest and most interesting of all."

I relayed the conversation to Sophie, who chided me for eavesdropping on the girls, but a few days later she had surprised Lucy with a miniature Yoda. *Feel the force*, Lucy would say in her raspy Yoda imitation, holding the little Jedi in her hand.

Was it possible that she had given it to the priest? I didn't believe that. It had been a gift from her mother, one she treasured, a talisman that, she once explained, when she needed clarity would help her find courage and truth. At the time, her words had stung slightly, as if my job had been appropriated by a child's plaything. And now it had appeared—all those months after her death. I couldn't imagine what that might mean or what, if anything, I should do about it. I cupped it in dry palms and ran a thumb over the small rough spot where once a section of a pale green ear had been affixed. When I returned home after my dinner with Father Gervase, I had been tempted to call Sophie and relate this latest development but on reflection had repressed the urge. What would be the point? To have her again fall into magical thinking and see this as some kind of mystical sign when in reality it was just one more mystery that, like our daughter's death, was unlikely to be solved?

Do you believe the dead have an ability to communicate with us?

Several months after Lucy's death, we had been lying in bed—this was before she had moved to the guest room—and I was just dropping off when Sophie spoke.

"What?" I'd said.

"The dead," she said, her voice fully awake. "Do you believe they have the ability to communicate with us?"

I'd pulled myself back from sleep and turned to hold her. "Don't do this, Soph."

"I'm serious, Will. Haven't you wondered too?"

"No. No, I haven't."

"But what if it's possible, Will?"

"It isn't."

"You're so absolutely convinced? So sure? I mean, people have experienced it."

"Documented, I'm sure," I'd said, not even trying to keep the cynicism from my voice. Although I understood Sophie's need to find some source of consolation, I wanted to shake her out of this delusional thinking. I saw only more pain and disappointment ahead for her if she continued to grasp onto this path of wishful thinking, more pain I was powerless to prevent.

"How can you be so sure? I've been praying, you know. I've been praying for Lucy to send us a sign."

"Jesus, Sophie," I'd said before I could stop myself.

Her voice had grown soft. "You know how she loved gray seals. When I walk by the harbor, I always look for a seal. I look for one to swim close to shore. Something to let us know she's all right."

How "all right" do you expect her to be, I'd thought. *She's dead. Dead and gone from us forever.* In the past months, people had told me it would get better with time, but that wasn't true. It actually got worse because there was no magical thinking. Lucy was never coming home. There would be no signs. No communication from beyond the grave. She was gone.

"Oh, come on, Sophie. Signs?" I didn't believe in that shite, the last resort of the gullible and desperate.

"Yes." Her head on the pillow was turned toward mine, and her face, lit by moonlight, shone with a hope I found both heartbreaking and infuriating and made me want to simultaneously hold her and shake her. "Signs of something meaningful," she continued. "A connection only those lost to us would know of. I remember reading of one instance about a woman whose father loved white owls, and on the morning of her birthday exactly one year after he died a white owl appeared in a tree outside her kitchen window. There are a lot of stories like that."

"Don't, Soph," I said. "Don't do this to yourself."

So I didn't phone Sophie. No matter how much she wanted to believe in signs and the sudden surfacing of clues to her death, I knew the mysterious appearance of Lucy's Yoda wasn't going to make a rat's ass of difference. Finally I rose, crossed the darkened room, and placed Yoda on the shelf where her other treasures remained displayed. At some point in a future I could not imagine I supposed we would have to empty her room, clear out the very last of her clothes from the closet and the dresser drawers. All would disappear. We would fold her favorite larkspur-blue sweater and place it in a carton with the rest, box up toys and treasures, her books and makeup. And with each item, over and over, Sophie and I would have the torturous conversation about what to do with it all, all those objects that held no meaning for anyone but us. I couldn't bear to think of another child having any of Lucy's belongings but found it equally intolerable to think of throwing away any of it, even a half-used tube of pink lip gloss. Someday, perhaps. But not then. Not then. The idea was beyond painful, and I knew enough not to bring it up with Sophie. In the past months I had experienced grief, but below and running through the grief I was left with loss. Loss was forever. There in my daughter's room the truth of that tightened my heart. My throat closed against a salty burn, and I left the room. I was not a crying man. Sophie had wept enough for both of us.

I spent a dreamless night. It was late morning by the time I headed out to the boat barn on the wharf. As I walked, I noted again how the landscape of the town had changed. Each year, new shops replaced older, long-familiar storefronts. I passed a yarn shop once the site of a small, independent five-and-dime. Next to it, in a space formerly occupied by a shoe repair place, stood a boutique decorator fabrics store. Farther on in the spot where one of the churches used to run a consignment store there was a coffee shop where a single cup cost as much as I paid for a sandwich. I approached the wharf, aware as always of the drone of the ice machines over at Cape Port Ice that hummed without ceasing. As I keyed the lock, I sensed a slight presence behind me but didn't turn. I was in no mood to see anyone, especially the little priest.

"Mr. Light?"

But it was not Father Gervase. I managed to conceal my surprise. "Hey there," I said, using a low tone I might have used to approach a wild and wary creature. I slid the door open and motioned for the boy to precede me. "I didn't expect to see you here."

Duane shrugged his thin shoulders, the perfected teenage gesture of apathy and indifference, one, I suddenly thought, that Lucy had never incorporated in her lexicon of body language. Would she have as she grew older? At sixteen? Seventeen? I didn't think so. I would never know. I studied the boy. "Let me guess. It wasn't your idea to come here today."

"Yeah." Duane looked around, watched while I set down my camera case, switched on the fans. "My mom was pretty insistent."

I could well imagine. I remembered Beth LaBrea's pushy attitude, the way she had bulldozed the boy, and again, as I had then, I felt a surge of protectiveness and an equally unexpected urge to comfort that surprised me. Sophie had always been more at ease, more *intuitive*, around teenagers and children than I had. I tried to remember what Sophie had told me about the boy. He had sung in the chorus. That was about it, although I had the sense that she liked him. "But what about you? Do you think you might like to give it a try?"

Again the shrug.

"Because if you don't want to do it, I can let you off the hook."

For the first time, the boy looked directly at me, and again I could see how much he resembled his mother. "How?"

"Well, let me see. I guess I could tell her I already have all the models I need."

"Do you?"

"Well, no." I laughed. "But no one has to know that."

Duane considered this and then asked, "What would I have to do?"

I kept my tone casual. "Very little, actually. I'd take some photos of you, studies really, focusing on your face and hands and feet. I'll tell you what—why don't you take a look at some of the studies I've already done. There are several pinned to that board on the wall over there and some more on the table." I was surprised by how very much I wanted Duane to say yes. "That will give you an idea of how I go about it."

Duane glanced over to where I was pointing. "Okay, I guess." He approached the table, his yellow high-tops moving silently on the wood floor.

"The completed project will consist of six panels," I told him. "There are seven saints represented in each panel." I reached for a folder from one pile and took out a small working sketch. "To begin I take a series of photos of each model and draw from them. For example, this is Saint Monica."

The boy bent over the sketch. "I know her." He took the sketch with slender fingers tipped with oval nails. "That's Mrs. Neal. From the bookstore."

"Right." I opened another folder. "Brendan, patron saint of sailors," I said.

Duane made a small sound close to a chuckle. "That's pretty funny. Seeing Leon Newell as a saint. I mean, isn't he kind of a—"

"Scoundrel?"

"Yeah." Duane smiled, and his face was transformed.

"Well, you don't have to be virtuous to be a saint. In fact, you'd be surprised. As it turns out, some were pretty rowdy. Prostitutes and thieves."

"Really?" Duane crossed to where I had pinned a draft of the panels on the rough planks of the wall. "This is bigger than I thought it would be," he said.

"Actually, this is a third of the size of what the completed work will be. When done, the canvases will measure sixty feet in height."

"Wow. That big?"

"We'll have to roll them and transport them to get them to the cathedral in a moving van. They'll be framed there."

Duane studied the six groupings. Beneath each figure was the name of a saint. He took his time, stopping once to say, "I never heard of some of these. I mean Crispin? Ambrose?" When he got to the last figure, he leaned in. "How come this one on the end has a question mark beneath it?"

"Because that one doesn't have a name. As Father Gervase put it, that figure is to represent the potential for sainthood in all of us."

"I'm not much for that stuff. I mean, my family is Catholic, but I don't go to church much anymore." The boy retreated, closed into himself. "I mean, when did that shit ever help anyone?"

"Belief in a faith is not a job requirement, Duane. Not for the models and fortunately not for me. Do you want to see which saint I had in mind for you?"

The boy leveled his eyes at me, coolly appraising, and for an instant I believed I had lost him. And then he said, "Sure. Why not?"

From the other bench, I retrieved an oversized book, which I thumbed open. Duane stared at the photo of the young saint lashed to a tree and pierced with arrows. "Jesus." The word was one soft breath. He pulled back. His reaction was not unlike my own when I'd first looked at the book Father Gervase had left at my home. The endless depictions of torture.

"Who is he?"

"Saint Sebastian. There's not a lot known about him. He was a soldier in the Roman army, and when he refused to renounce his Christian faith, he was shot with arrows and then clubbed to death."

"Jesus," Duane said again.

"Sebastian was an enduring theme for artists. Botticelli and Andrea Mantegna. And Antonello da Messina." I opened a second book, flipped to a page. "The one you were looking at is by El Greco. Here's one by Hans Memling."

Duane turned a few pages, looked at several of the other saints—Simon, Stephen, Sylvester—and then leafed back to Sebastian. "So back before—that day at the playground about a week ago. Remember? You said you wanted to ask me something . . ."

"Yes." I was taken by surprise that Duane remembered that afternoon.

"Was that all you wanted? To ask me to pose for you?"

"Yes."

"That's all?"

"That's all."

"Why?"

"Why what, Duane?"

"Why do you want me to pose? Why do you want me to be Saint Sebastian?"

I was careful with my answer. "It's hard to explain, but I saw something in you that drew me."

"Like what?" The boy's tone was wary, defensive, his face closed.

Again I considered. At the least I owed the boy honesty, and I wanted to define for him the qualities I had seen. "I guess I would say there is in you both vulnerability and strength."

The boy stared at me, then blurted, "That's exactly what Lucy said."

My lungs emptied of air. But of course I had misheard. I could not trust my hearing. When I finally inhaled, my breath came in jerks. "What did you say?"

"Lucy," Duane said. "She told me that too. That I was both vulnerable and strong."

Lucy. Lucy. Lucy. My ears rang with my daughter's name.

Duane was running on now, saying what a good person Lucy was, how everyone liked her, how you could talk to her, how you could trust her.

I sank on a stool, stared at the painting of the impaled saint. *Lucy.*

"Mr. Light?"

Lucy.

"I'd like to do it. Okay? I mean I'd like to pose for the painting."

I slumped over the table, barely aware of the light touch of the boy's hand on my shoulder.

CHAPTER THIRTY

~

Rain was slumped in her don't-give-a-shit slouch.

There was something off in the room, but she couldn't quite put her finger on it. She looked at the copper bowl full of candies and then at the table by her chair with the box of tissues. Her gaze swept the bookshelf and the clock that ticked away the minutes marking time until she could escape, the desk across the room. The little kneehole below. At least the room was pleasantly cool. Not frigid the way air conditioners could sometimes make a place, so cold you needed a sweater. And it was better than being at home, where suddenly Duane the Lame could do no wrong. Her mother who always thought he hung the moon was now acting like he walked on water and all because he was posing as a saint for Lucy's father. Duane the Lame as a saint. That was a laugh. If her mother only knew. Then it hit her. The off note. "So where's your dog?"

Dr. Mallory followed her gaze to the empty space beneath the desk. "Oh. I had to take him to the vet."

"What's the matter with him?" Not that she cared.

"They think it's a stomach flu. But just to be sure, they wanted to keep him overnight."

Just to be sure. In Rain's short experience, those were not good words. *Just to be sure, we'll run a few tests. Just to be sure, we want to admit him.* That was what they'd said to her grandmother when her grandfather went into the hospital. *Just to be sure.*

Dr. Mallory indicated the book Rain had returned and that sat on the table. "You needn't have returned it so quickly. I hope you had a chance to read it."

Rain pulled her attention back from the empty spot beneath the desk, back from thoughts of her grandfather. "Yeah."

"I'm curious to know what you think about it?"

"It's okay, I guess. I mean, it's kind of small for a real book."

"You're right. It is a very short book. Do you think it would have been better if Isak Dinesen had written a longer story?"

Isak Dinesen. Rain pictured the photo of the author on the back cover: those dark lips, the long fingers, one holding a book, the other a cigarette, the piercing gaze. She thought about this, taking her time, but the shrink didn't hurry her. "I don't know. Probably not."

"What did you think it was about?"

"What?" Rain asked. "I mean, what is this? A test or something? To see if I really read it?"

Dr. Mallory considered her questions. "In our short time together, Rain, you have struck me as quite forthright. Honest."

Forthright. Honest. The words warmed her, but she knew enough not to lower her guard.

"Why on earth would I think you'd lie about whether you read a book or not?"

Because everybody lies. "Well, I didn't. Lie, I mean. I read it. Okay?"

"Well, then," Dr. Mallory said. "It occurs to me that you might like to talk about it. I've found sharing with a friend doubles the pleasure of things. A meal or a book or a film."

This was true. For a fact. She and Lucy used to spend hours talking about a movie they'd seen together. And after they read *The Diary of a Young Girl* in freshman English, their conversation had gone on for weeks, long after all class discussion about the book had ended, covering everything from the horror of the Holocaust to Anne's amazing honesty about the other people in the annex, including her dislike of her mother. "Isn't it interesting that her last name is Frank and she's so frank in her observations about the others?" Lucy had said, which Rain had thought was such a clever thing to notice. For days they'd debated whether or not they could have stayed in the attic annex for two years without going outside. Rain didn't believe she could have; Lucy said she could absolutely if it were necessary. "We can do lots of things we never think we can do until we have to," she had said. When Lucy was first missing, Rain used to wonder if she had gone to a secret place. But of all the people she knew, Lucy had the least cause or need to hide or run away.

"Well?" Dr. Mallory said. "Shall we talk about the book? Like friends?"

"You're not my friend." *Take that in your honest pipe and smoke it.* The truth was she didn't have any friends. Not true friends. Her grandfather and Lucy had been her two best friends, and now both were gone. And so who exactly would be her friends? The girls that everyone at school thought were her friends really weren't, more like frenemies. For one thing, they could turn on you in an instant. Like the other day at the mall when they'd been trying on clothes, Christy had called attention to the roll of flesh around Meredith Banks's middle and said in a voice loud enough for other shoppers to hear, "That's not just a muffin top, it's the whole muffin," and then they all—even Meredith—had laughed in that totally fake way that was supposed to mean it was all in fun. Rain could only imagine what they would say if they found out she was seeing a shrink.

"We don't have to be friends to talk about the story."

"I guess." She might as well waste her parents' money discussing the book. It was better than having to talk about herself. Anything was better than that. Although on the way over today, she'd had a sudden urge to tell Dr. Mallory that she hadn't cut herself since their last session. Which would have been totally weird since they had never even talked about that subject. Which was also *seriously* weird since that was the reason her mother had done the total freak-out and dragged her there in the first place.

"So what did you think it was about?"

Rain thought for a minute. "A lot of things, I guess. Ya know? For a small book, there was a lot to think about."

"For instance?" Dr. Mallory leaned forward and picked up the candy dish and held it toward Rain.

Rain chose a butterscotch caramel and unwrapped it from the cellophane. "Choices people make. And art. I think it was a lot about art. Ya know. Babette being an artist and how important that was to her."

"Ah," Dr. Mallory said. "You are a very careful and intelligent reader."

Rain tightened her lips against a smile. "What do you think it's about?"

"You are correct in that it is about many things. Families and love and art. But one thing that struck me about the story the first time I read it is all the rules the people on the island lived by."

The sweetness of the caramel filled her mouth. "What do you mean?"

"There were rules both spoken and unspoken for all the people on the island. For instance, they were forbidden to enjoy earthly pleasures. Beauty, the pleasures of food. The sisters had rules that formed their lives as they were growing up, and they accepted them without question into adulthood. And they were constricted by these rules in every way."

"Like their clothes," Rain said, remembering the description of how the sisters dressed. "And how they couldn't go to parties or balls when they were young."

"Exactly. And you know, in that way, the people on the island are no different than any of us. We all have rules we grow up with. Even something as simple as how we are supposed to do the dishes."

Always put the forks in the dishwasher basket tines down. Rules. Don't get her started or she would have to stay there all day. *Make your bed before you come down to breakfast. Floss your teeth before you brush. Never wear torn underwear. Keep your elbows off the table when you eat. Write thank-you notes the same day you get a present.* "But why would Babette spend all her money on the dinner?"

"What do you think?"

"I don't know. It reminded me of something Lucy might have done."

"In what way, Rain?"

"Spend all her money doing things for others."

"I'd like to hear more about her."

Rain closed her eyes, near drowning in the loneliness of the past months. She swallowed the last of the butterscotch caramel. "I don't mean to make her sound too good or perfect or anything." That was one of the things Rain loved about Lucy, how just when she was a perfect goody two-shoes, she could surprise you with a naughty smile and a sly and spot-on imitation of one of the teachers. Her imitation of Mr. Marshall was so funny Rain had almost wet her pants. "Like I told you, she isn't a saint." *Wasn't. Wasn't a saint.* "But she always seems older than the other kids. Even as a freshman, she was elected president of SADD. Ya know. Students against Drunk Driving. She was always working to bring in speakers to talk to the kids about it."

"That's curious."

"What do you mean?"

"Well, often when we are drawn to a cause, to work for something, it's because we have had a personal experience. For instance, a girl whose mother has breast cancer might want to take part in a fund-raising walk for a cure for cancer."

"I guess maybe because of the accident last year when we were freshmen. After the junior prom one of the kids, a boy named Jared Phillips, crashed his car and all four passengers ended up in the hospital. One of the girls died." Rain remembered how on Monday when everyone was back at school, kids were crying, but Lucy didn't cry. She was upset. "She said drinking and driving was so stupid. Lots of things made Lucy upset."

"For example?"

"People being mean to each other. Or doing things for stupid reasons. Grown-ups who are cruel to their kids or their pets." Rain looked back over at the empty bed beneath the desk.

"It sounds to me as if Lucy had a strong moral compass."

Strong moral compass. Rain played the words through her mind, imagined a little compass occupying a space somewhere inside a person's body. Somewhere in the chest. Or belly.

"I want you to think about something, Rain."

Rain waited, not willing to commit.

"Do you think Lucy would have chosen for her best friend someone who didn't also have a moral center, who didn't share her values?"

"But I'm not like Lucy. Not in that way." She thought about shoplifting, about how she was mean to her mother.

"Sometimes it's hard to see our own best qualities."

Rain poked at the carpet with the toe of her sandal. The compliments made her skin itch, like sweat. "I really did like the story."

Dr. Mallory smiled. "I can see that."

"I kind of got lost in it. I—" She hesitated.

"Go on."

"Well, the other night, I couldn't sleep." She remembered the disastrous dinner, her mother's anger. "So I started to read the book, and somehow it made me forget to check the locks on the doors."

"Is that something you usually do?"

"Yes. You know. At night. To make sure they're all locked and the alarm system is on."

"Why?"

"I just have to."

"Don't your parents do that?"

"I guess. I mean, my father does, but I can't get to sleep unless I check."

"Is this something you have always done?"

"No. Not really." She could no longer taste even a lingering sweetness of butterscotch on her tongue. "Just since Lucy was murdered."

"Why do you think that is?"

Hello. "Well, obviously because he's still out there."

"Who?"

"The person who killed Lucy. I know everyone likes to say it was some stranger who did it, but what if it wasn't? What if was someone here? In Port Fortune."

"And it makes you feel better to know he can't get in your house?"

Duh. "Well, yeah. It makes me feel safe."

"I see."

"My mother thinks I'm crazy."

"What do you think she means by that?"

"Means by 'crazy'?"

"Yes."

"That's obvious." *I'm here talking to a shrink, aren't I?*

"Not really. When people say 'crazy,' they can mean a lot of things, Rain. They might mean foolish or goofy. Or irrational. Or mentally ill or not of right mind."

"I think my mother means mentally ill."

"Let me ask you something, Rain. Does it hurt anyone when you check the locks at night?"

"No. Except if you count that it makes my mother mad that my father spent a lot of money getting a security system because I'm so afraid but I still have to check the locks. But no, I guess it doesn't really *hurt* anyone."

"And does it make sense to you to lock the doors if it makes you feel safe?"

"I guess."

"I don't know who killed your friend or where this person is. But I do know it is a wise thing to do what we need to do to make ourselves feel safe."

"So not crazy."

"Not crazy at all. Perhaps irrational. But even if something seems irrational to others, it doesn't necessarily mean it isn't true."

What about a person who cuts herself? Did a sane, rational person do *that*? While Rain considered telling Dr. Mallory about her cuts, the shrink started to rise. Rain was surprised to see more than an hour had passed.

"I had another book in mind that I thought you might enjoy reading," Dr. Mallory said, "but I think we have more to discuss about this one the next time we meet. And I'll tell you more about the author. I think her life in Africa might interest you. She was a big-game hunter and a woman of courage, not afraid to follow her dreams, no matter what anyone thought. How does that sound?"

"Okay."

At the door Rain turned. "You never told me what I should call you."

"Whatever you'd like, Rain. My name is Sylvia, and I find most of the people I see prefer that."

"Sylvia?" Rain tried the name out.

"Yes." Dr. Mallory gave a little laugh. "When my nieces were very young they used to pronounce it Silly, but I have to say I didn't encourage that."

"Yeah, I bet. Anyhow, thanks. For today, I mean."

"You're welcome, Rain. You are very welcome. And thank you."

"For what?"

"For coming here. I know it isn't easy."

"No big deal." Rain snapped her shield firmly in place.

After the coolness of Dr. Mallory's house, the heat outside was like a wall. She knew her mother was waiting in the car and knew a flash of disappointment that she wouldn't have an excuse to walk, and maybe the good-looking Mr. Hayes would drive by and offer her a ride. But no, her mother would be there, sitting in the Volvo with her pathetic, hopeful look, as if one hour in the house with the shrink would transform Rain into the kind of daughter she wanted. Rain's face flushed with anger and resentment. If only she could run away from it all.

"Rain?"

The shrink was motioning her back, and she thought, *What now?* "Yes?" She looked down on Dr. Mallory's head. Her scalp showed pink through the thinning hair, and Rain felt a cruelty rise up, knew that she was no better than Christy and the others.

"Remember, dear, just because we can't always see our best qualities doesn't mean that they don't exist. Try to remember what Lucy saw when she chose you as her friend."

Rain stared at the perspiration that dampened the pale pink scalp, saw the horrid vulnerability of age. "Well, I think your dog is going to die." In the shocked silence that followed, she didn't dare look at Dr. Mallory. Fear and shame washed over her as the hateful words spun through the air like rabid bats. There was no way to recapture them, call them back, swallow them so they couldn't ever escape.

CHAPTER THIRTY-ONE

~

Father Gervase swallowed and looked out at the congregation, a host of faces both known and unfamiliar.

It was the end of July, and the oak pews were occupied by residents and summer people who attended the early Sunday Mass so they would have the rest of the day free for the beach. Or golf. Or tennis. Although why in the unrelenting heat one would even think of doing anything the least bit strenuous was beyond him. Beneath his white and red chasuble a film of clammy sweat coated his skin; the fans in the sanctuary did little more than move warm currents of air, and he felt slightly light-headed. No, this was not a day to be risking heat stroke by batting a tennis ball over a net. But then again, regardless of thermostat readings, the priest had always been drawn to activities more cerebral than physical. Even at ten Cecelia could outdo him at a backyard game of badminton. Or horseshoes. He pictured her now dancing with glee after tossing a ringer. *Cecelia.* Why, after all these years, were these memories rising? But he wouldn't think of her now. Couldn't think of her now.

An impatient rustling rose from the pews and broke into his musing. How long had his mind been wandering? He stared down at the homily printed on the pages in front of him. He had to rely on the pages now, following along the text with his forefinger, tracing his progress so that should he have a lapse of recall, all he had to do was glance down to reclaim his place. At one time, he could recall pages of a text without stumbling once or needing this crutch. Now he was no longer confident of his ability to recite the sentences and phrases, words he had labored over for syntax and precise meaning. He knew his satisfaction in the results was prideful, but he had always felt he owed this to the congregation, unlike Father Burns, who had not the gift for language and who dispatched his homilies in a manner one could, uncharitably he knew, call perfunctory. A second round of rustling from the pews, more pronounced now, flowed forward from the congregation. He adjusted his glasses, glanced down at the paper, slid his left hand under the scapular, as if seeking warmth in spite of the heat, and began.

"As many of you know—" He swallowed against a mouth suddenly dry and tried again. "As many of you know, one of our celebrated neighbors, the artist Will Light, has been selected to paint the art for the new cathedral, a series of paintings that will depict a gathering of saints." He ran his tongue over lips turned dry and paused to take a sip from the glass of water on the lectern's shelf, and then he inhaled deeply to shake off the faint light-headedness. "For this enterprise, the artist is following in the tradition of religious art that dates back for centuries. Like many of the masters, painters such as Caravaggio and Michelangelo and Rembrandt, he has decided to use as models for the saints the ordinary people of his town. Of our town." Another swallow of water. He slipped his hand from beneath the chasuble and grasped the side of the pulpit to steady himself. Perhaps he should have asked Father Burns to lead the Mass. Too late for that now.

"I know this decision has made some of us uncomfortable, even unhappy. After all, we might say, who among us is worthy of representing a saint?" He lifted his eyes from the text, unable to resist a quick glance toward the third row of pews where Lena MacDougall sat in her customary aisle seat, overseeing all. It took him several moments to regain his place in the text.

"We might ask: Who is a saint? What is a saint? It seems we ought to be able to give a simple answer. A holy person, we might answer. A pure being who practices the virtues of Christ to a heroic degree. One who has forsaken earthly pleasure in service to God. A martyr who has sacrificed all for his faith and in His name. And yet, these simple answers lead us to a sanitized version of sainthood that weakens our understanding of how grace works in the world."

He chanced another glance at Lena, who sat, mouth tight, disapproval an unnamed force of physics that radiated off her like smoke. Momentarily he lost focus. To calm himself, he took another drink, but the water was now tepid, and one swallow made him queasy. He soldiered on. "Among the legions of the saints, among the devout and pure of heart were crooks and thieves, con men and cutthroats, harlots and atheists. The thief Saint Dismas. The gambler Saint Camillus. Or the beggar Saint Benedict Joseph Labre. Or Saint Vladimir, the rapist. Thinking about these men as saints, we can feel uncomfortable, just as we might avert our eyes when we pass a homeless person on the street caught in the grip of poverty. Or alcohol. Or drugs. Why? Why does this person give rise to extreme reactions? Perhaps because we recognize the humanity in him, and so we are not let off the hook; perhaps she is a saint in disguise. We are then asked to release our judgments and accept the knowledge that there is no such thing as an unforgivable sin."

Unforgivable sin. He recalled a conversation with his confessor at the seminary. "How do we forgive?" he had asked the older priest. "Is there anything that cannot be forgiven?"

The old man had looked at him, a searching gaze as if to discover the question behind these questions. "To understand forgiveness," he had said, "it is first necessary to forgive ourselves."

Another rustling from the pews. He looked up at the congregation, thought he saw Will Light sitting toward the back, but the faces blurred and he was unsure. What would the artist think to know that the sketches he had been working on for weeks had inspired the homily this morning? He blinked again to clear his vision, relieved to be nearing the end of the text. "There are many pious people who believe themselves to be saints who are not," he read, "and many who believe themselves to be impious who are not." Lena snorted, a sound loud enough to rise to where Father Gervase stood. He carried on. "Simply put, the saints are us, all of us, in our full and flawed humanity. All it takes—" Another wave of nausea took him, and in spite of the heat, he was chilled. He thought again that he should have asked Father Burns to lead the service. He glanced toward the side door he used to enter the sanctuary in what now seemed like years ago and wondered if he should leave, but the distance to the door was daunting. He tightened his hold on the pulpit. His vision blurred, as if his eyes were filmed with oil. Off to his right, the candle flames wavered and shimmered. Where was he? "All it takes," he continued, "to convert a sinner to a saint is desire. Desire to do good, to be better, to try harder, to be open to grace." Now all he wanted to do was finish the Mass. He had completely lost his place on the page and tried to recall the last line. He closed his eyes and concentrated, willing the words to come. There was a rustling from the pews, not of impatience, but of concern, as if as one they were leaning forward in their seats, leaning toward their priest, sensing something had gone wrong. Something about a journey. Yes, a journey. And then it came flowing back. He remembered each word. "Our spiritual journey," he started. He stopped, inhaled deeply like a runner seeing the finish line. "Our spiritual journey is—or ought to be—a deepening realization of the possibility of sainthood in all of us."

Again Lena snorted, and that sound of her displeasure was the last thing he remembered.

CHAPTER THIRTY-TWO

~

Two hours into the trip to Maine, I remembered the portfolio I'd brought home from the wharf studio the previous afternoon.

I had set it on the hall table earlier that morning, and I definitely recalled seeing it next to my overnight bag, but had I picked it up and carried it out to the car? This I could not remember. Well, if I'd forgotten, it was too late to turn back now. It was already past one, and Sophie expected me around noon. I'd started out later than planned and hadn't thought about the crush of weekenders heading north, and so crossing over the state line from Massachusetts I'd been caught in traffic. I considered stopping to find a pay phone so I could give her a call. If I could even find a pay phone. One of these days I'd have to cave to the inevitable and get a cell phone. Welcome to the twenty-first century.

I'd been nervous all morning, and being late only added to my anxiety. My last conversation with Sophie had been easy, her voice relaxed and warm, and when we'd planned the weekend—not a day trip, we'd agreed, but an entire weekend—I'd felt an awakening to possibilities, but now I wondered if I had misread everything. The possibilities, the tender hope that we could begin again seemed just that, a hope and one too easily dashed. How did one begin again? Was it possible? Or had too much damage been done? Had we already crossed that line? There was so much I didn't know, but this I knew: I missed her and wanted her back. I wanted a return to our lives where there was no need for "space" and the unspoken threat that such a need gave rise to. The truth is, I loved her still.

Had I brought the damn portfolio?

I'd spent time poring over the working sketches from those I'd completed, hoping they would reveal to Sophie what I didn't trust words to convey. I had limited the selection to no more than a few, drawings I hoped she would be moved by. Elaine Neal as Monica, Leon Newell as Brendan, Harold Weaver as Simon, Payton Hayes as Vincent de Paul. I had included Mary Silveria, the young mother from the grocery store, the one I thought of as my first saint, sketching her even before I had known I would accept the commission. And there had been no question but that Duane LaBrea, my Saint Sebastian, would be in the folder. Thinking of the teenager, I wondered if Sophie would see the same haunting quality in the boy that I had. In the short time Duane had posed, I continued to feel protective of him, a pull to help the boy. Suddenly everything hinged on having the sketches to show Sophie. I pulled over onto the breakdown lane, clicked on the emergency flashers, and got out to open the trunk of the Prius. And yes, there it was, right next to my overnight bag.

A half hour later, I left the highway for a secondary road and recalled directions Sophie had recited the night before. "You'll pass a vegetable stand on your left and then a gas station," she'd instructed. "Shortly after that, look for a used furniture shop on the right. If it isn't raining, there will be some old chairs and bureaus lined up in front." I passed the farm stand, the gas station, and smiled, remembering a conversation we had once had about the difference women and men had about giving directions. "Men give it in miles, women in landmarks," she'd told me. I watched for the wooden sign that marked the lane leading to the cottage, and still I was almost past before I caught sight of it. "End of the Road." I backed up and made the turn. The lane was not paved, and tire ruts ran deep in the gravel. The Prius bounced over them, occasionally scraping the undercarriage. At least the roadbed was dry, and I thought that it had to be near impassible in winter and during the spring thaw. I rounded a curve, and as the lane descended toward the water, I saw first the one car—Sophie's green VW—and then the house. Just as she had described. White shingles with French-blue shutters, sharp peaked roof with narrow windows in the gable. Overgrown foundations plantings. A two-story farmhouse with a wing off to one side, but in the manner of many homeowners of places along the coast, it was referred to it as a cottage. Two Adirondack chairs sat on the lawn that sloped down to the cove that opened to the Atlantic, and even from afar I recognized the single figure seated in one. I scanned the yard, the columned porch that fronted the house, and was relieved to see that Joan Laurant was nowhere in sight. As I pulled up the seashell drive, Sophie rose and walked toward me, her movements full of grace. Her hair had grown longer and was pulled back, gathered in a low ponytail. She was wearing a blue halter top and a skirt of some gauzy fabric that traced the line of her legs as she walked. Longing thickened my throat.

I should have stopped for a bottle of French Chardonnay or a bouquet. Sunflowers, the blossom Sophie had chosen to carry at our wedding because, she'd said, they represented hope. Yes, sunflowers would have been perfect. But I had not brought her flowers. Or her favorite wine. I had brought her the only thing I could think to give. I was bringing her the saints.

I hoped I was not mistaken; I hoped it was enough.

CHAPTER THIRTY-THREE

~

There was something wrong. A mistake.

Father Gervase roused to hear two voices breaking through the mist. His father's? His mother's? A dream? He was still clothed in his vestments and lying on the sofa in the rectory with Father Burns bending over him. He attempted to orient himself, and this was when he saw, standing next to Father Burns—and he had to close his eyes again against the indignity of this—Lena MacDougall, her face no more than a foot or two from his, close enough for him to see a mole on the underside of her chin. He attempted to swing his feet to the floor, but Lena stopped him with a firm palm against his shoulder. "It's best you stay there for a bit. Get your bearings before you get up."

"Lena's right," Father Burns said. *Father Burns. In a golfing shirt. And a pair of those silly shorts with all the pockets. As if he were planning to hike, for heaven's sake.* "You need to rest."

Father Gervase looked around to see if there were others to witness his humiliation, but mercifully he was alone with just these two. Which was bad enough. Lena MacDougall, he thought again. Her of all people.

"Well," she said. "You gave everyone a bit of a fright."

Slowly, it came back to him. The Mass, the heat, his light-headedness. But to faint like this. He'd never passed out in his life.

"I wanted to call the EMTs," Father Burns said, "but Lena didn't think it necessary."

"My nurse's training," she explained.

Nurse's training? Lena? He absorbed this information. He'd known her for what—twelve years—and had never known this central fact. A failure on his part to see her only as a bossy, meddling busybody.

"Your pulse was steady and your breathing strong." She dropped her hand to his wrist, again checking his pulse with a competence he hadn't bargained for, though he should have expected it given the way she ran the Rosary Society. He was struck by the surprising coolness of her fingers against his skin, as if she had dipped them in cold water. "There you go. Nice and steady," she said, as if she was personally responsible for his normal pulse. "It was just the heat."

"Yes," he said. "The heat." Again he attempted to sit up, and this time she allowed it. He stood, hoping he was successful in concealing from them the wave of unsteadiness. To his relief, this passed after a moment. "No need to make a fuss. I'll just go change and perhaps lie down for a bit."

He saw Lena wanted to argue, to have him stay there with her where she could keep an eye on him. He could only imagine how long she'd dine out on the drama of it all, and then he recalled her fingers on his pulse, felt ashamed at the smallness of this thought. He crossed to the door before she could utter a word of protest.

"And it is important that you stay hydrated. Drink plenty of water." Her voice followed him, and for a moment he feared she would pursue him and so quickened his steps. In his room, weaker than he had admitted to Father Burns or Lena or even to himself, he stripped off the cassock, taking note of the dampness of the fabric. His hands trembled slightly as he folded the robe and surplice. It occurred to him that perhaps he should see a doctor, just a checkup. The church had good health insurance, and the priests were encouraged to undergo annual physicals, but Father Gervase avoided them. His father had distrusted doctors and, unreasonably, he knew, he had inherited this prejudice. He switched on the oscillating fan, slipped off his shoes, and reclined on his bed, not bothering to fold back the covering. Of course, Lena was right and he should drink some water, but that could wait. For now he just wanted to rest, to block out the memory of fainting in front of the congregation and then coming to with MacDougall leaning over him. Overhead, the fan whirred on and on, rhythmic and steady as a metronome.

A rap on the door woke him, and he was surprised to find the light in the room was now that of late afternoon.

"Father Gervase?" It was Father Burns.

"Yes?"

"Are you okay?"

"Fine." He cleared the rust from his throat. "Just resting."

"I hate to disturb you, but the family is waiting for you in the chapel."

"The family?"

"The Medeiros."

It came to him then. Gloria Medeiros. Following a year of treatments, her last tests had shown the cancer to be in remission, and she had returned home to an exultant family. Her children had requested the use of the chapel for a small service of prayer and thanksgiving.

"Shall I meet with them?" Father Burns asked.

For a moment he was tempted to turn his obligation over to his fellow priest but realized this would reveal a weakness he preferred to keep private. "No, no, I'll be right along." He took a fresh cassock from his closet and dressed. Mindful of Lena MacDougall's directive to hydrate, he detoured by the rectory kitchen and drew a cup of water, drank half of it, then went to his study to pick up the brief notes he had made for the service. On the walk to the chapel his steps were steady. Just a passing spell then. Caused by the heat. That was all. Inside the chapel, a small gathering awaited. Three generations. Gloria, her two sons and their wives, their four boys, her daughter Mary Margaret along with her husband, and, in Mary Margaret's arms, the baby girl who was the newest addition to the family. They turned to him, the faces of all but the youngest buoyed by relief and hope and faith. The chapel air was sweetened by the vase of honeysuckle and roses someone had brought to place by the altar.

"Oh, Father Gervase," Gloria said. "We were worried about you."

He smiled and said in what he hoped was a reassuring tone, "No need. No need." He reached out a hand to stroke the baby's brow. He'd christened the infant just two months ago and attempted to recall the name. Something unusual, he thought. *Kiara? Kiley?* But those names were faintly Irish, and perhaps he had confused this child with the O'Shea baby, whom he also recently christened. Unsure, he didn't chance a name. He looked now at Gloria, slip-thin from her treatments, her hair newly grown into short silver curls that haloed her skull, and he saw beneath the lingering ravages of illness the pure and shining essence of her.

"Father Gervase?" one of the sons prompted.

"Ah, yes," he said. For the occasion, he had chosen two readings. Some scripture, of course, Psalm 96, and then several lines of poetry. While meditating on the occasion he had recalled Frost's quote "the best way out is through," and that had led to pulling a slender volume of the poet's work from the shelf. When he came to "Birches," he'd stopped reading. Just the thing. Now he unfolded his notes. "Shall we begin?" he said. He opened with the scripture and spoke for a bit about this gift to the family of having their mother and grandmother returned to health and led them in prayer. Looking out at the gathering, at the infant and the young boys fidgeting on the pew, at the six adult children and Gloria, he was suddenly moved by the truth of life and was struck with the need to convey the fleeting preciousness of life to them. He leaned forward and veered off his prepared script. "No matter what span of days we are given," he began, "they are too few. An accident or illness. A single phone call. We never know when He will call us home, only that it is a call each of us will receive." One of the sons scowled and cleared his throat, and his obvious displeasure sent Father Gervase back to his text. But as he recited Frost—the lines about fate snatching one away not to return—he realized he had somehow misjudged his selection, and what had seemed perfectly appropriate in the privacy of the rectory had now missed the mark. In confusion, he returned to Psalms, repeating the verse he had already read. The scent of honeysuckle, so pleasant just moments before, now seemed too sweet, too thick in the air. And the faces tilted up toward him, which so recently had been filled with expectation, now reflected disappointment and anxiety. He should have let Father Burns substitute.

At last, the ceremony came to an end, and the family departed, politely murmuring their appreciation. "I hope you feel better soon," Gloria said when he took her hand. Alone, he sat for a moment in the front pew, welcoming the quiet of the empty chapel. His stomach rumbled, and he realized he hadn't eaten since morning and then it was something light. A soft-boiled egg. He'd feel better when he got some food. By now, with any luck, Lena MacDougall would have gone home and Father Burns would be off somewhere. Hiking, he thought, remembering those shorts with pockets on the hips and rear and legs, more than anyone could possibly have need of. As he rose to leave, he spied a rumpled Kleenex in the front pew where the family had gathered, and on the floor by the altar a few rose petals had dropped from the bouquet. He made a mental note to see if Mr. Jervis would arrange to come and tidy the place before his usual scheduled time on the weekend. As he locked the door behind him, a wisp of a thought sat on the edge of memory, too elusive to break through.

Mrs. Jessup had left a platter of deli meat and a second plate of tomatoes, sliced and lightly dressed with olive oil and salt. He was relieved to find that indeed Father Burns was nowhere to be seen, and so he fixed himself a dish and sat there at the kitchen table. The meal reminded him of those his mother and grandmother would prepare from the daily bounty of their summer gardens. Cucumber and corn and tomatoes and green snap beans. When the first crop of corn was ripe, the family would sometimes have a meal consisting entirely of sweet corn, ear after ear of it dripping with the butter his grandmother had churned herself, all of them delighting in the pleasure of that first taste of the season. Or blueberries. He could almost taste them. One time he and Cecelia had eaten almost a whole watermelon between them and been sick well into the night. At the memory of his sister, his eyes filled, and he wiped the tears away. He was turning into a sentimental old man.

When he was finished with his meal, he cleaned up the kitchen, poured himself a second glass of iced tea—Lena MacDougall's advice still echoing—and carried it to the living room in time to catch the first inning of the game, the second of a double header. As he stooped to pick up the remote, the thought that had eluded him earlier in the chapel stayed his hand. As clearly as if the scene were unfolding on the flat-screen in front of him, he recalled the day earlier in the summer. He saw himself sitting in the chapel where he had gone to work on a homily. He recalled the chill in the building, the coldness of the stone floor as it seeped through the leather soles of his shoes, and he remembered catching sight of an object half hidden beneath a pew. He had been working on a sermon. A sermon on the teachings of the apostle Paul. The power of hope and faith in the face of despair. Yes. That was right. So it had been in June. He remembered picking the object up and discovering it was a child's toy. The little figure that Will Light believed to have belonged to his daughter. *Where did you get this?* He saw Will's face across the table at the café. He knew the passing pleasure of solving a little mystery, and with this small victory, a win over elusive memory, the tribulations of the day—fainting during Mass, Lena MacDougall bending over him on the sofa, his failure to say exactly the right thing at the little ceremony in the chapel—all this receded. He clicked on the television and settled in with his tea to watch the ball game, making note before he turned his full attention on the game that he must remember to tell Will Light how he had come to have the little toy.

It was only later, after the game had ended—the Sox riding a five-game winning streak—and he was about to fall asleep that another question occurred to him. If the Yoda had indeed been Lucy's as her father believed, how had he come to find it in the chapel so many months after the girl's death?

CHAPTER THIRTY-FOUR

~

Sophie crossed the lawn to me, her body fit and tan, her step light, and I was ambushed by this thought: *This is the woman Lucy would have grown to be.*

Then she was in my arms, embracing me without hesitation, holding me for a long moment. "Hey," she said, her voice almost a whisper.

Another tsunami of longing swept me. There on the sloping lawn that led down to the cove, my wife in my arms, I had a deep sense of coming home. *Please*, I thought, *can we begin again?* "Sorry I'm late," I said. "I got caught in traffic." Much too soon, she slipped from my embrace.

"I was worried about that. Was it bad?"

"Yes. I completely forgot about weekend gridlock. I should have left earlier." *Is there still a chance for us?*

"It doesn't matter. That's one of the things I love about being here."

"What's that?"

"Oh, the way everything slows down. The way time is measured not by clocks but by the tides, moon, and sun."

"Sounds good." And it did. A timeless universe.

"Honestly, Will, it's amazing how when we stop paying attention to minutes and hours, they become nearly irrelevant. Sometimes this feeling is so strong I think we all must walk around wearing a mantle of stress or tension that we aren't even aware of." She looked at me. Her head slightly tilted in question. "Do you know what I mean, Will?"

"I do.

"And somehow, here, in the timelessness of this place, that tension dissipates."

I felt it too, the relaxation of being freed from ordinary demands. Or maybe it was being with Sophie. For a moment, and if that was all it was, one moment, I would take it and be grateful, for that moment, the world was nearly right. That day in Maine the inevitability of what lay ahead was as far away as Jupiter.

"Honestly," she said, "it makes me want to do away with every timepiece in creation. Without them, everything expands."

"Not everything." I grasped her waist playfully and encircled it with my hands. "Are you even eating, Soph?"

She threw back her head and laughed. "Oh God, yes. Joan and I eat like trenchermen."

Joan. I waved the name away, determined not to let anyone intrude on this time. "Not starving then?"

"No, but you must be. When it got late, I thought you might stop on the way up, but I waited on lunch anyway."

"I didn't stop." *I couldn't wait to get here.*

"Good. Why don't you bring your things into the house while I set out the food. And unless you prefer to be inside, I thought we'd eat outdoors." She laughed lightly. "By some miracle, the black flies are absent today. They must have known you were coming." I knew we were both remembering a long-ago vacation when I had declared war on the insects.

"Outside sounds perfect." Suddenly everything *was* near perfect. On the way to the car, I had the urge to shout this out. To let her know that this minute, here, with her was—well, not perfect, perfect would be another reality that was lost forever—but this was close, as close as it had been in months. I had changed, I wanted to tell her. And there, standing on that lawn, I really believed that was true. I believed I could be what she needed me to be. I believed by some miracle that summer, my anger and raging need for revenge had begun to dissipate, the grenade disarmed. But when I turned to tell her this, she had already disappeared into the house. As I retrieved my bag and the portfolio of drawings, I was aware of the quintessential sounds of summer in a way I hadn't been back in Port Fortune, as if with each mile traveled north, my senses had been sharpened. I heard the distant hollow slapping of a screen door against a doorjamb, the echo of voices across the cove, a chorus of birdsong from the grove of trees, and from somewhere not too far away the metallic clanging of horseshoes hitting a post followed by jubilant shouts.

The house was as I had imagined it. Summer cottage casual, a style Sophie once called shabby chic. Rag rugs thrown on worn pine floors. Furniture that had borne generations of use. A vase of wildflowers Sophie had gathered. The bookcase and the musty collection of *Reader's Digest* books. There were ashes in the fireplace, and on one of the chairs I saw a thin cotton shawl I recognized as Sophie's. I could picture her curled by a fire on a cool evening swathed in the lilac wrap. Again, as I had on arrival, I glanced around for a sign of Joan Laurant, but there was nothing I could see that suggested anyone else was staying here. From the kitchen, there was the clink of pottery and flatware. "Where do you want me to put my stuff?" I called.

"At the top of the stairs, the room on the right. But just leave it for now. Let's eat first."

I helped her carry out the trays. A green salad, cold poached salmon, and sliced cucumbers in a sour cream and chive dressing. The picnic bench where we sat was a repurposed kitchen table painted the same French blue as the farmhouse shutters, and it reminded me of a time we had spent one late August in Provence. A blue umbrella, its fabric faded nearly white from years of summer sun, threw a disc of shade. Sophie poured two glasses of limeade and handed one to me.

"This looks great," I said. And then, after a moment, "You look great."

"Thanks, Will. This time here has been good for me."

"I can see that. I'm glad." The limeade tasted faintly of mint.

She raised a questioning eyebrow.

"No, really. I am."

"Well, I'm glad you're glad." She reached across the table and laid her hand on me. "I know this hasn't been easy. I know you would rather I were home. With you."

"Yes." *When are you coming back? Are you coming back?*

"How are things at home?"

"Sweltering. It's been in the nineties for days." I didn't want to talk about the weather.

"And the work? How's that going?"

"It's going well. If you discount what a pain in the ass the bishop is."

She laughed. "I know you've told me a bit about who you've asked to pose, but I'd like to know more. How many models have you drawn so far?"

"Fourteen. I've completed the working sketches for the first two panels." I thought of the portfolio, waiting in the house. "In fact, I brought several of the sketches to show you."

"I'd like that, Will."

"And what about your project? How's that going?"

"I'm deep in it," she said. She paused, as if to add something, but then stopped. She held out the platter of salmon. "More, or are you saving room for pie?"

"There's pie, too?"

"Blueberry. I picked the berries myself."

"Keep this up and you'll have a permanent houseguest."

She started to answer but settled for a smile. We ate in a companionable silence. After a while she rose and headed for the house, turning at the steps to ask, "À la mode or straight?"

"You have to ask?"

"Two scoops?"

"Absolutely."

"Speaking of houseguests," I said when she returned. "Where's Joan off to today?"

She set the wedge of pie in front of me. The spheres of ice cream were already beginning to melt. "Technically, I'm the houseguest. Joan holds the rental lease. But to answer your question, she's away for a couple of weeks. Visiting friends up in Bar Harbor."

"So we're alone here. Just us."

"Just us." She didn't meet my eyes. "It's been great to be here with her though. We split up the cooking and chores. And we've been taking the kayaks out every afternoon at dusk. Almost like being in summer camp. She's trying to decide what the next chapter of her life holds."

"How's that?"

"She gave her notice at school and is leaving after this year, but she hasn't any definite plans beyond that."

"Hmmm." I didn't pursue the subject of Joan or her plans. We fell into a silence but again not an uncomfortable one.

"Can I get you another piece of pie?"

"No thanks. I'm good."

"Then I'll just clear things up."

I started to rise, but she waved away my help. "I've got it. You just relax." She pointed to the hammock strung between two pines. "I think that's calling your name."

I wasn't really wanting to laze in the hammock, but I wanted to please her and so let myself fall into it without a murmur and waited for her to come back, wondering as I stared up at the sky if the woven sling would hold both of us. When she returned, she had changed into a bathing suit, and at the sight of her my cock swelled.

"I'm going to take a swim. Want to join me?"

What I wanted was her. Then. "I don't think so."

"You sure? It might feel good after your drive."

"Maybe in a bit," I said. I followed her progress as she descended the worn path through the grass down to the narrow pier that stretched out into the cove. Her shape was still girlish. She hadn't thickened through the middle as many did in midlife, and I felt an irrational pride at this. She walked to the end of the dock and executed a perfect jackknife, then surfaced and called up to me.

"It's feels fabulous. Sure you won't change your mind?"

"Later. I'm feeling pretty lazy right now. I'll enjoy it vicariously." She had always been a good swimmer, and I took pleasure in watching her as she cut through the water, her strokes strong and rhythmic, hair wet and slicked close to her scalp. Otter-mother of our otter-child. Selkie woman.

I woke to a spray of salt water. Sophie stood over me, flicking drops on me and laughing. "You should have come in with me. It was delicious."

"Delicious." I stared at her, letting my eyes trail over her body. "Yes."

She blushed and avoided my eyes. "I'm going to change and then I'll bring us some wine."

"Why don't I get it while you change?"

"You look too comfortable to move. Stay here. I'll be right back."

Long minutes passed, and when she didn't return, I rolled from the hammock. I found her in the living room, still in her swimsuit, a circle of water at her feet. She was holding the portfolio, and when she looked up her eyes were wet with tears.

"Oh, Will," she whispered. "These are—I can't find the words."

"That bad, huh?"

"Don't joke, Will." Her gaze was steady and serious. "These are stunning. Truly, Will, they're the best work you've ever done. I don't know how you've done it. They are remarkable." She lifted the sheet with Saint Brendan. "Take this one of Leon Newell. It's Leon, but it's Leon elevated to something higher. And look what you've done with Duane." She indicated the drawing of Saint Sebastian. "You've captured something broken in him, something wounded, but he shines, Will. Do you know what I'm saying?"

"I'm not sure."

"You've drawn the saints, Will. You've conveyed them in all their humanness and their transcendent holiness."

"I just did what you said, Soph."

"I don't remember."

"I did it for Lucy." Lucy. The name that was a constant pain in my heart slipped from my lips with an ease I wouldn't have believed possible. "For Lucy."

"Oh, Will. She would have loved them, you know. She would have been so proud."

But she will never know, I thought. Unwilling to pursue this—to destroy the moment—I steered the conversation toward the safer topic of my technical decisions: having all the saints in robes of their individual periods, the variety of ways they clasped hands in prayer. I sensed the shadow that flickered momentarily over her at the shift in subject, but she followed my lead. No more talk of Lucy.

We cleaned up from the lunch, and Sophie suggested a walk. We began by strolling the cottage property and then continued past the overgrown bushes where Sophie had picked blueberries for our pie and ended up by following a narrow path to the point where the cove spilled out into the Atlantic.

Earlier, she had asked me if I wanted a copy of her finished chapters to take back to Port Fortune, but I'd said I would prefer to wait until she had completed the entire first draft, but the truth was I was not able to bear reading of murdered and disappeared children, bereft parents, and so, as if by mutual agreement, we had spoken no more of it. If she was disappointed, she concealed it.

We ended our walk by the dock, drinking Chardonnay and dangling our legs over the edge of the dock. Sophie had hitched her skirt up to her toned and tanned thighs. My chino cuffs were rolled to my knees. Water lapped our ankles. A lock of hair had fallen over her cheek, and I reached over and pushed it back. "Shall we go change and take a swim to cool down?" she asked.

The effort of going up to the house to put on a suit was beyond me, and I said, "Right now I'm enjoying this." And so we sat, sipping wine and staring across the cove, listening as the sounds slowly shifted from those of day to evening. The echoes of mothers calling their children in from play reverberated across the water. We were quiet, falling again into a companionable silence.

Sophie spoke first. "Lucy would love this."

My mind was far away as I'd been thinking about whether I should drive into the nearest town and pick up another bottle of wine or suggest that we go out somewhere for dinner. A shore dinner. Lobster and clams. The whole thing. And her words jolted me back to the present. *Lucy would love this.* Lucy. Our ever-present ghost-child.

"She would, you know," Sophie continued.

I closed my eyes at the truth of it, the sure and hard knowledge that Lucy would have embraced every moment of this day. Swimming in the cove. Long walks. The ease of cottage life and indolent August days. Picking berries. Eating outside on the painted table. Reading condensed stories from must-scented pages. And most of all of the three of us on holiday. Together. My heart was so heavy with sorrow it felt as if it were filled with knives.

"It never goes away, does it?" she said. "The loss. The pain."

I shook my head, not trusting my voice.

"I don't know how we could ever think it would. I think that's what's so hard for people who haven't lost a child to understand. As if it is even possible to forget. To go on like before."

From somewhere in the distance to our right came two voices, clearly drunken and raised in argument. A silvery shimmer of minnows curved through the water, circled our feet. At least I thought they were minnows, but my piscine knowledge was limited. My father wasn't a hunter or fisherman. His only hobby had been puttering around our home, fixing sills, teaching me the value of caring for belongings. For family. And at this I had failed.

"Do you know what someone once told me?" Sophie said. "'Life goes on.'"

"You're kidding me. Someone actually said that to you? Who? That bitch Alicia?"

"It doesn't matter. But it doesn't, you know?"

"Doesn't what?"

"Necessarily go on."

"I don't understand."

"I interviewed one man whose wife had committed suicide after their child was murdered."

"But you—you never thought of that."

"Actually, it did occur to me. I wanted to die. I wanted the pain to end. A broken heart still beats. Unless you stop it."

"But you didn't."

"No." She took a deep swallow of wine. "I never really could have, you know. Not only because it would be a sin. Perhaps the raw truth is I'm too much of a coward."

I thought of her facing interviewers, talking about the numbers of children lost every year, wanting to effect change, to weave even one positive thing out of Lucy's death. I thought of her out in the world doing her work in our daughter's name while I had retreated to my studio, to the false solace of alcohol. "That's one thing you are not.

You're not a coward, Soph." I took her hand. "I didn't know. I should have known."

She leaned her shoulder against mine. "Did you ever think about it, Will? Suicide, I mean."

I thought of that day in July when I'd met Sophie at the beach and how I had stared out at the horizon and felt the seductive pull of knowing how easy it would be to walk into the water and keep walking. But even then I'd known I would never take that road. As I sat next to Sophie on the dock I thought that the surprise wasn't that people commit suicide but that more didn't.

"No."

"Never?" Sophie persisted. "You didn't ever think of it?"

"Not really." *Murder.* I'd thought of murder, of finding and killing the person who took Lucy. Slaying that person. Such a biblical word, *slaying.* Shakespearean.

As if I had spoken, she said, "I read somewhere that suicide is rage and despair turned inward and that murder is the same turned outward." She swirled her toes through the water, scattering the minnows. "Do you think that's true?"

"I don't know." But I did know. I remember the nights I had lain awake thinking that if I ever discovered who had murdered our daughter I could kill that person without hesitation or regret, and I remembered the weapon in the empty paint can in the garden shed. At some point I realized I would have to find a way to dispose of it. "I couldn't have endured it if you died too." My throat burned. "I couldn't stand losing you too."

Both of us knew I was speaking now not of the past but of our future. The yodel of a loon reached us from somewhere in the distance. "Have I, Soph?" I finally dared to ask. "Have I lost you too?" My breath caught, held as I waited for her answer. With the easy effort of a teenager, she stood. Wordlessly, she took my hand, pulled me up beside her. As she led me up the grassy rise to the house, droplets of water from the cove dripped from our feet, marking our path in the August-browned grass as we progressed up the rise, past the Adirondack chairs and blue-painted table, across the wooden porch, through the living room, and up the narrow, age-stained stairs. Into the bedroom. Into her bed. It was only then that I fully let out a breath I hadn't been aware of holding—a long sigh that was the only sound in the room. And then the creaking of springs as we turned to each other at last. We held each other like young lovers, but lovers whose bones held marrow-deep sorrow. We moved slowly as we explored, touched, tasted, as if not only our bodies but the air itself was fragile and a misstep would shatter all.

I entered her, went deep, and knew that joy could be pain too.

CHAPTER THIRTY-FIVE

~

Ever since he recalled where he found the little toy figure doll, Father Gervase had been worrying over the information like an old woman fingering her beads.

Now, as he had for the past three days, he finished breakfast and headed over to Will's studio to deliver this information. Sometime in the night the oppressive heat had at last lifted, and this shift put him in an optimistic mood. He was hopeful that today he would find the artist and could tell him what he remembered about Lucy's little toy and put the whole matter to rest, but when he again found the double doors closed and locked his disappointment was acute, as if he had appeared with a gift carefully wrapped and the recipient was nowhere in sight. After a moment of indecision, he left the harbor and continued over to Fortune Street. The Lights' drive was empty of cars, but still he climbed the wide steps to the porch and rang the bell, recalling as he did the day months before when he had first approached Will about painting the saints—it had been, let's see? May? Yes. May. He remembered it clearly now, a spring day that in the fluid way of time seemed at once far distant and only days past. Well, one season had passed and another edging toward autumn. The priest realized he had reached that stage in life when time spun faster, months passing as if only days, years as weeks. Too fast. As fleeting as a child's giggle eaten by wind. Reluctant to accept defeat, he rang the bell a second time.

"He's not home."

The man in the neighboring lawn shouted over to Father Gervase. The priest looked over and frowned. In spite of the watering ban still in effect that restricted residents to watering lawns on the odd-numbered sides of a street on odd-numbered days and even-numbered houses on the even days, the man was spraying his grass with a hose. He looked vaguely familiar, but Father Gervase was unable to place him, but then his memory, never strong in the matter of faces, had grown more unreliable in this area.

"Do you happen to know when he's due back?" he called.

"Haven't a clue." The man barked a short laugh. "But then I'm not my brother's keeper, am I, Father?"

"Well—" The priest was considering how to respond—aren't we all our brother's keepers?—when he realized the man intended the remark to be some sort of jest. He was able to summon a weak smile. But the mystery of where Will Light was off to remained unsolved. Well, the artist had a perfect right to take time off. Perhaps a vacation. Perfectly his right. Still, the neighbor's remark irked him. He remembered a time when neighbors cared about and watched out for each other. "All right then," he said, but the man had already turned away, back to hosing the lawn.

Back at the rectory, mindful of the need to stay hydrated—the last thing he needed was another fainting episode—he headed directly for the kitchen for a glass of water, where he found Mrs. Jessup busy wiping out the refrigerator shelves.

"Good morning, Father," she said, and she heaved her shoulder in the silent way she had of letting him know he was interrupting her day, an attitude, he now realized, she never adopted with Father Burns and one that tended to make him feel like a tenant on her property.

"Is there something I can get for you?"

"No. No. I'll just get a glass of water, and then I'll get out of your way."

"Here. Let me get it." She poured ice water from a pitcher into a tumbler.

In spite of his promise to leave, he took the glass and sat, a bit concerned that the walk to the harbor and then over to Will Light's house had left him spent. He resolved, in spite of his bad hip, to start up again with the daily walks he'd abandoned during the worst of the heat spell. Beads of condensation rolled down the sides of the tumbler and pooled on the table. Mrs. Jessup swiped them away with a wad of paper towels. His mother had employed a stack of worn tea towels for all such tasks. He refrained from mentioning the wastefulness of paper towels. As he watched her mop up the condensation, his thoughts returned to Will Light. Certainly Will wasn't expected to punch in a time clock or report to him—it wasn't as if the cardinal had hired him for a regular nine-to-five job—but the artist's absence troubled him. Surely he hadn't gone off and given up on the project. The idea of having to face the bishop with that news made him light-headed. And he felt, too, the disappointment at not being able to tell Will where and when he had found his daughter's toy. Probably not important, but he couldn't rid himself of the thought that it might possibly be significant and that he should tell someone.

"Do you remember Lucy Light?" he found himself asking.

"Lucy Light?" she said. "Oh, you mean the child who was murdered. Lord, yes. They never did find out who did it, did they?"

"No."

"That poor, poor family. What a dreadful thing to happen. Absolutely dreadful. I can't imagine it."

Father Gervase didn't want to imagine it and in fact had deliberately tried, not always successfully, to keep any thoughts of Lucy Light's last moments from forming in his mind.

Father Gervase regretted bringing up the subject.

"It is hard to believe though," Mrs. Jessup continued. "I mean, this isn't one of those places where that kind of thing happens."

"No."

"But why did you ask about the girl?"

Unable to stop, he confided in her. "Well, here is the strangest thing. A while back, I found something in the chapel that belonged to the girl. As least, when her father saw it, he was certain it was hers."

"You found it here?" she said. This news caused her to pull a chair out from the table and plop down. "In *our* chapel?"

"Yes. Beneath one of the pews."

"When was this, Father?"

"Back in June. I was working on a homily and had gone there to write. I do that sometimes, and it was cold in there, you know how stone floors can retain the chill, and I remember wishing I had brought a sweater."

"What was it you found?"

"A toy figure. Of Yoda. Then I happened to have it with me when I was visiting with her father. You know he's painting the saints for the new cathedral?"

"Yes," she said. "And he thinks it's hers?"

Father Gervase nodded. "At the time I couldn't remember how it came into my possession, and then several days ago, during the small ceremony for the Medeiros family, I was sitting in the chapel and it came back to me. Since then I've been looking for Will Light to tell him, but he's nowhere to be found."

"But how did the toy—what did you say it was?"

"A little figure of Yoda." He recalled how the toy fit perfectly in the palm of his hand. "You know it? The little Jedi from the *Star Wars* movie."

"Well, how did it end up in the chapel? June, you say? And she was killed in—let's see—the fall it was, wasn't it? September? October?"

"Yes. October."

She went straight to the core of the matter. "Well, you must go tell the police."

"The police?" His voice trailed off. *The police?* The whole thing was spinning out of his control. What on earth had possessed him to confide in Mrs. Jessup?

"Of course."

"Well, I don't know."

"Shall I go with you?"

"With me?" he said, unable to keep the horror out of his voice. "No. No. There's no need of that."

She picked up his empty glass, took a last swipe of the table with the paper towel, and rose. "You should go right now. While it is all clear in your memory." She waited for him to get up.

Feeling bullied into action—Mrs. Jessup was getting to be as bossy as Lena MacDougall—he left for the police station. Recognizing it as a delaying tactic, he detoured by the harbor in hopes that he would find Will, but the building was still closed tight. Behind him, the day boats headed out of the harbor. He sighed in resignation. Might as well get it over with. No doubt Mrs. Jessup would be waiting for his report.

On the way up the steps, he met Michael Callahan exiting the station.

"Father Gervase," the officer said. "What brings you here? Someone stealing pennies from the alms box?"

"Oh no. No," the priest said before he realized that Michael, like Will Light's neighbor earlier that morning, was joking. It pained him to think he was completely losing his sense of humor. "Nothing like that. In fact, it is probably nothing at all, but I thought I should tell someone." Callahan held the door for him. A wave of cooled air bathed him as he entered the lobby. "It's about Lucy Light."

The patrolman's eyes narrowed slightly. "Lucy Light?"

"Yes."

"Wow. You surprised me there, Father. Why don't you take a seat, and I'll notify the detective in charge of her case."

"It's probably nothing," he repeated, but Callahan had already disappeared down a hall. Before he could gather his thoughts, he found himself ushered through the metal gate that separated the lobby from the inner rooms and sitting across a desk from a tired-looking man who introduced himself as Detective Gordon.

"Officer Callahan tells me you have some information about Lucy Light."

The feeling of foolishness increased, and he regretted not waiting until Will had returned from wherever he had gone. Let him decide what to do with this information. "Probably nothing," he said for the third time in minutes. The officer waited in silence for him to continue. In spite of his dry mouth, the priest found himself babbling on about the toy and how he'd first found it and how when Will Light had seen it, he had been convinced it had belonged to his daughter.

Gordon shifted forward in his seat. "And where is it now?"

"Will has it. He took it from me."

"And exactly when did you find it?"

"In June. The first week in June, I think it was." Again Father Gervase was unable to stop the flow of words. "I had gone to the chapel to work on a sermon—one on confronting despair—and saw something under a pew and thought I was seeing a piece of trash. We've had problems with kids using the place. And that's why we keep it locked. Hate to do that, of course. Hate to do that. The idea was to have it available day and night for anyone who might feel the need to sit in a place of prayer. But then we started finding trash in there—" He could not bring himself to mention the used condoms on the floor of the chapel, could barely stand to think of it himself. "And so it is now kept locked."

"I see. And how many people have keys?"

"Well, I have one. And Father Burns. And Wayne Jervis. The part-time custodian. He comes in each Saturday to clean."

"So there are only the three keys?"

"Well, there is one more. We keep it in the rectory office in case Father Burns and I are unavailable and someone wants to use the chapel. You just have to sign the register noting the time you take it and when you return it. We didn't use to bother with that, but we found people would forget to return it, and we would have to have another made up. You know. Over at the hardware store."

"So actually anyone can have access to that key?"

"Well, yes." As the conversation—the interrogation—went on and on, Father Gervase couldn't escape the sense of guilt, as if he had done something wrong, been negligible, which was ridiculous of course. "But as I said, you have to sign out for it."

"So you keep a register?"

"Yes. In the rectory office." He was back on solid ground. "A clipboard with spaces for the date, names, and times."

"I'll need to take a look at that."

"At the register?" Should he refuse?

"Yes."

Was this a matter of privacy for the parishioners? Would he be betraying them to turn over their names to the police? Should he check with someone first? A confusion of questions spun in his head.

The detective waited. "Father?"

"I guess so."

"Give me a minute to finish up here, and I'll drive you over."

A second wave of doubt swept over the priest. Perhaps he should check with someone about giving the register to the police. But who? Bishop Kneeland? No. Best to just go ahead and get it over with.

He was relieved to find Father Burns in the rectory office. When he explained the situation, the younger priest took over and Father Gervase was happy to turn the entire matter over to him.

"No problem. I'll just make a copy of the register pages you need," the younger priest said. "How many weeks do you want to cover?"

Gordon prodded Father Gervase to check his calendar and pin down the exact week of his sermon and when he had gone to the chapel.

"Give me the register for the week before, too," Gordon said. "Just to be sure."

"Right." Father Burns unclipped the pages from the clipboard and carried them to the copying machine. As the machine whirred away, spitting out the two pages, Father Gervase again was struck with doubt about the wisdom of giving the names out. There were seven names.

"Just these?" Gordon asked.

"Yes. It was early in the summer, so we hadn't begun to use it as much as we usually do. For small weddings. Christenings. That kind of thing."

The detective scanned the pages. "And these seven people are the only ones who had access to the chapel during those two weeks?"

Father Burns looked at the page. "Yes. Except for Father Gervase and me, of course. And Wayne Jervis."

"Jervis. You say he's the custodian?"

"Yes. Part-time." Father Gervase watched as Gordon penned in Jervis's name on the list. "He comes in Saturday mornings to do a little maintenance and to clean the chapel."

"Well, that should narrow the time frame for when the object was left there," Father Burns added.

"And the people on this list would all be parishioners?"

"Yes."

Gordon pointed to the last name on the list. "And this one too?"

"Well, the family are parishioners."

"But they aren't regulars," Father Burns said.

Father Gervase stared at the finger still pointing to the last name and was swept by a chill of foreboding.

Duane LaBrea.

CHAPTER THIRTY-SIX

~

"We are looking for Duane LaBrea."

Rain recognized the policemen standing at the door. They were the same two who had questioned her after Lucy disappeared, and then a second time after Lucy's body had been found in the woods at the edge of town.

"We understand you were her best friend," one of them had said, the one who'd made her nervous because he was the kinder and, she had sensed immediately, the smarter one. "We know how best friends tell each other secrets," he had said with a smile that hadn't fooled her for an instant. "We need to know anything Lucy might have told you. Even if you promised not to tell."

"No, nothing," she had lied. She'd thought that would be the end of it. Lucy's secret was safe with her.

Instead, to her amazement, they were now asking for Duane. Even surprised, Rain couldn't contain a smile. What the hell kind of trouble had Duane gotten himself into that brought police to their house? *The police*, for God's sake. So her mother's Golden Boy of the decade, the model for a saint, wasn't so damn perfect after all. Too bad her mother had gone shopping and wasn't here to witness this. But then her mother would probably have ushered the policemen in, offered them coffee, and waited for them to inform her that Duane was receiving some special, fabulous citizen-of-the-year award or something. That was how pathetically delusional her mother was. The only prize Rain could imagine Duane winning was for lamest seventeen-year-old on the planet. In the galaxy. In the universe. "Just a sec," she said and left them on the porch to descend to her brother's basement lair, where he was doing whatever the hell he did down there. Predictably, the door to his room was closed and locked. Apparently their mother didn't have a problem with *him* locking *his* door. Not Duane the saint. Oh, wait. The ex-saint.

"Duane?" She heard music. Something predictable lame. An old Queen album, the volume low per their mother's running order so she didn't have to put up with the noise. "Duane. I know you're in there."

There was a slight rustling on the other side of the door. The music stopped.

"Duane, damn it, open up."

"What do you want?"

"I'll tell you when you open the door."

"Just go away."

"And what? You want me to send the police down here to get you?"

"The what?"

"The police. The cops. There are two of them waiting on the front porch, and they want to see you."

The lock clicked open. Duane wore only a pair of old boxer shorts in a faded pink. Since he started doing his own laundry and no matter how many times their mother told him the correct way to do the wash—another of their mother's rules: *always separate the white clothes from the colored*—his clothes were weird shades of blue or red or, once, purple. There was a crease slashing his cheek where it had been pressed against the pillow. She avoided looking over at his bed. If he'd been down here watching porn and jerking off she sure as hell didn't want to know.

"Police?" His voice cracked like he was twelve. "Here?"

"Right."

"What do they want?"

"Have you gone completely deaf? They want to see you."

"Jesus." He thought a minute, then dropped his voice to a whisper. "Look, tell them I'm not here. Tell them you forgot and I'm at work or you don't know where I am. Okay? Just tell them something."

She wanted to tell him that she wouldn't lie for him, especially not to the police, but he looked so genuinely scared that she caved.

The two policemen hadn't moved from where she'd left them on the front porch.

"He's sleeping." Okay a lie, but not a big fat one. Not a *criminal* one. Definitely landed in the fib category.

"I see," the smaller one said, the one she instinctively was more leery of. "Okay, Rain. We'll wait while you go wake him up."

"You want me to wake him up?" She hadn't planned on their persistence. What the hell had Duane done?

"And if you don't mind, we'll step inside while you get him," said the other one. "Get out of this heat."

"Okay," she said. Though it was most definitely *not* okay. Without her knowing how it had happened, the power had shifted and they were running the show. She wished her dad was home. He'd know how to handle this. She descended to the basement, where she was again met by a closed door.

"Duane. Open the fucking door."

"Did you get rid of them?" Again the conspiratorial whisper.

"I told them you were sleeping."

"And they left?"

"No. They told me to wake you up. They're waiting in the front hall."

He yanked open the door. "Jesus, Rainy."

He hadn't called her that in ages, and suddenly it was like they were again children and had gotten in trouble with their mother. "Why are they here anyway, Duane? What do they want?"

"Shit, I don't know." He pawed through a pile of laundry on the floor and pulled out a pair of khakis. They were badly wrinkled, and there was a smear of chocolate ice cream on the thigh, but he stepped into them anyway. She looked at his concave chest, counted his ribs. When had he gotten so thin? Was he using drugs? Was that why he'd lost weight? Was that what had brought the police to their house?

"You should have told them you didn't know where I am." He pulled on a white polo he wore for work, one with the green Eastern Point Creamery logo embroidered on the breast. He shoved a foot in one yellow Converse, searched under the bed for the other. "This is completely fucked."

"Comb your hair," she said. *Stop looking so guilty.*

"Don't leave me alone with them, okay, Rain?" he said as they climbed the stairs.

"Why?"

"I don't know. I'll just feel better if you're there." Now he was acting like she was the older one, which she would have thought she would like, but it freaked her.

"Okay? Promise?"

"All right," she said in a tone that suggested she was doing him a huge favor. Actually, she had no intention of missing the action. Even though she had let them inside, it was still shocking to see them in the hall, filling the air with their presence.

"Hello, Duane. I'm Detective Gordon, and this is Officer Slovak."

"Hi."

Look them in the eye, Rain wanted to scream. Duane stood there all hunched and nervous and looking guilty as shit.

"We'd like you to come down to the station with us, son."

"The station?" Duane's voice did that twelve-year-old cracking thing again.

"So we can ask you some questions. Clear some things up."

"Jeez. I don't know," he said.

Rain could see she'd have to help him. Obviously. "Our parents aren't home right now." She was surprised by how loud her voice sounded. "I think they'd want him to wait until they are here and can go with him. Him being a minor and all."

The three of them turned and looked at her. Gordon in an appraising glance, the other one, Slovak, clearly annoyed at her interruption, and Duane with a look of such doglike gratitude she was both gratified and annoyed. She wished he would stand the hell up straight. "What is this about anyway?"

The men exchanged a look, and Slovak gave Gordon a what-the-hell shrug, which must have been some kind of signal between them, because Gordon started the questioning right there with no more talk of going down to the station. At least for the moment. He leveled his gaze at Duane.

"Can you tell us the last time you were at the chapel of the Church of the Holy Apostles?"

Rain snickered. Duane? At the chapel? Then she remembered one of the loser dopeheads at school saying it was a place where kids could score. *The locked bedroom door. Duane's thin body.*

"The chapel?" Duane looked confused. "I don't go there."

"Well, that's a little strange, Duane, because we have your signature on the register at the church. The one you have to sign to get the key."

Duane darted a glance at Rain, then looked back at the men. "Oh. Yeah. Right. Yeah. I forgot. I went there a couple of times. During final exams."

He did?

Gordon checked his notepad. "And that would be in June?"

"I guess. Yeah. That's right. June."

287

"Were you there alone?"

Duane shifted his weight, wiped a palm against his thigh. "Yeah. Alone."

"So no one was with you?"

Duh. That's what alone means, cone head. Rain nearly rolled her eyes. "No. I was by myself."

"Okay." He jotted a note on a pad that had appeared as if by magic. "Tell us how well you knew Lucy Light."

The words shot a current through the hall. Lucy's name reverberated. *Lucy Light. Lucy Light. Lucy Light.*

Duane shrank, actually took a step back. He shot another look at Rain, but after the first shock of hearing Lucy's name the significance of the policeman's phrasing hit her. Not *if* Duane knew Lucy, but how *well* he knew her, as if Lucy was his *girlfriend* or something, which was so ridiculous she nearly laughed.

"I knew her better," she blurted. "She was my best friend." Of course they already knew that. *We know how best friends tell each other secrets.*

"We appreciate your help, Rain, but we want your brother to answer our questions." They turned their attention back to Duane.

"We're trying to locate someone who might have had an object that belonged to Lucy," Slovak said. "We're hoping you can help us with this."

"An object?"

"Yes. Something Father Gervase found in the chapel that Lucy's father believes belonged to her. A little plastic figure of Yoda."

"Yoda?"

Rain knew exactly what he was talking about, had seen it in Lucy's bedroom about eight kazillion times. *Feel the force!* Lucy's Yoda voice was so clear it was almost as if she were standing right there in the hall with them. *Patience you must have, my young Padawan!*

"That's right," Slovak said.

"No," Duane said. He swiped his palm against his thigh. "No, I haven't seen anything like that."

Rain had always been able to tell when Duane was lying. He'd make a sucky criminal. The lie was so obvious she was sure the two policemen knew it too.

"That's too bad. We were hoping you could help us out here."

"Yeah. Save us some time," said the fat one, Slovak. "I guess we'll just have to send it off for DNA testing and fingerprints."

Now he was lying. Rain was just a living lie detector. The FBI should hire her. But she could tell by her brother's face that he totally believed the cop.

"I think you should come back later," she said. "When our parents are here."

Slovak opened his mouth to argue, but the other one—Gordon—said okay and, amazingly, just like that, they left. Their departure was so abrupt that she and Duane stood in stunned silence for several minutes.

"He was lying, you know." They were in the kitchen, and Duane was drinking a beer from the six-pack of Coors, his father's drink of choice now that he no longer drank scotch. He popped the tab right there in the open where either of their parents could walk in and catch him, a clear sign of how much the visit from the police had shaken him. "That stuff about the DNA testing and fingerprints. It's a lie."

Duane took a long swallow. Rain knew he had a beer now and then—who didn't—but the way he was sucking it down surprised her. He had the look of someone who intended to swim through the entire six-pack without hesitating to belch. "Do you think they'll really come back?"

"No doubt." Even though she didn't really like the soapy taste of beer, the yeasty smell of it, she reached for the can and took a foamy sip. "So you go to the chapel?"

"I did. A couple of times." He took the can back.

"That's a surprise."

He shrugged.

Once more she pictured his thin frame, the locked door to his room. "So what? Are you doing drugs or something?"

"What?" His voice rose in shock. "Drugs? No. Jesus, Rainy."

"So what was all that about Lucy and Yoda?"

He avoided her gaze. Drank more beer.

"Duane?"

"I had it. Okay? I guess I must have dropped it in the chapel."

"Wait. You had Lucy's Yoda?" Her voice was thick with disbelief.

"Yeah."

"What the hell, Duane? Did you steal it or something?"

"Steal it? From Lucy? Fuck no, Rainy. You think I'd steal from Lucy? Jesus."

"So how did you get it?"

Another long swallow of Coors. "She gave it to me."

"She *gave* it to you?" Rain reached for the nearly empty can.

"Yeah." Duane didn't bother taking it back but retrieved another from the refrigerator. Their mother the detective would know exactly how many were gone, but at the moment that was the least of Rain's concerns.

"Why? Why would she give it to you?"

He shrugged. "What does it matter now?"

"But why?" she persisted.

"Oh, Rainy." He closed his eyes and held the cold can against his forehead. "It wasn't anything. Just forget it. Let it go."

"Bullshit, Duane. Lucy loved that thing. Why would she give it to you?"

"It was kind of a secret, okay?"

"A secret? You and Lucy had a secret?" A sting of betrayal, the heat of jealousy caught her ribs. *Everybody has secrets.*

He started pacing from the table to the far counter, his face scrunched with concentration. "So do you really think those two cops will be back?"

A secret with Lucy? She fought to keep tears from welling. "Of course they'll be back."

"I don't know. Maybe they won't. I told them I didn't have the Yoda. That's all they wanted to know."

"Are you completely stupid, asshole? They could tell you were lying. You're such a shitty liar a blind man living on Neptune could tell."

"What? Are you mad at me now?"

"Dogs get mad, stupid. People get angry," she said in a singsong voice.

"So are you *angry* with me?"

"I wouldn't waste my energy. You know what? I hope they do come back. I hope they come back and drag you down to the station in front of the entire town and then lock you up."

"Lock me up? Jesus, Rainy. Why would they lock me up?"

"You tell me. You tell me why they would lock you up, Mr. Big Shot Secret Keeper."

He stared at her with eyes grown glassy from the two beers. "Jesus, Rainy, what are you thinking?"

"I'm not thinking anything. Should I be?"

"I didn't do anything to Lucy, if that's what you're thinking," he said. "I would never do anything to hurt Lucy."

CHAPTER THIRTY-SEVEN

~

A noise from outside the window woke me.

I was in an unfamiliar bed, and it was a moment before I remembered. Maine. Sophie. I turned and saw her still figure on the far side of the bed. I started to reach across the distance, but before I touched her I stayed my hand, my fingers that still held her scent. *Let her sleep*, I thought. Carefully, I slid out of the bed and descended the stairs. A nearly full moon lit the main room. I threw open a window, inhaled the damp air. I found the yellow plastic-cased flashlight on the table by the door and stepped onto the porch and went down to the dock, guided by the beam of its light and the moon. *Sturgeon moon.* The name came to me from memory's recesses. Once I had known the name of each month's full moon. Names, I corrected myself, for I knew each moon had many names, but I could only remember a single one of those for August. The stillness of night was broken by voices, drunken, I realized after a moment, and arguing, the same ones we had heard the previous afternoon. Suddenly a memory from childhood surfaced, the summer my parents had rented a lakeside cabin in New Hampshire for a week, unusual in itself because they seldom went away. Long before the word *staycation* had been coined, my father had been a proponent. "Why leave home when we have everything we want or need right here?" And yet, this one summer—I had been what? Twelve?—we had taken a cabin. The first night there we had eaten out, another rarity in my family. At the next table sat a family, mother, father, and daughter. The daughter was about my age, but it was the mother who fascinated me. She was tanned and dressed in a sundress with straps as thin as string, and she had struck me as exotic as a movie star. The man initiated a conversation with my father. They were from Ohio, a fact that had surprised me. Such an ordinary setting for the woman. This was their first time east, the man confided. Usually they took a place on Lake Michigan. Not long after we had ordered, the waitress arrived at our table with a bottle of wine. Compliments of that gentleman, she told my father. For a moment, I thought my father would refuse—my parents were not wine drinkers—but then my mother placed her hand on his sleeve and the moment passed. Much later, I woke to the sound of voices cutting through the night just as the ones did there in Maine. The father, clearly drunk, the woman too. And someone crying. The girl, I'd known. And as quickly as that, the scene in the restaurant seemed false. The memory of the dinner tainted. I'd vowed that when I grew up and had a daughter, I would never fight in front of her. Standing on the dock, I allowed myself that brief consolation. Lucy had never heard her mother and me argue.

After a while I returned to the house and replaced the flashlight where I'd found it. When I switched on the lamp on the table Sophie used as a writing desk, I saw the stack of manuscript pages. I reached for them.

The introduction was personal. I hadn't expected that and wasn't prepared for it. Sophie wrote of Lucy's murder, even writing of the day we had both stood and identified her bloodied book bag and ruined cell phone, the morning we had gone to pick out the coffin that would hold her ruined body. I forced myself to continue, reliving the horror, the shock, fighting a sense of violation. The book would be, she wrote, both our personal story and those of other parents of lost children, and an exploration of how our society had become one in which thousands of children disappeared each year or were murdered without an answering and sustained outrage. The first chapter related the story of a couple from Tennessee whose nine-year-old son had been kidnapped and his body found a week later, still dressed in his Little League uniform. The killer was never found. A tonsure-like circle at the top of my skull tingled, grew warm. I swallowed, continued to read the stories. The parents from San Diego. Their daughter had been eighteen when she disappeared, three years older than Lucy, and they continued to hold on to the hope that someday she would find her way home. The circle on my skull grew hotter, tighter. A phrase came unbidden to mind. *I blew my top.* The single mother from Key West whose son was fourteen when he was shot by another boy. Fourteen. Almost Lucy's age. The couple from Utah. Their child was two. Two. Rage spread through my chest like a stain. The buzzing in my head grew to a throb. Unable to endure any more, I dropped the pages and let my head fall into my hands.

"Will?" Sophie's hand was on my shoulder. "Are you all right?"

My rage, the anger that had retreated that summer, slumbering like a junkyard cur in the shadows, came back as hot and piercing as ever, so intense I didn't trust myself to speak.

She stood behind me, drew my head against her belly, still warm from sleep, and cradled it there. "I know. I know," she crooned and swayed, rocking my body. After a few minutes, she withdrew and sat beside me. "I'm sorry, Will. I wanted to tell you more about the book before you read it. Prepare you for it."

I still did not dare speak, swallowed the acridness of anger. Out the window beyond her head, the horizon was showing first light.

She took my silence as a sign to continue. "Some days when I'm writing, I just break down and sob. It is all so unbearably sad."

Usually so intuitive about me, she misread my rage for grief.

"Strangely," she said, "the work consoles me. At least when I'm writing. Of course when I'm done nothing has changed. It doesn't bring her back."

"Then why do it?" I asked, unable to conceal my bitterness.

"I need to know how is it possible that life has become so expendable, our *children's lives*, Will, that we are no longer even shocked when we read or hear of another killing, another child lost. Somehow the value of life has been profoundly cheapened." Her voice grew stronger. "Do you know how many children are murdered every year? Every day? Eight children and teenagers are murdered every day, Will. *Every day.* How could we let that happen? How can we make sense of how this is possible?"

A line from her introduction echoed: *What kind of people have we become?*

"I read somewhere that homicide has become the white noise in our society. We have to face that."

Her hope, her belief that she could change anything rekindled my anger. "And writing this book will change anything?"

She shook her head. "Perhaps not. But if I don't? Will that change anything? What was that old catchphrase? If you're not part of the solution, you're part of the problem."

"So it makes it more bearable then?"

"No. Not that. Never that. But we have to keep telling this truth, Will: violence begets violence."

Violence. My companion for so many weeks. All my dark middle-of-the-night thoughts of vengeance and retribution. The gun I had secreted in the shed.

"We must understand that," she continued. "We must come to grips with that. And there's something else. Talking to other families has made me more connected and less isolated in the grief."

I thought of all those months grief had been a chasm that separated us, not a bridge that brought us closer.

"Remember the story of the mustard seed?"

"Vaguely."

"The man sent in search of a home that has escaped sorrow. You are seeing this too. Think of the people who are posing. The story Leon told you about Louie Johns and the son he lost. Everybody has their share of loss. No one escapes. No protection against loss in this life, Will. It's what we do with the grief that matters. I think that you and I are each in our own way trying to do something good for Lucy's sake."

Lucy.

"I miss her so much," she said. "I never stop missing her. Not for one day. One hour." Her cheeks were wet with all the tears I was unable to shed.

CHAPTER THIRTY-EIGHT

~

Rain would rather walk shoeless over ground glass, step barefoot over fire, than face Dr. Mallory.

I think your dog is going to die. Her only prayer was that the shrink had forgotten what she said when she'd left the last time. Old people forgot all the time. And it wasn't as if Rain didn't have enough on her mind without dealing with this, because right now Duane the Lame, Duane the Once and Former Saint was at the police station where—as the detective said when he'd phoned their house last night—they were going to get to the bottom of how Lucy's Yoda ended up in the church chapel so many months after her death. Acting as if it were some important clue or something when it was just a dumb toy. Still, it was epically stupid of Duane to have lied about it. Earlier, at breakfast, he'd said he didn't want to go to the station. Don't waste your breath, she could have told him. No one is even listening to you. While Duane pushed his spoon around his cornflakes, their father for once stopped being Mr. Passive and said maybe they should contact an attorney. "Don't be ridiculous," their mother snapped. "Why on earth would we drag a lawyer into this? It just makes people look guilty, and Duane hasn't done anything wrong." Clueless as usual. Oblivious. Across the table, her brother had stared at his uneaten bowl of cereal and looked as guilty as the liar he was.

"Won't you tell me what's bothering you, Rain?"

Still, he was her brother. She concentrated on sending thoughts to him, as if by focusing hard enough her unspoken words could protect him. *Stand up straight. Don't look guilty.*

"Rain?"

Maybe her father was right. They should have hired a lawyer.

"Won't you let me try and help?"

Seriously? Like anyone could help. Especially this little shrink. She slipped her hand into the pocket of her shorts. *Shorts.* Not a skirt today. Or even capris. Shorts just long enough to cover her scars. One good thing about whatever trouble Duane was in was that their mother was too preoccupied to be the clothes police. Rain could wear a bikini to Mass and her mother probably wouldn't even notice. Her fingers closed around her Lucky Strike stone, the one Lucy had given her when they had exchanged stones last year and become chosen sisters, members of the Lucky Strike Stone Club. Total membership: two.

"Rain, dear."

"The police came to our house yesterday." The words were out of her mouth before she could stop them. "They were looking for Duane."

"Is your brother in trouble?" Dr. Mallory asked, as calmly as if Rain had told her that Duane woke up that morning and brushed his teeth. *Duh. They didn't show up to give him a medal.* "They wanted to talk to him." Too late, she regretted saying one word about the police and Duane. She should have realized that it would be opening a door best kept shut. Duane was a dweeb, but he was her brother. God, he'd looked so pathetic when they drove off to the police station. The thing was, there was no one to talk to about it. She supposed she could have gone over to see Father Gervase—she knew a priest couldn't tell anyone what you said to him in private—but she remembered Father Gervase was the one who started this by finding and bringing Lucy's Yoda to the police.

He should have just minded his own beeswax. And now, because she couldn't keep her mouth closed, Dr. Mallory knew.

"Rain? Is Duane in some kind of trouble?"

"So," she said. "What I tell you here. It's . . . What do you call it?" She stared at the copper bowl of mints as if the elusive word could be found there. *Confidential.* The word popped in place. "It's confidential, right? I mean you can't tell anyone what I say, right?"

Dr. Mallory considered the question. "I am bound by privacy rules, Rain. Rules that protect what is said in counseling sessions."

"Okay."

"So I'm bound not to divulge what you say, but there are exceptions. In certain circumstances it is permissible to disclose things."

Of course. There was always a catch. "Like what?"

"Well, for instance, if I determine that someone is a danger to others or to themselves. I am obligated to protect the health and safety of others as well as my patients. But anything else I am bound to keep confidential."

"And you can't tell my parents what I say, right? Just because I'm a minor?"

"What is it you want to say, Rain?"

She looked around the room, wondered what would happen if she just got up and left. No one could stop her. Her gaze fell on a leash hanging on the doorknob—Walker's leash, and a rush of shame heated her face. *I think your dog is going to die.*

Dr. Mallory followed her gaze. "He's fine, you know. Walker. He had an obstruction in his intestines, and the vet had to operate, but he's fine. He's coming home tomorrow."

Dr. Mallory's voice was normal, not angry, and Rain knew she should feel relief and couldn't figure out why it would feel better if the shrink had shouted or something. She tightened her fingers around the stone and hoped she wasn't making a huge mistake. "He lied to them," she said. "To the police."

"I see." Dr. Mallory closed her eyes a moment, thought. "Well, I wouldn't think lying to the police is the wisest thing to do."

"Everybody lies." She stared at Dr. Mallory, challenging her to argue the point.

"Tell me more about that, Rain. Why do you think everyone lies?"

"Because they do." Take her mother. She lied all the time. She even lied to herself. And her dad. She thought of the roster of people she knew for a fact had lied. Teachers. Friends. Even that policeman had lied when he told Duane they would send Lucy's Yoda out for DNA and fingerprint testing.

"And by saying 'everybody lies' are you telling me that you think I lie as well?"

Rain shrugged. "Why should you be different?"

"In our times together, Rain, do you believe that I have been untruthful?"

Rain shrugged again. "Well, Duane lied. He lied to the police, and he lied to our parents."

"Do you want to tell me more about that?"

Not especially. But it was like once she started, she couldn't stop. "They asked all these questions about him and Lucy. About how well he knew her, as if Lucy was his *girlfriend* or something."

"And he wasn't?"

Seriously. Lucy and Duane? "No. It's ridiculous they would think that." Maybe by now everyone was back home. Or at work. Duane at the creamery scooping Double Chocolate Chunk Cherry into waffle cones or the pink plastic dishes they had for little kids. Her father pushing papers at the insurance agency. Her mother cleaning or shopping or doing whatever it was she did all day.

"Did they say why they wanted to talk to Duane?"

"Because of Yoda." She told Dr. Mallory about Lucy's little toy and how the priest had found it in the chapel and that they knew Duane had been in the chapel that week and they wondered if he had been the one to drop the toy. "He told them he didn't. But the thing is, he did have it. He lied to them. After they left, when he was freaking out"—an image flashed of Duane standing in the kitchen sucking down beer—"he told me he did have it. He said Lucy *gave* it to him."

"And do you think that is true?"

"Why would Lucy give it to him? It was one of her favorite things." She slipped her hand into the pocket of her shorts and tightened her fingers around the stone, the stone that signified she and Lucy had been chosen sisters. "I mean, she barely even talked to him."

"Did you ask him that, Rain?"

"He said it was a secret."

"I see."

"Between him and Lucy. But I don't know how he would have a secret with Lucy. I mean, they barely talked."

"And if they did have a secret, would it hurt to think Lucy might have a secret she didn't tell you?"

"Everyone has secrets," she said in the same flat voice she had said everyone lies. That was what the policeman had said last October when Lucy disappeared.

"And your friend Lucy had secrets?"

She caught her bottom lip between her teeth, said nothing.

"Secrets are curious things, Rain. There are secrets that are benign, even fun. Like surprise parties and gifts."

Rain thought to when she was little and she and Duane had saved up to buy their mother a bracelet for Christmas. And the party she and her mother had planned to surprise Duane when he was ten. *I know I can trust you not to tell Duane*, her mother had said. *So he will be surprised.*

"Sweet secrets," Mallory said. "Things you only tell your best friend about." Lucy climbing into the front seat of Jared Phillips's green Jeep.

"Like boys you have a crush on," Mallory continued.

As if the little shrink knew the first thing about crushes. She probably didn't even have a date when she was in high school. It remained a complete mystery to Rain why the tall, good-looking man she had seen in the photo in the shrink's kitchen would have married her. And anyway, Lucy didn't have a crush on Jared. He only wanted to ask her something. *Don't tell. Okay?* Lucy had said. *I don't want my parents to worry. Because of Jared's reputation. And that accident where a girl died. But he's really a good person. A good person who made a bad mistake.* That was Lucy. Seeing the best in everyone. And that was Lucy too. Not perfect. Even telling a fib to her parents so they wouldn't know she was breaking her promise not to ride with Jared.

"And then there are secrets that are not benign, that can make us ill or warp our history."

Rain thought about the razor taped to the underside of her bureau drawer. But Lucy's secrets weren't that kind. Lucy's secrets were the ones she kept for other people. Like whatever it was Jared wanted to ask her the day she went with him. Or what Gabi Russell told her in the girls' room. Secrets she wouldn't even tell Rain.

They'd just finished third-period geometry and only had study period before lunch. They always sat together in the library, sitting at the same table by the window overlooking the center courtyard. Rain hadn't finished her take-home quiz for World Geography and was working on that when Lucy got up. "Be right back," she whispered. "Got to go to the girls' room." Rain wouldn't have thought anything about it, but as soon as Lucy left, Gabi Russell got up and followed her. Gabi was always trying to butt her way into whatever she and Lucy were doing, even though she was a grade ahead of them. *Get your own friends*, Rain always wanted to tell her. She returned her attention to the quiz, answered two more questions, waited for Lucy to return. She fiddled with her pen, flipped back in the text to find another answer, like it would ever matter in her entire life if she knew the leading crops of Ecuador. She shoved the quiz in her notebook and got permission to go to the bathroom. Mrs. Shepley was substituting for the regular school librarian, who would never have let them leave without grilling them first and then checking the clock every minute until they returned. She swung the door open, glanced around the empty room, and was about to leave when she heard someone crying. She followed the sound to the last cubicle. Gabi saw her first and clammed right up.

"Hi," Lucy said, as if it were perfectly normal to hole up in a toilet stall with a sobbing girl.

Later, at lunch she had asked Lucy, "What was that all about?"

"What?"

"Gabi. What was she crying about?"

"Oh, some personal problem," Lucy said.

"Like what?"

"I promised not to tell," Lucy said.

"Not even your best friend?" Rain teased.

Lucy had changed the subject.

In Dr. Mallory's office, Rain looked at the clock on the top of the bookcase. By now Duane and her parents must be on their way home. And even if the police didn't believe him about Lucy's Yoda, they couldn't prove anything.

"Are you worried about Duane, Rain?"

The fear that had been stirring beneath her ribs since the day before when the police arrived at their door to speak to Duane came out in a rush. "I'm afraid they might think he had something to do with what happened to Lucy."

"Do you?"

"No." But she kept seeing Duane, standing in the kitchen, sucking down beer and saying too insistently, *I didn't hurt her, if that's what you're thinking. I would never do anything to hurt Lucy.*

CHAPTER THIRTY-NINE

~

Although I had only been gone three days, our house had the staleness of a place shuttered and unoccupied.

I set my bag on the floor and walked from room to room, throwing open windows, letting in fresh air. It was not until after I'd showered, shaved, and changed and was back in the kitchen that I noticed the message light blinking on the phone. I pressed the message button and was so sure it was Sophie—who else would call? I hadn't gotten a message from anyone else in months—that it took a moment to recognize Father Gervase's voice. I erased it before hearing why the priest was phoning, knowing I wasn't up to yet another directive from the bishop, if that was his purpose. The second message was Father Gervase again, and again I hit the erase button, but when I heard the next voice on the machine, my finger, poised above the pad, froze.

"Mr. Light? Will? This is Dan Gordon. Would you please return my call when you get this message? I can be reached at the station house." He left the number.

Strength left my legs, and I sank into a chair. It could be anything. Anything. But I knew it wasn't. My finger trembled as I punched in the number. Gordon picked up on the second ring.

"Thanks for getting back to me."

"I was away for a few days."

"Yes, if you're going to be there for a bit, I'd like to stop by."

"Now?"

"When it's convenient."

"What's going on?"

"We have a new development around your daughter's face."

Lucy's face? I pictured the last time I had seen her. In the funeral home, before they lowered the lid on her casket. "Lucy's face?"

"Her case, Will. A new development in the case."

A new development. After all this time. I swallowed against the sour taste of coffee that rose to my throat, coffee I'd had with Sophie at dawn before I left Maine. "I'll be here," I said. While I waited for him, I debated whether or not to call Sophie but decided to wait until I learned what Gordon had to say.

He looked older, more tired than the last time I'd seen him.

"You said you have a new development?"

"Yes. Of course, it could mean nothing."

He wouldn't have called or be sitting there if it were nothing.

"Father Gervase called us. He said he'd been trying to reach you, and when he couldn't, he came to us."

I remembered the messages on the machine from the priest that I had erased. "I just got home and haven't had a chance to return his calls. What's going on?"

"He told us he found something in the chapel that he gave to you, something you believe belongs to your daughter. A toy figure."

Lucy's Yoda. "Yes. Yes, he did. But he couldn't remember when or how he found it."

"Yes. Well, apparently sometime during the past couple of days, he remembered. I'd like to take a look at it. If you still have it."

If I still had it? Of course I had it. It was *Lucy's.* I climbed to her room, slowly, as if scaling a mountain. I opened the door and glanced at the shelf, half expecting to find an empty spot where I'd placed it, as if it had all been a dream, but there it was. I cupped it in my hand, took a minute to steady myself before I descended.

"And you are sure this is hers?" Gordon said when I handed it to him.

"Absolutely." I pointed to the bottom of one of the little reptilian feet. "See here, those three *L*s—that is a mark Lucy made to put on things. Like a brand. I know absolutely that this is hers."

Gordon ran a finger over the looped letters. "Do you have any idea how it might have ended up in the chapel?"

"I didn't even realize it was missing from her room."

"So as far as you know your daughter didn't give it to one of her friends."

"No. No. Of course not. Why? Did someone say Lucy did?"

Gordon didn't answer the question. "And neither you nor your wife gave it to anyone?"

"No. This isn't making sense."

Absently, Gordon ran his thumb over the inscribed Ls. "As it turns out, a boy from the high school admitted that he had it. He said he must have dropped it when he was in the chapel. He said Lucy gave it to him."

That couldn't be true. Why would Lucy give her Yoda to anyone? "Who?"

Gordon didn't answer straightaway. "At this point, this person, this boy is only someone who knew your daughter and had this."

"Who is it?"

Gordon studied him, considered the question. "You understand, Will, we are only trying to sort things out here. As far as we know, the boy has done nothing wrong."

"Who is it?"

"Duane LaBrea."

"Duane?" I pictured the boy. Thin, lost, vulnerable.

"Did your daughter talk about him? Did they spend time together?"

I searched my memory. I couldn't even remember seeing them together except that time Duane had driven both Lucy and Rain home. "No. I can't even recall her mentioning him."

"So they weren't involved?"

Involved? "No."

"Is there a chance they might have been friends and you weren't aware of it?"

"No. We would have known. Lucy told us everything."

An expression I couldn't read crossed Gordon's face. "Not always," he said. "It's normal for kids Lucy's age to have a few secrets."

Not Lucy, I thought. *Not our Lucy.* "Duane told you that Lucy gave it to him?"

"Well, not initially. When we first questioned him, he denied it, but the second time we spoke to him, he admitted he had dropped it in the chapel." Gordon held out the toy. "So you have no idea why he would have had this?"

I stared at it. "None," I said flatly, and then a thought occurred to me. "Unless—"

"What?"

"Maybe Lucy gave it to Duane's sister, Rain, or something. They were friends. That's the only thing I can think of." But even as I said this, I realized it didn't make sense. Why wouldn't Duane just tell the police that? Why would he say Lucy had given it to him? Why would he lie about having it?

"Well, I guess that's it." Gordon rose.

"That's it?" I got up, a beat behind and let down that the new development had not been more significant.

"For now. Let us know if you or your wife remember anything. I'll stay in touch."

"Sure."

After Gordon left, I picked up the phone to call Sophie but set the handset down before I even began to dial. The coffee and conversation we'd shared at dawn, our lovemaking—for that was what it had been, tender and urgent and deep—all that felt as if it had happened in a dream. I needed some time to think about the information from Gordon. My portfolio was still on the table where I'd set it earlier. I opened it and flipped through the drawings until I came to the rendering of Saint Sebastian, remembering the day Duane had come alone to the studio and agreed to pose. *Why me?*, he had asked. *I see a vulnerability and a strength*, I had replied. *That's exactly what Lucy said.* That's what Duane had told him. *Exactly what Lucy said.* I had let it slip right by, hadn't paid attention.

It hit me then, something so obvious I wondered why I hadn't realized the significance of this before. Lucy would never have gone off into those woods with someone she didn't know. Someone she didn't know and trust. Never.

CHAPTER FORTY

~

Duane was off scooping ice cream at the creamery.

Rain crouched at the head of the basement stairs, close enough to eavesdrop on the conversation in the kitchen.

"The police are making a big deal out of nothing," her mother said.

"It was a mistake for him to have lied to them, Beth."

"What? Are you taking their side now?"

"Of course not. I'm just saying he shouldn't have lied to them."

"It's ridiculous. So he had Lucy's Yoda. That's no crime. The girl gave it to him."

"But what was he thinking? To lie to the police like that."

"Oh, for heaven's sake. Obviously, he didn't want to get involved. That's all."

"I don't know. Maybe it wouldn't be such a bad idea to talk to an attorney."

"That's your great idea? Get a lawyer? Do you even know how much they charge?"

"Oh, for Christ's sake, Beth."

"And it will just make it look like he has something to hide. Duane has nothing to hide, and we shouldn't run around acting like he does.

Like he has some big guilty secret or something. If we get a lawyer for anything it should be to sue the police for harassment."

Rain shifted her weight on the step. That was her mother. The Queen of D-Ni-Al. That was all she knew about her precious Duane. She slipped down the stairs and crossed to her brother's room, tried the handle, found it locked. Knowing Duane, he had stashed the key somewhere close by. She slid her fingers along the top of the doorframe. Nothing. So not in an obvious place. But where? Overhead, she heard the scrape of chairs against the kitchen tiles, the creak of the floor, the closing of the back door. Silence. Then her mother calling her name. What had she expected to find in Duane's room anyway? The answer to his dark secret? She should have forced him to tell her, should have kept at him until he gave in, but they'd only had a minute or two to talk before he left for work.

"You should have heard them, Rainy," he'd said. "They kept asking me about Lucy and that toy, and I thought about what you had said about them knowing I was lying, and so finally to shut them up I told them the truth, that Lucy had given it to me. I thought that would make them stop, but it didn't. I swear, they think I had something to do with what happened to Lucy."

"I don't understand, Duane. Why would she give her Yoda to you?"

"Cripes, I wish everyone would just forget about the fucking Yoda. I'm sorry I ever saw it." He yanked off his shirt, pulled a clean one out of a drawer.

Rain stared at his back, so thin she could see his spine, his winglike shoulder blades, and again wondered if he was doing drugs. He seemed a stranger to her. "I mean, it's not like you were friends or something. Why would she give it to you? Tell me that."

He avoided her gaze. "I can't—I can't tell you, Rainy."

She narrowed her eyes, considering, combing her memory of any-time she had seen Lucy even having a conversation with Duane. "Okay," she said. "I'll trade secrets." She shoved her hand into the pocket of her shorts and took out the Lucky Strike stone. "Lucy gave me this and I gave her one of mine and we swore to be sisters. Chosen sisters. That was our secret. Now I told you. You tell me what yours is."

Duane pulled on his clean shirt. "Christ, I'm going to be late for work. I'll probably get fired."

"Duane? Come on. Just tell me." She knew she was begging, sounded like a little girl, but she couldn't help it.

"I can't, Rainy. It's private, okay? Just forget it, will you?"

She stared at the locked door. There were about three thousand places he could have hidden a key. She could spend all day down there and she probably wouldn't find it, and even if she did, did she think Duane's *private* secret was stashed in his room somewhere? It was hopeless.

"Rain?" Her mother's voice floated down the stairs.

It's private, okay? She thought about what Dr. Mallory had said about secrets. Good ones. What did she call them? Benign ones. And harmful ones. Ones kept for the right reasons and ones kept for the wrong reasons. She wondered what kind her brother had.

"Rain?" her mother called again.

She thought of a game she and Lucy used to play when they were much younger. They would close their eyes and pretend to be invisible. She wished she could be invisible now. Just disappear. For the first time in days, she thought about the razor taped to the bottom of her bureau drawer. She climbed the stairs, stopping at the top to look back one last time at her brother's locked door.

CHAPTER FORTY-ONE

~

I did not hesitate.

It was as if I had been sleepwalking all summer and now had been shocked awake. My mind was clear, clearer than it had been in months with no doubt or indecision. Looking back now from this distance it seems like insanity, and I suppose in a way it was, but that day it seemed reasoned. I never thought of the consequences as I walked to the shed and retrieved the gun. Soon one year would have passed since the day Lucy left the house for school never to come home, leaving a hole that couldn't be filled. The abyss. Like a vital organ that had been removed from the center of my being—a crater occupying the center and one, I knew, that would soon grow larger. The weapon was where I had hidden it in the paint can in the shed.

There was a line at the takeout window at the creamery. Even now, and in spite of all that was to come, I remember that clearly. The line at the window that snaked along the front of the building. Off to the side of the lot, families gathered at the several picnic benches placed on the grass: a family of five; a mother with a double-wide stroller that held twins; a father wiping melted ice cream from his young daughter's chin. *Families*, I thought. The word was a bitterness on my tongue, as was the knowledge that my family was forever gone, taken from me in one evil act. I shut off the engine and waited, watched and waited. I didn't allow myself to think. To think of Sophie at that moment, of the days we had just spent, that last night of love, would weaken me. And to consider the future, the consequences of what I had to do didn't bear thinking of. There was only the present. Only what I had to do. Minutes passed. An hour. Cars came and went around me. Finally the door opened, and the boy in yellow high-tops walked out. I rolled down the window and called.

He turned, came toward my car. "Hi, Mr. Light."

"Hi, Duane." Purple-tinged shadows rimmed his eyes, as if he had not slept. Or was ill. "Hop in."

Duane set his hand on the passenger-side handle, hesitated only a minute. Had Lucy hesitated that final day? Had she sensed anything wrong?

"Come on. Hop in. I'll give you a ride."

He opened the door. So unsuspecting. Trusting. Just as Lucy had trusted.

I drove down Main Street, along the way to the harbor and my studio, Duane slouched in the seat beside me. "Where are we heading?" he asked as I drove past the studio barn.

I didn't answer. I drove on, on to Dogtown, to the woods where my daughter had been killed, her body left to decay. *Murder is rage turned outward*, Sophie had said over the weekend. Just one day ago. Another lifetime ago. When I had still believed it was possible to go on. I was relieved to see there were no other cars in the parking lot, an unpaved square carpeted with pine needles. I switched off the engine.

"So I understand you told the police that Lucy gave you her Yoda," I said. The boy shot me a look, and I saw the guilt in his eyes and any last doubt disappeared. "I was wondering why she would do that. Why would she do that, Duane?"

"I don't know."

"She loved it. Her mother gave it to her. Did she tell you that?" In the distance a dog barked. I wondered if someone else was in the woods. I remembered that it had been a person walking his dog who had found Lucy. "So I'm just wondering why she would give it to you."

The boy stared down at his sneakers. The top of one was smudged with chocolate. "For strength," he said after a minute. "She said it would give me strength."

The sun had disappeared behind a cloud, and the smell of peat, of decay floated through the car window. The last earthly odor Lucy would have smelled. "Why? I need to know why."

"Why she thought I needed strength?"

"Yes." The gun was heavy in my pocket. I was calmer than you would ever imagine you could be, the calmness born of certainty of what I must do. *What are we capable of?* I had wondered that back in the spring when I'd first looked at the paintings of the saints in Father Gervase's book. *What*, I had mused, *if tested, what would I be capable of?*

"I just want to know what Lucy ever did to you?"

"Did to me? Nothing. Nothing. I swear."

It was satisfying to hear the fear in the boy's voice.

CHAPTER FORTY-TWO

~

Everyone has secrets.

Rain collapsed on her bed and tried to figure out what to do. She'd made a promise to Lucy she wouldn't tell anyone that she had gone for a ride with Jared Phillips. It had seemed harmless enough when she made the promise. (They had been in her bedroom, sprawled on the bed and idly making plans for the weekend with no idea of what that weekend would hold.) After Lucy was killed, she'd continued to keep the secret because she didn't want to upset Mr. and Mrs. Light any more by letting them know Lucy had ridden in Jared's car when she wasn't supposed to. Now it didn't seem so clear. She didn't think it was *really* important. It wasn't like Jared had anything to do with Lucy's disappearance any more than Duane did. He was vice president of the student council for God's sake, and wasn't that a sign he had totally changed from the reckless boy who had been responsible for the deadly accident? But still the burden of the secret was heavy. Maybe if she told now, there would be one less secret to weigh on her and, it occurred to her, it would also deflect some of the attention from Duane. Rain fastened her eyes on the stain in the ceiling as if the answer could be found there. *Won't you let me try to help?* Dr. Mallory's words echoed, but Rain didn't see how she could help. She traced the brown sprawl of stain that ran from the corner above the window in toward the light fixture, the result of an ice dam over the winter. The icicles hanging from the gutter had seemed harmless (like secrets) until water leaked through her ceiling. *Won't you let me try to help?* It took a minute to find the card, and she let another few minutes pass before she keyed the number on her cell.

"Hello?"

"Dr. Mallory?"

"Yes."

"It's Rain."

"Hello, Rain."

"I was wondering if—"

"Yes. Go on, dear."

"If I could ask you something. It's about what we talked about. About secrets." As soon as she spoke the words she could feel the burden lifting, lifting, lifting.

At one time she could have walked to Lucy's home blindfolded. They'd practically lived at each other's houses, but she hadn't been there since a couple of days after Lucy disappeared, and it was strange to be back. Even the front porch felt different in some way she couldn't identify, as if the house itself were mourning. There were no cars in the driveway, and no one answered the door when she rang. She sank down on the top step and tried to decide how long she should wait. Now that she was there and had time to think it over, she wondered if she should have come. *You overreact*, her mother was always saying. *You're such a drama queen*, Duane accused. Well, she was not the one who'd been dragged down to the police station, was she?

A cricket hopped onto the bottom step and landed near her sandal. Her mother would step right on it, wipe it out before it could get into the house and drive everyone nuts with the chirping, but Rain found the sound cheerful. Her grandfather had told her crickets were considered omens of good fortune in China, and for that reason royal households kept them in cages, like pets. She leaned forward, wrapping her arms around her knees, and studied the insect. Such an odd, prehistoric-looking creature. She stared as it hopped off the step and into the grass, and her thoughts turned back to her conversation with Dr. Mallory. *We always feel better when we do the right thing.* But it was figuring out the right thing that was difficult. And then having the courage to do it. As mad as she was at Duane for his secret with Lucy, she believed him when he said he would never hurt her. He needed her help, and she would start by telling Lucy's parents everything she could, and she hoped they wouldn't be angry with her for not coming to them earlier. Courage. Like the writer Isak Dinesen. She would help Duane, she just wasn't sure what the next step would be.

The banging of a door startled her. She looked up and saw the man coming out of the house next door. Mr. Hayes. Payton, he had told her that day he had given her a ride, had saved her from Jervis the Pervis. It was clear then what to do. Mr. Hayes was a lawyer. Hadn't her father said perhaps they should get a lawyer for Duane? That would be a first step. She unwrapped her arms from around her knees and sat up. "Hi," she called.

"Hi, Rain. What brings you to the neighborhood?"

"I'm waiting for Mr. and Mrs. Light. Do you know when they're coming home?"

"I would guess they should be back soon," he said and smiled his killer smile, the one that made her wish she had worn something prettier than her old cutoff jeans and done something with her hair.

"Oh. Well, maybe I'll wait then."

"I guess it's been a while since you've visited them. I used to see you and Lucy playing badminton in the backyard."

"Really?" She was flattered that he remembered. She used to notice him too, playing hoops in the driveway by himself, dribbling the ball up and down the drive, twisting in for layups. She'd always had a tiny crush on him, although that was one secret she'd kept from Lucy.

"So why do you want to see the Lights?"

She noticed that the basketball hoop was no longer above the garage door. The window shades were lowered against the heat of the day. "I just remembered something Lucy told me before she—you know—before she was gone. A secret, and I think I should tell them."

"Oh?"

She tucked her feet in close to the step. At least she had shaved her legs. They still shone with the lotion she had smoothed on earlier. "Mr. Hayes—"

"Payton. Please. This 'mister' business makes me feel like my father."

"Payton." The name felt awkward on her lips. "Well, I was wondering if I could ask you something. It's something about Lucy."

"Sure." He studied her for a minute. "Listen, it's hot out here. Why don't you wait at my place? I'll get you a glass of soda, and you can tell me what's on your mind."

The kitchen was spotless except for a pile of paperwork on the little table. "It's nice and cooler in here," she said.

He checked the refrigerator. "Pepsi all right?"

"Just water would be great." Alone with him, she wasn't sure what to do. Sit? Stand? She nodded toward the papers on the table. "My dad does his bills in our kitchen too."

He handed her the glass. "Here you go."

"Thanks." She took a sip.

"So what is it you wanted to ask me?"

"What?"

"About Lucy. What was your question?"

He came closer to her. The water tasted metallic in her mouth, and she wished he would move back, out of her personal space. "Respect your personal space," Miss Laurant had told them in health, a mandatory class for all the sophomore girls that was totally stupid with the PE teacher talking about how to prevent getting pregnant, as if anyone over ten didn't already know stuff like that. Janice Linski had been excused from the class because her parents objected to the sex education part of the course curriculum, but everyone knew it was really because Miss Laurant was lesbian and Janice's parents protested against things like that. Of course last year the girls who got pregnant had all taken health, which just went to show how epically pointless it was. Miss Laurant had also lectured them about something she called Owning Your Own Power as a Woman. "If something feels wrong, some situation or person, don't ignore this feeling," she had said. "Learn to trust yourself. Always trust your instincts." She had said that often people explained away their gut feelings as foolish. Rain heard the echo of those words now, although she didn't know why—he hadn't *done* anything wrong—but it felt wrong, the way he was looking at her, the way he was standing too close. But he was an ordinary neighbor, for fuck's sake. A person Lucy used to babysit for, the kind of man her mother would flirt with. *Still.* There was nothing she could exactly name, but the gut feeling persisted. She regretted coming inside. She set the glass of water on the table and moved back.

"Can I get you something else?"

"Could I—could I use your bathroom?"

He hesitated, his smile slipping for only a moment, and then nodded. "Sure. It's down that hall. Last door on the left. Right past the bedroom."

Once in the powder room, she locked the door, leaned against it. Alone, her fears seemed foolish. She waited a few minutes and then flushed the toilet in case he was listening. She was being a baby. Completely paranoid. She was just not used to being alone with a man. *I used to see you playing badminton.* So he'd watched them. The thought made her feel funny but in a good kind of way, like when one of the men who sat on the benches by the harbor whistled when she walked by. She turned on the faucet and washed her hands, studied her features in the mirror, her ragged hair, her too-high forehead, trying to see what he might find attractive. Okay, so it was totally wrong to snoop, but she opened the mirrored cabinet, checked the contents, all so ordinary they mocked her fears. A box of Band-Aids, mouthwash and toothpaste—a brand that whitened, she saw and made note to buy some—a container of shaving cream, razor, aftershave. English Leather. She opened the cap, sniffed it. Although she wanted to, she resisted the urge to dab some on her wrists and replaced it on the shelf. She pulled open a drawer on the small vanity and saw a box of tampons, something the wife must have left behind when they got divorced. Or a girlfriend. A man so good-looking must have a girlfriend. She was taking too long, she knew, and he would wonder what she was doing. She closed the drawer and unlocked the door. On her return to the kitchen, she passed the bedroom, paused to take a look. The bed—a king-size bed that practically took up the entire room—was neatly made. She liked that. That he was not messy. Some men, if their wives left them, would let the house go downhill, dust everywhere, dirty dishes in the sink, yellowed sheets on the bed. Her father, for instance, didn't even know where her mother kept the vacuum. The closet door was partially open, and she saw a row of shirts hanging neatly. She pictured him in the morning cleaning the house and at night making dinner for himself, and she wondered what he liked to eat. And if he drank. Probably something like wine. Imported. She thought of him sitting at a table, imagined herself sitting opposite him, raising her wine glass. There would be candles on the table. Again she wondered if he had a girlfriend. The unease she had felt earlier disappeared. She had been being silly.

"Hey, Rain? You okay?"

"Coming," she called back. Shit. He'd think she'd died or something. She turned to go and caught sight of something on the surface of the bureau. She drew a sharp breath. Of course she was mistaken. It was a trick of light. From across the room it was easy to be mistaken. But as if pulled by a magnetic force, she entered the room, crossed to the bureau, picked up the stone.

"Looking for something?" He stood in the doorway.

"Where did you get this?" She held out her hand.

His mouth twisted in a smile that was not a smile. "Didn't anyone ever tell you it isn't polite to snoop around other people's rooms?"

"Where did you get this?" she asked again. She held her arm toward him, her palm upheld holding Lucy's Lucky Strike stone, the stone that contained the tears of the Apache women hiding in a cave. It was a mistake; she saw this at once. She should have pretended nothing was wrong. Rain glanced around the room, but there was no other way out except through the door that he was blocking.

"Where did I get it?" His voice was high, mimicking. "You're just like her. Meddling in where it is no concern of yours. You girls should learn to mind your own business."

He had changed right in front of her eyes. Turned into someone else. Something ugly. How could she have ever thought he was good-looking? She needed to make him stop talking. If he didn't tell her any more, she would be able to leave. She forced herself to be calm. Casually, as if it were no more than a beach pebble taken from the shore, she turned and put the stone back on the dresser. "It's pretty. I was just wondering what kind it was. My grandfather used to know all about the different kinds of stones."

It was too late. She understood that at once. He came toward her. Came for her. She stepped back until the bureau pressed against her spine. Her throat closed against a swift and fierce desire. She wanted her mother. Her mother who once could make things right, who had held her when she had nightmares or scraped her knee. But she was alone with no one to protect her. She remembered then a story she had heard on the news about a man, a convicted murderer, who had escaped from prison and had broken into a house looking for drugs. Somewhere in the South it had been. And a woman had been home alone and he had taken her hostage. He was going to kill her, and she had prevented him from doing so by reciting the Lord's Prayer.

"Our Father," Rain began.

CHAPTER FORTY-THREE

~

As Father Gervase left Rose Manor, he reflected, as he often did after these visits, about how very much the patients wanted to talk about their pasts, histories that in the telling assumed a surprising vitality and importance, more alive than the present.

Just this afternoon, after she had taken Communion, Mrs. Carlotto, now blind and confined to bed with the latest in a series of shattered bones, the pelvis this time, had kept him at her bedside talking, stories he had heard before of her days as a nursery school teacher. Staring with cloudy eyes into a place only she could see, she spoke animatedly about her students as if only yesterday she had stood in the classroom writing on the chalkboard. "Memories are all I have left," she had told him one day. "The thing is, I only remember the good ones." Father Gervase wondered if that were true, that unpleasant recollections faded. He hoped it was so, although it was his experience that the sins of his past, the disappointments and losses, remained as vivid as ever. The sins of commission and those of omission. It was the sins of omission that troubled him now. He thought of all the parishioners he had failed mightily over the years. And of course he thought of his one profound failure beside which all others faded. To understand forgiveness, his mentor had said, it was first necessary to forgive ourselves. Had he? Was it possible to forgive himself for failing Cecelia? His one big secret sorrow. *The secret sorrow the world knows not.* Who said that? Longfellow? Yes, he was pretty sure it was Longfellow.

"Hello, Father."

Deep in thought, struggling to recall the poet's full quote—he had known it once, but that was so true of many things now lost—Father Gervase did not hear the greeting. He limped along, the hip again paining him, his breath short as it was so often now. A half a block later, as often happened when he stopped struggling to pull something up from the depths of memory, the entire line rose up. *Every man has his secret sorrows which the world knows not; and often times we call a man cold when he is only sad.* And wasn't it the greatest misunderstandings, he thought, that came from our inability to see the grief hidden in the heart of another, to mistake it for anger or pride or coldness? He knew full well that each person carried a personal history of sorrow locked away in the chambers of the heart, burdens that bent one to their weight. Perhaps there was a homily that could come out of these musings. Something about the loss that was the human condition. Something about whatever our doubts or differences or inability to see into each other's hearts, our job was to love. But even as he considered these thoughts, they drifted away. He had grown tired of preparing sermons. Of preaching words that changed nothing. He passed the hardware store and saw Harold Weaver come out with a pole to roll up the awning before closing for the day. He continued toward Will Light's house.

He would not fail Will again. He had seen the danger the very first time he had gone to Will's house with the bishop's request and knew it was not too much to say the man's soul was at risk.

As he turned onto Prospect Street, he saw in the distance a girl walking from the Lights' house to the one next door. It took him a moment to place her. The LaBrea girl. She was walking up the steps to the home of the man he had watched flouting the watering restrictions during the worst of the drought. Rain LaBrea, he thought. From the back, she looked so like his sister. Not the hair—cropped so short while Cecelia's had been long—but the set of her shoulders, her gait, and the sight of her pulled the breath from his lungs. He remembered another day, a summer day much like this one when Cecelia had walked with another boy, climbed into a car while he watched. He hadn't called to her even though the instinct to had been strong. And later, it didn't matter how many people told him it wasn't his fault, that accidents happen and he wasn't to blame, he knew he should have stopped her from getting into the car. Why hadn't he? What had held him back? The question that had haunted him to this moment. His job had been to watch out for his sister. And at that he had failed.

But the LaBrea girl was not his sister. He was overlaying one distant memory onto this instant. He stood on the sidewalk and stared at the house she had disappeared into, paralyzed with indecision. If he followed his instinct and knocked on the door, what would he possibly say? He would risk appearing foolish. A meddling old man. Better to mind his own business.

And yet. And yet.

"Do not decide," Saint Ignatius had preached. "Discern. Discern what God is calling us to do. Follow the holy desire."

A wave of dizziness took him, clouding his mind.

CHAPTER FORTY-FOUR

~

"Our Father," Rain said.

The man was talking to her, rambling on and on, and Rain tried not to listen. She forced herself to continue. "Who art in heaven . . ."

He took a step into the room.

"Hallowed be thy name." She forced her voice to be calm, to go slow.

He took another step forward.

She moved to one side, her back still against the bureau. She raised a hand to brace herself and felt the stone, Lucy's Lucky Strike stone. She closed her fingers around it.

"Thy kingdom come . . ."

"'The Lord made of me a sharp-edged sword.'"

They both turned toward the door. "Father Gervase," she whispered.

"'And concealed me in the shadow of his arms,'" the priest intoned.

The man dropped his hands, confused.

"Let her go," Father Gervase said.

For years after, Rain would remember this scene. Standing by the bureau, reciting a prayer she had known since childhood, Lucy's stone clutched in her hand, the man, Payton Hayes, coming toward her.

Father Gervase, so much shorter than the man was, yet standing tall in the door, his hand reaching toward the man, his voice so big. *Let her go.*

"Go on, Rain," Father Gervase said in the voice not his. "Go on now. Leave the house."

Hayes froze in indecision.

"Go," the priest told her.

Rain slipped past the man, past Father Gervase, and ran down the hall, her shoulders braced for the hand that would surely grab her any second. She reached the kitchen—the clean and deceiving kitchen—and wrenched open the door.

She heard the echo of the priest's voice as she escaped from the room, ran from the house.

CHAPTER FORTY-FIVE

~

What stopped me?

His hands. I stared at his hands, needing them to hold the answer I had sought through the past months, wanting to wring the answer from them just as his hands had twisted Lucy's sweet throat, bloodying her face. They lay, palms up, limp and defenseless in his lap, the skin chapped and reddened from scooping ice cream, wrists so delicate they might have belonged to a ten-year-old. I wanted to deny the truth so obvious before me, pressing down on me, but I couldn't. He had not murdered our beautiful girl. Once again I was left impotent, helpless with the hard knowledge that I still didn't know who had killed Lucy, might never know.

We both sat for a long, immeasurable moment in the silence of the car. I shifted in my seat and the gun pressed against my thigh. Outside, the wind stirred the leaves in the trees. Duane spoke first.

"I didn't hurt Lucy," he said. "I could never hurt her."

"I know," I said. At last I turned on the ignition and as we backed out of the lot, I started to say more, but stopped and so we drove back through town, past the harbor, a charged stillness between us, thick with all that had remained unspoken. I dropped him at his house. Again he was the one to break the silence. "I'm sorry, Mr. Light." We locked eyes then, just the once as he got out of the car, but in that moment an understanding, a knowing without words, passed between us and an agreement was struck. We would not tell anyone what had happened. I knew that someday I would ask him how he had come to have Lucy's Yoda, why he had lied to the police, questions that didn't matter at that moment, just as perhaps someday I would be able to tell Sophie how often those months I had been wondering what we were capable of and what we were not, of the time in those woods with Duane, my Saint Sebastian, of how close I had come to destroying everything. Of course, before the day ended, I was to learn so much more about what we truly are capable of and what we can endure. Of what we are willing to risk. To destroy.

I watched Duane as he disappeared through the front door and then, with nowhere else to go, I headed toward home.

These thoughts were in my mind as I drove onto Prospect Street and turned into our drive and saw Rain LaBrea running from the house next door. She was crying, but between sobs she managed to get the words out. "It's Mr. Hayes," she cried. "He killed Lucy."

I couldn't process the words, my brain slowed.

"He did. Look." She held out her hand and the sun glinted on the silver chain. "He had this. He had Lucy's Lucky Strike stone. The one I gave to her."

I took the gun from my pocket and walked across his front yard. I followed their voices to the bedroom. Father Gervase saw me first.

"Will," he said.

Payton saw me then, and his eyes widened as I raised the gun and aimed at his heart. "Christ," he said.

Father Gervase stood between us, his hands raised palms upturned toward me.

"Get out of the way, Father," I said.

"You're not going to shoot me, are you?" he said and smiled.

"That's not my intention. But I need to you to step out of the way."

"You don't want to do this, Will."

Hayes made a sound, started to speak.

"Shut up," I said. "Don't say a fucking word." Vengeance was mine. All the months of being paralyzed by inaction and impotence lifted, and it felt so good. Try to understand that. One shot, I thought, one single shot in the chest. If justice were true, before his body was found our daughter's killer should rot on the ground, abandoned and alone as she had, but I would have to settle for his death. And then it would be over.

"You need to think this through," the priest said.

"I'm done thinking."

He smiled again, that gentle smile I remembered from the first time he came to the house in May, as if we shared a secret. "This isn't you."

"You don't know me."

"Vengeance is not yours, Will."

"I'll shoot, I swear I will, Father. I have nothing to lose."

"There is always something more to lose, Will."

"Why do you care?"

He didn't answer, but took a step toward me. "Stay back," I said.

But he continued walking to me, slowly but without hesitation. He reached for the gun, but I held it steady on him, and behind him, on Payton Hayes.

CHAPTER FORTY-SIX

~

"This is not your business," I said to the priest. "It has nothing to do with you."

Father Gervase started to speak but Payton cut him off. "You can relax, Father. He won't shoot me."

At the smugness in his voice, my finger tightened on the trigger.

Even now the weeks that immediately followed remain a blur, a filmy distortion of one man crumpled on the carpet, a circle of crimson, and later, the blurry confusion of the trial. Some parts of memory I am relieved to have blocked, details that cannot be borne or I would not be able to walk upright.

I do remember how Payton had laughed when I pointed the gun, his arrogance. "Go ahead, shoot. You'll be the one facing a murder charge, not me."

I did shoot him then. The report echoed, muffling the cry from Father Gervase, reverberating in my ears.

"Jesus," Payton said. He stared at his thigh, at the spread of blood on his clothes. "Are you crazy?"

I was satisfied to hear all the smugness gone, saw fear in his eyes.

"Give me the gun, Will," Father Gervase said.

I brushed aside his words. No one existed in that room except Payton Hayes and me. "Tell me why," I said, my voice steady, my purpose clear. "Tell me why or I swear to God, the next shot will go straight through your chest."

I saw him weighing his options. Saw the moment he believed me and then, instantly, trusted his own ability to save himself, to say what he needed to now and later deal with whatever the future held and, believed in his power to avoid answering to his sins.

"It was her fault," he said. "Your daughter should have minded her own business. Such a meddler."

He talked then as if he couldn't wait to get it out. How Gabi Russell had told Lucy about her secret affair with him, how he, and not one of the high school boys, was the father of Gabi's child. Lucy, trusting Lucy, who wanted only to help a friend and make things right, had taken it upon herself to confront him, to make him take responsibility.

I could see it, so true of our Lucy, so innocent, so confident of the goodness in everyone that she held not a speck of suspicion when she arranged to meet him when she should have been at the hockey scrimmage, not even suspicious when she got in his car and he had driven to Dogtown. What was his plan? Had he known even then that he was going to kill her?

"She said if I didn't confess about everything, she would do it herself," Payton was saying. "Who the hell was she to say that? I told her it wasn't her business, that it would ruin my life. I told her that but she wouldn't listen. Just kept insisting. Do the right thing she kept saying. As if it were that simple. It was the way she kept insisting, the way she wouldn't even consider my side of things that made me strike her. And when she started to run, of course, I had no choice but to kill her."

The way he spoke, the details told in such a matter-of-fact manner chilled me. In the relating of the story, his confidence had returned and with it his arrogance. "You should have taught your daughter to mind her own business," he said. "Then none of this would have happened."

There was a buzzing in my ears, blocking out sound for a moment, the sound of water rushing as if I were swimming in the sea. I raised the barrel and aimed true.

Beside me, Father Gervase cried out. Justice was served. The trial was a sideshow as I'm sure you can imagine.

Months passed. And gradually, but sooner than you might think possible given all that had happened, we adapted and we managed to carve out a precarious new normalcy. Sophie moved back home. She gained weight, her belly again slightly mounded in the way I loved, and I teased her that this was evidence of my good cooking. We smiled about that later. Eventually, not long after the trial, she got back to work on finishing her book, her way to honor our daughter, and I returned to the boat barn and worked on the panels of the saints, their faces holding both agony and ecstasy, sorrow and joy. Some days she would come with me and sit in the rocking chair I had carted there for her, and she would watch quietly as the saints grew to their sixty-foot fullness. And so both of us, in our own way, and in our own time, experienced the remarkable resiliency of the human body and mind and our capacity to not only endure but to heal.

Some nights, when my determination to block them was weakest, thoughts would creep in of all Lucy had endured those moments in the woods with Payton Hayes, and I would recall, too, the long-ago nights when I would wander around Port Fortune searching faces for a sign of evil, a mark to show me who had killed our daughter, and it sickened me to think he had been there all along. Right next door, nodding to me when we crossed paths, waving while watering his lawn, posing as a saint, evil concealed. For evil exists. It is not a theological question. It exists.

But so does goodness, so does goodness. I would remind myself of this on those dark nights of the soul. And in the darkness, as if they were talismans, I would draw close to me thoughts of Sophie and Lucy and Father Gervase, and the faces of the ancient saints.

EPILOGUE

~

"This is a most extraordinary day," Cardinal Kneeland intones.

On this extraordinary day, the archbishop gazes down on those gathered in the cathedral, looks out at the ordinary people who occupy the pews. Two years have passed since he set all in motion by sending a parish priest on a mission to ask Will Light to paint saints for this cathedral, although there are those who would say all that followed really started months before that with the murder of Lucy Light. Now, along with the invited dignitaries and the media, the governor and the members of the Arts and Furnishings Committee, they have gathered here, the curious and the faithful. And the people Will has painted.

There in the first pew, which has been set aside for the models, sits Mary Silveria, the young widow with three children whom Will has always thought of as his first saint. Her youngest, the infant he had saved from falling that distant day in the grocery store, is now a chubby toddler and sits next to his older sister, who has outgrown her love of red licorice. *Lick wish.* Next to them sits Constantos Anastas, who posed as Martin de Porres and to whom, within the year, Mary will be wed. The beekeeper and the baker and the clerk from the coffee shop are there. And Elaine Neal, the bookstore owner whose arthritis is now so advanced she is confined to a wheelchair, and Joseph Souza, who runs the bait shop near the harbor. Alonzo Americo has closed the bakery for this day and, with his wife and seven sons, sits with head tilted up, scanning the panels as if looking through a family album. It is his youngest son who first locates his father's face among the saints. Yes, there he is, the third figure in the first panel to the left of the altar. Saint Crispin. The widower Jules Cavanaugh sits alone. When he locates Saint Ambrose, he thinks of how proud his wife would have been at this moment, and his eyes grow moist. Next to him, Harold Weaver is moved to whisper a prayer. And him, not even a Catholic.

Lena MacDougall believes they should have been given better seating and leans over to whisper this to Miriam Endelheim, with whom, improbably, she has found more in common that she would have once believed possible. Miriam—Saint Elizabeth—smiles gently and pats Lena's hand in consolation.

Teachers and students from the school are there. And Coach Davis. And Jared Phillips, for whom Lucy had broken a promise to her parents and gone for a ride with him so they could talk about holding a fund-raiser for SADD. Tracy Ramos, Will Light's Rose of Lima, is here with her child. And here is the LaBrea family. Rain, now a high school senior, sits between her mother and Dr. Mallory, the family she was born into and the family she created, the mother who gave her life and the little woman who helped her return to life during a dark time of despair. She is clad, without a word of argument, in a dress. And heels. In one hand she holds the Lucky Strike stone Lucy had given her when they became sworn sisters. Her brother is here too, home from college for this celebration, and is accompanied by his partner, a boy who no longer remains Duane's secret, the secret he once confided only to Lucy Light. There is something in his hand, too. Yoda, returned to him by Lucy's parents.

The archbishop takes his seat, and the cathedral choir begins to sing. Will sits in his chair next to Cardinal Kneeland and lets the anthem wash over him, recognizes it as one Sophie used to teach the high school chorus for one of the holiday concerts. He scans the crowds, looking for each of his models, and then lifts his eyes to the six panels. Forty-two saints. A saint for everything and everyone, Sophie had once told him. Saints who, when tested, discovered what they were capable of and what they were not, as Will and Sophie have these past two years. He closes his eyes against the memory of that afternoon in his neighbor's bedroom, the gun in his raised hand, the barrel pointing straight at Payton Hayes. He had thought himself capable of it, welcomed it even, this act of killing the man who had murdered his daughter and left her body to lie in the woods. And only Father Gervase had stopped him, falling to the floor, crying out in pain.

Sophie is there. Will smiles as he looks down at her. And at their son, the child conceived that long ago weekend at the cottage in Maine.

There are those missing in this gathering, among them Leon Newell, who only last month died of stomach cancer, although Jossie has come. "Wouldn't for the world miss a chance to see old Leon as a saint," she told her friends. Cancer has also claimed Lorna Vogler who posed as Catherine. Payton Hayes is not there, of course. Nor the saint he was to represent.

Among the absent but ever present is, of course, Lucy. Father Gervase—the little priest who, shortly after rescuing Rain LaBrea, had died of a massive coronary and in doing so saved Will—is not here. But his presence, like Lucy's, is here. Will raises his eyes to look at the final figure in the end panel, the unnamed saint representing the potential in everyone, and gazes into the face of Father Gervase. From high above them the little priest stands, the only one among them with hands not clasped but with arms held wide, seeming to offer a benediction to them all.

Doughnuts in air.
Do not despair.

"Do you believe coincidence?" the priest had asked Will one day. And another time, if he believed in miracles.

"Not the kind you mean, Father," he'd replied.

"Tell me, then, what kind?"

"The fact that there exists in the desert a certain insect, the cochineal, that lives on cacti and the bodies of the female produce a dye the most stunning shade of red," he'd said. "That's miracle enough for me."

"Ah yes," the priest had responded. "Ordinary miracles."

The words seem to float down over the crowd, bathing each one. Sinners and saints.

Ordinary. Miracles.

THE END

ACKNOWLEDGMENTS

I owe a deep debt of gratitude to:

The artist John Nava. The idea for this book was birthed after I watched *Divining the Human: The Cathedral Tapestries of John Nava*, a documentary about the creation of Nava's massive and innovative tapestries that hang in the Cathedral of Our Lady of the Angels in Los Angeles.

The entire team at Lake Union, most especially my editor Kelli Martin, whose unwavering belief in and vision for this novel sustained me, whose brilliant comments guided me, and whose wit made the process a joy; copy editors extraordinaire Jessica Fogleman and Katherine Faydash, and artist Rex Bonomelli for the stunning cover. Working with them was an author's dream.

My agent Deborah Schneider, the best of agents who never stopped believing.

The Virginia Center for the Creative Arts in Amherst, Virginia, and the Ragdale Foundation in Lake Forest, Illinois, both of which granted me multiple residencies and the time and space in which to write a large part of this work.

The multitude of people who during the writing of this book and with great generosity shared their knowledge on a multitude of subjects that included art and religion, betrayal and forgiveness, doubt and faith, violence and its effect on families and communities, police procedure, adolescent therapy, and grief. In particular I want to thank Jack and Kathleen Mortell, Sandell Morse, Jane Hamilton, Ann Hood, Sara Young, Margaret Moore, Nita Finn (LICSW), Larry Thomas, Cleveland Morris, David Tierney, Lisa Boes, Father Marck Chmurski, Father Thomas Kelly, and Chatham Police Sergeant Andrew Goddard. The expertise is theirs, any errors of fact are mine.

My home team who helped keep the ship on course in both storms and fair skies: Christopher Mortell, Ignacio Mortell, Kate and Chris Harlow, Dr. Mark Griffin, Dr. Mita Gupta, Ginny Bernard, Kim Roderiques, Steve Crocker, Lane Byrd, Pete Higgins, Bob Vath, and computer guru Jimmy Fallon.

And, as always, my family: Hillary, Hope, and Chris.

ABOUT THE AUTHOR

Bestselling author Anne D. LeClaire has written eight novels, including *Entering Normal*, *The Lavender Hour*, and *Leaving Eden*, as well as her critically acclaimed memoir, *Listening Below the Noise: The Transformative Power of Silence*. Known for her exquisite and lyrical writing, the former op-ed columnist has been published in *Redbook*, the *Boston Globe*, *Yoga Journal*, and the *New York Times*.

A Distinguished Fellow at the Ragdale Foundation, LeClaire teaches creative-writing workshops around the globe. She is also a dynamic speaker—leading popular seminars and workshops exploring silence, creativity, and deep listening. LeClaire has been a visiting lecturer at Mount Holyoke College, the University of Tennessee, and Columbia College and was a featured presenter at the Lincoln Center.

A former reporter, print journalist, radio broadcaster, and private pilot, LeClaire lives in Cape Cod, Massachusetts, where she leads silent retreats, practices yoga, and plays the washboard.